GW00729126

30130500218544

About the Author

Kathleen Judd is married and has lived in both Spain and Italy. Now back in her native England she can indulge her lifelong desire to write. On discovering Regency Romance at her local library she had found the genre that inspired her.
One night she had a dream, and the rest, as they say, is history.

To my husband, who gets asked the strangest questions.

Kathleen Judd

FINDING DIANA

A CIP catalogue record for this title is available from the British Library.

ISBN 978 1 78455 544 3 (Paperback)
ISBN 978 1 78455 546 7 (Hardback)

www.austinmacauley.com

First Published (2015)
Austin Macauley Publishers Ltd.
25 Canada Square
Canary Wharf
London
E14 5LB

Printed and bound in Great Britain

Prologue

The cortège left the London house on its journey to the Earl of Selgrove's estate in Buckinghamshire. In the carriage following the body of his wife the Earl sat in the deepest depression. Why had this had to happen? What had caused this terrible tragedy and blighted his life. The light of his whole being had been his gentle young wife. They had been married for less than a year and she carried the early life of his child within her. It made no sense. The doctor could find nothing wrong with her but still she declined, slowly at first, then faster, until she had little memory and her body was wasted, too weak to stand, unable to feed herself. He had tried to visit her regularly but it was too painful, she did not even recognise him. This was not his wife, lying pale and vacant in her bed, her sister feeding her.

The retainers waited at the Hall steps as they arrived, the carriage with Madeleine's body, the coach with the Earl and the carriage with her parents and sister. The Hall was in darkness save for a few candles along the passageways. Tomorrow would be even worse, there would be friends and neighbours offering him their condolences, he was not sure he would be able to cope.

"I am sorry, My Lord, I understood you wanted to be alone or I would have made provision for your friends."

"I may want to be alone but I am not in the habit of refusing succour to my friends. You understood wrongly. Do you not know me by now?"

"Miss Ferndale assured me you wanted to be alone and I should admit no-one, sir."

"Miss Ferndale! Since when has my wife's sister given orders here?"

The housekeeper kept her had bowed. "Send someone to the local hostelries and see if any are there. Invite them back to the house."

"Yes, My Lord." She walked with purpose, the better to carry out his orders quickly.

He walked into the parlour to where his family, a group of distant and ancient aunts and cousins, sat with those of his late wife.

"Selgrove, why did you not invite your friends back after their long journey?" Lady Farthingdale, an ageing and infirm aunt with a temper to match was all he needed now.

"I expected them to come here. It appears they were told otherwise for reasons I do not understand." He turned to face Miss Ferndale. "Can you explain why?"

"You said you wished to be left alone, Albert. I was merely acting out your wishes."

"When I wish you to make decisions about my arrangements I will tell you."

"Have you not noticed who ran your house since your wife was ill?"

"My housekeeper."

"Not so, Albert, I have run it for you."

Albert Bursted, the Earl of Selgrove was disturbed and annoyed at the use of his given name from someone whose only connection was with his now departed wife. He excused himself and went to his study, with instruction to his butler to tell him if any of his friends had been found.

"Selgrove, what happened. We made to see you after the service but were told you wished to be alone."

"Carstairs, I am so glad they found some of you. I gave no instructions. I would rather have my friends here than those currently filling my parlour."

"Miss Ferndale seemed to be carrying out your orders. You will have to be careful or you will find yourself married to her, she appears to be a determined young lady."

"Miss Ferndale is not of my choice. I would rather not have had her in my house at all but Madeleine wished to have her family near her, they had no London house so I unwisely let them stay at Selgrove House. She is sitting there called me Albert! In front of my family. I have never given her permission to use my given name. Would that this day was over and I could travel far away from here to help put the pain behind me."

"What of her family, Selgrove? If you go away will they stay in Selgrove House?"

"No, I cannot allow that. I need that girl out of my house. Out of my life. I will speak to her father and ask them to make arrangements to find themselves somewhere to live. I need time, Carstairs. I have to come to terms with my loss. My life is too painful to bear at the moment."

"I am sure it will get easier, Selgrove. Your friends will help you, we know how much you cared for Madeleine and how great your loss is. If you need to, come to stay with one of us, a change of scene will help. Summer is coming and there will be house parties everywhere that will help to lift your mood. You can rely on us."

"No, papa, I will not leave. The Earl needs me here to take care of him."

"The Earl asked that I vacate his house with all my family. I have taken a house in Delcourt Avenue and you will come there with us. Your mother and I are almost packed and I expect you to accompany us."

"I will speak to the Earl myself."

The Earl was hiding from the packing and removal of his former in-laws. At least he would not be made to see that dreadful girl every time he walked around his house.

The housekeeper approached him with some concern showing on her face.

"What is it, Mrs Lever? Have they left yet?"

"Not quite, My Lord. I understand Miss Ferndale is resisting the move."

"I will not have her here, Mrs Lever."

"Nor I, sir. She gave orders as if she was the lady of the house." She pulled out a small box from her skirt pocket. "I came to ask you about this, sir. It appears the Countess's maid saw boxes like this in her room for some weeks before she died. They had disappeared when we went to clean. But we did find this trapped at the back of the commode. I wondered if you knew what it was and if it was important."

"I expect it was something the doctor gave her. I will ask him. Maybe Miss Ferndale will know, although I dread asking."

"Mr Ferndale is in the library, sir. I believe the move does not require him at the moment."

Ferndale was indeed in the library, a drink in his hand.

"I think I will join you."

"It is a great trial this moving but it must be done. We both understand the reason, Selgrove. It is the only way for all of us to make a fresh start. Unfortunately my younger daughter thinks otherwise."

"She may not stay, Ferndale. I cannot have her here."

"Of course you cannot. It would be unconscionable to expect it. You would both be compromised in the eyes of society."

"I will not be forced to marry where I have no affection. She seems to have some ideas in that direction, she keeps calling me Albert in front of family and friends. I have never given her use of my name."

"She is a headstrong girl. I can only think she wishes to take her sister's place to ease your loss."

The Earl poured himself a drink and moved to sit in the group of chairs where Ferndale sat. He held out the box.

"Do you know what this is? The maid has seen boxes like this in my wife's room recently but when they cleaned they had all disappeared. We are all at a loss. This was found where it had fallen behind furniture."

Ferndale took the box and studied it. "It looks as if it held some powder, there is residue still here. Perhaps the doctor gave it to her. I will ask my daughter if she remembers it"

"I would rather you did, I prefer not to do it myself. In the meantime I will ask the doctor."

The move was complete. They had all left, even the annoying sister. Why she had left so willingly in the end he had no idea. The doctor had arrived and been questioned about the box but it was not from him. He had spoken to Mr Ferndale for information from his daughter and assured the Earl he would check what it had contained.

The doctor stood rigid in front of the Earl.

"I went to ask about the box from the local apothecary. Apparently it had held arsenic. Miss Ferndale bought it for her complexion, she had said. I went to see the Ferndales to check what the Countess used it for. The illness of your wife is consistent with poisoning by arsenic, My Lord. Mr Ferndale was profoundly shocked. I was not content with the attitude of Miss Ferndale. You said boxes in the plural so I returned to the apothecary to ask how often she bought it. I also visited other apothecaries in the vicinity. It appears Miss Ferndale bought a regular quantity in increasing amounts starting some six months ago."

Selgrove stared at him, disbelief washing over him.

"She was poisoned by her sister." his voice was a whisper.

"I believe so, Selgrove. I suggest you contact Bow Street with some speed. The family know my suspicions although Mr Ferndale was excessively shocked."

Bow Street visited the house in Delcourt Avenue. The family had indeed moved in but had subsequently left at great speed. They had left no information as to their whereabouts. Bow Street would keep a record of this for the future. Somewhere there was a young lady who had deliberately poisoned her sister.

Chapter 1

London 1811

"My young childhood was happy to my memory. I had an older brother who took me everywhere with him, he taught me to swim and to fish when I was only four or five. We had a maze where we played hide and seek. I could never understand why he found me so easily but it was quite new and not very thick and he was taller than me, he still is. It was years before I realised he could see over the top. It's not so small now. The years have seen it grow as fast as I have. I still cannot see over it." Michael Pennington sat with a glass in his hand among his closest friends. Edward Ashford had come up from Kent to say goodbye, both of them staying with Robert Lansdale the third member of the close school friends. Michael had been a regular visitor to both their houses; especially the Lansdale's where Henry Lansdale had come to regard him almost as a second son.

"When did it change, what caused it?" Henry was concerned for this misfit.

"I have never been able to point to a certain occurrence. It happened slowly. I think Frederick was such an upstanding son, the heir to the estate and our father doted on him. If he did anything wrong accidentally he went and confessed. Father praised him for his honesty, but if I was with him, which I usually was, I was punished. If I confessed he said I was trying to get Frederick into trouble and got caned anyway. When you are only five you don't really understand. By the time I went to Eton he was seen as the perfect son. I still looked up to him, my perfect big brother. I never remember him being caned. I thought there must be something wrong with me."

"What kind of father canes a five year old, all children get up to mischief it's part of being a boy, I don't remember you caning me, father." Robert looked over to his father.

"There were times it might have done you good, but not at that age, and not with an older brother leading you into mischief."

"George and I were always up to mischief but we never told on one another and my father never caned me. I think George was caned, perhaps that's why he always blamed me if we were found out."

Edward Ashford, beloved of his doting parents, had offered Michael school holidays in peace and harmony roaming his father's estate, helping with the cows and sheep. He had helped with the wheat harvest when they landed up rolling on the ground in helpless laughter as they tried tying it into stooks. There had been good times, but not when he was at home in Northamptonshire.

"I just wish it did not have to be like this." Edward was the most outwardly emotional one, ready to give a helping hand whenever it was needed.

"What else could I do? I am never going to be able to support myself on my allowance. I couldn't at Eton. If it were not for you two I would have frozen or starved."

"It's just that I never saw you as a soldier, it's completely against your nature. You can never kill anyone."

"Then perhaps I shall be killed and the problem will have disappeared."

"Michael, don't talk like that." Henry Lansdale interjected. "Focus on what you will do when you come home a hero."

Michael burst into laughter. "I do not see me as a hero. Perhaps some General will give me his paperwork to deal with, that's more my forte."

Robert took Michael's glass to refill it.

"At least you are going in as an officer. I can't believe after all this time he stumped up for a commission for you."

"Nor can I, and after all the problem with not affording clothing for Eton he pays for the uniform, which is not cheap. He is obviously glad to be rid of me."

They sat in their own thoughts for a while.

"What will you do with your pay?"

"It depends on where I am posted and if I need to spend it. I expect my allowance will stop altogether now, sir."

"If not, why not let me invest it for you. You are going to need clothing when you come home. At least that way it would be inaccessible to your father or his agent."

Michael looked at Henry Lansdale and light came over his face. "What a good idea. Wentworth is the most inefficient agent but father can't see it. I wonder how long the estate will remain in funds with him managing the money. I will confront him over my allowance when I go up to say goodbye, which I suppose I must."

"You only want to show off your new uniform to the local young ladies."

"If there were any what could I offer them? No, the only one is affianced to Frederick and they are due to marry within the month."

"What a shame you will not be there at the wedding."

"I think I prefer it this way, a new life for everyone involved."

They sat late into the night talking of their school days, holidays and places they had visited together. The following day Michael donned his new uniform and set out for his family home. He would only stay a couple of nights then return to the Lansdale's ready for his departure from England.

There was a house party in full swing when he arrived; all the local gentry were there. His father rarely entertained like this, it must have something to do with Frederick and his upcoming marriage, Great Aunt Letitia was there. He missed his grandfather, Letitia's brother. For some reason he and father must have had a falling out because he used to visit his mother quite often and he had not seen him for a couple of years now. The last time was when he had visited him at Eton when he was sixteen. He would like to have said goodbye to him. Perhaps he would write to him while he was still in London at Lansdale's.

He was not welcome, he knew that. No-one actually ignored him but any conversation had to be instigated by him. After dinner when the port was handed round he listened to the tone of the conversation. There was some ribald mention of a new family in the area, the Firbecks. It was presumed they were in reduced circumstances, especially if you listened to the daughter Lucy talking about their previous residence in London, and you could not fail to hear what she said, she had one of those sharp whining voices that cut across everyone's conversation.

The men were joking about her obvious advances to Lord Williams, a distant cousin of Harwood who attended a dinner recently at Harwood's house. Michael thought the conversation not the kindest if the family were financially reduced. All it meant to him was that they had come from a much higher level of gentry than those pouring scorn. Mr Firbeck was not there, only his wife and daughter attended or they would not have been so free with their vindictiveness.

When the men joined the ladies Michael gravitated to his great aunt.

"Michael my dear, you look very handsome in your uniform."

"Thank you, Ma'am, I am grateful not to be in that of a normal soldier. I had not expected papa to buy me a commission."

Sharp laughter broke across their conversation as Lucy Firbeck dominated some group's discussion. Aunt Letitia gritted her teeth.

"I think I will retire shortly, would you escort me up to my room?"

"Of course, Aunt."

The tea was being served and the conversations stopped while cups were passed, emptied and returned to the tea trolley. Michael found it amusing when she announced she was going up and asked him formally to escort her.

Once in her room he went to ring the bell for her maid.

"Good gracious, young man, I am not ready to retire yet. I wanted to talk to you away from the mealy mouthed harpies downstairs. I do not know how your mother stands it. But then she has had a great many years with them so she probably does not notice any more."

She looked him straight in the eye. "Sit down and tell my why you chose to go into the army."

He was a little taken aback at her directness.

"What else is there for me? I have no future here, my allowance will not keep me dressed as a gentleman and I have no training for a profession, father would not have paid for that. The army at least gives me a life, food to eat, camaraderie and something to occupy my time."

"Why did you not go to Oxford and study?"

"Father refused to allow me. I am quite surprised he bought me my colours. I believe he expects me to be killed and cease to be a burden to him."

The old lady looked angry but made no comment.

"When do you leave?"

"I was intending to stay a couple of days but in the face of such a lack of welcome I believe I will leave again in the morning."

"Then I shall leave tomorrow also. Have you been to talk with your mama yet?"

"Mama refuses to see me any more. I do not believe I will upset her again by trying."

His aunt was genuinely distressed. He wondered whether to ask after his grandfather but decided not to distress her more by broaching what was obviously a sensitive subject.

"If you will excuse me, Aunt Letitia, I will leave you to retire."

"Good night, Michael. And keep safe."

He bent and planted a kiss on her cheek. "I will wish you goodbye, I expect I will have left before you come down in the morning."

She clasped his hand for a moment then turned her face away.

"Will you ring for my maid as you leave? I believe I will make a start on my packing."

Michael was up early and went down to breakfast before most. Diana Butterwick, Frederick's betrothed was there; obviously she also was an early riser. He made conversation with her, she was such a gentle, open girl with nothing of what his aunt had called 'mealy mouthed harpy' about her, unlike Lucy Firbeck who joined them a little later.

Frederick arrived and greeted Diana until Lucy dominated the conversation.

"Michael, up early as usual."

"Indeed, Frederick, do you happen to know if father is down yet, I wish to speak with him before I leave."

"You are leaving? I thought you were here for a few days?"

"I did think I might stay, but with such a cold reception I see no point. I will leave you to your revels." He turned to Diana. "I wish you happy, my lady." She smiled at him. Frederick was indeed lucky in his bride; he only hoped she could cope with his father's temperament. Maybe her gentleness would make him soften.

Not having received an answer from Frederick, Michael went into the hallway to find Wilson the butler. "Is my father down yet, Wilson?"

Wilson looked down his nose at him as did everyone in the house.

"I believe he is in his study, Master Michael."

It was, of course, said to rankle. He resisted saying 'thank you old man,' he was better than that even if they were not.

He knocked on the study door and was admitted by his sour faced father. He had such bad memories of this room and all the beatings he had been given.

"I came to ask a question before I leave."

"You are leaving?"

"I am not welcome, sir, and have no desire to stay. All I need to know is if my allowance will continue. I will need clothing when I return in order to find work. Unless you intend for me to die in a ditch."

His father looked rather surprised or was there more to his reaction.

"I suppose that is a good point. I will continue the allowance at the current level.

"Have no fear the money will go to waste, sir. If I am killed it will no doubt be returned to you. Call it an investment."

He turned toward the door. "Goodbye sir, we may never meet again."

Neither offered their hand.

Michael had his horse saddled and his saddle bags attached. He looked around at the land of his childhood and an overwhelming sadness came over him. He left the horse with the young groom and walked down towards the river. He had happy memories of swimming here. This was where Frederick taught him to fish.

He walked along the bank taking in the scene, absorbing the atmosphere, something to recall when he was far away. Turning back towards the house he would pass the maze on his way to the stable where his horse waited. It was so different now, so tall so ….he stopped. Someone was inside, the other side of the thick hedge. He had no wish to overhear but it was impossible not to.

"And when we are married I shall be rich and have everything I want." There was no doubt whose that strident voice was.

"But I thought he was betrothed, miss." Probably her maid.

"Oh don't worry, I've dealt with that."

He moved away quietly. What a dreadful girl, he pitied Lord Williams if she really had got her claws into him.

The Lansdales were not surprised to see Michael return so soon.

"I gather your reception was not very cordial."

"Worse than I expected. The whole district was there scowling at me. I had not a minute alone with any of my family except Great Aunt Letitia, God bless her. She singled me out to speak to."

"Did you have any time with your father?"

"I did speak this morning demanding to know if my allowance will continue. Apparently it will, at the same amount. I need to instruct Wentworth where to pay it. I still don't trust father to keep his word."

"All we can do is hope he is gentlemanly enough to do so."

"I will instruct Wentworth tomorrow after enquiring about my departure."

"One thing you know, Michael, you are always welcome here."

The first call in the morning was precluded by a letter announcing his departure the following day, obviously a good thing he had returned early. His visit to Wentworth was now the only necessary call for him.

Wentworth worked from rather meagre rooms in one of the cheaper areas of London, not exactly disreputable but definitely not somewhere you would choose to visit.

The first person he met on entering was Allan Tucker whose father was a tenant farmer with a large farmhouse and productive land on the Pennington estate. Allan had been a clever boy and asked to be articled in order to have a profession not working the land as his father did. Unfortunately he mentioned this to Michael's father who arranged for him to be articled to Wentworth, in his opinion the worst place for him.

"Allan, still here? I thought you would be out of your indenture by now."

"Well technically I am, but I need to find another chambers to take me on and having trained here they are not enthusiastic." He gave a rueful smile. "Do you have an appointment?"

"No, I just need to see him for a few minutes, I leave for France tomorrow."

"I will arrange it if you will wait a while, he has someone with him at the moment."

Michael sat on the proffered chair and wondered what he could do about Allan's situation. Perhaps he could ask Lansdale to make a few enquiries on his behalf."

"Ah, Mr Michael." He had an oily voice which raised Michael's hackles. "How nice to see. You look splendid in your uniform. How can I help you?"

"I leave tomorrow, Mr Wentworth. My father has agreed to continue my allowance; I shall need clothing if I return."

"Of course, well I would expect you to have your money when you return." Did he look a little guilty? "I will take good care of it until you are twenty one."

"No, Mr Wentworth, it will be sent to this account." He handed over the direction for the payments to Lansdale for investment.

"You have made arrangements?" He oiled

"I have, be so good as to honour my instructions, sir."

"Of course, Mr Michael. I wish you a safe return."

"Thank you." With that he rose, shook his hand and left.

Allan Tucker called after him.

"Are you going to lunch, Tucker?"

"I am, why not join me." He looked serious.

"Is there a problem?"

"I would like to have the opportunity to speak with you."

They made their way to a rather seedy looking inn where they took a corner table at Allan Tucker's direction. They enquired after the food and ordered a beef and ale pie, with a glass of ale each.

"You seem very serious, Allan, is this about your position?"

"No. It is several years since I saw you so I have not had any opportunity to speak with you. Did Wentworth tell you about your money?"

"My allowance? My father has agreed to continue to pay it."

"Not your allowance, your money."

"I have no money, Allan."

"I discovered your file in the records; your grandfather gave you money to go to Oxford."

Michael stared.

"Grandfather, when?"

"Over two years ago. He left it with his investor. It was to be free under your direction, but your father had it removed to Wentworth and has been administering it ever since."

"Wentworth said he would look after it until I was twenty one. I wondered what he had meant."

"I had the feeling you had not been told. Your father could not stop your allowance, it is your money. He used it to buy your commission and your uniform."

Michael was angry, very angry.

"Grandfather wanted me to go to Oxford and father stopped me. Allan, I think I need to make some provision for my money. By the way, how much is it?"

"It started out as twenty thousand pounds but is obviously less now."

The pie and ale were delivered but Michael had no appetite.

"I can only thank you for telling me, my father has kept this from me for over two years. He has changed my life and damaged my future. If I survive this war I will have retribution. I will speak to someone and see whether he can find you a new position. You have been a good friend."

They sat for a while longer talking about Allan's father and his work on his Pennington tenancy until it was time for him to return to chambers.

"He gave you *How Much*!"

"Twenty thousand pounds but nobody told me. Why did Grandfather never write to me?"

Henry Lansdale leaned back in his chair. "Perhaps he did. How many letters did you receive at home?"

"None, even Robert and Edward's rarely arrived."

"I think that answers your question. Why not write to your Grandfather and explain why you never thanked him for his gift."

Michael made up his mind. "I will, and in the event of my death I will leave my money elsewhere, to Allan Tucker, I think. It will remove him from the clutches of Wentworth and my father."

"Who is Allan Tucker?"

Michael spent some time explaining his indenture to Wentworth, his belief in a poor training and his inability to find a position. "His father may not always be able to work the land and Allan had hoped to be able to offer him a home."

Lansdale took him to a local solicitor who drew up a hurried will for Michael to sign. The evening was spent writing a long overdue letter to a very generous and caring grandfather.

The following morning he reported for duty and was introduced to his regiment prior to leaving for France. His future was now in God's hands, but where he had previously been prepared, even willing to die, now he wanted to come home to exact his retribution.

Chapter 2

The weather was foul when Captain Michael Pennington knocked on the door of Henry Lansdale's house. A much older looking man answered the door.

"Captain Pennington! How good to see you returned safely, sir."

"Hello, Nesbit. You still recognise me then?"

"Indeed, sir, although we are all somewhat older. I must say you were always slim but now your physique is somewhat more developed." He showed Michael into the library. "Mr Lansdale is at his office at the moment but will return shortly. We had no idea of when to expect you. There is a decanter and glasses if you require a drink. Shall I arrange food for you?"

"No thank you, Nesbit, I have eaten. Although a shot of brandy will not go amiss."

"Your usual room is prepared for you whenever you require it."

"Thank you. It is good to be back to somewhere ordered and predictable."

"I imagine you will enjoy the respite, sir."

"Indeed I will. How could I not surrounded by books. I have had little to read in over four years now. I believe you have delivered me to heaven."

Nesbit smiled, the most any good butler would allow of himself, and then retired. Michael walked around the room, paused at the decanter to pour himself a drink, then extracted a book and settled himself in a chair to read. It was like this, book in hand, drink at his side, that Henry Lansdale found him several hours later.

"I suppose I should not be surprised." he laughed "You always were a bookworm; I am surprised there are any here you have not read before."

Michael stood to greet him. "It is so good to see you again, sir."

"I am just relieved you came back alive and uninjured if my eyes see correctly."

"Indeed, physically uninjured, mentally, well that I can't answer for."

"I can barely imagine what it has been like for someone of your gentle personality. We can only hope time and rest will heal that, to some extent at least." Lansdale released his hand and indicated a chair. "Do you have any plans as yet?"

"Not really. I suppose new clothes if I can afford them."

"You can indeed, although you do not have as much as I had hoped. Your father stopped your allowance a year ago. Perhaps he thought you dead, did you communicate in any way?"

"I wrote to Frederick quite a few times but never received a reply."

"Did you receive much mail in France?"

"Oh yes, you and my grandfather wrote to me regularly. Not every letter found me but many did, rather belatedly of course. It depended on where we were and how big the company was as to whether there was direct contact with England."

"Both Robert and I answered your letters but we never knew if you received them all. I know you did some as you responded to questions several months later. It became a game to work out which questions you were answering. We had to make copies of what we had written."

Michael finished his drink and put down his glass.

"A refill?"

"No I think not. I may have been in France but brandy such as this was never available to us, we mainly drank the local wine. Your brandy is a little potent on an empty stomach."

"Were you not offered food?"

"Yes, do not blame Nesbit for anything. I had eaten before I arrived but I am not used to large meals at the moment. We were glad of anything we could find."

"Dinner will be shortly. I would suggest you change ready for it but you have nothing to change into, unless you can find some of your old clothes that still fit you."

"You still have my clothes?"

"Of course. We had no idea how soon you would return. My valet has kept them in as good order as possible. They will be rather out of fashion but better than your uniform no doubt. Unless you are so attached to it, that is?"

"No, I am definitely not. I will be glad of clothes that are in better repair." he stood up and stretched. "I will investigate my armoire and see what will still fit me. If you will excuse me, sir."

Dinner was a very long-winded affair. Madam Lansdale, Henry's wife and their daughter Jane were eager to hear of his experiences and the places he had visited, so eating took some time and the food was not always hot when it reached his mouth. It was difficult to explain, as he told Lansdale later, how one battlefield seemed similar to another. Sometimes you noticed a Church which was more ornate but otherwise one Spanish village looked like every other, all French towns seemed alike when you were occupied in trying to stay alive. You noticed places where anyone could hide or for a possible ambush; roads, entrances, overhanging balconies, they were what you concentrated on, not the architecture.

If you were lucky you slept in a building, if not you slept in a ditch or a barn, always someone had to be on guard.

"It will be some time before I will sleep easily through the night."

When Lansdale felt Michael had talked all he could and was just a little foxed he dispatched him to bed.

"I shall go to my office in the morning as usual, I may see you at breakfast, if not, enjoy your first foray into the life of a gentleman."

First he needed clothes. Wearing what fitted him he ventured first to the outfitters where he could buy a basic wardrobe, then to where he could be measured for clothes which were tailored to his new more muscular frame. He returned with a hackney full of parcels.

"Goodness me, Captain, you have been diligent!"

Michael laughed. "These are only what is available, Nesbit, there will be more when it has been made. I had not realised just how much a gentleman needs to be ... a gentleman." he finished. "I will change before leaving again, I shall not require lunch."

"Very good, Captain."

The best he could buy to wear today he now unpacked. He chose breeches of a tan colour with a jacket, fairly loose around his slender waist, in a dark brown. His shirt felt good after the well-worn and much washed one under his uniform jacket. The material was soft and fitted his shoulders better. He had a dark green waistcoat with pockets into which he put a pocket watch.

The watch was a sacred trust to him. Its owner had died in his arms asking only that the watch be given to his young son. Somehow he had to find the family and honour his promise.

Presenting himself at Lansdale's rooms he was shown into Robert's office.

"Michael!" Robert sprang from his chair to clasp his hand. "Father said you had arrived. I wondered how long it would take for you to come here. Have you eaten?"

"Not yet. I wondered when you took a break."

"Now. Come and tell me about everything over a bite and a drink."

The two friends spent the next hour in avid conversation. Robert was married, Michael knew that, it had been mentioned in more than one letter.

"Come to dinner tonight. You must meet Henrietta she will be so pleased to see you. What a pity Ashford is so far away, you must go down to see him."

"I have a few errands to do before I am free to visit, Robert. I need to find out about my money, it looks as if I am in need of an occupation to keep me."

Leaving Robert to continue his work with a promise to visit that evening, Michael took himself to Wentworth's chambers and presented himself before the clerk.

"I wish to see Mr Wentworth."

"Do you have an appointment, sir?"

"No, but he will see me."

"He is rather busy at present."

"Then tell him Captain Pennington has returned from the war and requires him to report as to what he has done with his money." The look on Michael's face told the clerk the importance of his errand. He knocked cautiously on Wentworth's door.

"A Captain Pennington wishes to see you, he seems rather insistent."

"Then show him in."

Wentworth was a little concerned but this was only Michael.

The man who entered was not the boy who he remembered.

"I will come directly to the point, Wentworth, why did you stop my allowance, or have to wasted all my money?"

He hardly knew how to answer. "Good afternoon, Michael."

"Captain!"

"Captain, I don't know what you mean. Your allowance has not been stopped."

"Then why has it not arrived for the last year? I would like to know the state of my bequest."

31

"Well, if you come back in a few days ..."

"NOW! Mr Wentworth. Unless I am satisfied I will be calling on legal acquaintances to bring a case against you. Where is my money and how much is left?"

"Well there was the change of account last year."

"Who changed my account?"

"Well, your father."

"I was over twenty one, Mr Wentworth, why did you take orders on my account from him?"

"I had wondered if you had been killed or were missing, sir."

"So what account have you sent my money to?" Michael had no intention of letting Wentworth avoid answering. "You must have details of my holdings, I suggest you stop prevaricating and produce the relevant details. I am not leaving this office until I have what I want."

Wentworth was a little pale. He opened the office door and requested his clerk to fetch papers. Very quickly he returned with a file. He shuffled through the papers until he pulled out a letter which he handed to Michael.

"Is this the only letter from him recently?"

Wentworth was definitely unhappy.

"Well."

"Is it?"

"No, sir."

"Then show me any others." he looked down at the letter while Wentworth searched the file. "This is my brother's account."

"Yes, sir, Captain. I thought something must have happened to you."

"If it had you would have been shown a will giving you leave to release the money. What have you there?"

Wentworth held a letter as if it would burn him. Michael took it from his fingers.

"One thousand pounds. You transferred one thousand pounds of my money to my brother's account!"

Wentworth was silent.

"You will produce the current extent of my holding with you and you will not leave this office until you do. Do you understand me, Wentworth!"

He nodded, being unable to speak, and lifted the file with shaking hands. The clerk was dispatched to find and calculate the exact worth of Michael's investments.

"You do realise this is theft?"

"Your father gave instruction."

"Oh make no mistake, Wentworth, he will be beside you in court for the same crime. My money was never given for him to administer. He stole it and blighted my life. He will pay, Wentworth, as will you."

Michael had never felt so angry in his life, but his was not the hot anger most people experienced, this was an ice cold determination that seemed to come right from the core of his soul. He had talked of retribution but now he was not prepared for talk, he intended to act. Something had awoken inside him that demanded he defend those like him who had been used and abused by men like his father and Wentworth. He had not fought all these years and seen good men die for people like this to escape justice.

Michael stared at the figure. "Nine thousand four hundred and thirty eight pounds. This is all that is left?!"

"The investments have not been doing well."

"But your fees have. I see your fees are more than the interest on my investments." He fixed his eye on Wentworth. "You will write me a note for the whole of my money. NOW!"

"But."

"No buts, Wentworth. Or would you prefer I call in Bow Street to have you arrested?"

With shaking hands Wentworth wrote the promissory note and handed it to him. Michael nodded curtly, turned on his heel like the officer he was and marched out of the chambers in full military style. He waited for his anger to subside, for his gentle reticence to return but it did not. So a newly determined Michael took himself back to Lansdale's house to change for the evening with his old friend.

"If he is doing this to all his clients they will soon be without funds."

Michael nodded. "After all his kowtowing to my father, I wonder how long before he finds out the state of his investments."

"That depends on how well the estate is doing, I suppose. Oh, by the way, did father tell you about Allan Tucker?"

Michael was surprised. "No, what do you know of him?"

"Father took him in and trained him for a year then found him a position working for Lord Williams. He is extremely satisfied with him, he deals with his investments and most legal matters, a great asset was how he described him. I believe his father is moving in with him and his wife."

"His wife!"

"Yes, he married about a year ago."

Michael lifted his glass of port. "To Allan Tucker, good luck."

Robert laughed. "What do you do next?"

"First I need to see my father and obtain evidence he thinks he is still administering my funds. I doubt my arrival will be welcomed, so it will be good to show him I have survived and intend to take matters further over my money. I am not the gentle scholar that left four years ago. Then I have an obligation to a fellow officer." He pulled out the pocket watch. "He wanted his young son to have this."

They were both silent. Then Robert said "It must have been unspeakably harrowing for you, Michael. I thought of you every day you were away."

"And now I am back and must make a life for myself, after I deal with my family. They have more than a few crimes to answer for.

Michael waited until his tailored clothing was delivered. He intended to look the gentleman he was when he arrived.

The journey into Northamptonshire was not a pleasant one; there were no happy memories to look forward to rekindling. Childhood had gone.

Chapter 3

The land did not look as green and productive as in his memory. The house itself had changed not at all, the gardens well tended if a little sparse, as if there were less men employed in their maintenance. Michael wondered if that were the case. Was Wentworth's bad money management beginning to show in the upkeep of the estate?

A groom came to take his horse and recognised him at once.

"Mr Michael, Captain. Welcome home sir."

"Is it? Do you think I will be welcome?" He handed the reins to him. "I doubt it myself. Have my bags brought in will you."

"Yes, sir, Captain."

Wilson answered the door and had difficulty being polite.

"You are returned, Master Michael."

"Indeed I have, and I am Captain Michael Pennington, Wilson. Remember that unless you wish me to make your life difficult."

He walked past him into the hall.

"Have my room made ready for me."

Wilson was unnerved by the change in Michael, whose attitude and bearing he could not recognise.

Michael walked into the library, poured himself a drink and settled in a large leather wing chair to await the arrival of his family. He needed the drink to calm the internal turmoil caused by this character he was endeavouring to portray. He had no intention anyone should see his real self when they met, which he expected would be very soon.

Frederick was the first and seemed genuinely pleased to see him.

"Michael, you're alive, I am so relieved. We had thought you dead."

Michael rose and Frederick grasped his hand.

"Why would you think me dead, you had no notification?"

"Well not having heard from you in four years, when father heard a Pennington had been killed at Villefranche we presumed it to be you."

"But I did write, Frederick, every few months. You never answered my letters but some must have arrived, I had regular correspondence."

Frederick looked rather perplexed.

"Before I leave remind me to tell you about Villefranche, I guarantee you will find it very interesting."

The door opened and a young woman entered.

"Lucy, come and see who has arrived."

Lucy stared at Michael in horror. Michael stared at Lucy in confusion.

"My wife, Lucy, you did meet her before you left."

"You were betrothed to Diana Butterwick."

"There was a little trouble I'm afraid." Frederick began.

"A little trouble!" Lucy interjected. "A great deal of trouble, I am still finding items are missing."

Michael looked from one to the other.

"Frederick, will you please explain to me clearly and concisely what happened and when?"

Lucy went to answer but was silenced by the hard stare Michael gave her.

"How long have you been married?"

"More than four years now."

"You never married Diana then?"

Lucy leapt in "No he did not and a good thing too. She was a thief."

"Lucy dear, Michael asked me to explain."

"And have you tell only half what happened."

Michael held up his hand.

"I wish to speak to my brother for the first time in over four years, madam. Either leave the room or keep quiet. Surely you have duties in the house to attend to."

"I have maids who work for me, I do not have duties."

Michael looked at Frederick. "Is mother dead?"

"No, why should you think so?"

"Your wife speaks as if it were her house."

"Mother does keep to her room, she is increasingly ill." He had the decency to look a little sheepish.

"Shall we walk in the garden, I am finding the library a little confining?" Michael walked to the door and Frederick followed him, giving his wife an apologetic smile. "I am sure your wife will make sure you tell me all the salient points."

"So when did this happen?"

"It was the day you left. You may not remember the small figurine in the parlour. Apparently Diana was excessively taken with it the previous evening. The morning you left it was discovered to be missing."

"By whom?"

"I think a maid mentioned it to Lucy."

"And Lucy came to you?" Was this beginning to sound familiar. "Did you speak to the maid?"

"Well there was no need to."

"Why?"

"Because it was found in her belongings."

"What did she say?"

"Who?"

"Diana."

"Well she denied it, of course."

"Did you search the whole house, everyone's belongings?"

"Well no, we knew she had been taken with it so we started with her."

"Who suggested looking in Diana's things; it could have been dropped and broken?"

Frederick looked at him strangely. "Why are you being so pedantic about this, the girl was a thief."

They were close to the maze and Michael heard the voices in his head. *'Oh don't worry, I've dealt with that'.*

"So a maid nobody spoke to is supposed to have told Lucy who told you it was missing but you never checked. Lucy told you about her being 'excessively taken with it' the night before, and Lucy suggested you check her belongings. Do I have that right?"

"Well, yes."

"What happened to her?"

"She was turned out."

"By father, I imagine. You did go to father with the tale?"

"Yes of course."

"When you say turned out, what exactly do you mean Frederick? Was she sent home? Did her parents send her away?"

Frederick looked almost guilty.

"Her parents were here, you know that. Father opened the door and evicted her."

"What, just as she was?"

"Yes."

"Did anyone give her a wrap or a cloak?"

"No."

"Did she have walking shoes or those pretty blue house slippers she wore at breakfast?"

Frederick stared.

"What happened to her, Frederick? Where did she go?"

"I don't know. Nobody saw her after that."

"You mean a gently bred girl was turned out dressed for a house party and left to die in a ditch or become a whore because you never thought to question the maid?"

"But we found it in her belongings."

"I wonder how Lucy knew to direct you there." Michael said thoughtfully.

"Now look here, Michael, I will not have you say anything against my wife."

"You were happy enough to listen to the lies at school. Did you ever come to my room. Did you ever see how I had to live. In a tiny attic with no furniture except a small bed and no fire all through the winter, because you repeated to father all the lies the boys told you, and he beat me. No, you never cared. The boys knew you, naïve and gullible they called you. Even the masters knew but they never knew you told father all the lies nor that he told the whole neighbourhood. When did you last see Grandfather? Have you ever seen him since I left.?"

"No." Frederick's voice was quiet.

"You never checked if anything was true, father believed everything you said because you were the honest, upstanding son who never did anything wrong. But Grandfather checked.

"I thought when you went to Oxford the lies and the beatings would stop and they did until the brothel incident. Who told you I was involved, did you ask. No, you wrote to father. Luckily for me Grandfather was here and came to Eton to check. We were with the house-master that night discussing until well after curfew. He had to give us a pass in case we were stopped. Grandfather saw it, saw the way I lived.

"I was never punished at Eton, do you know that, Frederick, because I never did anything wrong. I loved my study. The headmaster hoped I would go to Oxford and become a Don. He thought I was that accomplished. But father hated me. You went to Oxford and for what, to make father feel good. Your gullibility has ruined my life. I never hated you because you were too innocent, you never realised what you were doing, there was no malice. But now your gullibility has taken an innocent girl's life. You will not believe me but I will tell you of a conversation I heard the day I left. '*And when we are married I will be rich and have everything I want – but I thought he was betrothed miss – oh don't worry, I've dealt with that.*' Do you need me to tell you whose voice it was? Who had 'dealt' with your betrothal to Diana? If Diana had loved that statue so much she only had a few weeks to wait and she could see it every day for the rest of her life. Why steal it and ruin her future?

"No, Frederick, I am not the only one in this house who knows you to be naïve and gullible."

They walked in silence.

"Why did you never tell me?"

"I did, but by the time I realised what was happening you all thought so badly of me. I never understood what I was being beaten for when I came home. He beat me harder for not knowing or denying it. I came to hate this house and everyone in it, just as everyone here hates me."

"No they don't, Michael, only father."

"Have you seen Wilson speak to me. 'Oh it's you, Master Michael,' and that was today. Mother hates me because father taught her to."

Frederick looked surprised.

"Had you never noticed that mother ignored me? She has never spoken to me since I was fourteen. The boys told me I was not given a decent allowance like you because I was a by-blow, so I made the mistake of asking father. I never ate with you for a week because I could not sit on a chair. I think that was the moment I realised what true hate was."

Frederick had nothing to say. How could he when he had so many emotions going through him.

"I will only stay a couple of days. I need to find employment if I am to survive. I was offered a promotion if I stayed in the army but I have had my fill of killing. I was never meant for a soldier."

Frederick remained silent.

They came to a bench looking down to the river where Michael sat. He put his hand to his waistcoat pocket and withdrew the pocket watch. Frederick looked at it.

"That's new."

"Actually it is not mine. I have taken an obligation to return it to the son of an officer who died in my arms."

"Where was that?"

"A question, Frederick? Are you sure you want to know? It was at Villefranche. A small village had been overrun by retreating French soldiers. They took all the food they could find, raped the women and any men not enlisted at gunpoint were shot. One man refused to go because he was responsible for several families. His wife had died and he had both their elderly parents and the children of more than one family to feed. They shot him.

"We arrived and they ran away, the villagers were relieved to see us. We treated them well, shared what food we were carrying. The women worked in the fields with the old men helping if they could as there were now no men. The boys did nothing. A teenage boy, old enough to have been enlisted, marched them around calling himself their General. Most of them were afraid of him, he was the quintessential bully and I should know how to recognise one.

"We stayed there three days. We were tired. It was not a battle, Frederick, it was two captains and their platoons resting. The main forces were spread out but we knew where to head for. On the third day my fellow captain put down his gun and removed his jacket to wash in the stream that ran through the village and from some balcony the young bully shot him in the back.

"I held a court martial. He could be dealt with as a civilian and hanged for murder or treated like the general he made himself out to be. He chose to be a General thinking it would give him immunity. He was put before a firing squad. Every member of Newman's platoon wanted to be part of it. The villagers shook our hands when we left. We buried Captain Newman in the churchyard, the villagers helped us.

"I did write a report to go to the General but I later found out the messenger had dropped his bag in the river when he had been shot trying to cross, so the report never made it.

"No one knows about Villefranche, Frederick, except the men who were there. But I told you about it in the letter I wrote. Yet you say you never received it, never received any of them. So where did the name Villefranche come from as the place I had died?"

Frederick sat with his head in his hands. "You must hate me."

"No Frederick, there was no malice in you. It just makes me sad that you could do that to me, and now you have the life of an innocent girl on your conscience, too. Why does Lucy say she is still finding items missing? It is over four years and Diana came here only rarely. How would Lucy know what was here before she replaced her?"

Frederick shook his head. "I don't know."

Michael stood. "Shall we return to the house, I am sure your wife has things to say and father will be waiting to glower at me for daring to be alive."

Dinner was a strange meal that night. Frederick rarely spoke, what his father said was less than friendly and Lucy poured venom on him. When they rose for Lucy to leave Michael declared he would take no port but retire to the library to read. His father was scathing.

"You would have me join you in the drawing room to allow your daughter-in-law to spend the evening hurling insults at me?"

"It is no more than you deserve."

"For what, for being alive, sir?"

His father glared at him.

"I quite understand, sir. It would have eased your conscience, no doubt, if I had died in France." He rose from the table. "I shall be in the library should anyone wish to speak with me."

Later in the evening while engrossed in a book Frederick arrived to tell him everyone had retired. It was rather early, Michael thought, but perhaps there was only so much of each other's company that they could bear.

Chapter 4

Michael breakfasted early. He had spent a restless night making plans. Once his horse was saddled he rode to the village to speak with the innkeeper Willy and the local shopkeepers.

"You are an early bird, sir. Will you be wanting breakfast?"

"No, Willy, merely a tankard of ale and some information."

"Mr Michael! Captain Pennington, I hardly recognised you."

Willy was a local man, the son of the previous innkeeper and married to a local girl. He was rather more rotund than Michael remembered and definitely had less hair. While he filled the tankard Michael asked "Willy, four years ago when I left, my father threw out a young girl, Diana Butterwick. What happened to her?"

"That were a long time ago. We did hear about it but none of them told us what happened."

"But you heard later?"

"Well, yes, but we didn't believe it. She were a lovely, gentle sort of girl, whereas that Mrs Pennington – well, none of us like her."

"Did anyone see or hear where she went? Who took her in?"

"No-one that we heard of. It's not like it used to be, Captain, everyone is bitter and miserable, none of them smile at you or wish you good day any more."

"This is important to me, Willy. Was there ever a body found in a ditch anywhere?"

"No, sir. I would 'av 'eard if so. Unless one of them found her and buried her quiet like. But their workers would have known and said something."

Michael dropped a coin on the table. "Thank you, Willy. Does Mr Frederick come in here often?"

"Not often, Captain, but more than 'e used to. Likes to get away from 'er, I expect. She's a demanding one with her trips to London and her fancy clothes."

Michael was not hopeful for the rest of his day after what Willy had said. His next call was to the vicar.

He was shown in to the Vicar's study with some haste.

"Am I intruding, Vicar, do you have guests that I interrupt?"

"I have no guests. Say what you have come for, I must admit we thought you had been killed."

"Indeed, so I understand. Another of my father's inaccuracies about me that he has always loved to spread."

The Vicar looked shocked.

"Your father is an upright and honest man. You would not understand that concept, of course."

"And my father is the Magistrate and also pays your stipend. Your loyalty speaks well for you, even if it is misplaced."

The Vicar's face was reddening with anger.

"What happened to Diana Butterwick? Did you take her in?"

"That little thief, no I did not."

"Did it never occur to you she might not be guilty?"

"Of course she was, they found the proof."

"They found what they were supposed to find. Your attitude is not one of a man of the cloth."

"How would you know with your character? She was as bad as you."

Michael was growing cold inside with the anger he felt.

"I take it you do not consider this girl's life to be on your conscience?"

"She deserved it."

"To die in a ditch."

Michael rose and picked up his hat.

"You, sir, do not know me, only the lies my family told of me. I have nothing on my conscience to be ashamed of, whereas you are not fit to call yourself a Christian. I studied religion a great deal at Eton, you do not have any of the attributes required. I studied other religions too and I have decided to stop 'turning the other cheek', something you have never done. I intend to follow another creed 'an eye for an eye and a tooth for a tooth.' Diana died because there is not a Christian among you, I will have 'a death for a death', Vicar. My father will hang for murder. Will you be his willing follower then."

He turned to leave while the Vicar stood dumb.

"I am leaving before the evil of this house should pollute my soul as it has yours."

The next visit was to the Turnbulls who had also been at the house party. He was refused admittance so he went to the Harcourts. Instead of his name and card he announced "Pennington to see Mr Harcourt."

He was shown into the parlour where both Mr and Mrs Harcourt sat.

"You!"

"Indeed, sir, in spite of my father's latest lie I am still alive."

"How dare you come here?"

"Easily, I have nothing in my life to be ashamed of, whereas the residents in this area are steeped in guilt. I find the lack of any Christian morals in the district a weight upon me."

He looked from one to the other.

"I am come to hear what happened when my father evicted Diana Butterwick without any questions being asked."

"She was a thief, the evidence was there."

"Oh the evidence, all of which came from the same person. Tell me, how often do you discuss that day?"

Mrs Harcourt was belligerent. "Regularly and we have reason to with all that Mrs Pennington is finding."

"Ah yes, Lucy Pennington, who had never been in the house before that day, knows every ornament in every room and still finds things missing. If your maid broke an ornament in a guest bedroom would you even notice? These are items you acquired, not ones in a house before you lived in it. What kind of item is the latest loss, may I ask?"

"The latest one is a beautiful woven ceramic basket in pink and blue from the guest suite."

"If it disappeared before Diana left how would Lucy know?"

"I imagine the maids told her."

"Oh the maids nobody ever questions. As it happens I know the piece you mean. Lucy must have seen it at some time since her marriage for it was not in Diana's possession on that day."

"It disappeared before."

"No Mrs Harcourt, it did not. My Great Aunt Letitia was staying in that suite at the time. I visited her shortly before I left and I remember picking up the basket and holding it, it was so delicate and intricate. Diana was not a thief, merely a young girl who stood in the path of a viper who wanted her removed. Who knows if she expected her to die but someone will hang for her murder, my father being one. Others like you will no doubt be allowed to live, but your soul is now blackened for all time.

"I take it you have no knowledge of where she died, dressed in her house slippers and only a muslin dress? You must be so proud of yourselves."

He turned to leave the room. "Goodbye, I shall be leaving the area very soon, I doubt I will ever return. I wish to live with honest and decent people, not here in this domain of Satan. But do not think you will escape. Fate has a way of extracting retribution."

The cold inside Michael was oozing through him. He needed to escape from here for a while. He rode away to the adjoining parish with another inn where he was not known.

Ordering a hot pie and ale he sat surveying the occupants of the tap.

"You passing through?" The innkeeper asked.

"In a way. I am searching for information about a girl, but from four years ago."

"Where've you been for four years?"

"In France with the army."

"Oh, and this girl was she local?"

"The next parish. They have no news of her."

"Do you think she might be married?"

"No, I think she might be dead in a ditch."

The innkeeper sucked in his breath through his teeth. "She were in trouble?"

"Not in the way you think, someone lied about her and she was not given an opportunity to defend herself. They just threw her out."

"Was she a maid or just an outdoor worker?"

"Not a maid, a gently born lady."

"Who would do that?!

"My father, and when I find how and where she died he will hang."

The innkeeper looked uncomfortable. "Per'aps you should talk to the Vicar. He'd know if he buried anyone."

"Thank you, I will."

The Vicar was of no help. He took out the register of burials and checked but there was none of an unknown woman. Thanking him Michael had one more call to make before his final confrontation with his father.

The Butterwicks were at home. The Butterwicks were always at home, they had nowhere to go, no-one to visit. The astonishment that someone was calling brought them all to the parlour where Mrs Butterwick was taking tea.

"Good afternoon, Mrs Butterwick."

"Do I know you, you seem familiar?"

"It's Michael Pennington." Felicia snarled. Mrs Butterwick spilled the tea.

"I am returned from the war to find an appalling injustice has happened. Your innocent daughter was criminally treated."

"Criminally! She was a thief and we are shunned because of it." Felicia bit out. Her mother was trembling close to tears. "Oh Mama still thinks her maligned. She has not had to suffer the nasty remarks and the public cuts from everyone. I can never marry because of her."

The door swung open and Mr Butterwick strode in. There was a cold icy aura about him.

"What are you doing here? Have your family not done enough to punish us?"

"I arrived yesterday and learned what happened. I came to see if you had any news of her."

"News, why should there be news, the girl was a thief, she deserved it."

Mrs Butterwick was in tears. No one in the room seemed to care about anyone else.

"I believe her innocent."

Butterwick looked at him in contempt.

"Then you are as big a fool as my wife."

"Do you not care about what happened to her? Is this bitterness what you intend for the rest of your life?"

"How would you know, you are not in a position to understand with your background."

"Why does everyone refer to my background? All you know of me are the lies my father told and you believed them." He had taken the pocket watch from his pocket and made a show of putting it on the table.

"Mrs Butterwick, a cup of tea would be most acceptable if you are pouring." He scooped the watch into his hand and walked to the tea table, dropping the watch into the basket of sewing beside Felicia's chair.

"You at least have some manners, Ma'am." He turned to face Butterwick.

"I intend to find out what happened to Diana. If she died in a ditch then I intend to report my father for murder. I understand you approved of your daughter being put out with nothing, not a cape nor proper shoes and no money. It will be the responsibility of the authorities to decide if you also are guilty and must hang. What will become of your family then, sir?"

Mrs Butterwick had collapsed back in her chair but Felicia never went to help her.

"I suggest you leave, sir."

"Captain! I am Captain Pennington and I have seen better men than you die for their country." He put his hand in his waistcoat pocket.

"My watch!" He looked around. "I put it here on the table. It belonged to a dead comrade and is to be returned to his family. I insist you return it!"

"We have not taken your watch."

"So where is it? You all saw it a few moments ago"

"None of us have been near the table."

Michael looked around. "I accuse … you!" he pointed to Felicia who leapt up in anger.

"I will search your things." He went to the sewing basket and lifted it to the table, tipping out the contents, revealing the watch.

"I never took it! You put it there. Your are trying to make me a thief like my sister."

"No, indeed I am not. I have just demonstrated what happened that day and why Lucy Firbeck knew exactly where they should search. Diana was no more guilty than you."

He placed the watch back in his waistcoat.

"Be aware, sir, I intend your daughter to be avenged. If I could punish every family in the neighbourhood then I would. If she is dead then someone will die, hopefully my father. If they hang him I will happily go and watch."

He bowed to Mrs Butterwick and left. Now he had the hardest interview of all, but the cold filled him and he knew exactly what he should do.

Chapter 5

Dinner that evening was no better. Hardly anyone spoke except Lucy and his father to complain at him. Frederick was silent which they blamed on Michael. When the meal drew to an end and the covers drawn Lucy rose to leave and Michael recognised his father's intention to speak severely to someone.

He took out the watch and looked up into Frederick's eyes.

"I find the atmosphere here decidedly icy; I believe I will take myself to the inn for some warmer companionship. I will be leaving in the morning."

The look on Lucy's face was a picture. More than one person could play the viper in this house. He had few clothes with him; it would take little time to pack.

He knocked on his mother's door to be admitted by her maid.

"Madam has not quite finished her dinner, sir. Would you like to come later?"

"I will wait."

He sat on a chair near the door where he could see his mother while she could not see him. She was looking older, her hair was thinning, there were loose hairs on her shawl, too many to be normal.

The maid took a box from the dinner tray and placed it on a side table with bottles such as the doctor prescribed. The maid then removed the tray and assisted his mother into a more comfortable chair.

Michael stood and came to bow before her.

"Good evening, Mama." She said nothing.

"I am aware you will never speak to me. I came to say goodbye. You will never see me again but I would like to tell you to your face, I am not what you have been told. A better son could not have lived nor a more maligned one."

His mother waved her hand to her maid. "I would go to my bedchamber." The maid assisted her as she turned away from him without any recognition of his presence.

He waited.

"You should go, sir. Your presence upsets her and she is increasingly ill."

Michael crossed to the table with the medicines and picked up the small box of powder.

"What is this?"

"To help her."

"It is not a doctor's box."

"No, sir, Mrs Lucy brought it, her mother found it most useful."

Michael replaced the box and noted the position to the left of all the others.

"And no doubt she suggests she takes more as the weeks go by."

"Indeed sir.

Michael turned to the door to leave.

"What will you do when your mistress dies?"

"Oh she is only a little unwell, she will recover, sir."

"Not if she takes that powder. You may be in need of a position sooner than you realise."

An hour later, waiting in the library, Michael heard his father go into his study. He put down the now empty brandy glass.

Suitably determined he knocked on the study door.

"Come."

He entered to the astonishment of his father.

"What do you want? An apology will get you nowhere now."

"I never thought it would, but then I never had anything to apologise for. Grandfather knew that. That is why he gave me the money."

His father looked up sharply.

"I found out the afternoon before I left for France. I am over twenty one, I want a paper to Wentworth to tell him you relinquish any rights to it."

"And if I don't?"

"I will go to the courts, even if it costs me every penny."

Michael stared into his father's eyes, his father gave in first. He took out a sheet and wrote instructions for Wentworth, handing the paper to Michael who read it and folded it to place it securely into his pocket.

"Now you can leave."

"I think not. I have just this one time, after which I will never see you again. Thank you for the paper, it will be used together with the letter Grandfather wrote giving me my money under my control to allow me to go to Oxford. I have the letter you wrote to the agent when you removed the money to Wentworth. By the way, Wentworth said the money would be mine at twenty one. Why did you pay my allowance to Frederick. I was over twenty one and you have never been informed of my death?"

His father was having trouble finding the right words.

"Come now, I don't have all night, I have much to say. Was Frederick short of money, his wife does seem expensive to keep."

"She is."

"So why did you give him one thousand pounds from my account?"

"She wanted to go to London for a season."

"And that is a good reason to give him my money, is it?"

His father sat silent.

"I have never known you so quiet. Usually you are shouting at me as you beat me for offences I never committed. But you didn't know that, did you? You believed everything Frederick said. It must have been a shock when Grandpapa proved it was all lies and I was not the evil son you thought.

Any decent father would have made amends but not you. When you opened my letter from Grandfather telling me about the money you never gave me a penny from then onwards. Everyone thinks you a generous father burying my colours but you did not, did you? You used my money. You opened every letter I received and kept the knowledge from me. You stopped me from the study and position I was most suited for. I also have the letters changing the allowance payment and transferring the thousand pounds. It should make interesting reading to a lawyer. I did warn Wentworth I intended to sue for theft and embezzlement.

"My twenty thousand pounds is just over nine thousand now. Wentworth's investments bring in less than the fees he charges. I wonder if they do yours too, if so you may be running out of money soon, especially with my money no longer paid to Frederick, and Lucy so expensive. But first I wish to recall the day I left for the war."

His father cleared his throat. "What about it?"

"No one came to see me away."

"Is that all."

"That is of no import, but I might not have walked the places that held such memories of my young life before I left. When I passed the maze I heard women's voices. 'And when I marry him I will be rich and have everything I want. - But I thought he was betrothed, miss. - Oh don't worry, I've dealt with that'. I thought Lucy Firbeck was referring to Lord Williams whom she had tried to entice at Harwood's dinner the week before. It seems it was Frederick, and she did deal with Diana, with your help. Did anyone check the maid? Did anyone hear this avid interest in an ornament. I told Frederick, why steal an ornament when in a few weeks she would live in the same house and see it every day. Nothing makes sense. But then sense was never your good point, was it. You 'evicted' her; that was the word Frederick used. Dressed for a party in her slippers you pushed her out to die. You bullied her father into agreeing with you, destroying every member of her family. Still they are isolated by the venom that viper spews at every possible occasion.

"By the way Frederick now realises that I wrote to him regularly and you withheld all my letters, just as you had mine."

"I did no such thing." it was just bluster.

"What about Villefranche, you said a Pennington was killed there. How did you hear of it?"

"It was in the news sheet."

"That is another lie. Villefranche was not a battle, just two platoons resting in a village. The report never reached the Colonel's office. No one knows of Villefranche except me and the letter I wrote to my brother. How much of this will I need to convince the authorities you are not fit to be a magistrate. Will I tell them before I find out what happened to Diana Butterwick? You will have to wait and see which comes first, the denouncement, the court case for theft and or the case for murder."

"Murder!"

"What did you think would happen to a gently bred young miss dressed in her party clothes in the countryside with nowhere to go? You knew she would die and you cared nothing. You made sure nobody assisted her. To me that constitutes murder."

His father was staring in horror.

"You may not live long enough, of course. When Lucy learns there is no more money and Frederick's allowance is reduced by the loss of mine, be careful what you eat. It is so easy to die from a serious stomach upset. What will happen to your wife then? Will her marriage agreements be there or will she be removed before you. Of course, when Frederick inherits and finds there really is no money, how long before a poor grieving Widow Pennington takes what she can and searches London for another wealthy husband?"

"You go too far."

"Do I, sir? Whether you choose to believe me is up to you, but I would give you a little advice. When people are poisoned with arsenic their hair falls out. I should check the white powder mother sprinkles on her food as a tonic given by Lucy.

The box lies to the left of the doctor's medicines; you could get him to check it.

He went to the decanter to pour a brandy for both of them. Putting the glass in front of his father he made his final point.

"I will give you a forecast for the future. Unless you act, in the next few weeks mother will die. Depending on your finances you will be dead within a year, Frederick a matter of months, perhaps weeks after you. Within the next day or two Lucy will demand you cease my allowance as they need it more, and I will be accused of a heinous crime which she will never expect you to investigate. It may be something in the war which she could never have known; perhaps I am supposed to be dismissed for some evil reason. If you wish to check, my Colonel wanted me to stay on, I was to be promoted. It won't matter what, because she knows you too well. You are a bully, but she is a cunning viper."

He finished his drink. "I will never think of you as my father, you are neither a gentleman nor a Christian.

"I will retire now; I leave very early in the morning. It will be pointless to try to find me; I am too ashamed of the name Pennington. I would rather lose the title Captain than keep the hated name of this family. If you survive long enough you may see me in the crowd when they hang you."

With that he left the study where his father sat stunned.

He walked silently through the hall to the stairs making sure Frederick and Lucy never heard. If he had this well enough planned the little viper would fall into the trap he had devised when he announced his visit to the tavern.

He rang his bell to summon a footman and ordered hot water to be brought at six in the morning. Breakfast was not important; he could stop on the way. Anything eaten in this house now would choke him.

Chapter 6

Lansdale let him alone the first day. The second day something was definitely wrong and it was eating into him. The third day he sent Robert to see if he could get through to him.

"Pennington."

"Don't call me that ever again!"

Robert thought out his response.

"Michael, what name shall I call you?" Best not ask too many questions yet. "Have you thought of one yet?"

"No."

"I hesitate to ask why; your family have never been the happy supportive kind."

"I feel cold inside."

"Do you need something hot or some brandy?"

"No, I've felt like this for days."

"Something happened didn't it?"

"Yes."

"I won't ask if you don't want to tell me."

"I went to threaten him over the money, to find out why Frederick was given it." He looked down at his feet. "I feel ill now and so cold." He leaned back in his chair, he was definitely uncomfortable. "I remember once your father said I only went to say goodbye to show off my uniform to the young ladies. I remember clearly saying there was only one and she was to marry Frederick within the month."

He put his head in his hand. "I think I will have that brandy."

Robert poured one for them both.

"Here, sip it, it will help warm you."

"I doubt anything could at the moment. The day I left I spoke with Diana at breakfast. I thought how lucky Frederick was, she was such a gentle girl." His eyes had clouded over as he looked into the past. "She wore a dress of pale blue muslin with lace at the edges and dainty slippers to match, definitely only of any use in the house.

"Frederick came in then and spoke but he let this dreadful girl interrupt. She dominated any conversation. I heard she had tried to catch Lord Williams the week before, so when I heard her talking in the garden it never bothered me and I left." He took a gulp from his glass.

"Sip it, Michael."

"When I arrived I found Frederick married to the dreadful creature. She had told her maid she had dealt with someone's betrothal. It was Frederick's. She had planted an ornament in Diana's belongings then made it look like theft. You know my father, she had no chance. He opened the door and pushed her out dressed as she was. No one took her in; no one has seen her since. I have searched. If she died of hunger and cold, which is most probable, I intend to accuse him of murder"

"Murder? That is a big step to take."

"How many steps could Diana take in those slippers. They knew what they did, all of them. Of course you know who Lucy told, who never checked but went straight to father."

"Frederick."

"Yes. He knows the truth now, if he can live with it."

"Someone must know where she went."

"No-one. I went to the village, to the inns, to the neighbouring parish. I even asked after bodies in the ditch.

"Have you asked everyone who was there?"

"Those that would speak to me."

"What about the maids."

"The staff don't speak to me, the butler won't allow them to. He hates me."

"Your mother?"

"No, she ... Aunt Letitia was there! She said she would leave if I did, she called them mealy mouthed harpies. I went to see her before I left."

"Where does she live?"

"Not far from Grandfather Arnott. That's it, I will be Mr Michael Arnott. How do I do it legally, do I have to? Can I still be Captain?"

"You need to ask someone from the regiment?"

"I'll ask the Colonel. I want to see if he can find me some employment, possibly with the foreign office."

"If you do something positive it might help you to feel better."

"I'll send a note and ask for a meeting."

Robert patted him on the shoulder. "How about a walk in the park to get some fresh air and check out the latest curricles?"

"Curricles or their occupants, Robert?"

"Michael. I'm a happily married man." he laughed.

Henry Lansdale sat back in his chair and contemplated his son.

"Was he sweet on this girl, do you think?"

"She was to marry his brother so he would tell you not, but he described the dress and slippers she was wearing over four years ago."

"I would take that as a yes, then."

"It has certainly hit him hard. He feels icy cold inside, that's the way he described it. He's going to see the Colonel to ask if changing his name will mean he is only a Mr. He wants a job too."

"I doubt there will be any jobs, there are too many already at the Foreign Office whose usefulness ended with the capture of Bony."

"What could he do? Is he really in the best state of mind to choose a lifelong profession."

"He can stay here but I feel he will only get worse. Could he go to visit anyone?"

"He could go to see this Great Aunt he was going to write to. She lives near to his Grandfather so a visit there might help him. He has that watch to return also. I hope he remembers to ask for the direction of the man's family."

"Are you trying to get rid of me?"

"No, Michael, you can stay here as long as you wish, you know that. I just think your Grandfather would like a visit now you are home. You can visit your Great Aunt, too."

"She is a crotchety old lady but with a heart of gold. Now I think about our conversation that day, she was trying to find out if I knew about the money, I'm sure."

"Then go and see them. They are your good family; you have even taken his name."

"That was easier than I thought. I am registered as Captain Arnott Pennington for the records but I don't need to use Pennington if I don't wish. I can just be Captain Arnott or even Mr Michael Arnott, I like that. Nobody asking about the war.

"Take today, I decided to take tea in Bond Street and someone remarked on my looking like her cousin who was a soldier. I said I had been a soldier and she expected me to know her cousin. Then someone overheard and wanted me to tell her how her brother died, as if I were there. People have no idea about war and the number of men involved. I think next time I shall say nothing. Mr Arnott of no fixed abode."

"There are too many like that now. You know you are welcome here, Michael."

Michael set out for his Grandfather's estate in a happier frame of mind. It felt better to be doing something not just thinking. He would go to his Grandfather, visit his Great Aunt then continue north to the Newmans' to return the watch. The only cloud on his horizon was how to avoid telling Grandfather his money was so depleted he needed an occupation. Best not to say anything if possible.

It had been during his early childhood when he last visited. Usually things seem smaller when you see them as a grown man, but not this estate, somehow it seemed to have grown.

He handed over his horse and knocked on the door which was opened immediately by an elderly butler.

"I would like to see Mr Arnott."

He handed him his card with pride.

"Oh, Mr ..."The butler looked confused.

"If you will wait a moment, sir."

The elderly man walked sedately down the hallway and knocked at a door. After a brief conversation he returned.

"If you will come this way, sir. Please try not to tire Mr Arnott too much."

Michael smiled at him. "I will try."

He entered a comfortably large study, a man who looked like a steward sat at the large desk, his grandfather sitting in a comfortable chair his knees wrapped in a blanket. He looked old and frail.

"Grandfather."

"Michael! It is you. But your card says Arnott."

"That is my name now, sir. I still own the Pennington name but have no wish to use it."

"You have argued with your father?"

"As usual, sir, over several things which I will not worry you with at present. I am just happy to be here."

"We must talk further, how long will you stay?"

"As long as you wish, sir."

"Oh good, then that is settled. Call Tranter, will you?" He indicated the door which Michael opened and called. The butler arrive almost instantly.

"Have Mrs Tranter arrange a room for my grandson, will you Tranter? I think the blue room, don't you?"

"Of course, Mr Arnott."

"Fletcher, can we continue this at another time. You can show Michael what we do here, I'm sure he would be interested." Then rather belatedly. "This is Fletcher, my steward as you heard. My grandson, Michael, who has just returned safely from the war, for which I am exceedingly thankful."

The men shook hands. He seemed a very genuine man with an open smiling face, but then he worked for a very generous employer.

"I think we could do with some coffee, or would you rather something stronger?"

"Coffee will do nicely, thank you, sir."

"Would you care for Fletcher to show you the estate tomorrow morning, some of it at least? It would take all day to see all of it."

"I would indeed. If you are free, Fletcher."

"I will meet you at eight if that is not too early for you."

"Not by my usual hours, it sounds very reasonable."

"Until tomorrow then." He bowed to Grandfather Arnott, then Michael and took his leave.

"I usually spend most of my time in here, although we can go to a more ornate room if you wish?" It was so unusual to Michael for someone to address him so jovially.

"The study will suit me well enough, Grandfather."

"Then sit down and tell me all your news, where you have been, who you have met. Not all today, of course. We have plenty of time."

Michael settled in a chair facing the old man.

"How are you, sir? It is so many years since I have seen you."

"Rather older and weaker than the last time. I had hoped you would come while you were at Oxford, but you never managed to go, I understand. It hurt both of us your father concealing the letters. It worried me, I have to admit, when you went to the war. You were never destined for a soldier, Michael. Was it hard, the life in France?"

"It was not easy I have to admit. If life before had been easier it would have been more difficult. Some came from happy homes and an easy life and the shock was sometimes more than they could handle. The biggest shock to most was the lack of accommodation and food. We had to find our own food and often slept in ditches and haystacks, anywhere available. When you were detached from the main army there were no tents."

"How did you feel sleeping in the open?"

"Well …" Michael said sheepishly. "I had so little after I left Eton that when visiting friends I never had the money for inn rooms, I usually slept where I could, wrapped in my cloak."

His grandfather rubbed his forehead.

"I'm sorry, sir, I have distressed you."

"No matter, Michael, I need to know. Was there much hand to hand fighting?"

"Oh yes, there were set battles, of course, but often we had to take a Spanish village or a mountain pass. The larger the town the more likely you were to run against your own forces when you moved through the streets. Someone asked me about the villages, what they were like. I told her, when you are fighting to save your life the architecture is of no importance."

He took the watch from his waistcoat. "I want to return this to the family. Newman died in my arms, shot in the back while unarmed in a safe and friendly place. He was a good friend with somewhat similar family problems to mine. It was never safe wherever you were; it was hard to accept that in the beginning." His head fell forward. "Sometimes I feel tired to my soul, sir."

A knock on the door brought the coffee with some delicious looking biscuits.

"I really can't get used to having good coffee and biscuits such as these. It's only when you return that you realise exactly how much you have missed simple things."

The footman had poured the coffee for Grandfather as usual and placed it on the desk beside him.

"Will that be all, sir?"

"Yes thank you. My grandson will help if I need it."

"Your staff seem very friendly, sir."

"So they should be. I am not the ogre your father is, they have little to do now I do not entertain. Now you are here we will make them work a little harder, I believe." His eyes sparkled. "So tell me how long you have been home and where you have been?"

Michael knew what the question meant. Had he been home to Pennington.

"I have mostly been in London with Lansdale. My friend is married now but his father insists I am welcome to stay with him as long as I wish."

Should he mention the money? "I had need of clothes which took some time. I am a rather different physique than when I left." He puffed up his chest and patted his firm flat waistline. His grandfather chuckled.

"You are indeed a fine figure of a man. The ladies will be chasing you."

He saw the shadow of pain as it crossed Michael's face.

"What is it, boy? Has some girl hurt you?"

He wondered how to tell him without upsetting him too much. Maybe today was too soon for such a revelation.

"Can we talk of this another day, Grandfather?"

"Of course. Today is a happy day, not one to be spoiled by sad thoughts. Drink your coffee and I will show you my library."

Dinner was taken in a small dining parlour which was the only room apart from the study that his grandfather used. He was slow in his walking and a footman came to give him his arm as support. They talked a little as they ate but his grandfather was tired and excused himself to retire early.

"I hope I have not tired you too much, sir?"

"This has been the best day for many years, my boy, a little tiredness does not bother me, I am used to it. Enjoy your ride with Fletcher in the morning."

Chapter 7

Fletcher and Michael fell into an easy companionship as they rode the fields and farms. He was introduced to several tenant farmers who seemed genuinely pleased to meet Mr Arnott's grandson home from the war.

His father may not have told him about estate work but his time spent with Ashford on his father's estate had given him a surprisingly wide knowledge. Fletcher was quite impressed.

It was spring now and there were lambs in the fields with shepherds in close attendance.

"Are the sheep a large part of the estate?"

"Not the major part. Mr Arnott likes to have a good variety in the event of a bad harvest or a disease among the animals. We also have chickens in the home farm. You might want to see the kennels. We keep few dogs now but we continue to shoot birds for the table. The coverts are on the other side of the estate where the major woodlands are. You will meet the gamekeeper in a day or two, I expect."

Grandfather had spent the morning resting in his chair in the library before the fire, which meant he had spent most of the morning asleep. They took lunch a little late when Michael had returned.

"So tell me what your plans are now?"

Michael was relaxed and not thinking closely of what he said.

"Well I have to return the watch, see you and Aunt Letitia then find a job in London, possibly with the Foreign office if I am lucky."

"Do you mean an occupation to fill your time or work to bring in payment?"

Michael suddenly realised what he had said. His grandfather, however old, was still astute.

"I gather from your silence that my gift has been seriously depleted. Is there any left?"

"Just over nine thousand pounds."

"What did he spend it on?"

"My allowance, my commission and you have to realise he never gave me a penny since I was sixteen, it all came from my funds."

"Was your allowance that good?"

"No, he never raised it from Eton days. He gave it to Wentworth to invest, the interest was less than Wentworth's charges." He took a deep breath. "Then there was the money he gave to Frederick."

His Grandfather sat quietly."

"I see, how much?"

"My allowance for a year plus one thousand pounds."

"Why?"

"He has an expensive wife."

He sat and thought deeply, Michael said nothing.

"Do you like her?"

"No, she's a viper."

"Well that was honest enough. But there is something more."

"It will distress you too much, Grandfather."

"Not as much as it distresses you. Tell me."

"She planted an ornament in his fiancée's belongings and told Frederick it had been stolen. You can guess the rest."

"Frederick went to his father?"

"Yes."

"What did he do?"

"In Frederick's words he 'evicted' her, with nothing."

"What did the local gentry do?"

"Nothing. Believed him, agreed with him."

"What was she wearing, do you know, was she dressed for travel?"

"A pale blue muslin dress with short sleeves, lace edges, matching slippers suitable only for indoors."

"Cloak, money?"

"Nothing. I have been trying to find her. If I find she died hungry and cold in a ditch I intend to report him for murder. I told him so."

"You have found your strength of character in France, Michael. I am proud of you. Is there no sign of her?"

"None. Great Aunt Letitia was there, I want to ask her if she has any information, she might have seen something." The old man looked sadly at him. "All my letters never arrived, did they? Aunt Letitia died last year."

Michael put his head in his hands and gritted his teeth. "I will have retribution for her. They will not win!"

Grandfather sat back in his chair and remained thoughtful.

"I told him I intended to take a court case against him and Wentworth for theft and embezzlement. I will see him unseated as a magistrate if I manage nothing else."

"You remember the girl well, Michael. Is this the young lady who you were thinking of yesterday?"

"Yes. She was gentle, unassuming, honest and helpful, and Frederick was due to marry her. I was a little envious, even if I could never afford a wife. It appears he cared nothing for her or he would have fought to keep her."

"You could ask Letitia's maid, I suppose. She must have been there and maids do talk."

Michael perked up a little. "Do you know where she is?"

"Not exactly. Your aunt had a companion for several years. A woman with no family or friends. She left her money to make her independent but she has no home. She went as a companion to the Smeaton's daughter, I am sure she took the maid with her."

"It may not prove useful but it is something to give me hope."

"I will write to Smeaton before you go, give him some warning. I would not like you to cause any trouble for the girl; she has a difficult life on her own."

He rang the bell to order tea then laid his head back and fell into a doze. Michael made up the fire and relaxed a little. It was only a small hope, but it was better than nothing.

The next morning Fletcher took Michael riding the estate again. This time they went in a different direction, towards the woodlands and mainly arable land. The fields were ploughed and seeds were being sown. They discussed the amount of grain per field and the overall amount required. Michael had been to Ashford's in the spring but not since before the war, he was interested in how they gained an even spread throughout the whole field. They rode past barley fields already seeded, young boys in evidence everywhere as they tried to keep the birds at bay.

The woods were dense in places, in others they had been coppiced. The gamekeeper had a cottage on the edge of the woodland but he was in the pens with the new chicks and those about to hatch.

"Freddie, come and meet Mr Arnott's grandson."

A wizened man emerged to shake Michael's hand.

"Michael Arnott. You are the gamekeeper I take it. Will it be a good year for the birds, do you think?"

"Not unless the weather improves. If they cut too much wood there will not be enough cover for them. They need it to shelter from the rain and sun. I says it every year, but do they listen."

Fletcher chuckled and patted him on the shoulder. "You do, Freddie, but every year you manage quite sufficient birds."

"Is there enough woodland to supply all the household needs?"

"We manage well enough. If we were to set aside land for more wood we would lose out on the cereal harvest which has always been lucrative. There is talk of coal becoming more accessible. If that happens the wood will be of less importance. Come, you have yet to see the river. Where it comes down to the higher pasture we have a lake to ensure a regular supply of water. We have sheep on the highest pasture where the grass is coarser; we take them up when the lambs are weaned and need less supervision."

Michael felt a new peace riding this well-tended land of his grandfather. It was no wonder his funds were better than the Penningtons', he cared for it and for the people who worked it.

The river was quite high at this time of year. The fishing would be good, no doubt there were good places to swim in the summer.

He spent some time staring into the depths, lost in his memories while Fletcher waited, quietly watching over this troubled young man. The old man was right, it would be some time before his grandson would find peace. He could barely imagine how a gentle scholar would feel thrown into the horror of war, but he had time, his grandfather would make sure of that, and he was more than willing to help.

After lunch Fletcher came to the study to discuss the progress of the barley, it was late in germination, the wheat late in sowing due to the heavy wet ground. Michael asked after the tenant farmers' land, how productive it was, did it need any improvement, did they have their own plough horses. The discussions lengthened until Fletcher noticed Grandfather's eyelids drooping.

"Enough for today, sir. You are tired, I will come again tomorrow unless you send other instruction."

Grandfather nodded and waved his hand. "Indeed"

The two men sat alone and silent. When he was sure he was asleep, Michael stole quietly out of the study and went to the library to find a book. His Grandfather had a good selection. Taking down an interesting looking history he returned to the study. There was no fire to keep him in the library, but he had no intention of leaving him on his own, he may need something.

The days fell into a pattern, riding in the morning, discussing the estate in the afternoon and a quiet evening reading after Grandfather had retired. After a little over a week

Michael was more relaxed, more contented but the problem of finding Diana Butterwick's fate still hung over him.

"Grandfather, if you have no objection I would like to visit the Smeatons you spoke of."

"I wondered how long before you would feel driven to go."

"Driven, sir?"

"Indeed. You have a driving need for retribution which will not easily be overcome. Best you go and find out what you can."

"You have written to them?"

"Yes I have, they are expecting you, no doubt Miss Newby will have been informed of your upcoming visit. You will return here?" It was not so much a question as a plea.

"How long will it take, shall I be away for long, do you think?" In truth he was loath to leave the old man alone now.

"Only two hours the way you young ride. If you go early you may be back in the day, or at least the following day."

"Then I will take your directions and leave in the morning. Miss Newby, you say. Was she with my Aunt long?"

"Several years. She was very good to her at the end when it became hard for my sister to live with her illness. Miss Newby was a true gift to her, she deserved everything Letitia left her."

"Was it much?"

"Five thousand pounds, enough to keep her comfortably but not enough to buy and staff a house. She is not a servant, Michael, she is given no remuneration, merely a place to live in exchange for friendship and comfort."

Chapter 8

Only two hours, the directions lay in his pocket, his cape around his shoulders against the damp weather. They would have difficulty sowing today. He pulled up the collar of his cape to stop the wet dripping from his hat down the back of his neck, the front of him low to shield his face. What a strange spring it was.

He passed through villages and a good sized town. There was a large emporium, now defunct, obviously the owners had lost their money. If they had died surely there would have been some family to continue. The only reason he noticed was because of the name, now faded, painted on the front. Newby. Was this why his Aunt's companion had no money and no family.

There were a range of houses he passed, some larger than others, the Smeatons' was not one of the largest but it was obviously that of a gentleman. Michael wondered how Grandfather had known them.

He handed over his horse and presented himself at the front door.

"Mr Arnott to see Mr Smeaton." It was still early for many ladies to be down.

A man about his father's age came to meet him.

"Come in young man, your Grandfather wrote to me." He led him to the drawing room where a lady, obviously his wife, rose to greet him.

"Newby, can you arrange coffee for Mr Arnott. You do drink coffee?" She had turned to Michael.

"Yes, Ma'am, I do. Thank you."

The butler's name was Newby, could he possibly be a relation?"

"I understand you have come for information about Miss Newby and her maid."

"Yes indeed, sir."

"I will tell you what occurred."

Michael was puzzled but was inclined to listen.

* * *

The butler opened the door as she stood feeling rather alone. It was good for both of them to have someone now Aunt Letitia had died.

The Smeatons, she had been told, had a daughter who needed a companion to lift her from the ennui into which she was sinking. She had declared she no longer wished to go out into society and hardly left her room.

Her parents were at a loss. She had been so happy, looking forward to a loving marriage, the agreements had been drawn up, until the day she announced she would not marry him. Nothing her parents said would change her mind, but she refused to say why. It did not help that her intended seemed to feel the same way. From that dreadful day two months ago she had become increasingly silent.

They had invited friends to visit but she refused to see them. They organised a visit to her Grandmother but she refused to go. In asking for help from close relatives someone had suggested a companion, a young lady who could sit quietly with her or read to her, just someone to prevent her from shutting herself completely away.

As it happened they knew of just such a young lady. She had been a companion to Mrs Fortesque, old Mr Arnott's sister. Mrs Fortesque had recently died and although not needing employment she did need somewhere to live. Mr Arnott was applied to, Mr Smeaton, who was a little acquainted with him, rode over to discuss the suggestion.

So here she was, alone with only her maid standing at the front door of a strange house.

As she lifted her hand to knock the door opened.

"Good afternoon, Miss Newby, you are expected. If you would care to come this way."

He turned to the maid nearby. "Take Miss Newby's maid to her room and show her also where she will sleep, Mary. The trunks will be brought up shortly."

He led her down the hall to the drawing room and announced "Miss Newby, sir, madam."

"Thank you Newby. Do come in Miss Newby. I feel this is going to be a little confusing. Our butler is called Newby."

Mrs Smeaton had risen to take her hands to welcome her.

"Come sit with me. It must be difficult for you, suddenly alone like this. It will feel strange to begin with but I am sure you will soon feel at home."

"Thank you Ma'am. It does feel a little daunting."

"Would you like tea, Miss Newby?"

"Yes Ma'am I would but please, if you call me Diana it will no doubt solve the problem with your butler."

"Indeed it will. Diana is such a pretty name and it suits you. I understand you have been a companion to Mrs Fortesque for some years?"

"Yes, Ma'am, she was very good to me."

"And you to her, from what we hear." Smeaton noted

"The household have been instructed you are not a paid servant but a guest, even a member of the family, and should be treated as such."

"Thank you, Ma'am."

"When we have taken tea I will take you to your room. How soon would you like to meet Geraldine, my daughter?"

"Quite soon, Ma'am. If she does not take to me it would be of no use to unpack my trunk."

"Goodness me, Diana, and where would you go. No, I am quite cognisant of your position in life. You need a home and we will allow time for Geraldine to become acquainted with you."

"Thank you Ma'am."

"You are very quiet, is there any problem?"

Mr Smeaton joined in. "Not if you would let her settle Francis. You have barely given her a moment." Then turning to Diana, "I believe you are just the gentle companion my daughter needs, my dear. Do not let my wife talk you into silence. When you know us better I expect you to be able to converse freely enough."

Her room faced the garden where the roses were blooming and the colourful flowers nodded in the breeze. It had a pleasant symmetry with some evergreen hedges and trees. The sun, she was told, shone in the window in the early morning until just before lunch. That pleased her, she was an early riser and often sat and read before going downstairs. The furnishings were light, not the heavy dark drapes often found in guest rooms and the bed felt comfortable.

Eliza hovered outside the door until Mrs Smeaton encouraged her in.

"You are Miss Diana's maid, I believe."

"Yes, Ma'am."

"You are older than I would have expected, have you been with her long?"

"No ma'am. I was Mrs Fortesque's maid."

"Oh, I see. What is your name?"

"Eliza, Ma'am." Turning to Diana she asked "Did you not have your own maid?"

"No, Ma'am. Aunt Letitia, Mrs Fortesque wanted me to but there was really no need. I needed only a little help from Eliza and I was already helping her with Mrs Fortesque."

"Diana, you called her Aunt, was she your family?"

"No, ma'am, but she treated me as if she were. It pleased her to be called Aunt."

Mrs Smeaton went to the window where the sun was throwing heavy shadows from behind the house. "If you are ready, Diana, I will take you to meet your companion."

Geraldine's room was only two doors away. Mrs Smeaton tapped on the door then opened it to enter.

"Geraldine, dear, I have brought someone to see you. This is Miss Diana Newby, she is staying with us for a while." She took Diana's hand and drew her into the room. Diana curtsied.

"Good afternoon, Miss Smeaton." She was not quite sure what else to say, what did Geraldine know about her coming.

"Sit down, Diana, I am sure you and Geraldine will get along very well once you know each other. I will leave you to talk. Martha will be outside if you need any assistance."

She shooed the maid out and left the two young women staring at the floor in embarrassment. Surprisingly it was Geraldine who spoke first.

"I do not want a companion."

"But I do." Diana replied. "I have no family and nowhere to go. I am grateful for your family giving me a home if only for a while." She subsided into silence. Geraldine was obviously thinking.

"No family at all?"

"No."

"But where do you live?"

"I have no home now Mrs Fortesque has gone."

"Was she your family?"

"No. I was her companion. She gave me a home."

"Are you totally alone?"

"I have Mrs Fortesque's maid with me."

"What work are you qualified for?"

"I have no need to work."

Geraldine looked surprised. "But surely you are being paid?"

"I have my own money, my dowry is invested to give me sufficient. I need only a home to live in, for that I offer friendship and whatever is asked. I believe I have more need of you than you have of me."

Diana walked to the window, the view of the garden was the same as hers, the sun throwing the shadow of the house across the terrace and nearest flowerbeds, the distant colours glowing in the afternoon sun.

"The garden looks delightful, do you walk there often?"

"No, I keep to my room."

"Then I will walk alone unless you require my company indoors." Geraldine sat silent. There was a novel laid on a table. Diana went to it but thought she might upset her if she touched anything, so she returned to her chair and sat.

"Do you enjoy reading?"

"Not often."

"If you are not disposed to read for yourself I would willingly read for you. I always read for Mrs Fortesque. It helped to fill the days, she said."

"Then perhaps you would read for me." My my, progress this early.

"Do you have a favourite book?"

"Not love stories."

Oh dear, there was a problem of the heart here.

"Then I shall read a history or a travel book. Travel can be very helpful in sending your thoughts to far away places."

"Do you enjoy far away places, Miss Newby?"

"Diana, please call me Diana, it will save the confusion with your butler, and yes, I enjoy reading of distant places where everything is different. I imagine what it would be like to be there, it helps me to fall asleep at night."

"Do you have trouble sleeping too?"

"Oh yes, especially when it is winter and reading is not so easy. I like to read at night before I sleep and early in the morning before anyone is awake."

"I wake early too but there is nothing worth leaving my bed for so I lie and stare at the walls."

"Then if you would like I will come early and read while you are in bed." Geraldine smiled. It was the first time and Diana hoped she could encourage many more as the days passed.

A gong sounded to announce time to dress for dinner.

"That is for your benefit, Diana, it does not normally happen."

"Then I will go and prepare. If you will excuse me Miss Smeaton."

"Geraldine. If I am to call you Diana you must call me Geraldine."

"Do you go down to dinner?"

"Not often, but perhaps today I will."

"Dinner was strange for everyone. Diana was in an unknown house, Geraldine mostly did not come down, Mr and Mrs Smeaton were not sure what to say to either of them.

Mrs Smeaton tried to make conversation. "Have you always been alone, Diana? Were you educated at a school?"

"Oh no. I was educated at home."

"You did have a home once. Did you have parents?"

"Yes Ma'am, and a sister."

"But now you have no-one."

"No Ma'am."

"How old were you when you lost them?"

"Seventeen, Ma'am."

"Oh, I see. Was it a carriage accident?"

"If you please, Ma'am I prefer not to speak of it."

Mrs Smeaton looked embarrassed. "Of course, my dear." But still she went to ask more. "Was no provision made for you?"

Diana looked down at her plate.

"Enough, my dear, do not press her. It is painful for her." God bless Mr Smeaton.

"You must not allow my wife to question you, Diana, it is for her own curiosity only." He patted his wife's hand. "She likes to know everything but sometimes it causes her distress when she does." He smiled at Mrs Smeaton. "That is so, is it not, my dear?"

"Yes it is. I do not mean to pry or upset you, Diana. I will not press you again."

After dinner she asked to see the library.

"You wish to read tonight?"

"I would like to take a book if I may?"

"Certainly you may, although I do not know if we have any of the novels you young girls read."

"Oh no, sir. I look for a travel book."

"Travel, then this section here is what you need." He moved the candle he held across the titles on the covers. Diana put out her hand and took one.

"It really does not matter which. I cannot know which is the most interesting until I have read them."

Mr Smeaton laughed. "What a practical young lady you are."

"I hope so sir. Fanciful ideas will not help me through life."

Early the next morning when the birds were shouting their welcome to the day, Diana put on her robe and took the book to Geraldine's room. She tapped on the door and opened it slightly.

"May I enter."

"Yes do." Geraldine sounded in low spirits, the night had obviously not been good.

"I have brought a book about ..." she read the title " *Across Africa on foot.* Oh it's about Africa. Goodness me, I hope he had good boots if he was to walk all that way. I believe Africa is quite large."

Geraldine giggled, that was the only word for it.

Diana opened the book in the centre. "I never start at the beginning with travel books; they spend so much time preparing. I can read that later if I want to know. This book is interesting.

"'*The camels were being loaded with everything we would need. Water was the most important. The camel knelt down to allow us to climb onto its back.*' What an accommodating animal. Have you ever seen a camel?"

"No."

"Nor I, I wonder how large they are to carry so much. I have never seen an animal kneel down.

"'*It is for a good reason they are called Ships of the Desert.*'"

Diana giggled. "What shape are they if they are called ships. Perhaps they are very wide and pointed at the front."

Geraldine's giggles were getting out of control, this was real laughter.

"I think we shall have to visit your library and find a book with drawings. I cannot take an animal seriously who is a ship that can kneel down."

They were both laughing now.

"I know little of what a desert is like, do you think the book will tell us or should we search the library for that too? Oh, here we are.

"'*The desert sand went on as far as the eye could see in all directions.*' Well not behind them obviously for they had only just arrived. Why are they on a camel when the book is called *Across Africa on Foot*? It is written by a man, of course, we women are the only ones who think before making such mistakes.

"'*We travelled for several hours. The heat was unbearable but we had been warned to cover our skin and wear a hat. The wind blew the sand into our faces until we were so wrapped we could barely see. There were some of the local ladies in a special covered seat surrounded by cloth of some kind. It must have been very hot and dark inside. By the time we reached the first oasis I felt as if my bones had become separated and were moving in all different directions at the same time.*'

"What is an oasis, have you ever heard of it?"

"No."

"It must explain it somewhere." She read on.

"'*There were only a few very tall trees around the tiny waterhole, the grass growing very sparsely.*'

"Oh, that is what an oasis is.

"'*The bearers pitched the tents for us to rest. I would rather have let the air to my skin and to allow my hair to dry from the perspiration but we were infested by insects which seemed intent on biting us. I enquired why we were staying there but was informed the wind was bringing a sandstorm from which we must be sheltered. It was hours before the wind relented and we could leave the tents.*

"'*The doorways were not blocked but the rear of the tent which had faced the wind was piled high with sand, the small waterhole at present invisible. I was reliably informed sandstorms can sometimes continue for days, we had been lucky.*

"It was dark by the time we reached the small cluster of houses around another waterhole. At least tonight we could sleep inside, the night time temperature in the desert feels as cold as winter when a tent is your only protection'" Diana concluded.

"I'm thirsty." Geraldine said. "Shall we ring for breakfast?"

"Oh I never have breakfast before dressing. I will ring for you if you wish, then I will return to my room. We can continue our foray through Africa a little later."

Geraldine was disappointed but Diana had no intention of encouraging her to stay in her room the whole time.

Once dressed and prepared for the day ahead, Diana went down to the room indicated by the footman as to where she would find breakfast. A footman waited to serve her tea or coffee while she lifted the various covers to make her choice. Kidneys, eggs and some sliced ham with toast; that would keep her full for the whole day, although she thought they would expect her to eat again at lunchtime. She must be careful not to outgrow her gowns.

Mr Smeaton arrived and was surprised. "You are an early riser, Diana."

"I am, I often take a walk before breakfast is served."

"My wife is rarely down for breakfast. Like many ladies she stays in her room."

They ate in comparative ease with each other. He seemed to be trying to compose a question.

"You met Geraldine last night, I understand."

"Yes, sir, I did." What was he trying to ask, whether they liked each other, whether Geraldine would accept her?

"I was reading a little of the book to Geraldine this morning, the travel book you so kindly allowed me to choose in the dark last night."

He looked up surprised. "Oh, you have seen Geraldine this morning?"

"Yes, sir, and I hope she will accompany me when you show us where in your library we can find a representation of a camel."

Mr Smeaton leaned back in his chair and looked at her as he registered the wording she had used."

"Indeed. Perhaps I should insist upon it."

"No, sir. She must wish to do it herself."

"What a capable young woman you are, practical and capable. I begin to feel more hopeful for my daughter's future. Should you need any information do not hesitate to ask, my dear." He smiled and indicated to the footman to pour him more coffee.

The door opened slowly and hesitantly Geraldine entered.

"I thought I might join you."

"Come in, my dear."

Diana stood to meet her holding out her hands. "I had the most wonderfully tasty breakfast, what can I help you to. Eggs, ham?"

"I normally eat little, perhaps some toast."

"Very well, toast, my lady. This conserve is delicious"

Geraldine laughed. Her father turned his face to hide his surprise. Had his daughter just laughed for the first time in months? Whoever Diana Newby was, she was a remarkable young lady.

"Papa, can you help us in the library?"

"Of course, my dear, what are you looking for?" As if he had not already been told.

"We wish to know what a camel looks like and why it is called a 'ship of the desert'."

"That I can answer, it is very difficult to walk in a desert, no coach could go there, no horse has the right hooves, the camel has big splayed feet that can walk on the shifting sand. Everything that is transported must be carried by them, rather like a ship transports goods from one country to another."

"How interesting." Diana said." We must see what else the desert can teach us."

"But what do they look like, papa?"

"That we must investigate. I have a letter to write so I will join you there when you have finished your breakfast." Diana thought how sensible he was not to give her an opportunity to avoid eating.

There were various books with drawings, some of them coloured paintings of various animals and flowers but none of a camel.

"Are they only found in Africa, sir?"

"Oh no, I think they are in other countries too. They say the three wise men rode camels, I believe. Perhaps we have a drawing in one of the bibles."

He went to another section. "Here we are. I remember this from when I was small." He held a battered copy of a bible with pictures for children. "There we are; camels." He answered triumphantly.

The girls stared at them. "They are a strange shape, they have lumps on their backs. How would you sit on them?"

"I believe you sit between the humps." Diana said innocently.

Mr Smeaton looked quickly at her then smiled to himself.

Chapter 9

The days followed a regular pattern. Diana read to Geraldine, they discussed things then went to the library to find information.

After a few days Diana encouraged Geraldine into the garden to read. The discussions now included the flowers in the garden and whether they had come from a different country. More research in the library. Gradually Geraldine was coaxed further away from the house and towards the surrounding woods and pond area.

Eliza and Martha were both allowed a little time to themselves. Martha had family in the nearby town and was sometimes taken on the cart to visit them. Eliza was interested in the town and what shops it had to offer, so it was arranged they would go together, leaving the girls to look after themselves.

Eliza was aware of there being a problem with Miss Smeaton and was not surprised when Diana asked her to take note of anything Martha said that could help her.

"Shall I ask, Miss, or just listen?"

"Well, be careful not to make her suspicious; just ask if she knows why her mistress never married. There is a problem here and I need to know what it is. If she will not tell you do not worry, she may tell you at another time."

"Very good, Miss. Is there anything you need me to buy for you?"

"No, not if you can find that ribbon. Just take note of anything available I might need in the future."

"Yes, Miss."

So the maids left on a bright sunny day, the horse and cart trundling down the road.

Morning was no different to normal. They discussed, researched in the library and walked in the gardens with the brightly coloured flowers among the roses.

"Have you a favourite flower, Geraldine?"

"Not really, I like roses but they do not always last long enough. Do you have one?"

"Not really a flower, I like many especially if they are yellow, it is such a sunshine colour. It makes little difference if it is a buttercup in the field."

"You like buttercups?"

"Yes, why not? They are God's flowers too."

Geraldine was somewhat surprised. "Well, fancy that!"

Diana had to laugh.

After lunch the sun was too hot to sit close to the house but not wanting Geraldine to find an excuse to stay indoors she suggested the woodland.

"We can see how many yellow flowers there are in the wood."

Geraldine had not visited the woodland for quite some time. The last time had been with Andrew when flowers were the last thing on her mind.

Diana was aware of the change in her, the sadness returning.

"Now don't forget to count."

"Does it matter if I don't know the names?"

"Of course not, many flowers have more than one name; I don't know most of them.

They were walking the path through grassland.

"Buttercup, I know that one." Geraldine stepped onto the grass to pick some.

"What's that called?" She pointed to some flowers in the grass like straggly yellow daisies.

"Fleabane, I think." The path led past the edge of the pond where they did not venture too close.

Geraldine pointed. "I recognise that." She pointed to the tall plant near the edge of the water.

"Loosestrife, and there is bird's-foot-trefoil, look at the shape of the petals, there are three rather like clover."

"That is a cowslip, and is that broom? There aren't many flowers."

"I think it has finished flowering for this year."

"Dandelion, we have a maid who says her mother makes a drink from the root. I don't think I would drink that."

Diana laughed. "Most medicines are made from plants. Those who can't afford the doctor rely on plants."

"Oh do they, how strange."

They had reached the edge of the wood; she had to keep up Geraldine's spirits.

"That is Creeping Jenny."

"I can't pick that, it's too small."

"These are anemones. They don't seem to have as many flowers as the white kind." They walked further through the open woodland.

"The problem with wild flowers is they never last long when you pick them."

"But they are beautiful, look at that tall one."

"What colour would you call that?"

"Yellow, well it is darker than that, more of a gold colour."

"It is called goldenrod."

"Oh look at these aren't they beautiful."

"They are St John's-wort, I think, that one over there may be Celandine."

Geraldine walked towards the Celandine where the ground was covered with growth. "Oh look, this is the biggest buttercup I have ever seen, I will pick it for you."

"NO!" But it was too late. Geraldine had stepped into the greenery, her shoe sank into the shallow water sliding on the wet ground beneath. With a wild flailing of arms she landed face down in the mud.

When she was once more on the dry path they both stared at her ruined dress and dirty face and legs.

"Marsh Marigold."

"I thought it was a buttercup." Geraldine wailed.

"We need to get you home and into dry clothes, although looking at you a hot bath might be needed, you can't see your hair."

The housekeeper was alerted as they walked across the side terrace.

"Miss Geraldine, what happened to you?"

"I think I took a swim in some mud, Mrs Trimdon."

"A hot bath for you, we can't have you catching cold."

Up they went to her room where she suddenly remembered she had no maid to call.

"Don't worry, I will be your maid, Miss." Diana curtsied and made Geraldine laugh. They removed her dress and wiped off as much mud from her face and arms as they could. The maids brought the bath tub and the pails of water began arriving.

Geraldine sank into the warmth of the water and rubbed at the brown stains on her arms and face.

"Shall I wash your hair, Miss?" asked maid Diana.

Geraldine laughed. "Yes please, Martha."

Diana struggled to lift the pail of water and emptied it accidentally all over both of them. By the time Geraldine was clean the room and Diana were both covered in water. She helped her out of the tub and wrapped a towel around her, rubbing down her back and legs, another she wrapped around her wet hair.

"If you will put on your robe until I return I would rather like to put on a dry gown myself."

Geraldine assisted in opening the back of Diana's dress before she tiptoed to her room to change her clothes.

'Well,' thought Diana, 'if I wanted to distract from the sad past memory of the woodland that was certainly a very effective way.'

It was an afternoon tea time. Geraldine rarely went down to the parlour, her mother and any callers were apt to try to ask questions she was not prepared to answer, or they just stared at her as if she was guilty of something.

Today was different. She was informed her friends Miss Shenton and Miss Littlebeck had called to see her.

She refused to see them.

"Geraldine, do you object if I go to meet your friends."

"If you wish."

Something was definitely wrong and her friends seemed to be involved if she had read her reaction correctly.

Diana entered the parlour where Mrs Smeaton sat with two young ladies.

"Diana, Miss Newby, is Geraldine not with you?"

"No, Ma'am, she is resting, she had a headache."

"Oh dear, well come and meet Miss Littlebeck and Miss Shenton." They rose to touch fingers with her.

"We heard you were here, of course. I am pleased to meet you Miss Newby." Miss Shenton was a quiet ladylike young lady of about eighteen or so. Her friend who was dressed a little more expensively took charge of the conversation.

"Miss Newby, how strange, you have the same name as the butler."

"Yes it is strange but I am not from around here."

"Oh, are you not, nor am I. I came to visit a few months ago and like it too much to leave." There was something about her voice that grated on Diana. "I hope you are settling in, it is so hard for a companion, but Geraldine is a lovely girl, we became friends as soon as I arrived."

Diana's teeth were on edge.

"Miss Shenton, have you always lived here?"

As she opened her mouth to answer Miss Littlebeck answered for her.

"Oh she has, we are distant cousins which is why I came to stay."

Diana had no desire to continue any conversation but it would be rude to leave now.

"We came to invite you to a garden party." Miss Shenton ventured to say.

"Yes do come, and make sure dear Geraldine comes, too."

This girl was probably the reason Geraldine had refused to come down.

"That would be a pleasant outing for you both." Mrs Smeaton said with more hope than she would have previously had.

"Thank you, I would like that, whether Geraldine will come will be her decision."

The conversation continued for some time but most of it was by Miss Littlebeck, Diana declined to join in further.

When they rose to leave Miss Shenton came close and quietly said. "Please call me Ann; I would like us to be friends."

"Thank you Ann, you know I am Diana."

She smiled as a voice behind her said. "Yes, we knew your name was Diana, it is much more pleasant to be on first name terms don't you think."

"Yes of course, Lucy."

"Lucy! My name is Victoria."

"Oh, I am sorry, you must remind me of someone else."

As soon as possible she escaped up to Geraldine's room to pass on the information.

"No I will not attend, but you go, it will introduce you to everyone around here."

"Geraldine, is it Victoria Littlebeck you wish to avoid?"

"Not just her, please do not ask me to explain."

"I will not press you, I promise."

The garden party was being held at the Shentons' house only fifteen minutes' walk away. Mrs Smeaton was only too pleased to accompany her and was surprised when Mr Smeaton also announced he would attend. It was at breakfast when Mr Smeaton was again the only other occupant of the room when he admitted his intention that afternoon was for a specific reason.

"You are a very astute young lady. How much my daughter has told you I have no idea but I am not surprised she will not attend, I expect Andrew Harsley, her former fiancée will be there. She no doubt would wish to avoid him. I fear my wife is likely to stir up problems with her curiosity and I believe you will have more success if you are left to make your own enquiries."

Diana thought for a moment.

"The problem is, sir, she has told me nothing. It is quite obvious she is suffering with a broken heart but until now I did not even know the name of her intended. I believe Miss Victoria Littlebeck to be part of the problem."

"Victoria! Shenton thinks her a good influence on Ann who is rather shy."

"I consider her the worst thing to happen to someone like Ann. She barely lets her speak."

"You met her once for a few minutes and yet you have assessed her character."

"I have met one such as her before when I was quiet like Ann. I did not survive, sir, I aim to see Ann does."

The garden party was well attended, apart from the young people most of the gentry from around the area were there. The most notable absentee was Geraldine.

Diana was introduced to everyone, Mrs Smeaton made it her undertaking. When all had met her Diane drifted towards where Ann Shenton sat. Victoria was not with her. Mrs Smeaton still by her side she looked over to where Mr Smeaton stood watching. He came strolling over.

"Come, my dear, let Diana join the young people. She needs no more introductions."

"Oh yes, I suppose so." Mrs Smeaton seemed a little surprised by his intervention.

Diana joined Ann where she sat watching some of the younger set engaged in an archery contest.

"You do not care to play, Ann?"

"Diana, how good to see you. No you have need of a partner and I have none."

"I see Victoria is playing, who is her partner?"

"Andrew Harsley."

"Geraldine's fiancée!"

"Yes, that was so sad. He used to be a very light-hearted young man, full of fun, I quite envied Geraldine. But now he is so serious."

"Victoria does not seem to mind, the way she is hanging onto his arm."

"I think she sees it her task to see him happy again."

"In what way, Ann, does she have designs on him?"

Ann looked shocked. "No! Well, I don't know. She complains he is slow to respond and she may have to do something drastic."

"Compromise him, you mean?"

"Oh, I. Well. Possibly. I never thought of it that way/"

The match had finished and the players spread out across the lawn. Victoria and Andrew Harsley were heading their way.

"Diana, how pleasant to see you again. Have you met Mr Andrew Harsley?"

"No, I have not had the pleasure."

"Miss Diana Newby is Geraldine Smeaton's companion."

Diana watched as the pain crossed his face. It seemed Geraldine was not the only one with a broken heart.

"Miss Newby." He bowed stiffly.

"Come, Andrew, there is boating on the lake and I wish you to row me."

They set off for the small lake leaving Ann alone again.

"How rude of her to leave you here alone."

"Oh it is of no import, Diana. I would rather be alone than in company with Victoria, she dominates my whole life. I wish she would go back home to London."

"Then we shall have to arrange it." Diana smiled at her, her eyes sparkling with mischief.

"I have someone I wish to speak with, if you will excuse me, Ann."

Walking slowly not to attract attention she made her way to the terrace where Mr Harsley sat with a glass and a cigar, surveying the garden. He did not look overly happy.

"Mr Harsley, I would speak with you privately."

He stood to greet her.

"Miss Newby. Of course if you wish." He placed his glass on the table and indicated a quiet area of the terrace.

"Is this about Geraldine, have you any news?"

"No, Mr Harsley, this is about you. Please will you smile and look as if we are having a pleasant conversation."

He looked at her as she fashioned her mouth into a smile. He copied her.

"That is better, sir. Now tell me, how will you like to live with Miss Victoria Littlebeck for the rest of your life?"

He turned to stare at her.

"Smile, Mr Harsley."

"I take it this is a joke."

"No joke, Mr Harsley. I believe Victoria intends to trap your son and he is too distressed to notice or care."

"Why should you think so? You have only just met us."

"Victoria reminds me of a girl I once knew. She moved to a new area and decided she wanted a man who was betrothed, so she arranged it with lies that the betrothal was broken and everyone believed the innocent girl a thief."

"How do you know she was not?"

"Because it was me, Mr Harsley. I am alone in the world because of her lies. I will not see it happen to another. You did not answer my question. How would you feel, do you like Victoria?"

"No, I can think of nothing worse. I will speak with my son."

"No! I will tell you how to alert him. Discuss with him where he will live when he is married or if he means to put you out of your house for you cannot live with Victoria. Perhaps you could alter the house to make two apartments. I believe he will be shocked and deny there is any possibility of him marrying. Tell him she is letting it be known she intends to have him. I will try to find some way to help with Geraldine."

He led her back towards the house.

"Smeaton was right about you, Miss Newby. You are a remarkably astute young woman."

Diana walked down to where Ann was talking with a young man.

"Diana, I would like you to meet Mr Arthur Cardine. This is Miss Newby, Geraldine's companion."

Mr Cardine bowed. Ann was a little flushed, she noted.

"You are at the Smeatons then, a very pleasant family."

"Do you live nearby, sir?"

"Not near enough. I would come more often if every move were not organised by Victoria, Miss Littlebeck."

"Can you not avoid her?"

"Unfortunately Shenton believes her a paragon of virtue and allows her to dominate the house. She does not approve of my association with Ann."

"Oh, then I shall have great pleasure in disabusing him. Have no fear Ann, I will not abandon you. Can you never get away on your own?"

"Yes, for a short time but it would not be proper for me to meet Arthur alone."

"Then you must come to the Smeatons. Do you rise early?"

"Sometimes, Victoria likes to take breakfast in bed and is late coming down, so I have time to myself in the morning."

Then come to the Smeatons at nine thirty each morning and I will chaperone you, perhaps Geraldine will join us."

Ann grasped her hands. "I knew when I met you that you were a kind person." There were tears in her eyes.

"I see Victoria bearing down upon us, will you escort me, Mr Cardine."

He bowed to Ann who gave him a very private smile, and held his arm to escort Diana to the tea table for some refreshment.

Chapter 10

True to her promise at nine thirty Diana and often Geraldine walked in the garden or sat in the parlour with Anna and Arthur. Mr Smeaton became aware of what was happening when he regularly found Ann's maid waiting in the hallway. Eventually he decided she should have some company and directed a maid to take her below stairs for company and refreshments. After several days Ann informed them of a change in Victoria's attitude. She had become angry and complained at everyone. Even Mr Shenton was surprised at the change in her.

Nothing having altered with Geraldine, Diana once more applied to Eliza for information.

"She knows and is upset, Miss, but she won't tell me. Perhaps if you speak to her."

"I think I just might, Eliza." So one morning when Geraldine had gone down to breakfast believing Diana already there, Diana went to Geraldine's room where her maid was arranging her clothing.

"Martha." She tapped at the door then opened it slowly. "Martha I need your help."

"Yes, Miss Diana, how can I help?"

"This is difficult for me to explain. I believe someone told Miss Geraldine a lie. She did it so she could steal Mr Harsley away. Mr Harsley is very unhappy so she told him a lie about Miss Geraldine. I fear if she compromises him into marrying her it will cause Miss Geraldine to go into a serious decline or even harm herself."

Martha gasped in shock.

"I do believe it, Martha, once he is married she will not wish to live."

"You think it was a lie, Miss?"

"I am convinced of it, but she will not tell me and I fear time is running short."

Martha was nearly in tears.

"What did Victoria Littlebeck say to her, Martha? You must tell me if you want me to save her."

Martha was trembling. "You won't tell her I told you, will you Miss."

"I promise I will not tell her, Martha."

"Well Mr Harsley went to London for a few weeks to stay with a friend. A few weeks later Miss Littlebeck arrived and told her he had found his true love, a Mary Pulman in London. He intends to set her up as his mistress once he has married to produce an heir. Geraldine is his family's choice and when she is with child he will move to London to be with Mary."

Diana sat and thought. "A dreadful thing to say to a young woman so much in love. It was so cruel, Martha. But now I know how to proceed. Thank you for your confidence."

There was to be another garden party, this time at the Harsleys', a quiet suggestion to Mr Smeaton had brought quick results. There were those who hoped Geraldine would attend but now Diana knew the reason she had no such expectations.

The Harsleys' was a little further away so a carriage was required. Mrs Smeaton had no idea of anything unusual happening.

"I do wish Geraldine had come. I am sure once they see each other again this will all blow over."

"We can but hope for a happy outcome, my dear. But do not try to force things, leave Harsley to deal with his son. Any interference from you will only cause further problems. Promise me you will do nothing."

"Well if you really think so."

"I do."

Mr Smeaton was looking at Diana when he spoke.

The company was pleasant, there were games on the lawn but the grass was a little soft after the recent rain so bowling and croquet was not possible, so they sat on the terrace and talked. Victoria was trying to sparkle.

"I am surprised you are here again. What have you been doing recently, Miss Newby. Tell me, what does a companion do?"

Diana knew this was meant to insult her.

"I do everything a young lady would do."

"Yes but your time is not your own to decide, now is it?"

"Of course it is, why should it not be?"

"Well you are paid to be with Geraldine."

"Victoria, Miss Littlebeck, I am not paid by anyone. I have my own money. I am here as a friend but am under no obligation. I read and walk in the garden, I study in the library and Geraldine joins me when it pleases her. Did you think me a glorified maid?"

Victoria was silent.

Tell them a story.

"The only time I acted like a maid was when our maids were both in town and we walked in the wood. Geraldine wanted to pick a flower for me. It was a Marsh Marigold, surrounded by water and floating greenery. I took her home covered in mud so I helped to bathe her. Her hair was covered in mud. I am the most inefficient maid, by the time I finished we were both soaked and so was the floor. I needed a maid to remove my wet clothing, we laughed a great deal over that."

Was it her imagination or was there a strange look on Andrew Harsley's face, almost fear of what she was going to say.

Tea was announced and they went to collect their plate. Andrew walked close to her.

"I was nervous you would say too much."

"Too much, Mr Harsley, too much what?"

"About Geraldine."

"I don't understand you, sir."

"I presume you saw her."

"Saw her, in her bath, of course I saw her. She is a very beautiful young lady, a little thin because she will not eat, but that is your fault."

"My fault!"

"How is Mary Pulman?"

"Who? Mary Pulman, how would I know? Ask Victoria, she is her grandmother."

"Grandmother! You wish to make an old lady your mistress while you use Geraldine only to produce an heir!"

He stopped dead and looked hard at her.

"Where did that lie come from?"

"Victoria Littlebeck I believe. What lie about Geraldine did she tell you?"

He looked uncomfortable.

"That she was not properly formed; could never be a normal wife."

"Oh dear, the vipers of this world have been spreading unhappiness to more than just you, Mr Harsley. Will you stay quiet while I tell a lie on your behalf?"

"What lie?"

"That you have signed the betrothal forms and can marry no one else without great expense."

He stared at her. "Why would you say that?"

"To save you from a breach of promise court case which would involve Geraldine."

Others were catching up with them or passing them on their way back with filled plates.

"Can I help you to some fish, Miss Newby?"

"Thank you Mr Harsley, if you will."

The tea was eaten and cleared away. Andrew had joined his father to wish goodbye to some older ladies who were leaving.

"You were close with Mr Harsley." Victoria almost spat the word out, jealousy written on her face.

"Why not, I feel sorry for the man."

"Sorry?" Phillipa Cardine, Arthur's sister queried.

"Well the poor man can never marry now, neither of them can."

The group stared at her.

"Why not?"

"Well the forms are signed; save for the church blessing they are married. It would cost a great deal of money and a friendly Bishop if not the Archbishop for either of them to be free."

"That is a lie. He never told me that."

"Why should he?" Arthur Cardine said. "There was no reason for him to tell you. He was never interested in you."

"That's not true. He told me …" She stopped.

"I told you what, Miss Littlebeck? I told you nothing, unlike the lie you told me." Andrew Harsley had arrived quietly behind Victoria, the better to hear what she was saying.

Diana looked around. The anti-Victoria plan had taken on a life of its own, everyone seemed part of it. Accusations were being thrown from every side until she stood and stalked to the house to order her carriage.

"You just lost your ride home."

"Then I will not go." Ann giggled.

"We came by coach." Phillipa said, "we could take you."

"You could come in the Smeaton's coach, but I suspect you would rather go with the Cardines?" Several looked expectantly at them and Ann blushed. Arthur spoke for her.

"Victoria did not approve of me or at least of Ann's association with me so I have been unwelcome of late."

Diana smiled, she was not about to give away their secret meetings.

Mr Andrew Harsley called to see Miss Geraldine Smeaton the next day while she was walking in the garden. Diana did not need to hear what had been said, the look on Geraldine's face said more than any words could.

Less than a month later they were married. At the wedding Diana was quietly informed that Mr Shenton had given leave for Andrew Cardine to marry his daughter Ann.

Victoria Littlebeck had returned to London.

* * *

"Her name is Diana?"

"Yes, did you not know that?"

"No. She is twenty one or two years old?"

"That is right. You look shaken, Mr Arnott. Is something wrong?"

"No, sir. The question I came to ask of her maid concerned the whereabouts of a girl who disappeared over four years ago. Her name was Diana."

"I gather her name was not Newby."

"No, sir."

"We did come to believe that was not her real name. Whatever happened to her was traumatic but it made her into a very accomplished young lady."

Michael stood up in a daze.

"Thank you for your information, sir. Is she still here?"

"No, she left last summer. We had a friend whose eldest daughter refused to marry so we suggested Diana as a companion."

"If you will give me their direction I would like to see her again."

They went to his study where he wrote the direction for the Cobden family. Thanking them profusely he stopped only to speak to the butler as he showed him out.

"Newby, has that always been your name."

"No, sir. I was brought up in an orphanage. They called me John but there were many of us so I was John twenty one. I disliked being a number. When I arrived here I passed an empty building with the name Newby painted on it, so I decided that would be my name."

"Thank you, Newby; that explains everything."

Rather happier than he had been for some time, he set out on the two hours' ride home to his grandfather.

Mr Smeaton smiled at his wife. "I think I will write to Cobden and tell him of this young man. He seems very interested in her and she deserves some happiness."

It was late that night when he arrived home to his Grandfather's estate. He could ask nothing until the morning but his mind was teeming. Had his Grandfather known who she was? Did he send him to hear about her? Did he know about what had happened? There were so many questions.

He expected to sleep badly but in fact he fell into a peaceful sleep and awoke refreshed in the morning. Was that the relief that she was alive and well, that he might have the chance to see her again?

Grandfather was in the study by mid-morning, Fletcher was no doubt out on the estate checking what the previous day's rain had done to the ground.

"Good morning, Michael. Did you come back today or last night?"

"I came home last night, sir." He noted the use of the word home Michael had used without thinking. That pleased him.

Michael was obviously wanting to ask him something but was having trouble finding the words.

"Before you ask; no I was not sure but I did wonder. Judging by the happier state you are in this morning, I gather Miss Newby is the Diana you are looking for."

"I believe she is. When they told me her name was Diana I did begin to wonder. Now I believe she probably is Miss Butterwick."

"I understand she has moved to another family."

"Yes, why did you not tell me she was not there?"

"It was important you went to find out for your own peace of mind. If you want to find her you needed to know where she moved to. I expect Smeaton told you that."

"Yes, he did. I have the direction, a family called Cobden, a distant friend of theirs. They have a need of a companion for their eldest daughter. I hope she is finding some peace there. She had so little time to settle into the Smeaton's home and she deserves some quiet time to herself even though she was well treated. Mr Smeaton was very impressed with her. I hope she has not been sent into a problem like she found at the Smeatons."

"The Cobdens, I have heard of them, although it was years ago and I have not been in touch recently. Maybe I will write to Smeaton and ask him of the circumstances. I would not like you to think she was not happy there."

Michael returned to the routine he found so soothing, riding the estate with Fletcher every morning, discussing the estate in the afternoon.

Grandfather was true to his word in writing to Smeaton to enquire after the reason the Cobdens needed a companion, but the reply was not to his liking. His daughter refused to marry the man he had chosen for her and until she did he refused to allow her younger sister to marry at all. It was a dreadful situation to pressure one sister using the other. He would be lucky if the sisters did not come to hate each other. He had to tell Michael without making him upset. Perhaps suggest he go and visit. Smeaton did say he had mentioned Michael to Cobden so perhaps a visit would not be too surprising.

Michael was not averse to a visit. He had no wish to leave at that moment but Grandfather seemed convinced. What did he know that he would not say?

"I will be away at least three of four days, Grandfather. I hate to leave you for so long."

"I have managed all the time you were away at the war, Michael; I believe I will manage a few days without you. But I will look forward to your return."

Chapter 11

The house was slightly larger than the Smeatons' and rather more pretentious. Someone had taken a solid old house and added not only a wing on one side, totally unbalancing the façade, but also a Greek portico which ill-suited the style of the building.

Michael arrived at the front of the house down a long curving drive which gave the stable lads adequate time to see a visitor coming and for a groom to be there when he arrived at the portico to take his horse.

He knocked on the ornate knocker and waited for the butler to answer, which he did in record time.

"Mr Arnott to see Mr Cobden."

"If you will wait here, sir, I will see if he is receiving."

Michael waited as the butler walked with a slow measured step to somewhere down a corridor. The house and everything in it had a look of grandeur above its station. The furniture was over ornate and too large, the decoration too fussy for the size of the hallway. He had the feeling this family considered itself above those in the district and this was the way to show it. He hoped this was not true, it would make his enquiry difficult for him and Diana, if she was still there. Perhaps they had not liked her. She was not pretentious like this house.

It was a pleasant surprise when a man of Smeaton's age came smiling at him down the corridor.

"Arnott, how good to meet you. Smeaton wrote and told me you may call." He took Michael's hand in a warm clasp.

"Come into the drawing room, I believe my wife is there."

They entered the second door to the left on the long hallway and were in somewhere that could have been a room from a French château. Again the over ornate and gilded furniture was too large for the room, the wall covering too fussy and the fireplace big enough to have come from a baronial hall.

A small lady sat insignificantly on one of the sofas supported with cushions, her embroidery on her knees with a wicker basket by the footstool at her feet.

"Ann, my dear, this is Mr Arnott. You remember I told you Smeaton said he came asking after Diana."

"I do remember, Frederick. You are welcome, Mr Arnott. Can I offer you some refreshment? It is almost time for tea; we shall take it a little early today since you have arrived."

Michael thought it very strange that tea was taken at such a precise time she felt it necessary to explain that it was being taken early.

A chair was indicated and he sat stiffly while Mrs Cobden gave orders for the tea to be served. Cobden sank into his usual chair extremely relaxed.

"Now, Arnott. You came to know why we offered Diana Newby a home. I presume you know everything that happened at the Smeatons."

"I do, sir." He tried to ask if she was there but had no chance.

"The problem was my younger daughter was pressing to be allowed to marry. I was not completely sure of her young man hardly having met him. My elder daughter I had made a match for with Lord Langdale who seemed an excellent man with a tidy estate and a London House. She would have been well set up for life, I felt, but having only met him once she declared she would rather stay single than marry him.

"I quite despaired of her, so I hit upon the idea of using her sister to persuade her. Until her elder sister married she could not. I thought it would encourage her. It caused a rift between them that may never heal and is something I bitterly regret.

"We heard of Diana from one of Smeaton's friends who suggested we offer to take Diana as a companion for Beatrice, my eldest. I have to admit I was surprised when she arrived, she was so young and I quite thought Smeaton had exaggerated."

* * *

Diana stood outside another house with Eliza her maid and waited for the butler to answer the door.

"It looks very grand, Miss."

"It does, doesn't it? I hope they will not think me too fancy for a companion. Some families often want them to be inferior. It depends so much on how they expect me to behave. I will not be used as a servant, Eliza."

The door opened and prevented any further discussion. The butler led her to a very fancy parlour where he announced her as if she were being presented at court. '*Oh dear*' she thought, '*I do hope this will not prove to be too much for me.*'

Mrs Cobden sat perched on a large ornate sofa but never made any effort to rise. Mr Cobden was a rather overbearing man who bowed to her with condescension. She was urged to sit but no mention was made of any refreshments.

Mr Cobden began.

"I hope you understand why you are here, my dear."

"Yes, sir. I am to be a companion to your elder daughter Beatrice."

"What we expect you to do is to make her see reason and marry Lord Langdale. She is being so awkward about this."

"You are insisting on her marrying against her wishes?"

"Well that is your job, Miss Newby, to make her see the benefits."

"Sir, I understood I was being offered a home in exchange for being a companion. I am not a servant to be told what I will do. If you wish to change the terms of your offer then I will decline and leave immediately."

Mr Cobden looked quite shocked at her outburst.

"But Smeaton said you cleared up the problem with his daughter."

"I may have helped, sir, but it was not an obligation and they were both in love with each other. It was obvious to me what was required. I did not force her and I will not force your daughter. If you will excuse me I prefer to leave now."

"But we understood you had no home."

"If the carriage is still here I will return to the Smeatons, if not I will go to an inn until I find a position as a companion, sir. You do not offer what I was expecting. If you require someone to do your bidding then hire someone and pay them. I would be ashamed in your place to be forcing unhappiness upon my own daughter."

Diana rose to leave.

"I understood you were a quiet young lady not the outspoken female I am seeing."

"And I understood you to be a gentleman, sir, not the opinionated condescending man I am seeing."

She turned and walked to the door which opened as she reached it. A young lady of almost her own age entered and smiled tentatively at her.

"Are you my companion?"

"It seems she declines to stay."

"I decline to do your father's bidding, I was offered a home in exchange for companionship; I will not be used to spy on you or bend you to his will."

"You will not? I gather he has told you of our disagreement. Please stay, Miss Newby. There is no-one in the house to whom I can talk, they are ordered to lecture me at every turn. I need someone who will be my friend not my enemy."

"We are not your enemy, Beatrice, what a dreadful thing to say."

"But you care nothing for me and my future happiness, only your advancement in marrying me to a Lord." Then turning to Diana "If I had anywhere to go I would leave here, Miss Newby. I sorely need someone who will not condemn me with every word they say."

Diana held out her hands and took Beatrice's in hers.

"Then I will stay and we will be friends and have laughter and happiness not sadness and disapproval."

Her room was not close to Beatrice's. The house having been extended she was put in the long wing some way from the original house. These rooms were usually for visiting guests, the top floor housing their maids and valets. Even so, it was a pleasant room if a little dark in its furniture but the outlook had possibly the best view of the garden available from that wing. She had the whole floor to herself; the only footsteps she was liable to hear were those of the maids doing some perfunctory cleaning during the daytime.

Beatrice was indeed besieged. The first consideration was gaining not only her friendship but also her trust. Everyone in the house seemed upset with her and it took very little time to understand why. When the gong sounded for dinner she made her way to the main staircase and descended slowly. She was not disappointed, Beatrice was indeed looking for her. They entered the dining room together and sat side by side at one end of the impressively long table. The Cobdens, it seemed, liked to invite guests to dine, quite a few if the size of the table was anything to go by. A younger girl came in and stared hard at both of them, then with a swirl of her skirts she plonked herself onto her chair.

"I hope you can make her see reason or I can never marry and I will hate you too!"

Diana was rather taken aback with this outburst, the first words said to a stranger. She was even more surprised at the lack of reproof from her father. Needless to say the dinner was a rather uncomfortable meal; she ate very little and set her mind to wondering how she would survive this angry, unhappy house.

When they left the table Mr Cobden retired to his study and the ladies went into the parlour to await the tea trolley. The younger sister began again.

"Of course, papa could just throw you out, what would you do then, with no employment?"

"Miss Cobden, I believe you are under a misapprehension. I am not employed and can well afford to keep myself in lodgings while I find someone who needs a companion and to whom I will be useful."

Beatrice put her hand on Diana's arm. "You are useful to me, Miss Newby. I have need of a companion."

"That is the reason I stayed, because I realise how much you need a companion. It seems you sisters are not close." It was the first tentative step she had tried to take in finding out the reason for the animosity.

The tea trolley arrived and nothing was said in front of the servants. When the tea cups were removed everyone sat waiting for the next accusation.

Diana turned to Beatrice. "You will need to tell me of your daily habits and the normal workings of the house. I would not like to cause the staff a problem by arriving too early for breakfast."

"We do not come down for breakfast, we stay in our rooms." Beatrice informed her.

"You stay upstairs half the day so you can avoid Papa. What kind of woman is prepared to stop her sister from ever marrying." Gertrude bit out with some vehemence.

"I do not understand your meaning, Miss Cobden. It is not your sister who is stopping you. Surely it is your papa who makes the decision."

"He will not let me marry until Beatrice does and she refuses to marry Lord Langdale."

"Surely that is her choice not yours. Would you have her unhappy the whole of her life so you can marry early? I am sure your papa will allow you to marry eventually."

"But what if Harold finds someone else!"

"If he truly cares for you he will wait. If not then he would not prove a faithful husband."

"You are hateful!"

"No, that is not true. I know little of the problem having only just arrived, I am merely looking sensibly at the little information I have."

Gertrude glared at Beatrice. "You will have to marry him, Papa will make you." With which parting retort she stormed out of the room.

After a few moments silence Diana asked, "Is your sister always this angry?"

"She never used to be, we were always friends."

"Do you think she could be jealous your papa chose a Lord for you to marry?"

A noise between a snort and a laugh reminded them both Mrs Cobden was there. Beatrice turned to speak to her mother.

"Do you think that could be the reason, Mama? If so why does she not offer to marry the Lord?"

Mrs Cobden spoke for the first time in Diana's hearing. Her voice was quiet, her demeanour without confidence as if she were afraid to voice an opinion.

"I have no idea, Beatrice. She seems very taken with this man Harold. I cannot imagine why your father is so adamant."

"Can you not, Mama. He wants a Lord in the family. You know how much his status in society means to him. A Lord would raise him above any of the surrounding families. He thinks he may even be invited to dinner with Earls and Dukes. My happiness is of no concern in comparison."

Diana stifled a yawn.

"You are tired, Miss Newby?"

"Indeed, I am a little. I have had a busy day with the travelling. Would you excuse me if I retire early tonight? What time do you rise in the morning?"

"We stay in our rooms until past ten o'clock."

"I am an early riser and prefer to be out before breakfast. Can you tell me what time breakfast will be served?"

"I have no idea exactly when. We have breakfast after nine in our rooms."

"Then I will walk in the garden if the weather is fine."

"At this time of year!" Mrs Cobden was surprised.

"Indeed, Ma'am. A garden is a pleasure at any time of year if you are dressed correctly."

Although she walked steadily to her room she had wished it would not have been impolite to run. She shut her door against the household and wondered what she had walked into. She rang for Eliza to help her dress for bed; she needed a friend herself tonight. There was not even a lock on the door to give her a feeling of security.

Diana rose early the following morning and wrapped herself in her cloak to combat the coolness of the hour. She found a footman who showed her the way out into the garden where she walked among the late summer flowers, the few there were. When she saw a man tending the garden she went to speak with him.

"I imagine the roses are beautiful during the summer. Do you not have under planting to bring colour for when they are not flowering?"

"No, miss. Mr Cobden likes it clean. He thinks the annual plantings look blowsy. We only have them in the formal beds near the house."

"Mr Cobden. Does Mrs Cobden have a favourite area?"

"I don't know, Miss. It's Mr Cobden what gives us our orders."

"Is it really, how unusual."

She explored the formal long borders which still held those flowers hardy enough to survive the morning chill. The borders all seemed to be of one colour only. In some areas they had been cleaned ready for winter and were only bare earth.

As she returned to the house there were pansies flowering in the narrow borders between the gravelled paths. All one colour. What a strangely uniform structure the garden had. There was little to lift the spirits. It seemed to reflect the mood of the house.

As she re-entered through the side door she was greeted by a stern woman who identified herself as the housekeeper.

"Mr Cobden requests that I give you the rules of the house, Miss Newby."

"The rules. I am afraid I do not understand you."

"This house is run in as orderly fashion as any aristocratic establishment. The ladies do not come down before ten o'clock, they take their breakfast in their rooms. Lunch is at one thirty precisely and tea is served at four o'clock. Dinner is always at seven."

"Are those Mrs Cobden's rules?"

"No, Miss Newby. I take my orders from Mr Cobden."

Diana had a cold feeling in the pit of her stomach.

"As I am already down, does that mean I am forbidden breakfast?"

The housekeeper looked surprised at her tone of voice.

"No, I am sure Mr Cobden will accept that you had not been informed before, but I believe he will expect you to adhere to the rules now."

"Will he now. Tell me, why are the vases filled with only one colour flower?"

"It is how Mr Cobden likes it, the maid has her orders."

"And what of Mrs Cobden. Does she not see to the flowers?"

"Oh no. She is not involved in such mundane work."

"Could you show me which is the breakfast room, I presume Mr Cobden takes his breakfast there?"

"Oh yes, he is there now, so if you would care to wait until he is finished."

"Tell me, if I were a visiting Duchess would you give me rules and orders."

The housekeeper looked shocked. "Of course not."

"Then do not give them to me. I am a guest here, not a servant to be ordered around. I believe if I leave Mr Cobden's friends would be surprised at the reception he gives his guests, or does he believe this is how aristocracy behaves."

Diana walked to the room indicated by the housekeeper and opened the door with a flourish. Mr Cobden sat at the table with a footman hovering close by.

"Good morning, Mr Cobden." Diana was taking the offensive with this obviously dictatorial man.

She walked to the covers to see what was on offer. Very little. He expected to be the only one there.

"You keep a very meagre table, sir. I have never seen so little. It seems I must make do with only toast." She turned to the footman. "Tea, if you please."

"There is no tea; I only drink coffee at breakfast."

"But I drink tea. In all the houses I have lived in and visited I have never been informed I was not allowed down to breakfast. I find your rules dictatorial, like those of an uneducated workman." She used the analogy to cause him to react.

"I find you most impertinent, Miss Newby."

"I did not think you would even notice after the way you allowed your younger daughter to address a newly arrived guest at dinner last evening. You gave her no censure. It seems you have a special feeling for your younger daughter who is allowed to marry where her heart leads, while your elder daughter must have an arranged marriage to suit you. Just because yours was an arranged marriage you presume Beatrice will accept such a loveless union."

"How dare you. I chose Ann because I held her in high regard."

"And did your wife have any choice, sir."

"It was a mutual attraction."

"Then at sometime since your daughters were born you turned against her."

"I will not discuss my marriage with you, girl."

"No, I expect you will not, for you have no marriage. I wonder if you know what aristocratic wives do."

"They are there to grace their houses and accompany their husbands."

"No sir. They run their houses, arrange flowers, order tea when they wish it. You sit in the parlour in a chair which fits you. There is no furniture comfortable for a woman; you must have bought it with no thought for your wife or daughters' comfort. Your wife is no more to you than another '*ornate sofa*', she has no duties, no pleasures and no confidence, nothing worth living for."

"How dare you. I have a mind to throw you out."

"Then do, sir. I will go to the Smeatons and ask them to help me find a position where there are real people not dolls for you to play games with."

Mr Cobden realised the consequences of his proposed action. This girl was held in high esteem, she could do a great deal of harm to his standing, if Lord Langdale heard of it he could possibly break from the agreement.

Having taken part in an argument with this outspoken young girl he was at a loss how to proceed. Diana then turned the conversation.

"Tell me about Lord Langdale, what is so special about him."

Cobden looked surprised. "He is a very superior gentleman with an estate some miles from here and a house near Grosvenor Square in London."

"Near Grosvenor Square, I see. But that tells me nothing of the man only his property which could be tied up with debt. What of his personality?"

"I do not understand you."

"No, I believe you are unable to see beyond property and title to the man's character. What do you know that makes you think him a suitable husband for Beatrice? Is he a young buck gambling in London or an older man looking for a young wife?"

"He is about thirty years old. His wife died in childbirth a little over a year ago. The estate is entailed so he needs an heir."

"Was his wife from around here, or did they meet in a London ballroom?"

"What strange questions you ask. I believe she was from this county, I never knew her."

"Thank you. I doubt you have any further knowledge that is of interest. I will go to my room and request my maid fetch me some tea since your rules extend even to the food and drink the unlucky occupants of this house are allowed."

She rose from the table and left the room quietly. She did not slam the door however much she wished to.

Cobden sat in silence; the room seemed empty as if all life had drained from it. It was a strange feeling and it unsettled him.

Diana rang for Eliza with a real sense of apprehension. Perhaps she should write to the Smeatons as they had been so kind to her.

"Yes miss."

"Oh Eliza, do not be surprised if we have to leave suddenly. I have been very outspoken with Mr Cobden, he was very angry. I believe I will write a letter shortly, but could you manage to persuade them to let me have tea. Mr Cobden drinks only coffee and no-one is allowed downstairs for breakfast except him. All I have had is some dry toast, not even conserve."

"I will see what I can do, miss. I must say I would not be sorry to leave. They are an unfriendly lot downstairs. Nobody talks, everyone stares at the floor when I pass."

"Oh, then I am afraid I have just made it worse. I gave the housekeeper my opinion of the house rules."

Chapter 12

"Good morning, Miss Cobden, I hope you slept well. Do you have any plans for today?"

"I have not made any, although no doubt Papa will give his orders as usual."

"Your father tells you what you must do each day!"

Beatrice smiled at her. "Well he tries."

"Ah, then we will upset him some more, I have already arrived for breakfast to be told I may not come down until after ten. If he thinks he will incarcerate me in my room then he thinks wrongly. Tell me, do you have a lock on your bedroom door?"

"No-one does except papa. He says there is no need, we are only family here."

"If you could leave, Miss Cobden, would you?"

"Please, my name is Beatrice, you remind me of my papa whenever you speak my family name. And yes, I would leave if I could."

"What of your mama, does she approve of your father's attitude?"

"She says nothing. Everything changed about five years ago after a visit they made to London. We have all been unhappy since then."

"I would like to thank the Smeatons for their kindness to me. Is there anywhere local where I can send a letter?"

"Oh no, except for letters he sends to London, all are taken by a messenger."

"Oh dear, then I am unable to write without his knowing. I could not be sure the letter would be sent."

"Maybe one of our neighbours will send it for you. If you write your letter we will take a walk which just happens to pass a neighbour's house."

"A very good idea. If you will excuse me I will write immediately."

Diana retraced her steps back up to her room where she prepared for a very difficult correspondence.

'*Dear Mr Smeaton*

I write to thank you for the friendship and understanding you gave me. It is greatly appreciated. I could only wish this house held as much care as you showed for your daughter, for a more unhappy place cannot exist.

Beatrice, to whom I expected to be a companion, is to be married to a man she dislikes and I am here to force her, which you know I will not do.

The match was made because of his social standing and yet his character is unknown. Mr Cobden feels it unnecessary to ask, he is a Lord with land therefore he must be of superior character.

I would ask your help for a very unhappy young woman. If you have any contacts in London who could ascertain his character I would be most grateful.

His name is Lord Langdale and I understand he has a house 'near Grosvenor Square' although how near I do not know. He is about thirty years old and had a wife who died in childbirth just over a year ago.

I have no idea how useful this information will be, for I have been outspoken and it is possible Mr Cobden will send me away very soon. I will not adhere to the rules by which he controls the whole household. I most certainly could not stay if I did not feel an obligation to Beatrice to whom no-one is allowed to speak kindly.

I look forward to hearing from you. If you feel you are unable to help I will understand.

Yours Diana Newby'

"Miss Cobden, Beatrice, I am prepared."

"Come into the parlour until Papa leaves. He has asked the butler to arrange a messenger and will no doubt be in the entrance hall in a few moments."

They waited silently with the door slightly open in order to hear when he came. When he spoke his voice was angry.

"Is the messenger arranged?"

"Yes, sir, where is he to go?"

"I have a letter to Smeaton I want taking immediately."

"He will be here within the next few moments."

The footsteps retreated down the corridor. Diana and Beatrice stared at each other.

"He is writing to complain about me, I am sure. Could we catch the messenger and give him my letter."

"We must be quick."

They walked purposefully to the front door where the butler waited.

"We are taking a walk. Just so you know where we are when Papa looks for me." The Butler was confused at Beatrice's outburst as he stood there, the letter in his hand. He made no effort to open the door so Diana did so and walked outside leaving the butler to close it after them.

A young man on horseback came around from the stables and dismounted at the door.

"I understand you are to deliver a letter. I have one to the same person I would like you to deliver. Will you take it?"

"Yes, miss. Do you know where I am going?"

"The butler will tell you." They walked away as the door opened and the butler came forward with the letter.

"This must go to the Smeatons immediately. Do you know their direction?"

"The Smeatons, yes sir I do."

He made as if to ride away as the butler watched, but stayed near the corner of the house where the ladies had walked. She handed up the letter which he added to his bag.

"Thank you so much, young man." He was startled that anyone would smile at him and his face lit up with the pleasure it gave him.

"My pleasure, Miss."

Then he was away down the long drive to the road.

Beatrice held out her arm. "Shall we take our walk, Miss Newby?"

"Diana."

"Diana, will you walk with me?"

Arm in arm they walked away from the house which made them both unhappy.

* * *

William Smeaton was surprised when the messenger arrived with two letters. One he expected from Diana, he knew she would write but this was too soon. She had only left the day before. The messenger had brought it, a strange habit Cobden had, so the other must be from him he did write occasionally. What he found in the letter disturbed him. The whole tenet was unexpected. Diana was not rude or opinionated. What rules would she be expected to follow and why was he so displeased after one day?

He put the letter aside and opened Diana's. Ah, here was the answer. Cobden must have thought he could force Diana into following his orders. The man must have changed a great deal from when he had known him. Francis and Ann had been friends before they married and corresponded regularly until about five years ago. Whatever had happened Diana seemed to be stirring them up. He laughed to himself as he remembered the instant way she had assessed their problem. No doubt Cobden's problem, like theirs, was not what he thought. Diana did seem able to see beyond the apparent difficulty to the real cause.

What did she want, information on Lord Langdale. Well he could always pay a visit to Dursley for a couple of days. It should be easy enough to find the details on a Lord; the *haut ton*, the London high society was full of the latest goings on of any eligible aristocracy.

The Dursleys were at home, thank goodness. If they had been away it could have been difficult.

"Smeaton, what brings you here?"

"I hope it is not inconvenient, Dursley. I have an errand in London and hoped you would accommodate me."

"You are more than welcome, Smeaton, you should know that. We see too little of you these days. Have you come alone?"

"I have, I only expect to be here a couple of days."

Mrs Dursley and the housekeeper fussed around preparing him a room and he sank thankfully into a chair in Dursley's study.

"Do you have an appointment or are you free for lunch at the club tomorrow?"

"I have no appointment and it is your help I shall probably need."

"Are you in some trouble?"

"Not me. I have had a request for information from Miss Newby which I would find if I can."

"Ah, Miss Diana Newby. The remarkable girl you wrote to me about. What kind of information?"

"I believe it would be best not to spread the information, but she has gone to the Cobdens as a companion and there are already problems after only one day."

"That does not surprise me. We used to see him sometimes when he came to the Walfords. It was just unfortunate they gained him an invitation to a ball. Since then he has had the strangest ideas of how the aristocracy live. He has Walford baffled with his pseudo aristocratic lifestyle. I doubt he has seen him in some years now, I certainly have not."

"It appears he has made an arrangement for his daughter to marry a Lord Langdale. She dislikes him and refuses to marry. Cobden expected Diana to force her to. You can guess Diana's response, the house seems to be in uproar. She needs to know the character of this Lord, which Cobden has no interest in ascertaining. Surely a Lord of around thirty in need of a wife, the ton will know everything of his character."

"I am sure they will, we can make enquiries at my club tomorrow, although I believe it is the ladies who will prove most informative. I suggest we ask Melissa after dinner, she can make enquiries of her friends tomorrow."

So with the organisation in place, Smeaton relaxed and enjoyed the company of his friend and an excellent dinner with him and his wife Melissa. They spent little time with their port and joined Mrs Dursley in the parlour where she sat alone since their daughter had married and their son had his own rooms.

"We have a request of you, my dear, and I dare say it will be of interest. Smeaton wishes to know about a Lord Langdale who has a house near Grosvenor Square. Have you any knowledge of him?"

Melissa Dursley looked thoughtful. "You know I dislike the tales one hears about the ton although I have heard the name before and it was not in a positive context. If you wish I will call on Felicia tomorrow and ask what she remembers."

"That would be useful, my dear. We will ask at the club at lunchtime, see what the men say about him."

"Is it for your family, William? I thought you daughter was married?"

"Indeed she is, and very happily, all due to Miss Diana Newby. It is she who is enquiring of his character for the family where she is now a companion."

The tea tray arrived and after general discussion of their family and friends they retired early. Smeaton was more tired than he expected after the rough ride to London.

The two men entered Dursley's club a little before twelve when many congregated to talk before taking lunch. Dursley signed for Smeaton to accompany him as a guest and looked around for any faces he knew well.

"Dursley, over here."

A group of three gentlemen of a similar age sat with a glass in or near their hand.

"Billings, just the man I need. Have you met my friend Smeaton before?"

Billings looked closely. "I believe I may have but it was some years ago."

"Indeed, it is quite a few years since I visited London."

"Sit down and make yourself at ease." he waved the steward forward to arrange a brandy for them both. "What brings you here?"

"Information." Dursley answered. "Information on a Lord Langdale."

"I know the name but he does not belong to this club."

Another of the group had better information.

"I see him occasionally if I go out for the occasional game of cards. I think he is much younger then we are."

"So I understand. Do you know anything of his character?"

"His character? He does not seem to be a habitual gambler. He has a family, I believe."

"A family!"

"Yes, I have seen him with a woman and children quite recently."

Smeaton was confused. "I understood his wife died in childbirth over a year ago. He is to marry shortly."

The third member of the group leaned forward. "I should ask the ladies as to his character. He is rarely in the ton; I understand he frequents the gatherings of the demi-monde."

Dursley and Smeaton exchanged glances. "You believe this woman is not his wife? His sister perhaps?"

Simpson burst with laughter. "I doubt that unless there is a case of incest. Billings is right, ask the ladies of the haut ton, they will know all the details."

By the time they left the club they were both seriously worried.

"The demi-monde. We can only hope Melissa has some more detailed knowledge."

They expected to wait until after dinner when they could talk easily but Melissa had other ideas. They were sat in the library reading the latest news sheets when she arrived in a flurry of agitation.

"My dear, what has you so upset. Come and sit here and calm yourself."

She was persuaded to a chair before she started her outburst.

"Whoever is to marry him, she must not!"

It was said quite vehemently.

"Now keep calm and tell us what you have heard. Does he have a house near Grosvenor Square?"

"Oh yes. And he lives there all the time; he very rarely goes to his country estate. He lives there with his mistress of many years. She has children by him and is expecting another soon, I am told."

"But what of his wife who died last year."

"He hardly ever saw her. She was never in London, well where would she stay! I knew there was a reason I remembered his name. Winifred brought a young debutante to an 'at home' a few months ago. She was his wife's sister. She stayed a great deal of the time at the Hall as his wife was so lonely. From the day he knew she was carrying his child he never saw her again. He arranged a London doctor for her and forbade the staff to call the local man, they must have had a disagreement of some kind. She died before the doctor arrived from London. It was nearly two weeks she lay in the chapel waiting to be buried, until he found the time from his pleasures to visit. Her sister hates him; the whole ton seems to have been told of his treatment of his wife. He cares nothing. He intends to marry again for an heir and she must have a decent dowry."

The men sat silent.

"Do you know who he is to marry, William?"

Without thinking he responded "Cobden's daughter."

Horror showed on her face.

"Then you must tell him."

"Tell him I can, but whether he will take notice is debatable. At least I have information for Diana. I can only hope she can arrange something."

"Diana?"

"Diana Newby."

"Oh, the remarkable young lady you wrote about."

"Yes. Cobden knew of her success and thought to use her to pressure his daughter into marriage against her will."

"Then the daughter must be warned"

"Don't worry, Melissa. I intend to do just that."

The following morning William Smeaton returned home.

* * *

"Francis, I have some business which calls me away. As it takes me past the Cobdens, I wondered if you would care to accompany me. We could visit for a day or so and you could see Ann. It is many years since you saw each other. We can see how Diana is fairing."

"Oh William, that sounds wonderful, but what if we are not welcome."

"I will write first, or course. After so long I would not arrive unannounced, we were not that close friends."

So William Smeaton wrote to announce his possible visit and ask if the Cobdens would receive them.

Cobden's answer was exactly what he expected. They were very welcome and he hoped they would stay a day or two. What he actually hoped was that Smeaton would see how dreadful this Miss Newby was. Smeaton, of course, knew his motives and wondered how he could aid Diana in whatever course of action she had decided.

Chapter 13

The days improved for Diana and Beatrice as they deliberately broke Cobden's house rules. Each day Diana went downstairs early and walked in the garden. Each day she made a fuss in the breakfast room that a guest was not allowed tea. After a few days Beatrice joined her as her confidence grew. Their logic went like this. 'Diana was a guest and could not be punished for breaking the rules although she could be sent away. Beatrice could be punished but how, she was already denied any friendship or family life, she could not be sent away. If he hoped to change Beatrice's mind, sending Diana away would do completely the opposite to what he hoped. Between them they had him confounded.

The flowers were the next attack. Cobden had no aesthetic appreciation of flowers. The blue room had blue flowers; the white room had white flowers. They were unnoticeable, they blended in. First they changed them over putting the vase of blue flowers in the white room and the white flowers in the blue room. He noticed, of course. Everyone noticed, that was the whole point of a vase of flowers.

One morning they picked pansies from the garden and arranged them in a small bowl on a low table. The effect was wonderful, the room came to life losing its bland appearance; until they disappeared.

Each day they were expected in the parlour at four o'clock for when the tea arrived. There were insufficient upright chairs for both of them and Gertrude arrived early to occupy the best positioned one. The sofas were far too deep and high for either of them to sit on so one of them sat on a very low foot stool. Mr Cobden was annoyed. They must sit on the sofa.

Each day he complained, each day they ignored him.

After the first week Diana sat on a sofa, in the corner at the back with her feet tucked under her. He was scathing with his complaint that it was not ladylike.

"What am I supposed to do, sir, cut off my legs and leave them on the floor, for I am not a man and cannot reach from here."

"Then sit forward like my wife."

Mrs Cobden said nothing, her arm laid over the arm of the sofa to hold herself upright."

"You may force your wife to have an aching back, sir, but you cannot force me."

After that he stopped complaining.

There was an increase of maids in Diana's wing and she was informed they were expecting guests. Mr Cobden had informed no-one except the housekeeper.

The Smeatons were both apprehensive during their carriage drive. William wondered how Diana was coping with Cobden's pseudo aristocratic rules. Francis was worried that Ann might not be pleased to see her. She was not sure how to proceed.

"William, I am worried about how to behave. You know how I say things; ask too many questions, what if I upset them."

"My dear Francis. You have my permission to say whatever you think and ask as many questions as you wish and upset whoever you like. If Diana wishes us not to mention something she will tell me." Francis looked at him thoughtfully.

"There is a reason for this visit which you have not told me."

"I cannot tell you what I do not know. We must wait until we arrive to find out if she needs our help. Just be your natural self, my dear."

As the coach pulled up by the ornate portico the front door opened, the grooms taking the horses heads to steady them.

"The house looks a little ..." She could not find the words.

"Yes it does, let us see if the inside is as ostentatious."

It was.

The butler led them to the parlour and announced them as if they were royalty. Cobden rose to meet them. Ann made no attempt to rise until she saw her erstwhile friend. "Francis! What are you doing here?"

Smeaton, realising she had not been told of their visit answered for his wife.

"We are here for a couple of days while on a business errand."

Francis held out her hands and took Ann's. "It is so long since I saw you I could not resist accompanying William."

Cobden not wishing to be left out insisted that they were seated and indicated a sofa to Francis. She tried to sit on it but being smaller than Ann she had to wriggle to sit and her feet came nowhere near the floor. As she leaned over she lost her balance and fell backwards, arms and legs flailing. Cobden stared. William Smeaton rushed to return his wife to an upright position.

"I believe you need cushions, my dear." he looked toward Ann sitting primly clutching the arm of her sofa.

"Cushions! They would ruin the line of the sofas. They were very expensive, a copy of those at Versailles."

Smeaton stared at him.

"Then send them back there, Cobden, my wife cannot sit on them." he brought an upright chair forward and seated her on it pulling the footstool beneath her feet.

"Where do callers sit when they visit your wife?"

"Callers? Occasionally one of the neighbours calls, I usually take him into my study."

Francis had barely regained her composure.

"I think you need a little tea to revive you, my dear." He patted her hand and looked at Ann, who looked back at him.

"Tea, Smeaton! Tea is at four o'clock like any superior establishment."

Smeaton faced Cobden. "What balderdash, Cobden. Tea is taken when it is required, where did that idea come from?"

Ann slid off the sofa and went to ring the bell. "The housekeeper will show you to your rooms." Her voice was quiet and she made no mention of tea.

After an embarrassing silence the housekeeper arrived to take them upstairs. Smeaton took note of everything he saw. The overdone wall covering, the oversized furniture, the flowers of one type and colour only, the sad and dutiful staff, the serious hard-faced housekeeper ....

Their rooms were down the long extension wing, their footsteps echoing on the highly polished floor.

"Take care you do not slip, Francis." He offered her his arm, then decided he should gain as much information from the housekeeper as he could.

"Is it usual for you to have tea only at four o'clock?"

"Oh yes, sir. This house is run on aristocratic rules. We serve the tea at four and dinner at seven."

"Does Mrs Cobden never ask for tea earlier?"

"There is no need to ask, we deliver it at four."

"Why did she arrange that, do you think?"

"Oh Mrs Cobden is not to be concerned with mundane things. Mr Cobden gives me my rules and I run the house accordingly."

Smeaton and his wife were looking at one another.

"Here we are. This is your room, Ma'am, your husband's is further down the wing in the Gentlemens' rooms.

"Why do we need two rooms?"

The housekeeper looked at them with amazement.

"You sleep in the same room! Mr Cobden will not approve of that."

"What does our sleeping arrangement have to do with your master? Does he rule everything in this house?"

"Yes sir. Of course he does. He is a man of superior understanding, he takes care of everything."

William and Francis sat in their room, he in the chair, she on the bed, reclining on the pillows.

"Did you know Frederick was like this?"

"Not this bad, I have to admit, although I knew he had strange ideas of the aristocracy."

"Why did he want Diana here, because he has several daughters?"

"Two daughters. Diana was invited to persuade the eldest to marry the Lord he has picked out for her. She is refusing."

"I hope Diana is not in any difficulty. Should we take her home with us, do you think?"

"Francis, my dear wife. Now you know why I care so much for you, you are indeed the kindest person I know." In spite of their long marriage, Francis blushed a little at the compliment.

"Diana wrote to me with a request. I doubt she would leave until she has accomplished whatever she is planning." He took out his watch and checked the time. "Perhaps we should go down. If we miss the four o'clock tea I doubt there will be any until after dinner."

They arrived shortly before four and found the upright chair and footstool occupied by Gertrude. Smeaton looked at her pointedly but she never moved, so he fetched the second chair and seated his wife within the family circle.

He gesticulated to Gertrude. "Do you mind, Miss Cobden, my wife has need of the footstool."

Gertrude stared at him. "So do I."

No one spoke.

The door opened and Diana and Beatrice entered.

"Mr Smeaton! Mrs Smeaton! She held out her hands as she moved eagerly towards them, taking his hand and bending to kiss Mrs Smeaton's cheek. Mrs Smeaton wobbled.

"Oh you need the footstool."

"I'll get it." Beatrice went to take it from beneath Geraldine's feet.

"I need it."

"No you don't, Gertrude. Usually Diana or I sit on it." She pulled it from her feet and delivered it to a grateful guest. Diana introduced Beatrice to their visitors, something Cobden had made no effort to do.

"I think we have to use a sofa today." They both took off their slippers and climbed up to sit with their feet folded beneath them.

"You will have to hand around the tea today, Gertrude. You have the chair, I dare not move or one of us will spill tea on papa's precious sofa."

Mr Cobden sat silently as he watched the interplay between the Smeatons and the two girls. This was appalling behaviour; they were acting like low born girls. This would not do for the wife of Lord Langdale. His dilemma was how to chastise them with the Smeatons there. He would use Geraldine.

"Since you appear to be the only young lady of manners here, Geraldine, you must be the hostess and hand around the tea." It was intended that Geraldine would be pleased at the praise. He had miscalculated.

"Why should I do it just to save your precious sofa?"

The knock on the door brought the tea trolley loaded with biscuits and tiny cakes and the very best of china Cobden could find. The highly coloured plates and cups of Crown Derby porcelain were garish against the whiteness of the room.

Francis was nervous of dropping something and causing the ire of Cobden. Did he make everyone feel like this?

Eventually Beatrice went to climb from the sofa. Diana put out her hand. "No, I will do it. The Smeatons are my friends. I can easily stand to drink my tea." She slid to the front of the sofa and dropped to the floor, replacing her slippers. As Mrs Cobden poured the tea she handed around the cups, first to Mrs Smeaton, then to Mr Smeaton. As he took the cup she smiled.

"Welcome to Brobdingnag Mr Smeaton." her eyes laughing at him.

When she handed a cup to Mr Cobden he said "What the devil are you talking about?"

"Ah, you have obviously never read Gulliver's Travels have you, Mr Cobden?"

He huffed.

"Do you know what she is talking about, Smeaton?"

"I have indeed read Jonathan Swift's writings."

"A children's book!"

"Indeed no. Children can enjoy it in its simplicity but it is a serious comment on society. You would do well to read it yourself."

"I have no time for frivolities, Smeaton. I have a house to run."

This was too much for Mrs Smeaton not to comment on.

"Surely your wife runs the house. That is what wives do."

"Obviously you know little of the aristocracy, Ma'am."

This was too much for Smeaton. "The aristocracy are either in parliament or running their estates. Why would they want to run their houses as well? I think you have misinterpreted things you have heard, Cobden. No wonder your housekeeper is so full of strange ideas."

Diana carried her cup to the window. "It has been a fine day today. I hope it will continue tomorrow."

"Do you walk in the garden every morning as usual?" Mrs Smeaton had enough confidence to speak with Diana if not others.

"I do if the weather is good."

"Is it a pleasant garden?" One of Mrs Smeaton's awkward enquiries.

"Not particularly, there is no aesthetic pleasure there, merely fresh air."

Cobden was nonplussed.

"What do you mean no aesthetic pleasure? A garden is for growing flowers for the house. You see what I mean, Smeaton. She is rude and outspoken."

"Outspoken, perhaps, but I expect she speaks the truth. Who sees to the garden?" He looked towards Ann.

"I do, of course." Cobden was getting truculent.

"What does your wife do, Mr Cobden?" With all the outspoken conversation Francis had asked the question which puzzled her most.

"Do? Why should she do anything? She is a gently brought up lady and is treated as she should be."

Diana turned to him. "As you believe aristocratic ladies should be. Like your sofas, Mr Cobden." Only Cobden knew the reference to a previous conversation.

The teacups had been returned to the trolley and Cobden rose to ring the bell for it to be removed. Gertrude excused herself and left with a scowl on her face and the two girls offered to show the Smeatons the garden walks close to the house where the late afternoon sun was still shining. Francis asked Ann to accompany them but she refused. As Francis remarked later, it was as if she felt she was not allowed and might be punished.

The gong sounded at 6 o'clock to announce time to dress for dinner. "I hope I have brought an elegant enough gown."

"Your gown will be quite adequate, Francis. However Cobden wishes, we are not going to a ball."

Dinner was tense, the discussions mundane and stilted. When the desert was served Geraldine remarked "Quince tart again."

"It is the time of year for quinces; no doubt we have a surfeit."

"We had it only two days ago."

Beatrice intervened to remind her. "Cook only has so many dishes to choose from; perhaps this is the only one for the quince season."

To try to lighten the atmosphere Diana added "Mrs Fortesque's cook always made conserve when she had too much of one fruit. That way it was available the whole year: until it was all used up, of course."

"Is that why we have hardly any conserve, Papa? Did you tell cook she should make some? I doubt if you realised when you gave her the list."

After dinner they sat in the parlour, the two girls curled up on a sofa again. The Smeatons asked Cobden about mutual friends and they shared information. In all this time Ann remained silent, as if she knew no-one and had nothing useful to add. Francis wondered if she was even interested.

They retired early; it had been a tiring day. As they made their way up the stairs Smeaton turned to look at Diana. "If you walk in the garden before breakfast I may join you."

Diana knew his reason and inclined her head. She hoped he had useful information for her. "Goodnight Mrs Smeaton, Mr Smeaton. I hope you sleep well."

Diana was in the garden early, wrapped in her cloak against the cool of the morning. It was not long before she heard footsteps behind her.

"Good morning, Mr Smeaton."

"Good morning, Diana. I have an answer to your question."

"Good. I need to know more, I am at a loss to know how to proceed."

"She must not marry him. Make sure she understands. He kept his wife in the country while living with his mistress and children in London. He left her completely alone when with child. The London doctor arrived too late to help."

Diana was shocked. "She was just to provide an heir?"

"And a dowry. The ton do not approve of him, the wife was never presented to them. He left her body in its coffin without burial until he found the time from his pleasures. Make sure she understands, Diana."

She was quiet. "Don't worry, I will."

They arrived at the breakfast room together. With Smeaton there Cobden had requested a range of food which Diana helped him eat. When Cobden arrived there was little left. He scowled at the empty plates and sent the footman to request more.

"Tell him to bring tea also." Smeaton called over to him.

"I do not drink tea at breakfast."

"But I do. I find it refreshing." Diana knew he normally drank coffee and smiled to herself.

When Beatrice arrived a little later she was surprised. "Tea. How lovely. Thank you, Papa." He went to enlighten her but changed his mind.

After the breakfast confrontation Cobden wanted to distance himself from his house and all its trouble. Too many were now challenging his view of how life should be. It was a relief when Smeaton agreed to ride out to be shown the local area and meet the odd neighbour.

Neither of their wives had yet appeared but Smeaton went to tell Francis where he would be. He found her dressed, the maid removing the breakfast tray, and planning to spend her morning with Ann.

"We will be out riding. Why not take the coach, take her out of this house for a while, then she may talk to you."

"I will try. I know something must be done she is so unhappy. I feel the pressure of this house leaning on me."

"If you do, think of how Ann feels. Do what you can for her, my dear."

Cobden took them on a long ride passing the most prestigious of the local houses. They passed The Major out for a ride and exchanged pleasantries with him. He was an elderly gentleman who had taken no part in the recent troubles with Bonaparte. They rode to where the local stream joined the river.

"As you see, we have a fair number of wealthy families in the area."

"What contact do you have? Do you entertain them?"

"Not really. They come to me when there is something to discuss. I believe they feel the need for my decision."

Smeaton refrained from another confrontation. Cobden was already in a very strange mood.

"If we follow the river a little way we come to the village with its church. I have something there I would show you."

They rode in silence, not particularly peaceful but in a harmony that came from a shared past and mutual friends.

On the driveway to the church was a carriage with a driver Smeaton knew all too well.

"I do believe that is my carriage. Francis must be visiting the church. Perhaps Ann has come with her."

"It is getting late in the morning, I do hope she will not be late for lunch."

"Do you never forget your rules, Cobden? Can no-one enjoy anything without being reminded of them? Shall we see if they are both there?"

As they passed the side entrance to the churchyard it was possible to see the two women at the far end.

"My wife is obviously showing your wife the mausoleum I have had built for when we die."

"You have a mausoleum ready!"

"Well I doubt Ann would be able to arrange it sufficiently if I died first, and I have no intention of going to a common grave like the local serfs."

"You astound me at every turn, Cobden. You have such an opinion of yourself as if you were the high born aristocrat you aspire to be. We are no different you and I, nor are most of your neighbours. Why do you feel the need to be above everyone else?"

"It is a matter of standards, Smeaton. My wife appreciates how much I strive to maintain an acceptable level for the sake of all our future happiness."

"Is Ann happy?"

"Of course she is. She at least never complains, unlike my daughters. She knows the value of what I am aiming for and appreciates the sacrifices I make."

They arrived at the church lych gate and dismounted, tying their horses to the rail.

"It is not quite the church I would have liked but it is the best there is for miles so it will have to suffice.

The women had entered the church by the side door before they arrived, the heavy door was ajar. As they went to enter Smeaton laid his hand on Cobden's arm. Francis was talking.

"Ann, it is a sin for which you would be sent to hell. You cannot!"

She was upset, her voice pleading.

"I already live in hell, Francis. How do you think it feels to be useless, ruled by a cruel man? I am not even allowed to read, he does not consider it ladylike! Sometimes my back aches so badly I take a book to the nursery and read. They are the only chairs not too large for me. At first I had cushions made but he took them away. Everything is to his liking, his ideas, his pleasure, even the food I eat. You think I will be sorry to lie in unhallowed ground. I would rather lie there than in that dreadful mausoleum. He aims to control me even after death. Well I can at least choose when I die and he cannot stop me."

"But think of your soul in hell for eternity."

"I have no soul. Frederick took possession of it years ago. Let him lie in his mausoleum alone, at least I will not be there to be ordered how to sit, how to dress, what to eat, when to eat it. Let him stare at his empty sofas for eternity. They mean more to him than I ever have.

Cobden went to enter but Smeaton put a hand on his arm and drew him away. He was ashen white and trembling.

Quietly in a voice the ladies could not hear he urged him away. "Come Cobden. Let us return to your home. I believe you need a drink."

While they rode they were silent, Cobden almost in a trance. They passed several neighbours houses with their gardens full of nodding flowers in a riot of autumn colours. He stared at them as if he had never noticed them before. When they reached his house they passed empty borders bare of even greenery.

Chapter 14

They sat silently in Cobden's study with a rather large glass of brandy each.

"The aristocratic ladies live this way, why not Ann." His voice was thin and reedy.

"No they don't, Cobden. They spend their days arranging the menus with their housekeeper, shopping in Bond Street, visiting and receiving visitors in the afternoon. Dinner with friends then going to a ball at about ten o'clock at night. They arrive home at possibly two o'clock in the morning. Many of their husbands then go gambling or to their mistresses and their wives entertain one of the young bucks of the ton in their bedrooms. Very few are awake early enough to come down before ten o'clock. Is that the life you see for Ann?" He waited a moment then continued, "In the country it is totally different. Lady Bostock regularly passes our house in the pony and trap at eight in the morning. We all eat earlier, usually around six, and retire earlier. The exception is at a country house party. They often stay up later but breakfast is a very jovial meal with everyone except the elderly ladies there. Where did you acquire these ideas of yours?"

"We went to a ball. I heard the ladies talking and I asked after their habits."

"I bet they never mentioned their night time visitors."

Cobden was shocked.

"But they are superior people."

"No Cobden, they are merely born or married to a title and have enough money to indulge their passions. Many lose their whole fortune in the gambling hells. That is hardly superior."

He was thoughtful for a moment. "Why did you buy such large furniture?"

"I saw it in the furniture makers and it looked so aristocratic. So I employed them to decorate the downstairs rooms."

"But they are so big!"

"They looked normal size in the store. They were expensive and the cushions made them look ordinary."

"But it made them comfortable. What else did you learn at the ball?"

"The flowers were all one colour and one type. The whole room was blue and silver, it looked so superior. The ton ladies said they had white and gold or pink and green."

"Pink and green would have been an improvement. They are the colours they pick for the décor at their balls, to impress their guests. They often have a theme, Greek or Egyptian. Sometimes a masked ball. Would you have made Ann wear a mask her whole life? I just do not understand why you insist on making every decision. Did Ann never complain?"

"She did at first, but I was so busy organising everything."

"Like the garden. Does she ever walk in the garden?"

"Not now."

"Ladies organise their houses, Cobden. They have visitors in the afternoon and ring for tea when they arrive. Often they go out for tea with friends. You insist Ann must be there to pour the tea, how can she go visiting? When did she last see a neighbour, how long is it since anyone called?"

Cobden looked down into his glass. "I don't know. Not since the rules, I suppose."

"How long is that?"

"About five years, I don't know."

"So, for nearly five years you have not allowed her any friends, no comfortable seat, nothing to do. You changed her garden to grow your flowers and what is this about reading?"

"Only bluestockings read, Smeaton."

"Not so. There are so many books that ladies read these days; all ladies of every rank: romances, travel books. Miss Newby - Diana - read a travel book to Geraldine and it brought her out of her ennui. She reads a great deal, perhaps that is why she has the ability to understand the real difficulty. I think she saw not your daughter's refusal but your intransigence as a problem for the whole household."

"She is too outspoken."

"I have never known her to be so, but maybe she feels this is the only way to make you see there is a problem. My advice would be to speak to your wife. Ask her to run the house again, tell her she must say if she dislikes something with the promise that you will listen and talk to her. The alternative is too dreadful to contemplate."

"Diana Newby said I had no marriage."

"Then she saw your wife's unhappiness very quickly. Try talking to Diana, she is always early to breakfast, we were often the only ones there. If you listen to what she is saying you will learn a great deal from her. I know I did."

"Will she persuade Beatrice to marry?"

"That I cannot predict. Of course it depends on the Lord. Some are quite acceptable, but what the ton accept and what good God fearing folk accept are often different. They accept a man keeping a mistress and spending a deal of time with her, showering her with jewels and money. But they are outraged when he keeps her in his house and lives openly with her. Simpson, a friend of Dursley who I met when in London recently, was telling me of a Lord the ton disapprove of because he has lived with his mistress and children for years in his London house near Grosvenor Square. He is not acceptable to the ton even if he does need a wife. He gave the last one none of his time, she was shut away alone on his estate and he rarely visited. The ton never saw her."

"He must be a very poor specimen."

"Indeed he is, but there are more like Lord Langdale than you realise."

Cobden froze.

He stared at Smeaton.

"Who!"

"Lord Langdale. Simpson often sees him in the park with his mistress and several small children, another one coming soon, it seems."

"He never goes to the ton balls?" It was a hesitant query.

"No, he and his mistress are part of the demi-monde."

With the men away from the house Diana and Beatrice were in the library. "I really do not see what Papa has against us reading. He seems to think it is not ladylike. I know Mama always read when we were younger. I have such a limited number of books I have to keep re-reading them." Beatrice was wandering around peering at the shelves with their musty old books with obscure titles.

"I can't imagine who would want to read these old books. The smell alone is enough to put you off. Does your father never read?"

"Yes I believe he does. I wonder where he keeps those books."

"Well not in here. Could they be in his study?"

"Oh I dare not go in there."

"Well I will. It will only take a minute to check."

Diana checked no-one was about then quietly opened the door. The study was almost as big as the library with rows of newer looking books. She scanned along the shelves, took out a book and retreated back to Beatrice in the library.

"A few of the books are almost as old as in here but mostly they are newer ones." She held up her prize. "This is quite well read, he obviously likes this one. '*Taking The Grand Tour*'" she read.

Beatrice looked puzzled. "What is the Grand Tour?"

"When rich men or aristocrats are young they are sent on a grand tour of foreign lands, France, Spain, definitely Italy and sometimes Greece. They take tutors with them to explain things and they buy paintings and sculptures to bring back, furniture too. Do you think your father read about it before he bought your sofas or afterwards?"

Beatrice laughed. "I think it would be a good idea to read that."

While she was relaxed and they were alone perhaps now was the time to speak plainly.

"Beatrice, you must not marry Lord Langdale no matter how much your father tries to force you."

Beatrice looked surprised. "Well I don't intend to, but if he makes it impossible for me what can I do?"

"I will take you away with me if the need arises. You must not marry him."

"Do you know something about him?"

"I do, and it is not pleasant. He wants you for your dowry and to bear an heir. You will never go to London and he will leave you on your own in the country estate. Like I said, another sofa. I will not allow you to become a sofa."

"Why could I not live in the London house where I could visit people?"

"Because his mistress and their children live there. His wife died because of his neglect and because he is like your father, only the physician he says can be called. If they had called the local doctor his wife may well be alive now."

While they sat talking they heard the men's footsteps down the corridor to the study, the door shutting firmly behind them.

"That was close; I did not expect them back yet. I wonder where Mama and Mrs Smeaton are?"

"No doubt having a happier day than your mama usually has."

But in that thought she was totally wrong.

Lunch was strange. The girls were feeling quite light-hearted, Ann Cobden was as silent and serious as usual, Mrs Smeaton was in some distress and hardly ate anything, Mr Smeaton seemed concerned and Cobden was in shock. Nobody spoke.

After lunch the girls went to the blue lounge to avoid the dreadful atmosphere. Smeaton suggested they all walked in the garden while it was still warm enough. The ladies were dispatched to fetch their cloaks and put on walking shoes.

"Cobden, while we are alone I would suggest that if you intend to save your wife you must speak to her soon, today if possible. Now she has spoken of her intention I believe it may happen very soon."

Cobden rubbed his neck with the tension.

"Where do I start, Smeaton?"

"First we go around the garden and the vegetable garden and see the house flowers. Ask her what she would like the gardeners to grow."

The ladies came down the stairs to the men waiting in the hall. Both were serious and ashen-faced. They walked first towards the roses; they were not in flower of course. They had been pruned low after the flowering had finished, the ground around them was bare and some of them bore the mark of disease.

"I had not noticed they were in such poor condition, we shall have to talk to the gardeners, eh, my dear."

Ann Cobden made no reply; she had not registered her inclusion in his statement.

The long borders were mainly bare now, most of the summer flowering over. Cobden looked at his wife. "We must ask why the flowers all finish so early. There must be a reason."

Ann never responded.

Some little way further and they came to the wall of the vegetable garden with its wooden gate. As they entered they expected to see a hive of activity but there was nobody around.

"Where are they all?"

"Perhaps in the glass houses," Francis said helpfully.

There were only a few flowers growing at the far end of the enclosed garden. There was a range of glasshouses and sheds built against the south facing wall. A man emerged from one of them and came forward to greet them, He was old and a little slow and Cobden was surprised to see him.

"Old Tom, are you still working here?"

"I has to eat, sir. Do you wish to see anything in particular?"

"I was wondering why there is no-one in the vegetable garden working"

"That was done this morning when we dug the vegetables for cook. We work on the flowers most of the day now."

"Why are there no flowers growing here?" He indicated the far end of the plot.

"All gone over now. Only some pink and yellow left at this time of year and we don't grow them."

Cobden turned to his wife. "Shall we go into the glasshouse and see what is there?" She stared blankly at him. Francis stepped forward and took Ann's arm.

"Let us go and see if we can bedevil the gardeners."

There was no response but Francis had not expected it. At least Ann walked with her.

Inside the first house it was not at all as they expected. Rows of pots stood on the shelves, most were empty but a young gardener was planting bulbs.

"They smell like onions." Smeaton remarked.

"They are, sir. We grow them for their flowers in the winter. This is the white house."

"You have another?"

"Oh yes, the blue house. We have to keep them separate for the seed to come true to colour."

Cobden was looking amazed. Smeaton asked if the glasshouses were heated.

"Oh yes, sir. We have to regulate the temperature or they don't flower. We have to provide lamps to make like it is daylight longer. When they are well grown we put them into a cooler house and it makes them flower. We have a boy as stokes the fire at night and another in the day."

"But that takes a huge amount of fuel!"

"It does, sir, but if you want your flowers in the winter it 'as to be done."

"I had no idea. Are these the only winter flowers?"

"There are the dried ones but they take a deal of work."

"Are they difficult to dry?"

"Oh no. Tis not the drying, tis the dying them blue. We loses a great many with the dying."

"You dye flowers!" Smeaton was now caught up in this strange tale.

"We have to dye them blue, they don't none of them grow that colour."

Cobden was in shock. "How many do I employ for these winter flowers?"

"Well there is me and four boys plus the two gardeners who normally look after the flower garden."

"Who is in charge?"

"I am, sir."

"What happened to … er."

"Dick, sir? He left. his brother got him an under-gardener's job at some Lord's estate."

"An under-gardener" Cobden was quite angry. "He was head gardener here."

"He gets paid nearly as much and a house to live in free, and food from the estate. He got a job there for my grandson to train. They grow special fruit in the glasshouses."

"Special fruit?"

"From abroad, it won't grow in the garden."

"Oh, exotic fruit." Francis was intrigued.

"That's right. Oranges, peaches and something called a Pine Apples we never grew those. They send them up to his London house."

Cobden was now pacing up and down. It was Francis who remembered the problems with the roses.

"Mr Tom. What is wrong with the roses?"

"They has an illness, Ma'am. It gets in when we cut the thorns off."

"Why do you cut the thorns off?"

"So as no-one catches their clothes. It's Mr Cobden's rules, Ma'am."

"Well how else do you stop anyone getting scratched, especially children." He was fully defensive now.

"We used to have box edging growing around before."

"Before what?" Francis asked.

"Before the rules." Smeaton muttered.

They suddenly realised Ann was staring blindly out of the window and had taken no part in any of the discussions. Smeaton looked pointedly at Cobden.

"Speak to her."

Cobden was unsure what to say.

"Ann, my dear. What flowers would you like to have the gardeners grow? Do you have a favourite?"

Ann slowly turned in answer to her name but stared at him blankly.

"Do you have a favourite flower, or a favourite colour?" He said hopefully.

She was slow to answer. "I don't remember." Then she turned back to stare outside again.

Cobden turned to Old Tom. "What grows in the winter, Tom?"

"Precious little and we have none that does. There's only greenery."

"Then add greenery to the house flowers. Will it make more work, is it possible to reduce the number of flowers now."

"Oh yes, sir. The onions can just be eaten. There's greenery a plenty in the area. Then we have the dried flowers, of course."

"Shall we see the dried flowers?"

Tom led them through the garden to another gate in the wall where there were sheds on the north side. Inside one the roof was hung with bunches of drying flowers of many hues. For the first time Ann looked up and raised her fingers to touch them.

"They lose some of their colour but they are a pleasant mixture. The yellow and pink are particularly rich in the dark days and they last for the whole wintertime."

Everyone stared at the fingers touching the flowers and a small voice said. "I like pink." And everyone held their breath.

Chapter 15

It was time for the gong to dress for dinner when they arrived back at the house. The Smeatons and Ann Cobden went up immediately but Cobden went to his study and called for the housekeeper.

"What cushions do we have in the house?"

"Cushions Sir. We don't have cushions."

"There were once, what will have happened to them?"

"There may be some in the guest bedrooms or perhaps in the attic."

"I want them found during dinner. If you can find no cushions then we must make do with pillows from the guest rooms. I want them on the white parlour sofas when we leave the dinner table."

The housekeeper looked belligerent but left in silence. Cobden went to change. He dressed quickly and knocked on his wife's door.

"Ann, dear, are you dressed yet?"

Her maid opened and curtsied. "I was just finishing her hair, Sir."

He walked over to his wife sitting at her dressing mirror.

"I have come to escort you to dinner, my dear. That is if you are ready, if not I will wait." She was staring at him in her mirror.

"I ..."

Her maid came to her and lifted the lid on the jewellery box. "Oh yes, my necklace. I almost forgot."

He stood aside while the maid fastened the clasp and she stood, turning slowly to face him. He held out his arm to her.

"Shall we go down to dinner?"

The girls were already waiting when he escorted his wife to the table and seated her. Everyone was stunned by what they saw. There was still silence when the Smeatons entered and took their seats. Ann was gazing up at Cobden in quiet disbelief.

The food was served but only the Smeatons noticed what the dishes were, everyone else had eaten the same dishes several times in the last couple of weeks so they hardly relished it. Ann kept taking a mouthful then putting down her fork and staring at her husband.

While the desert was being served, a perfectly acceptable apple tart, if only it had not been the same as three days before, Cobden amazed everyone by asking his wife what meals she liked best and if there were any she wished the cook to prepare that were not their usual. It took a while before an incredulous Ann quietly said "Pheasant. I like pheasant."

"Do you really, I had no idea. I will ..." he stopped. "You must speak with cook and see how to acquire one."

Gertrude was sitting with her mouth open, Beatrice was gripping Diana's arm. When the silence stretched Smeaton asked what the young ladies of the house had been doing. Gertrude said she had been sewing ribbons onto a dress. Beatrice was looking slightly guilty so Diana answered. "We have been in the library looking at the books. They are all very old and smell musty. It must be a long time since there were any new books added."

"Do you not have a regular subscription, Cobden?"

"Not at present. I ... We used to purchase books when we went to town but since we rarely go, I am afraid I have rather lost the habit. Perhaps we should make a visit to town, my dear, and see what novels the ladies are reading these days."

Ann looked up into her husband's face. "Am I asleep?"

"No, my dear, but it seems I have been for far too long."

The gentlemen were not long with their port and joined the ladies in the parlour where there was much activity. It seemed the housekeeper had found a variety of cushions from somewhere and augmented them with a few pillows from the guest rooms. Ann Cobden was sat supported by several but when she sat back they slid apart and allowed her to fall backwards. Diana was speaking.

"What you need are really big cushions so you need only one."

"How big?" Beatrice was helping Francis Smeaton to lift Ann from where she had disappeared amongst the shiny silk.

"Try the pillows." They put two pillows behind her back and she sat comfortably. "That big."

"They would have to be specially made."

Cobden took in the scene. "Why not? The sofas were recovered locally, I am sure they could make cushions."

"What a good idea, if they have any material to match they would enhance the sofas."

Smeaton smiled to himself. Cobden looked at him in surprise.

"I told you to listen to her."

Eventually everyone was seated and the conversation turned to the following day.

"Perhaps we could all rise a little earlier and drive into town tomorrow." Cobden suggested. "We could arrange about the cushions and perhaps some footstools to match, then we could visit the booksellers."

Gertrude in particular was staring at him. "What, all of us?"

"Why not. When did you last visit the town? We could have lunch at the Four Oaks."

"I would appreciate that. I could attend to my business while you make your calls and meet you for lunch."

"You have business there?" Francis was surprised.

"I told you that was the reason for coming."

So plans were finalised as they drank tea and the exceedingly bemused ladies left for an early night.

Before breakfast the next morning Diana walked in the garden where Smeaton joined her.

"What happened, what have you told him?" she asked.

"I told him of the way aristocracy often live and how bad some Lords can be. I dropped his name into the conversation just as an example. I never let him know I had heard the name of the Lord in his marriage agreement."

"But why has he suddenly changed his rules. There is more than you have said."

"You are too astute, Diana. This is a confidence you must not betray, although you should know the reason because we will leave possibly tomorrow. We came upon Francis and Ann talking in the Church before we entered. Ann Cobden is, or was, intending to end her life. It has had a profound effect on him. You may need to watch her. I have advised him to talk with you, I hope he does." Diana also was profoundly shocked.

"Mrs Cobden was more unhappy than I realised. I will do what I can to help."

"Thank you, Diana. I hate to leave you with a problem this great but if anyone can help them it is you."

Diana blushed. Smeaton turned his head to save her embarrassment.

"I believe it may be time for breakfast. We must not be the ones to delay the departure.

Diana and Beatrice rode with the Smeatons. The coaches were left at the Four Oaks while they made their calls. Smeaton excused himself and walked in the opposite direction. In truth, he had no business to attend to but he did have an idea for an errand of his own.

He passed various shops selling ribbons, jewellery, shoes and amongst them a solicitor's office. He checked he had not been followed then entered the chosen premises. He wished he could have been there when they chose the cushion material but this errand meant a great deal to him.

The furniture maker and upholsterers was a large premises with a shop front where you could purchase material or arrange for work to be carried out.

Cobden was remembered.

The young man dealing with two ladies choosing material excused himself for a moment and called for the owner to help. The owner was not only pleased to make the cushions, he was overjoyed. The material of the sofas was expensive and had been ordered from London on Cobden's insistence. He was relieved to use the rest of the bales which had sat there unsold ever since.

Ann Cobden was encouraged to pick the footstools she preferred with help and encouragement from Beatrice and Francis. Diana added a mention of the footstool that already existed and the style of the sofas that made the decision much easier. Then they started toward the book sellers. But there was a strange occurrence on the way. As they walked— Beatrice and Diana arm in arm bringing up the rear—Diana noticed a man who turned away as they passed. When she looked back he was staring after them. The reason she noticed was the tremble of Beatrice's arm and her lowered head. They had met this man before when out walking and the same had occurred, Beatrice trembled and looked down, he rode past and ignored them then turned to stare after them. She had no idea who this man was but Beatrice knew him well enough.

She found out at lunch when Gertrude made a remark intended to upset Beatrice.

"Did you see Peter Sedgefield?"

"No, I did not." Beatrice looked away as she spoke.

"He was with a very pretty young lady, perhaps he has married."

"No he was not!"

"I thought you never saw him."

Diana made a mental note to find out about Peter Sedgefield, he could be useful.

Dinner at the Four Oaks was a subdued meal. Gertrude and Beatrice were actively hostile, Ann Cobden was overwhelmed with the change in circumstances, Francis was concerned for Ann and consumed with wonder at what business her husband had in this particular town. Cobden and Smeaton were the only two in a talkative mood, Diana being concerned for Beatrice and Gertrude's sudden real hostility.

After lunch they strolled around the town returning to the Four Oaks to take tea before the carriage drive home.

At dinner that evening Smeaton declared his intention of leaving the following day which brought consternation to both the Cobdens. Diana felt the weight on her shoulders but decided she must see this through, if it grew impossible she had decided to leave and take Beatrice with her. She could always send to Mr Smeaton again. No, she must do this herself. She hoped her relationship with Mr Cobden had improved enough to be able to talk sensibly to him.

The Smeatons left after breakfast leaving the family at a loss as to how to occupy their time. Mr and Mrs Cobden retired to the library with their newly acquired books, which caused more consternation for the sour-faced housekeeper who never expected anyone to need more than a minimal fire there.

Beatrice and Diana wrapped themselves in their cloaks and went into the garden. Gertrude was to be seen sneaking quietly out of a side gate to visit her friend's house, which happened to be where she had met her friend's distant cousin Harold Filton.

There were few flowers now except the pansies, boldly fighting the cold nights in the lea of the house.

"The kitchen garden will be more sheltered."

"Have you been there?"

"No, not for a long time. I was not sure if the gardeners had been warned to exclude me."

"Then let us find out. The rules certainly seem to be much reduced at least." They entered by the side gate the group had used a few days before. There were a couple of young men digging up vegetables, presumably for dinner.

"I wonder what new dish will arrive today. Mama did ask for pheasant but it may be a little too soon to have arranged that."

They wandered over to the glass houses and surprised Old Tom as he was instructing a very young man.

"Oh, Miss Cobden, Miss. I never noticed you. Have you come to see the flowers?" He opened the door to the glass house wide enough to allow them in.

"Now we can use other colours we are preparing to bring some bulbs into early flower. Do you like the dried flowers I sent?"

"What dried flowers?" Beatrice looked perplexed.

"I sent them yesterday as instructed instead of the large blue and white ones."

"They have not appeared in the parlour, I know that. I will ask the housekeeper. Maybe the maid does not know how to present them."

"That could be it, Miss."

They thanked him and wandered on. When they were nearing the house Diana had a thought.

"Suppose we pick some pansies again, they could go on the hall table where they would cheer everyone, even the servants."

"They are very serious. It must have been difficult living under Papa's rules."

"No doubt it has been." Diana had a thought which troubled her about the missing dried flowers.

When they entered the house Beatrice found the small vase from the blue parlour in which to arrange the pansies for the hall. Diana took her cloak up to her room where she found Eliza sitting miserably on the bed.

"I brought you this, Miss. Mr Smeaton asked me to give it to you after he had gone. She pointed to the letter which sat on the top of her dressing table together with a small box. Eagerly she opened it.

'*Dear Diana*

I know it would be impossible for you to accept this gift if I were there, so I have arranged for you to receive it after we have left.
It is a thank you from my wife and I, also from Mr Shenton and Mr Harsley for everything you did in aiding the happiness of our children.
If I can be of any use in the future please feel able to contact me.

She lifted the small box and opened it. It contained a gold chain necklace which was the first and only jewellery she owned. She turned away so Eliza could not see her tears.

"Thank you, Eliza, it was kind of him and no, I would not have accepted it if he had given it to me before he left."

She became more aware of Eliza's long face. "What is the problem, for you are not normally so sad?"

"You can't ring for me any more, Miss. The housekeeper has moved me to another room. There is no bell and no-one will fetch me."

Diana tightened her mouth. "I think you should show me, then we need to have a serious talk."

Lunch having finished Diana went into the hall and checked. Yes she was right; the bowl of pansies had disappeared. Beatrice intimated that she was going up to her room which gave Diana the freedom to act as she knew she must.

She tapped quietly on the study door and waited until she was called in. It was upsetting to have to do this; she had to hope Mr Cobden was genuine in his desire to save his wife.

"Mr Cobden, may I speak with you."

He stared at her intently. "You want to leave."

"Not just yet, sir, although there are those who would prefer it if I did. I wanted to ask you a couple of questions."

"I suppose there is a reason so go ahead."

"Have you told your wife how much you love her yet?"

"I beg your pardon." He was rising angrily from his seat.

"The reason I ask, sir, is that wives need to hear it, especially when the house will return to its strict rules now the Smeatons have left."

"How dare you! I will not let that happen."

"But you believe you run this house and can change things as you wish." He had sunk back into his chair. "You do not.

Your housekeeper does and she believes in the rules. Have you instructed her things are to be changed?"

He looked bemused. "Why do I need to instruct her? I have changed things by giving orders to cook about the food and to her about tea times and breakfast."

"Then everything will remain the same."

He looked at her closely. "What makes you so sure?"

"The flowers."

"The flowers, what flowers?"

"Did you like the dried flowers the gardener sent?"

"They have not arrived yet, he has not realised how soon they were expected."

"Indeed he did, they were sent yesterday. Then there are the pansies."

"What pansies?"

"The ones Beatrice and I picked this morning. Beatrice put them on the hall table before lunch. They are gone."

Cobden leaned back in his chair thoughtfully.

"Is that the reason for the anger at my housekeeper, for anger I perceive."

"What do you know about what happens below stairs and why the servants are unhappy and leave?"

"Do they?" This had surprised him.

"Since I arrived the housekeeper has believed it was wrong for me to be here and has actively tried to cause me to leave. I take breakfast downstairs now, although tomorrow morning I expect there to be only enough for you. I am allowed only dry burnt toast and cold tea. My maid is not allowed to eat with the servants, your housekeeper believes me a servant and servants do not have maids. She is fed only what is left over, sometimes from other peoples plates. She has now been moved from her room to the top attic in the main house. The room is full of old furniture; it is exceedingly dirty, cold and damp. There is a wet patch above the bed where the rain soaks in. From now on she will sleep in my room if necessary, I will not have her treated so. Did you instruct her to stop Beatrice's maid from speaking to her?"

"Her maid, no."

"The servants are sent to check she says only 'yes' and 'no' to Beatrice or she is punished. No wonder Beatrice wants to leave. It is not pleasant washing in cold water and impossible to dry your hair without a fire. Would Lord Langdale marry an unwashed lady with greasy hair?"

"Are you sure this is correct?"

"I am. I help her to wash her hair which her maid used to do in a hot bath. Neither of us have hot water or fires. Do you visit your neighbours often?"

He was having trouble following everything she was saying.

"I ask that because I wondered if you recognised any of their maids or footmen. There is contact between the servants of the local area. When anyone requires a servant one of your staff is mentioned. Most of your maids are new and very young now. There is a list waiting for places to be available. Shall I come back to the flowers? When Beatrice and I changed the flowers between the blue and white parlours and introduced a small vase of pansies, the flower maid was blamed for not removing them quickly enough and given a beating." Cobden looked shocked.

"Yesterday when the gardener sent the dried flowers she asked what she should do with them. Your housekeeper believed she should not have accepted them and beat her soundly. She is walking out with one of your gardeners who is now under-gardener for a neighbour. He fetched her away last night. Gertrude's maid has asked them to find her a position. With the way they are treated and Gertrude now always angry and growing vindictive, she wants to leave.

"If your wife tries to take up running the house again what success will she have? You will need to support her or she will not be able to cope, she needs to know you are there to encourage her. I say again, tell her how much you love her, how much you thought the rules were to help her be like an aristocratic lady. Tell her how much it matters to you she is happy now, she needs that."

Diana rose from her seat and quietly left the study with Mr Cobden lost in thought. She could not go any further until he made a decision.

Chapter 16

Cobden sat for a long time. He knew now he had been blinkered believing in the rules, not taking notice of his wife's needs, not understanding the working of the house and the garden. Ann had always run the house and it had been a happy home. He remembered days in the garden, Ann laughing as the children ran to pick flowers then worrying they would be chastised. He had wanted to make her happy, to make her like the ladies of the ton aristocracy who danced at balls and took tea in Gunters. It had taken this outspoken young lady to make him realise his mistakes. Diana and Smeaton. Did he really have an errand in that particular town or was it in response to his letter complaining about the young lady he held in such high esteem. He did not doubt her honesty with the leaking roof but why had he not been informed. He opened his study door and called the butler.

"Send someone to the village to ask Banton to come and check a leaking roof."

The butler noted his mood, bowed and left quickly.

What did he do about the housekeeper? Was it all true? He needed to put the housekeeper to the test and he had a good idea how.

The girls were again in the library when he informed them tea would be taken early. Beatrice thought he was giving orders again. Diana was thoughtful.

They were all seated before half past three when he encouraged his wife to ring for tea. The request went to the kitchen and they waited, and waited.

"I wonder if cook will manage to prepare the pheasant in time for dinner." Cobden was trying to fill the silence. "We shall have to wait and see; if not then it will be mutton with apple sauce. Are you looking forward to a change?"

Ann looked up into his face and smiled. "Oh yes, Frederick."

And they waited.

At four o'clock precisely there was a tap on the door and the tea trolley entered pushed by a very young and frightened maid. Cobden took a note of her.

"Are you new?"

She blushed and trembled.

"Yes sir."

"Do you know why the tea has taken so long to arrive?"

She looked terrified. "It's four o'clock, sir."

"But we rang over half an hour ago."

She was dumbstruck. Diana, understanding his enquiry, tried to help the maid to be less afraid. "We are not cross with you. Do not be afraid of us. Did you bring the trolley because Mrs Cobden rang or because of the time?"

She looked gratefully at Diana. "It's four o'clock, Miss. We had to wait 'til four."

Dinner was a serious meal. After the débâcle of the afternoon tea Diana had kept her own counsel, not making any remark to Mr Cobden. What arrived was not pheasant, nor mutton with apple sauce but the usual stew that arrived several days a week. It was followed by Quince tart, again. Cobden sat tight lipped.

When they retired to the parlour the pillows and cushions had disappeared. Ann Cobden was distressed so Beatrice and Diana ran up to the spare bedrooms to fetch pillows.

Cobden's lips tightened.

He made only one comment. "This will not do."

Breakfast was again served for only him, there was no tea. Diana ate her dry toast as usual.

"At what time does your maid go for your breakfast?"

"Eliza goes down by nine a.m., sir, but it never arrives before nine thirty."

He nodded and continued his silent thoughts.

At nine o'clock he went to his wife's room and watched for her breakfast to arrive, eggs and ham, toast with butter and hot chocolate. Gertrude's maid was the next to arrive, hot buttered toast with boiled eggs and hot tea. Beatrice's maid brought dry toast and tea but he waited in the long corridor for quite some time for Eliza to bring Diana's breakfast, burnt dry toast and cold tea.

He went down to the study with the intention of calling his housekeeper but the butler was waiting for him.

"A Mr Banton to see you, sir."

"Ah, the man about the roof. Have the housekeeper join us in the upper attics will you."

It was unprecedented for the master of the house to escort a rough workman up the main staircase and even more so for him to enter the servants' staircase up to the roof.

He opened several doors, each room filled with furniture but there was no problem with those ceilings. The last corner room was the coldest being the most exposed. The furniture had been piled on one side to allow access to the bed above which the sloping ceiling showed where the rain had soaked in.

"This is been goin' on for some time. I'd say several years."

The sound of footsteps brought the housekeeper.

"Did you know about this?" Cobden asked, indicating the damaged ceiling.

"It has been like that for several years, sir."

"Why was I not told?"

"Well no-one uses these rooms now."

"That is not the point. This needs repairing or it could cause more problems. If you knew of it you should have informed me." He was really angry now. "Barton get this dealt with will you."

"Of course, Mr Cobden."

Barton eyed the housekeeper warily and made his way down the servants' stairs.

Cobden turned to his housekeeper. "I will see you in my study in half an hour."

He left her there staring at the empty, unused bed.

Diana never knew what he said to her or how she answered, the butler kept everyone away from the study where his master's voice was raised in anger. Eventually a tight-lipped housekeeper came out and Cobden ordered the small carriage for one hour later. It took the housekeeper and her trunk to the town where she could take a stage or a room, he cared not. It returned without her that was the main thing.

Lunch was a little delayed due to the mayhem in the kitchen but none of that showed in the dining room. Dinner that evening was mutton and apple sauce with suet pudding and cream custard to follow, all of which was served by surprisingly happy footmen.

For several days there was confusion as the servants tried to work out what they had to do and whose orders they had to follow. The butler eventually asked Cobden if they were to have a new housekeeper. Cobden went to his wife and asked for her advice on the matter.

"Well, Frederick, Braithwaite's wife is still here with her husband, she has been very loyal despite all the rules. I am sure she remembers how the house used to be run.

Mrs Braithwaite was sent for and interviewed by both the Cobdens. Having been assistant to the previous housekeeper she did remember the way the house was run and how happy everyone had been. She would be honoured to take her instructions from Mrs Cobden and to train the new young maids. So Mrs Braithwaite was promoted to housekeeper and together with her husband, as butler and housekeeper, they took over the running of the Cobden's house. Everyone hoped they would bring proper order to the confusion below stairs.

It was several days before Cobden began to ask questions of Diana when she arrived for breakfast. They were never direct and it was a puzzle for her to work out exactly what was troubling him. The best way would be for her to ask questions and see what she could discover.

The next morning she had her first questions ready.

"Mr Cobden, may I ask you about someone I have heard of but only in name. We have passed him several times and he never acknowledges us, but it is clear to me he knows Beatrice and she knows him. His name is Peter Sedgefield. Gertrude mentioned his name when we were in town at the Four Oaks."

Cobden looked a little troubled.

"Ah, Sedgefield. He and Beatrice were quite close once. That was before she was promised to Lord Langdale. Has she mentioned him?"

"No, sir, not ever."

"He came to ask for her, but he is only a second son and his elder brother has married into trade. I had decided on the agreement with Lord Langdale so he was refused. I forbade Beatrice to speak to him again."

"That was a little harsh, Mr Cobden, if they had been friends for some time. But I understand you wished to force her into accepting Lord Langdale. Did it never occur to you that might be the reason she refused him."

Cobden looked surprised. "Do you think that could be the case?"

"I do, sir. Until Beatrice knows Lord Langdale better she will never agree."

"Yes, Lord Langdale. I have heard something a little worrying about him but I have no idea how to resolve the problem. If it is true I would rather Beatrice not marry him but he will demand a marriage or sue for her dowry. I am at a loss."

"Is it true Gertrude's young man is a friend of Lord Langdale?"

"Yes, I understand so. I know nothing of him which is why I wanted to delay any agreement. Gertrude is still rather young."

"It seems everyone needs to become better acquainted before anything can be resolved."

Cobden sat quiet and thoughtful for a while, then he seemed to make a decision.

"Smeaton suggested I should talk to you. That you could help me. If Lord Langdale proves to be an unsuitable husband for Beatrice, how do I withdraw from the contract without giving up her dowry? If I did that she would have nothing to take into any marriage."

"You cannot withdraw, sir. He would bring a court case against you for the money. It would probably bankrupt you. Either you pay, with or without the marriage, or he must withdraw."

"He must withdraw? Why would he do that?"

"I have no idea. Perhaps in a day or two some course of action might suggest itself. Shall we consider it for a while?"

Cobden waited to see what this forthright young woman might suggest. What she suggested made no sense at first.

"A Houseparty!"

"Yes, we invite as many people as you can accommodate including Lord Langdale and Mr Filton. See how they behave, what they are like. People relax at a houseparty; they often show their real character."

"Who would we invite?"

"The neighbours. What a pleasant way to re-introduce your wife into the social life of the area. Surely there are other young men and women who could be included to encourage our potential suitors to show their true colours."

But what of Beatrice's dowry?"

"Leave that to me, Mr Cobden. There is nothing you can do about that at the moment."

All the ladies sat in the parlour in deep discussion.

"A houseparty! How will we manage that?"

"Don't worry, I know what must be done and if we all work together it will not be a burden on anyone."

All the ladies were looking at Diana in shock.

"You will get to see all your old friends, Mrs Cobden, then you can invite them to tea and go visiting again. Gertrude and

Beatrice will see all the young people they grew up knowing. It will be the start of a whole new way of life for all of you."

Gertrude looked angry. "Why should I be involved?"

"You don't have to be if that is your wish. But your Mr Filton is being invited."

"Harold, you mean Papa has agreed?"

"He has."

Diana had only organised small parties before, it was all Mrs Fortesque could cope with. Sometimes Diana had thought they were only to teach her how to arrange everything. Right now she was very grateful for all the training she had been given.

The three ladies sat by a bureau where Mrs Cobden prepared to write the list. "We need a list of lists, really. First the list of things to be done, then lists of people and rooms and food. It seems a great deal but if we work slowly through everything it will not be as difficult as you think." Diana had to give strong encouragement to Mrs Cobden who was becoming increasingly worried. "First we make the list of things to be done. How many bedrooms have you and are they small enough for one or large enough for a couple?"

"I am not exactly sure."

"Never mind, that is not for you to worry about, it is your housekeeper who will do that. Write down 'Ask housekeeper for list of available rooms plus maids and valets' rooms.' Now we cannot make a list of people until we know."

"Will Mrs Braithwaite manage, do you think?"

"Of course she will, Mama. She had maids to help her."

"Yes, I suppose she does."

"Now, note the stables must be readied for the extra horses. That again is up to them to make arrangements. Any extra help they require they will apply to your husband not you."

Ann Cobden beamed up at her. "Oh I see. We just organise everyone else."

"Exactly. Now, how long will they be here, we need to know what number of meals."

"You suggested Friday afternoon until Monday morning." Beatrice remarked.

"Well it can be whenever you wish."

"Oh I think Friday to Monday will be perfect." Mrs Cobden was beginning to enjoy the whole idea.

"So, three breakfasts, three lunches and three dinners." Mrs Cobden dutifully wrote it down. "Don't forget teas, we will need plenty of cakes and biscuits for tea." Ann Cobden noted. "We will speak with cook when we are ready. She will have ideas I am sure." She was really quite excited now.

"Drinks will be needed, for the gentlemen especially. Your butler can speak with Mr Cobden about that, including the wine with the meals." Ann Cobden dutifully wrote it down.

"What will they do all day; the weather will be too cold to walk outside."

"Perhaps a good job by the look of the gardens at the moment." Beatrice tried to stifle a giggle but gave up when her mother joined in.

"Write down, 'list of games to play.' Do you think we should have a ball?"

"A ball! Well I don't know. What do you think Beatrice.?"

"A ball. I'm not sure. It would have to be a small one; we don't have a large ballroom. Where would we hold it?"

"If you rolled up the carpets in the blue parlour you could have dancing there. It would only be a small affair. You need not decide now. Write down 'Ball?' then 'musicians'. I think the only difference between dancing at a party and a small ball is who is playing for the dancing. If your neighbours are all staying there will be no need to invite anyone extra."

"How much more?" Beatrice was reading the list over her mother's shoulder.

"Well a guest list and clothes."

"Clothes? What clothes."

"Well, clothes for a party and clothes for a ball. Do you have suitable clothing to be the elegant hostess, Mrs Cobden?"

She looked up surprised. "No, I suppose not. New clothes, and somewhere to wear them. That is the best part of all." She beamed.

Beatrice had a very relevant question. "When do the cushions arrive? We can't have a party before then."

"No, I suppose not. We can start with the clothes and the cushions and ask the housekeeper to count beds before we choose a date."

"Then we start on the guest list. You can be of little help with that, Diana, you know no-one."

Diana just smiled.

The dressmaker was sent for first. Mrs Cobden required several dresses. Beatrice needed fewer, but Gertrude demanded more than her fair share.

The first of the cushions, the white ones, would be there the following week, the blue ones less than two weeks later.

Mrs Braithwaite was rather concerned at dealing with a houseparty so soon after taking up her position, but she hid it as best she could. She would use the extra work to train the younger maids.

They started to clean in readiness, checked the linen presses and listed the rooms, starting with the guests' then giving the maids some responsibility in preparing the servants' rooms.

Cook was sent for and after the shock had worn off, she was encouraged to suggest various dishes that would be appropriate.

Cobden kept abreast of how the preparations were proceeding.

"Next comes the list of guests, Frederick."

"Do you have any idea of who you will invite, my dear?"

"Well we need a variety of young and older, I believe."

"Indeed we do. Try to find enough younger ladies and gentlemen so Lord Langdale and Mr Filton will feel at home. It would be uncomfortable for them to be the only young men."

"Oh yes. Of course. Lord Langdale and Mr Filton. We need to balance the amount of ladies and gentlemen." She looked over to Diana. "Perhaps we could do that tomorrow morning." Diana nodded at her.

Beatrice had turned away in some anguish. Perhaps it was time for Diana to start asking her questions.

"Beatrice may I talk with you?" Diana had gone to Beatrice's room where she had retreated after tea.

"Lord Langdale is coming, do not expect me to take any more interest in the houseparty. You are doing what Papa wants."

"No Beatrice. That is why I came to speak to you." She pulled her to the chair to sit down "Your Papa is beginning to realise Lord Langdale will not do; that you will never accept him and maybe that would be best."

"So why is he invited?"

"Because he cannot withdraw from the contract without him taking your dowry; he does not know how to proceed. It is up to us to make Langdale withdraw. I will not tell you how until the time, but I do have a plan. Please do not be downhearted; it will come right I am sure. I will make it come right." She smiled at Beatrice who relaxed a little.

Next she went to find Mrs Cobden.

"Mrs Cobden, may I have a word with you in private."

"Diana, come in. I am amazed at how someone as young as you knows so much."

"Mrs Fortesque trained me as a hostess, Mrs Cobden. She wanted me to be able to help in the houses where I lived."

Ann Cobden smiled. "Well you have certainly helped me. Do you wish to tell me something?"

"No, Mrs Cobden, I wish some information from you. How attached was Beatrice to Peter Sedgefield." Ann Cobden turned to stare at her. "I know Mr Cobden refused him permission to address her, so he was very committed. He still is from the way he reacts when he sees her. "

"Do you think so? He was very angry at the time."

"But how did Beatrice feel?"

"My husband forbade her to speak to him."

"I know that, he told me. But was Beatrice as attached to him as he to her, Mrs Cobden? This is important to the whole family."

Ann stared at her. "Why?"

"I cannot tell you at present but I do need the information."

"She was very attached to him. She refused to speak with her papa for several weeks. I feared the whole family would end in misery for every one of us because of his addiction to the aristocracy. Why it has changed I have no idea, but it has happened since you arrived and I am so relieved."

"Your husband said he is the second son but the elder has married into trade. Which trade, Mrs Cobden?"

"Her father runs his own coal mine and has an interest in several cotton mills. He is extremely wealthy."

"I believe Mr Cobden believes you should have an estate or large investments only. I fail to see the difference."

"I doubt there is any. Peter runs his father's estate on his brother's behalf but that is not enough for my husband, I am afraid."

"Thank you for the information, Mrs Cobden. Now I know how to proceed."

Chapter 17

Over the next few weeks preparations went on. The first cushions and footstools arrived and everyone went into raptures over how they suited, even Cobden. The guest list was prepared and matched to the rooms. Lord Langdale and Mr Filton were in the gentlemen's section at the end of the long corridor. One room was left vacant but Diana refused to say why.

The day came when the invitations were written and sent out. The district began to buzz with the surprise that the Cobdens were holding a houseparty with a small ball. There must be a reason and everyone wanted to be there to see. Everyone accepted.

Then came the wait to see if the central characters would answer. It was almost a week later when Lord Langdale replied. He was returning from somewhere and could manage a weekend on his way home. He was very condescending.

"I begin to thoroughly dislike the man," Cobden remarked at breakfast.

"If you please, Mr Cobden, I have an important errand. Would it be permitted for me to be taken by carriage, it is quite a distance."

Cobden looked surprised. "This errand, is it pertaining to my problem with the dowry?"

Diana glanced away. "Yes, sir, it is. You may not be pleased with what I wish to do but it is the only way forward I can find."

"Then of course you may have a carriage. When would you require it?"

"Directly after lunch, if you please."

"If it is quite a distance, when will you return?"

"I will not be here for tea sir, but I will be back for dinner."

The arrangement being made, Diana went to prepare.

The afternoon was cold and somewhat damp. Diana was wrapped in her warmest cloak but the coach was not warm and the roads were rough and muddy. It took until three thirty to arrive at the Sedgefield's house. It was smaller, more solid looking than Cobdens. It had no pretentious additions but it stood strong and settled in the landscape. She thought it must be a beautiful sight when the evening sun caught the large windows and made the façade glow.

The butler answered the door and was surprised to see a young lady standing alone.

"I have a letter for Mr Peter Sedgefield and I would be grateful to speak with him once he has read it."

The butler showed her into a small parlour to the right of the front door. She heard the raised voices of two men arguing and was apprehensive of the outcome of her errand.

An older man entered the parlour and she stood to meet him. Well she had started this so she must face it.

"Which one of you is angry, sir. You or your son?"

He was taken aback by her directness.

"You are Miss Newby who wrote the letter?"

"I am, sir."

"Without it I believe Peter would have torn up the invitation. Who does it come from?"

"It comes from me, sir. I am Beatrice's companion and do not wish to see her life in danger to save the family."

Mr Sedgefield stared at her quite hard.

"Why should Peter care what happens to the Cobdens?"

"Not the Cobdens, sir, Beatrice. And I know he cares for her."

"After what they did to him!"

"I understand that Mr Cobden was probably rude and unpleasant. The whole family have suffered because of it. If your son does not come the whole houseparty will be pointless and I will have failed to save her."

"Come with me, young lady. I think you need to explain to my son."

He led her to a pleasant room where light streamed in through the large windows even on this dark afternoon.

"This is Miss Diana Newby who wrote the letter. My son, Peter Sedgefield."

Diana curtsied.

"I've seen you with Beatrice, are you family?"

"No sir, I am a companion. I was invited by Mr Cobden, erroneously, to persuade Beatrice to marry Lord Langdale. I will not do it. She refuses."

"What do you expect of me? I am not of a mind to help him."

"I quite understand that. I knew a letter would be insufficient to convince you that is why I have come in person. I know you still care for Beatrice and she for you."

"You are mistaken. She ignores me."

"And you ignore her, but you watch her with a longing in your eyes that is unmistakable. Beatrice is forbidden to speak to you but she trembles when you pass and is unable to hold a conversation for some time afterwards." Both men were looking at her wide eyed. "Mr Cobden has realised his mistakes. The edicts that ruled the house for the last five years have gone. He now knows that Lord Langdale is not the upstanding man he thought him to be, but he has signed a contract for Beatrice to marry him."

"He will make her."

"No, sir. I know he wishes the contract withdrawn. Beatrice will never marry him but she will have no dowry to marry any other, and so will be forced to remain single her whole life. Langdale will demand the dowry or sue in court and bankrupt them. Beatrice could be thrown onto the streets or forced to marry a man she hates to save them."

Peter turned and walked to the side table to where his glass sat untouched. He took a large swallow. His anger was now real pain.

"What do you want of me?"

"Lord Langdale has no real wish to marry Beatrice, she is to bring him a dowry to spend on his mistress, and to give him the heir he needs. His first wife was abandoned most of the time and died in childbirth alone because of him. He does not deserve Beatrice. The only way is for him to withdraw. It will be to your advantage, sir."

"How do you make him withdraw?" Mr Sedgefield was perplexed. This young woman seemed convinced it could be done.

"Mr Sedgefield, you have to look at the reasons he wants her. Any woman of good birth will do, preferably with a large dowry. He needs an heir. If he finds Mr Cobden still insisting on the marriage while Beatrice is showing a marked preference for someone else, can he be sure the child will be his. I want you to come and openly court Beatrice, and for her to respond to you, which she will. When Langdale withdraws, and I am convinced he will, Mr Cobden will be in no position to refuse you Beatrice's hand."

They both stood silently trying to absorb what she was saying.

"You think he will relent?"

"I do, sir. He has more to do to placate his wife for the last five years; a happy daughter is just the beginning."

Mr Sedgefield began to laugh. "When did this change begin, Miss Newby, before or after you arrived?"

"After, sir."

"Then I begin to believe it could work, Peter."

Peter smiled for the first time.

"Of course I must not *actually* compromise her, although the idea is very tempting."

It was Thursday, the day before the houseparty was to begin. The food was organised, the cushions and the gowns had been delivered. The gardener had done wonders with the bulbs and flowers, where he had obtained them nobody dared to ask. Mrs Braithwaite had organised her maids and trained them to clean until the whole house shone and smelled of beeswax. All the beds were made; it only needed the arrival of the guests.

So far Diana had said nothing about her plan to anyone in the house but Cobden was getting restless. At breakfast he all but pounced on her.

"When are you going to tell me what you expect to happen? I need to know."

"Mr Cobden, if I told you no doubt you would make some comment accidentally. You have to remember only one thing, you expect your daughter to marry Lord Langdale and you are not intending to withdraw from the contract."

"But that is not true. I must tell him."

"Then be prepared to be sued and face bankruptcy."

"Why bankruptcy, it is Beatrice's dowry we are trying to save."

"You really do not understand a man like Lord Langdale. He will take as much as he can, regardless of how it leaves you. Unless you wish your family destitute then Beatrice must be forced into marriage to live and die lonely and uncared for. You must hold to the contract until he withdraws. When he does, be careful not to be too overjoyed, he must leave here determined to see his solicitor."

"Am I to be told nothing else?"

"No, sir. You are to act as you normally would, show the normal reactions to those around you, including anger. For I fear you will be angry at some point."

"About what?"

"If I told you that, you would not act normally, sir. Trust me and I believe it will come right."

Mrs Cobden was fussing with the flowers.

"Diana, come and look at what the gardener has brought. There are more to come tomorrow morning." She had a large, ornate container in which she was arranging various greenery and branches with berries into a huge arrangement. "Where shall I put this?"

"Perhaps in the hall, Mrs Cobden."

"Oh yes, what a good idea. It will not be knocked there and everyone will see it as they arrive."

Diana stood silently waiting for the right moment.

"What is it, Diana?"

"I must tell you, Mrs Cobden, because I cannot let your husband know and he will be very angry." Mrs Cobden turned to face her warily.

"I have invited Peter Sedgefield."

Mrs Cobden's eyes opened wide and her hand went to her mouth. "The empty room."

"Yes the empty room was always for him, I just had to encourage him to attend. Do not be disturbed at what takes place; it is for the best I assure you."

"He will be angry."

"I know, but Peter Sedgefield will make Lord Langdale withdraw from the contract and the family finances will be saved."

"My husband does not know?"

"No, he must act normally which will include anger. It is the only way to convince Lord Langdale it is genuine. He would sue your husband and leave you destitute if he knew. Please tell no-one."

A maid was heard arriving at the door so Diana put her finger over her lips and quietly left.

In spite of what she had told the Sedgefields she was not sure how Beatrice would react. She must be sure she understood what could happen and how important it was. Regardless of what she had said, perhaps Beatrice would not accept a marriage to Peter after the weekend, she must instil into her how important this was and that the outcome with Peter was her decision.

"Beatrice, may I come in and talk to you." Lunch was finished and they had retreated to their own rooms.

"I presume you are going to tell me about this weekend and how I must be pleasant to Lord Langdale."

"No, not at all. First I must tell you what I told your father and how he will react. I told him he must stick to the contract and his intention for you to marry him."

"You promised me, you said Papa had changed his mind. You lied to me!" Beatrice was shouting. "No, Beatrice. Calm down. It is what your papa must do. Let me tell you what would happen if he withdraws from the contract."

When Beatrice had calmed enough she explained how a Lord like Langdale would react. He was used to getting his own way; the family could be left destitute and homeless unless she married him. To avoid this she had a plan.

"What plan?" Beatrice was very low in spirits now.

"You must make Lord Langdale not want you."

"Will he care, he wants my dowry."

"No, that is only a bonus to him; he needs you to produce an heir. If he thought a child of yours might not be his child it would make him very unsure, unwilling to take the risk."

Beatrice was horrified. "Why would he think that!"

"I have invited someone to come; I kept the spare room for him. He is to court you openly and I hope you will respond to him. It will make Lord Langdale angry at you, but he knows your reluctance to marry him and will believe the worst."

Beatrice was staring at her open mouthed. "You expect me to allow a stranger to court me all weekend. Be close to me; make everyone think badly of me. What if I don't even like him."

"He is not a stranger, Beatrice. I have invited Peter Sedgefield. He is willing to put aside your father's treatment of him to help you; I believe he is looking forward to being able to court you openly. Of course, after the weekend it will be your decision whether to cease his attentions. I know he hopes success with Lord Langdale will make a case for his suit."

Beatrice had her hands wrapped in her skirt and was gripping it tightly. She was visibly trembling, and then the tears started to roll down her cheeks.

Diana sat quietly staring out of the window until Beatrice had control of herself.

"Peter is coming here tomorrow." She was having trouble speaking.

"Yes, Beatrice, he is, and eagerly." When she looked at her Diana saw the flush on her face and the shine in her eyes.

"How you and he conduct yourselves is up to you, so is the future you decide upon."

Beatrice leaned forward and clasped her hands. "How did you find out? Who told you?" Diana laughed. "You did, Beatrice. Every time he passed us you trembled and became upset. I found out his name at the Four Oaks when Gertrude was nasty to you."

"I hope it works for her and her Harold or she will be even worse."

"What will you care if Peter Sedgefield whisks you away?"

Beatrice blushed deeply. "Do you think he will?"

"I know it is exactly what he hopes will happen."

They stayed in her room until she had become her normal self and they were able to go downstairs to tea.

"The flowers are beautiful, Mama."

"There are so many to do."

"Why did you not say, we will help if you wish."

"Oh yes, that would be a help. The gardener is bringing more in the morning. They are for the console tables upstairs."

"Do we have enough vases?"

"Yes, there is a variety in the garden room; they have been shut in a cupboard for years. We always had flowers on our landing and in the corridor when anyone stayed there."

Cobden was listening avidly even though he faced the other way. He felt rather mortified over his previous behaviour. His family seemed more eager to forgive him than he would have been in their place. This weekend would be a trial on his nerves he knew that. He had been less than close to his neighbours recently; he could only hope they were forgiving. At least he could talk to Smeaton, and Ann would have Francis to help her, although with Diana Newby there she may not be needed. What a capable girl, so different to any he had met before. That is what Smeaton had called her, capable.

He was glad he had listened to her for he now had more hope
than a few weeks ago.

Chapter 18

The morning brought a flurry of work in checking all was prepared and finishing the flowers for the upstairs. Diana found two small vases not being used in which she made posy like arrangements. One she gave to Mrs Cobden's maid to put on her dressing table, the other she herself placed in the Smeaton's room.

Lunch was early, buffet style to allow the ladies time to change and prepare for the guests to arrive.

With everyone in the hall with the oversized tables it was too crowded, so Diana drew Beatrice into the parlour doorway to be available to step forward when required.

Lord Langdale arrived and Beatrice was called forward to curtsey to him. His friend Mr Filton came at the same time, his eyes wandering around the maids scurrying about under the housekeepers orders. Gertrude appeared from where she had kept watch and insisted on accompanying him to his room. He seemed amused. He was older than Diana had expected, nearer to Lord Langdales' age than the youthful suitor she had imagined.

The arrival of Peter Sedgefield almost caused a problem. Cobden was not expecting him and reacted badly.

"What are you doing here?" Mrs Cobden stepped forward to calm matters.

"Good afternoon, Mr Sedgefield, you are very welcome." She steered him to the housekeeper who had him escorted to his room. What a good job Diana had warned her.

Beatrice gripped Diana's arm, her eyes were shining.

Guests were returning downstairs to the parlour for tea and to meet everyone, the Smeatons were the last to arrive.

"I will show them upstairs, Mrs Braithwaite."

"Thank you, Miss Newby." She was relieved to return to her other duties.

"You have the same room as before." she opened the door and encouraged them inside.

"Oh look, flowers." Francis exclaimed. "Now I wonder who brought those." She turned to smile at Diana.

Smeaton was a little more serious. "Do you need any help, Diana? Do you have anything to tell me?"

"You are too quick, sir. I hope everything will work easily but I may need you to help if Cobden becomes a problem or if Lord Langdale has ideas of his own."

"Such as.?"

"If he decided to compromise Beatrice into an early wedding."

"Do you think he might?"

"I know nothing of him, Mr Smeaton, I can only guess at his actions."

"So what have you arranged?"

Diana smiled, "You know me too well." It would be good to have someone else who could watch for problems. Mrs Smeaton needed to be told to avoid her innocent but awkward questions.

Diana spent a few minutes explaining the problem of the dowry and fear of his suing them. He smiled to himself when she related her discovery of a previous suitor more to Beatrice's taste.

"How far do you expect them to take their courtship in public, Diana?"

"That is up to them. I can only plan and encourage. How everyone reacts will no doubt become apparent."

"I will watch to see Langdale's reaction and restrain Cobden from ruining the plan."

"Why did you not warn Frederick, dear?" Francis said innocently.

"I feared he would accidentally betray what was happening."

"I think you are right, he could not carry it off. I will monitor him."

"Thank you. I will see you downstairs when you are ready."

Lord Langdale and Harold Filton stalked the drawing room and stood gazing out of the window with a superior attitude. Filton's distant cousins met him and enthused over his presence there, which he found embarrassing with Langdale there. He excused himself to return to the window.

Gertrude hovered, not sure what to do as she handed around plates of biscuits and passed him as often as possible.

"Well yours seems eager enough." Langdale noted.

"Wait until she finishes with the tea. You'll have more than enough attention then. More than you want."

"How well you know me, Filton."

The Smeatons had arrived downstairs and he steered Francis to a seat close to the window and sat facing away.

"Why don't you just marry Millie? She has already given you one son. It would save this farce."

"Millie has not the blood line for an heir to the estate. The aunts would be scandalised."

"More than they already are?"

"A good point. Unfortunately I have signed a legal agreement. She would sue."

"Then prove her unsuitable in some way."

"Unsuitable, look at her, the picture of an aristocratic wife. Who would believe me?"

More people moved to the window and they had to curtail their quiet discussion. Smeaton had caught enough of the conversation to make him smile. So perhaps Diana's plan would work better than she realised.

The teacups were returned and the trolley removed. Cobden welcomed everyone and announced the time for dinner and the ball. There would be cards for those who wished in the library during the evenings, and for any who wanted he had a billiard room for the gentlemen to entertain themselves.

"Thank goodness for small mercies." Langford remarked. Heard only by Filton and Smeaton.

The tea over, Beatrice was free to circulate and talk, until her fingers were captured by Peter Sedgefield. "Miss Cobden, Beatrice. I have missed seeing you." Beatrice looked up shyly into his face.

"But you have seen me, Mr Sedgefield. It seems you ride this far from home rather often."

He looked seriously into her eyes. "I couldn't keep away, even though I thought you had turned against me." Beatrice went to argue. "I know. It was your father's orders, Miss Newby told me."

Someone nearby coughed and they became aware he was still holding her fingers. He dropped them quickly but offered his arm. "Would you care to stroll a little?"

She smiled up with shining eyes. "Thank you, sir, that would be very pleasant."

Dinner was a slow affair. The servants were not used to this number of people to feed. The dishes were slow in arriving but this gave the guests time to talk. The seating had been deliberate; Lord Langdale was sat next to Mrs Cobden, Beatrice at the side of her father with Peter Sedgefield at her side. Lord Langdale was therefore facing Beatrice and well able to see her blushes and interaction with her neighbour. He was not sure whether to be affronted or relieved.

The ball followed and everyone inspected the blue parlour with its musicians and small dance floor. Some of the older ladies sat to watch, some retired to the white parlour to talk, their men going to the card tables in the library. The younger guests waited eagerly for the ball to begin.

It started with a slow waltz, quite unusual for outside London. Mr and Mrs Cobden were naturally the first couple on the dance floor, she looking up into his face with pleasure, he puffed up with pride.

Lord Langdale solicited Beatrice's hand to join them, it was expected of him. She never smiled up at him and was rather heavy footed, almost ungainly, not what he was used to.

When he next saw her dancing a country dance she seemed much more light and elegant.

Filton danced with Gertrude and she was glowing with happiness.

After a short time the two men took themselves to the billiard room to join other escapees.

Diana danced with Mr Smeaton then any of the young men who asked. At supper time she helped lay out the food in the adjacent dining room. The men in the library mainly stayed with their cards and brandy but most of those in the billiard room felt obliged to join them.

"I've missed you, Harold." Gertrude was by his side. He supposed he should be more affectionate toward her but in truth he was growing tired of her innocence and clinging nature. He had expected greater results from his hint of marriage, but she was too innocent to realise what he was expecting and he never had enough opportunity alone with her. He supposed he could initiate her while he was there but it was risky in her father's house, and he was really not sure he was that interested in her now.

After supper the dancing resumed but with fewer taking to the floor. Two of those missing were Beatrice and Peter. Below stairs in the garden room with the vases and the dried flowers Peter Sedgefield was pursuing his future. He had kissed Beatrice before but this was different. He held her close and stroked her, feeling her body press against his. He explored her back and moulded his hands around her soft bottom, his lips now more demanding, hers more willing as he encouraged her against his growing erection. He really should stop now; it was too soon, he could frighten her. How far should he go this weekend? Right now his brain was not functioning; decisions were being made by a different part of him.

The distant sound of music ceased and he pulled away from her.

"I think the ball has ended, maybe we should go back."

"I suppose so, or the butler might lock us in here."

"I wouldn't mind that, although I think the table would be rather hard as a bed." Beatrice trembled with anticipation at the idea. Maybe he should reconsider his plan.

They tiptoed quietly up to the blue parlour where everyone was saying goodnight and retiring, all except some of the men in the library and billiard room. Walking from parlour to parlour as people left, Smeaton noted the wanderings of the couple. Cobden had thought Beatrice in the billiard room with Langdale, Smeaton had encouraged him to think that.

Most of the ladies had retired now so Smeaton went up to the landing outside the Cobden family's rooms. There were candles down the long corridor and on the landing at the top of the stairs but it threw dark shadows to the doorways of two cupboards, deep enough to stand in and be unseen. He went to tell Francis a little of what he was doing, took off his shoes and went back to stand in the farthest recess.

Eventually Beatrice arrived escorted by Sedgefield.

"Don't go."

"I have to; your maid will be waiting." While they stood silently wrapped together the sound of footsteps coming up the stairs made him pull her to the other shadowed doorway.

"Make up your mind, Langdale. If you want her why not get it over with tonight? She can't say no then and you can leave her in the country like you did Arabella." They were both more than a little foxed.

"Are you going to yours?"

"I don't think so, I've lost interest. There are better available, I'll look around tomorrow." They continued down the corridor. Peter steered Beatrice to her room.

"Lock your door."

"There are no locks."

"None!"

"No. I'm frightened, Peter." He held her for some time then made a decision.

"Go to your maid, when she leaves I will be here waiting." They parted reluctantly, she to be prepared for bed by her maid, he to remove coat and boots and return to wait in the silent shadows.

Smeaton was cold and weary but had lost his chance to move away unseen and had to wait until her maid had left and Peter Sedgefield was eagerly admitted to seal their future.

Francis Smeaton thoroughly enjoyed the rest of her night.

The breakfast table was dominated by talk of a ride. The weather being cold it was mainly the young men involved. Few women had arrived yet although Diana, as always, was up early.

Filton was paying attention to her. He had noticed her last evening at the ball and during supper where she seemed to be helping the servants. He made an effort to speak to Smeaton.

"Were you in the ballroom last evening or did you take to the cards in the library?"

"Neither in particular, I moved around generally, sometimes dancing, you have to keep your wife happy."

"And your daughter, too. Are you related to Cobden, I saw your daughter helping at supper."

"My daughter! My daughter is married and definitely not here. No we are not family, merely acquaintances."

"I thought she was your daughter." He indicated Diana who was assisting one of the older men choose his breakfast.

"Oh Diana, No Miss Newby is Beatrice's companion. I know her well as she was companion to my daughter before she was married. She is a very helpful young lady."

Gertrude arrived and came directly to him. "Good morning, Harold. Did you sleep well?"

"I did, and you?"

"Quite well, although I think Beatrice was having bad dreams, I heard her shout out. I believe she is sleeping late." She turned her eyes to Lord Langdale who sat opposite and feigned a lack of interest. Smeaton smiled to himself.

With Gertrude hanging on his arm Filton decided a ride was definitely a good idea.

A buffet lunch was provided for when the men had all returned from their ride and the ladies had made it downstairs.

Langdale and Filton then escaped to the billiard room once more.

Everyone mostly sat and discussed in small groups until the tea trolley. Beatrice then had to leave Peter to assist her mother. Langdale ambled close to where Peter sat.

"You seem very close with my intended." It was said to bait Peter but made no impression in the circumstances.

"We have known each other a long time, Langdale. I have not seen her for a few months so we have a great deal to catch up on."

"Make sure it remains only friendly discussion." He wandered on. Peter smiled to himself, it appeared the ploy was working, he was jealous and beginning to worry.

After dinner they played charades. Everyone was involved, even those not willing to move from their chairs. They played in teams and Filton found himself once again in close proximity to the clinging Gertrude; she really had no idea how to behave with a man like him, he thought.

Lord Langdale found himself in a team which included Diana, while Beatrice had managed to be with Peter Sedgefield, again. By the time supper was provided everyone was laughing except for Filton and Lord Langdale, who was getting extremely upset with Peter Sedgefield's obvious attachment to Beatrice and more so Beatrice's attachment to him.

Cobden saw the jealousy in him and began to worry, making his way toward Sedgefield to have serious words with him. Smeaton steered him into his study and shut the door.

"Leave it, Cobden."

"But he is getting quite jealous and Beatrice is behaving disgracefully."

"I can see just what is happening, the same as you, but I have faith in Diana's plan. You are the worried father who wants the marriage, so behave that way."

"What do I do? Has Diana told you what her plan is?"

"She has and I suggest you continue to be a worried father and make peace with Lord Langdale. Make him believe she will agree to the marriage by the end of the weekend that Sedgefield knows of her future marriage and is helping you convince her."

"Oh, that seems plausible, is it true?"

"I have no idea." Lied Smeaton.

Cobden played his part. Smeaton had told him what to do and last time it had saved Ann, hopefully this advice would save Beatrice. When the party broke up and retired some stayed drinking in the billiard room, including Langdale. He may not have wanted Beatrice when he came but he was not being pushed aside by a man like Sedgefield. He would wait until the house was quiet then go to Beatrice's room.

Smeaton had watched again. Once more he had seen Sedgefield enter Beatrice's room and he heard the scrape of furniture as he moved some piece as a barricade, no doubt. Once again he was cold, so he went to his room to don his dressing gown over his clothes for extra warmth, then wedged his bedroom door slightly open as he watched and waited.

It was not long before he heard the quiet footsteps and saw the figure stealthily making his way on his nefarious mission. Smeaton waited until he reached close to the stairs then followed in stocking feet.

He watched Langford open Beatrice's door then heard his expletive as he found himself face to face with Peter. The confrontation was violent but hissed and he turned in fury only to meet Smeaton.

"What were you intending, Langford?"

"She is my intended, I have every right."

"To take her against her will. There is a word for that, and no you do not have any right." Cobden opened his door at the angry voices.

"What is going on?"

"It seems Langford was intending to force himself on Beatrice."

Cobden was confused, was he supposed to be angry or pleased. All he could do was open and shut his mouth.

Langford turned angrily to him.

"I will speak to you in the morning. Your daughter has no morals, sir. Good night!" He stalked off up the corridor. Smeaton calmed Cobden and encouraged him back to bed.

"In the morning, not now Frederick. I'll tell you what happened then."

They went back to their rooms and the house sank once more into quietness. Cobden was not aware of Peter's presence in Beatrice's room.

There was a slight scrape as the chair replaced the barricade at the door, and then all was silent.

A little before dawn Peter stirred to pull Beatrice closer. She stretched and came awake with the pleasure his hands were creating.

"Tell me again about babies, Peter." He smiled inwardly.

"Well." his hand roamed "The baby grows in here ...." He slowly stroked her stomach. "And it comes out here ...." His fingers moved and Beatrice squirmed in growing need. "You make milk in here ….. and the baby suckles it like this."

Her panting was growing, her fingers gripping his upper arms as he tortured her breasts and nipples. He nuzzled into her neck. "And it all starts when I put my seed in like this ….."

Could it get any better? Beatrice was his.

She sighed deeply and slid back into sleep.

"Put your night rail on, my love." It was quite a fight with her deep satisfaction leaving her boneless. He dressed himself and lifted the chair away from the door a couple of feet, then sat in deep contentment to await the expected visit.

Chapter 19

As the light of a grey day dawned Cobden rang for his valet. He was thinking over what had happened last night. What did Langford mean, Beatrice had no morals. Surely it was him who had tried to enter her room. Why was Smeaton there?

"Can you see if Smeaton is up, Shilton?"

"Of course, sir."

He waited while his valet went on his errand. Smeaton was behind Langdale so who was in Beatrice's room stopping him from entering.

With dread in his heart he opened Beatrice's door. It hit the chair and the seemingly sleeping fully clothed figure of Peter Sedgefield who leapt to his feet, one hand on the door one on the wall, effectively blocking his entrance. Cobden blinked.

"What are you doing here?"

"What does it look like? I'm guarding Beatrice, it seems someone has to."

"Oh." He was not sure how to react. His valet arrived with Smeaton still pulling on his coat.

"A problem?" He took in the chair blocking the entrance with Peter in front of it barring anyone from entering. It seemed to Smeaton that Peter knew exactly how to manage Cobden, he was fully clothed.

Smeaton took charge. "Your study, Cobden. Are you coming Sedgefield?"

"I'll ring for her maid; I'm not leaving her alone. I need to change.

"What happened, Smeaton?"

"Langford talked to Filton, both Sedgefield and I heard him say he intended to violate her so she had no option but to marry him. He would put her in his country estate like he did Arabella. I watched for him, it seems Sedgefield was prepared to go further."

"Where is Langdale. Is he down yet?"

"I'll check."

There were quite a number in the dining room, including Langdale and Filton. Langdale's face was black as thunder, Filton's was damaged.

"Are you leaving with me?"

"I see no point in staying." Filton looked around. "They have such violent servants here."

Several of the men looked horrified, the couple of ladies there went into a huddle to discuss it. Langdale noticed Smeaton and almost growled.

"Is Cobden down."

"Yes, in his study."

Langdale turned on his heel and stormed out. If Cobden had wanted the marriage it would have been the worse for him. Langdale railed at him as if it were Cobden's fault. "If you think I am prepared to be cuckolded by a man like him you are mistaken. There will be no marriage, your agreement is finished, Cobden. Try to sue me and I will finish her, no decent family will acknowledge her."

"You intended to force her, Langdale, no gentleman would do that."

"What do you know of the aristocracy and what we do."

"If that is the case then I am glad to be rid of you. Pack your bags and leave."

Cobden was still shaking when Smeaton returned. "This is Diana Newby's fault. What did she plan."

"To make him believe it would not be his child."

"And in doing so she has ruined Beatrice. Is she at breakfast?"

"No. Which is unusual for her."

"She said I would be angry. She is hiding from me, but not for long." He strode angrily out of the study and made his way up the stairs with Smeaton hurrying after him. At Diana's bedroom door he rapped hard and opened the door.

"Don't bother to hide. I know … " He stopped. The room was a mess. The sheets were pulled off the bed, the upper one torn; the side table was on its side, the candlestick, which usually stood on it, was in the middle of the floor the opposite side of the bed, together with a pillow. Cobden bent and picked up the candlestick.

"There's a sliver of wood missing and dried blood." Smeaton took it from him and examined it, he was frowning deeply

"We need to find her."

"I'll get Braithwaite to find her maid, she should know."

They returned to the study via the hallway where Braithwaite was instructed to find Miss Newby's maid urgently as Miss Newby was missing. Then they sat in the study to wait.

Cobden went to the decanter of brandy. "A bit early, Frederick, isn't it. You've had no breakfast yet." "I have a feeling I am going to need it." He replied.

They sat in silence for almost ten minutes until there was a knock on the door. It was not Eliza who stood there but the housekeeper with the doctor.

Cobden looked between them.

"You had better come in." He returned to his glass. "Where is Miss Newby?"

The doctor replied. "Asleep in her maid's room."

"Why are you here?" he was dreading this. Smeaton was leaning on the wall for support.

"I called him. Eliza came for me early this morning. I could see Miss Newby needed a doctor so I sent for him."

"It is not quite as bad as you are fearing. He did not succeed." The doctor assured them. Smeaton visibly sagged. "From what I have been able to make out, a man came to her bed in the night and tried to rape her. She fought hard and she has some very bad bruises on her legs and body and fingermarks on her arms. He appears to have held his hand over her mouth to keep her quiet; she has bruises coming on her lower face. Judging by the bruises on her knees she must have hurt him. Then he put a pillow over her face to suffocate her." Smeaton took a step and collapsed in the nearest chair. "She hit out and rocked the table which luckily knocked the candlestick onto the bed near her hand. She hit him hard several times around the head, she believes. She must have hurt him because he let go and she escaped, but in fleeing she hit her foot on the leg of the bed. She appears to have broken at least one toe. Her foot is twice its normal size and throbbing. I have given her laudanum to make her sleep and deaden the pain. I would suggest later you arrange for her to be carried to her room where she will be more comfortable. "

"Did you manage to talk to her, was she able to tell you all this."

"She has spoken to all of us at some time. She was still shaking when I arrived some three hours after. She is in deep shock."

"Why did it take so long?" Cobden looked at Mrs Braithwaite.

"Eliza dare not leave her for over an hour, she said. Her night rail was torn and when I went to help her I found all the bruises so I sent for the doctor. If she is brought to her own room I will have a truckle bed brought for Eliza. She should not be left alone."

Cobden sat and rubbed his forehead. "Did she know who it was?"

"No, but whoever it was will have damage to his head or face at least."

"Thank you, doctor."

"I'll call later to check on her."

He left leaving the fretful housekeeper waiting to be dismissed.

"Shall I prepare her room, sir?"

"Yes if you will, Mrs Braithwaite. It is rather a mess."

Smeaton put his head in his hands. He had sent her there and she had had nothing but anger and unhappiness, and now this. He should have let Francis take her home with them as she had wanted.

"We need to find some man with injuries."

"You'll find him in the dining room." Smeaton's voice was dead with the anguish.

Cobden strode purposefully, running up against Gertrude in a highly excitable state. "Harold says he is leaving, papa. You have to stop him. One of the servants hit him, you must dismiss him."

Cobden succeeded in bypassing his daughter to where he faced the men at the table.

"Who saw to your wound, Filton?"

"My valet."

"He took the sliver of wood out?"

"Yes, and it was painful." He lifted his head arrogantly.

"Do you always try to rape guests at houseparties?" There was a sharp intake of breath from the room.

"She's only a servant."

"And you believe servants are there for your use?"

"It is expected."

"Not in my house. And Miss Newby is a guest not a servant."

"If you pay her she is a servant."

"I do not pay her and I do not like your attitude. Pack your bags and leave."

"You think I'd want to stay in this place with country bumpkins like you?"

Geraldine was in anguish. "Harold don't go. Why didn't you come to me?"

Everyone turned to stare at her.

"What have you to offer that I might want?" With that he stalked out of the room.

Everyone sat silent, waiting.

Less than an hour later they were gone.

Some of the guests went to church but most stayed quietly talking. Those who went reported the vicar had preached on David and Goliath and how sometimes the small man may not want to fight but they feel they need to, and the bully loses. Like against Bonaparte.

The lunchtime discussions saw how the Cobdens had fought against the ton bullies. Smeaton was not quite sure the analogy worked, after all it was Diana who had fought by organising this and look what the bullies had done to her.

Everyone was eager to hear of her progress. Cobden had to ask for a report from the housekeeper.

"I am pleased to say Miss Newby has been taken to her room and is awake. She has eaten some lunch. Her foot still hurts a great deal, obviously, but she is calmer now."

"May I visit her?" Beatrice had been inconsolable all morning.

"If you stay only a short while. It would be better if she slept until the doctor returns."

A gentle tap on the door and Eliza opened it to find Beatrice outside.

"Is she awake?"

"Oh yes, Miss Cobden. I'm sure she will be pleased to see you."

There was a fire burning in the grate to keep her comfortable. Something lifted the covers away from her foot making the bed look as if she was lying downhill.

"I won't ask how you feel. It must be awful."

"I must look awful. Eliza says I have bruises on my cheeks."

"You look as if your face needs a wash. Oh Diana, It all worked so well until this."

"Has he left?"

"They both have.

"I imagine Gertrude will blame me."

"I expect so, you know her. She said something dreadful about him going to her instead of you, everyone is scandalised. His cousins, the Timms, are horrified. It appears Filton is courting a rich aristocratic widow in London, he never intended to marry Gertrude, they were surprised she thought that he would. You knew it was him?"

"Not until Eliza told me, it was too dark. Oh Beatrice, I've never been so frightened in my whole life."

"Now, Miss Diana, don't get upset again." Eliza broke in.

"I'm sorry. I upset you Diana. What hurts most?"

"My foot. The bruises have not really come out yet. I'll no doubt be sore for days. If it were not for my foot I would be thanking God for my lucky escape."

"From what we heard it was more than luck. I hope you hurt him a great deal."

"I think my knees did more than a little damage. That's what made him so angry." She went to laugh. "Oh, that hurts."

"I'd better go, I promised not to stay long." Beatrice rose to leave.

"I'll give her a little more laudanum now Miss, she'll sleep then."

The report Beatrice gave was that she was in good spirits despite her painful foot which helped everyone to relax. Dinner was a happy meal without the presence of the two arrogant ton members.

The evening was to be musical with the ladies entertaining everyone. Prior to them beginning the doctor appeared and spoke with Cobden. A footstool was set before his fireside chair, pillows on it for comfort, and a burly footman carried in Diana. There were exclamations from everyone. The doctor held up his hand for quiet.

"Miss Newby wished to join you for the music. She must only stay for a while and be left quiet. Please do not all press her for information, she needs rest."

He spoke with Diana, nodded to Cobden then left. Beatrice and Peter came to sit close to keep her company.

The evening was a great success, the piano and singing being well received and when supper was announced Diana was found to be peacefully asleep. She was returned to her room very gently amid smiling faces as if she were sleeping beauty.

She would not be down to see them all leave in the morning.

The breakfast room was buzzing with conversation. The maids and valets were busy packing; those without help were hurrying upstairs to make sure they were ready. By mid-morning the carriages began to arrive, horses were saddled or tied on behind and one by one the families left. The Smeatons being from farthest away could not be late in leaving with the days getting so short. They visited Diana to ascertain she was still improving, which Eliza assured them she was and had spent a quiet night.

Then everyone had gone, the Cobdens were alone again. Except for one person. Peter Sedgefield was still there with Beatrice at his side.

"Mr Cobden, may I have a word with you." As the two men left Beatrice looked at her mother, who smiled.

"I'm sure it will be all right."

Peter followed him into the study.

"Mr Cobden, I wish to ask for Beatrice's hand. My expectations have changed, my father has bought the Gilpins estate for me as a means for me to marry."

"I understood the Gilpins estate is in ruins. If not, why has it not been bought before, it has been for sale for several years?"

"The house is only small and in need of repair. The land is large but laid out to parkland similar in style to a grand aristocratic estate by Capability Brown. He spent all his money on the landscaping. There is no income from it beyond the venison it produces. With no house and no income it has not encouraged buyers."

"So what good will it do you?"

"It abuts my father's land which I oversee on his behalf. Starting from our border we can revert to farming using my father's workers and horses. That way we can bring back income until it is sufficient to support me and repair the house. In the meantime I have my father's house to live in close by."

Cobden walked behind his desk and sat down, leaving Peter standing.

"The problem is, Sedgefield, I hoped for more for Beatrice."

"More than happiness, sir?"

"But would she be happy with you."

"Yes, sir, she would. It is what we both want."

"I shall consider it, of course, but after your behaviour this weekend I do have some concerns."

"My behaviour! You mean my putting aside your treatment of me to save the family from being ruined. You mean to let the neighbours see me as prepared to compromise Beatrice and then walk away and leave her."

"I'm sure they realise she is not actually compromised. I'm sure her husband will accept the circumstances."

"Miss Newby asked me to save Beatrice, appearing to compromise her. How we did that was left to Beatrice and I. We made our decision. I intend to marry her with or without your approval. Whoever you imagine to marry her to, I doubt he will welcome the child she may be carrying. I was told you had changed, that you cared now, but I see no change and no care. I will inform Beatrice of your decision."

Cobden stared after his retreating back. Had he sunk back into his dictatorial ways? What would Ann say? What did he do now?

Peter Sedgefield strode into the parlour to the waiting Beatrice.

"His answer is no. He wants someone better for you. I will have the carriage brought round. If you still wish it, then fetch your cloak. Your maid can follow with your clothing."

Beatrice launched herself into his arms in floods of tears. In a muffled voice she said "I will fetch my cloak."

As she ran to tell Diana and her maid, Peter stood stony-faced.

"He refused!"

"Yes, Mrs Cobden. I am taking Beatrice to Scotland to marry. We did fear his dislike for me may be a bigger obstacle than Diana thought."

Ann rose to take his hands which were rigidly fisted at his sides.

"He will not stop you, Peter. I will see to that. He will have cause to regret this."

"Thank you, Ma'am."

Chapter 20

.

Cobden sat in his study for a long time. He heard Peter Sedgefield's carriage arrive and leave.

When he went into the parlour there was no-one there. At lunch only Gertrude appeared. He went to his wife's room but was not admitted. Beatrice's maid was busy packing; there was no sign of his daughter.

He had two visits he needed to make, however long it took. He sent for his horse to be saddled, even if he was still out in the night.

First he went to the vicar and asked for the Banns to be read. Then he went to the Sedgefields. He was admitted to the small parlour inside the door and left to wait. It was Peter's father who eventually came.

"It seems I find it hard to change. I had not understood the depth of my daughter's feelings. I thought she was just grateful to him for saving her."

"She will not return with you, of that I am sure. She is very distressed."

"I would be grateful if you will give them both a message. I have asked the vicar to read the Banns. They can be married here in three weeks' time."

Sedgefield was dumbfounded. "You mean this?"

"I do, sir."

"Than I am relieved. It is never comfortable to have parents and children divided. It leads to disharmony in the district."

"I suppose that is possible. I think I am unable to see things clearly. I will not stay longer. If Beatrice should wish to return home there will be no arguments from me, I am sure her mother would wish to be involved in the wedding preparations."

Beatrice did return home to her mother and to the ever improving Diana. As the wedding grew closer the neighbours visited Ann and discussed avidly.

"You say Miss Newby organised all this?" Mrs Wilson was intrigued.

"Yes, indeed she did. She knew just how to organise a houseparty at short notice. She suggested the ball."

"My daughter Elizabeth could do with her to help her organise their Christmas. Since the baby was born she cannot cope, even with her sister there to help." Mrs Wilson had two daughters; the elder had caught the eye of Arthur Petersford, a wealthy man with a strong connection to the aristocracy. Mrs Wilson was not able to give her daughter advice, being the daughter of a vicar and unused to such high entertainments.

The nearer it came to the wedding the more bitter Gertrude was, especially to Diana.

"I must look for another position now, Mrs Cobden. It will be very unpleasant for everyone if I stayed any longer than necessary. I believe I would prefer an elderly lady where there is no problem with marriage and jealousy. If you know of anyone I would appreciate that."

Mrs Cobden spoke with the ladies who came to tea. It was a distant cousin of the Clintons who knew of an old lady, rather crotchety and infirm, by the name of Lady Farthingdale. Enquiries were made. Lady Farthingdale's present companion would be leaving when she returned home from Bath after Christmas and would be pleased to accept a younger lady who came so highly recommended.

"I must find somewhere to go until then."

"You must stay here, Diana. I know I have not been the most amenable gentleman; I did not always appreciate what you were doing to help me, I do now. I would not have you alone over Christmas."

"Thank you, Mr Cobden, we have not always agreed but I hope we now understand each other better."

"Mrs Wilson has a married daughter who needs help to organise a Christmas party. She has a new baby and is finding it hard to cope. Perhaps you could teach her how to organise like you did us." Ann Cobden had a great deal to be grateful to Diana for.

"A married lady sounds less problematic than a single one." Which amused even Cobden.

Beatrice was married and left with Peter Sedgefield, a gloriously happy couple. Diana wondered if she would ever have the chance to meet anyone to marry. Even Frederick had not been her choice. She had liked him and been a willing fiancée, but if she had been able to choose … but that life and everyone in it had gone.

* * *

"She has moved on?"

"Indeed she has, Mr Arnott. Are you acquainted with her?"

"I knew her in the past but I have been away fighting in France."

"You were in the war. What rank were you?"

"Captain."

"But you do not use it."

"The war is over, sir. It was not a pleasant experience, I have no wish to be reminded of it every day."

Cobden was surprised. He thought a rank as good as a title and found it hard to accept.

"Thank you for the information. If you have Lady Farthingdale's direction I will visit her there."

"I'm afraid I do not know it. We are not acquainted with the Clinton's cousins and the family are in London at present. I can give you the directions to the Petersfords, Mrs Wilson's daughter. She was taken there in my carriage."

He wondered if he would be offered lodgings for the night but judging by the face of the young lady who had joined them he preferred not. This must be Gertrude and any mention of Diana brought more anger to her face. He was grateful for the information and took his leave eagerly. He could find a bed in the village inn.

Perhaps the first thing he should do would be to visit this Mrs Wilson. She should be able to tell him if there had been any problems for Diana. She might even know the address of Lady Farthingdale. The innkeeper was able to give him directions there.

Mrs Wilson was rather flustered at his call as Mr Wilson was out riding and she would have preferred him to be there. He was introduced to the younger daughter Eleanor, but she seemed unwilling to discuss Diana with him.

"Tell me, Mrs Wilson, was Miss Newby happy there. She has had such a difficult time recently."

"Well I think she was happy enough. She is such a pleasant girl it is hard to know if she is happy or not. She was very good to my daughter Elizabeth, she helped her a great deal."

"Your younger daughter seems unwilling to speak of her."

"No, we do not discuss her stay with her sister any more."

"Do you happen to know the direction to Lady Farthingdale's?"

"I am afraid not. Arthur will know, of course. He had his carriage take her there. He was so grateful to her, but he will no doubt tell you when you arrive."

With no more information to be gained, Michael left on the next part of his journey. At least he was moving in the direction of his necessary call at the Newmans.

The Petersfords were at home, the butler informed him. They were in the garden.

Arthur Petersford was an obviously wealthy gentleman of the ton, his clothes marked him out as such. His wife was a pretty young lady in her early twenties with a child playing on the grass, watched by an ever vigilant nursery maid.

"Arnott, come in. To what do we owe this visit?" Michael found it strange he seemed almost to expect him.

"Were you advised I might call, sir?"

"No, not at all. I presume you are one of Farthingdale's cousins."

"Does Lady Farthingdale have cousins named Arnott?"

"I believe so, although I thought them all elderly. How can I help you?"

"I have come for directions to Lady Farthingdale, I understand Miss Newby has gone there as her companion. The Cobden's were unable to give me assistance."

"Indeed she has. Do you know Diana?"

"I have known her in the past, but that was quite a few years ago before I went to the war. I would like to see her again."

Elizabeth Petersford stood by her husband and gripped his arm.

"Oh how wonderful, a young man interested in Diana. She deserves some friend of her own; she is always such a good friend to those who need it."

"Do you have a bed for the night, Arnott?"

"Not at present."

"Then stay here, stay for dinner and I will give you all the directions you need."

"You are most kind, sir."

"Not at all. There is so little I can do the thank Miss Newby for all the help she gave us."

"I understand she came to help with a Christmas houseparty?"

"That was my wife's parents' intention."

The small baby on the grass had rolled until he reached a bush and was in danger of poking himself in the eye. Mrs Petersford and the nursery maid both rushed to rescue him.

"It was all my fault, of course. I was so upset after his birth, it was such a difficult time for Elizabeth and I was so distressed for her I found it impossible to see what was happening."

Another house, another problem no doubt. This one was much more elegant than she had stayed in before.

"I hope this is not like the Cobdens. I don't think I could bear that."

"I know I couldn't, Miss. It was a terrible place. At least you left them happy, Miss Beatrice married and Mrs Cobden in charge of her house."

"I feel quite weary, Eliza."

The butler ushered them into the hall and led Diana to a most elegant parlour where a young lady a little older than her sat checking through some papers at a small bureau.

"Miss Diana Newby, Ma'am."

"Come in, Miss Newby. Let me ring for tea, you must be tired after your journey." She went to the bell to summon a footman.

This was a better start; at least she was being offered tea.

"I understand you are organising a Christmas houseparty."

"Yes, I am. Though why my mother thinks I need help I do not understand. We hold house parties regularly and I have never needed help before."

"She seemed to think you could not cope after the birth of your baby."

"I must admit I was tired for a while, it was a difficult birth, but that is not a problem now. I am quite able to carry out any duties I need to." She had a look on her face which intrigued Diana.

"Then I will find somewhere to go if I am not needed."

"Oh no! I did not mean to make you feel unwelcome. You are very welcome here, just not needed to train me in what my mother considers is required. There may well be areas where you can be of help."

"I understood your younger sister is here with you. Is she not helping you?"

The look on Mrs Petersford's face told Diana a great deal.

"If you wish to tell me something I will keep your confidence, if not I will assess your problem for myself."

Mrs Petersford turned to look at her. "You believe there is a problem?"

"That I will see when I have met your sister and Mr Petersford. If you did not tell your mama there was a problem then someone else did."

"The someone else being my sister. I will leave you to decide if you can be useful. I have to admit I have no idea how to deal with my problem." She looked suddenly sad, as if she had dropped the façade she was hiding behind.

Dinner was a more aristocratic meal than Diana was used to. There were more courses and they were more elaborate than she expected. Mr Petersford was not as old as she had envisaged and seemed concerned that his wife had rested during the afternoon. Eleanor Wilson, her sister, was much younger than she had been led to believe. She could not be more that seventeen, but still she tried to dominate the conversation.

"Mrs Sheldon was asking after you, of course. I told her how tired you were and how difficult you were finding the running of the house. She was pleased I was here to take the burden from you. She seemed very concerned, did she not Arthur?"

Arthur Petersford looked concerned at his wife. "Indeed she was, my dear, but then they all are."

His wife took a deep breath. "That is very kind of them Arthur, but I am not at all tired. I do wish you would not keep telling everyone that I am."

"But you are not able to go calling, you said yourself."

"I am busy with the house and the coming Christmas gathering, although I could go out occasionally if there were a carriage available." She looked pointedly at her sister.

"Well how am I to go out without a carriage? We cannot wait every day for you to be ready, can we Arthur?"

Petersford looked unsure how to respond.

"Tell me, Miss Wilson, do you go visiting every day?" Diana was gathering information.

"Of course we do. We leave Elizabeth to her rest."

"I understood you were here to help her, which of her duties do you help with?"

Eleanor was a little nonplussed. "Well, a great many. I often deal with the servants, they need telling what needs doing. It is so hard for them with Elizabeth so unable to cope."

Diana wished Arthur would stand up for his wife. He did not seem an indecisive person, she must find out more of his character.

"Have you lived here all your life, Mr Petersford, was this your parents' home?"

"Yes, Miss Newby. I went away to school, of course, but it was always a pleasure to come home to this house. Has Elizabeth shown you around yet?"

"No, sir. I have not been here long enough. I would be very pleased if you could show me around, I always think you learn more from someone who has lived there and knows the house intimately."

Eleanor looked a little put out.

"It is a little dark now, perhaps after breakfast in the morning."

"That would be very kind of you. At what time do you take breakfast?"

"I rise early but breakfast is available from eight until ten. Of course if you prefer to take it in your room then send your maid."

"No, sir. I prefer to come down to breakfast."

"Then I will be in my study until you are ready."

Diana thought it best not to tell them how early she usually arose or Eleanor might deliberately make sure she was there, if she read her character correctly.

Early morning saw Diana arrive at the breakfast table as soon as there was light enough. She wished she could have walked in the garden but it was too cold and dark at this time of year. She was, in fact, the first.

Not long afterwards Arthur Peterford arrived in the breakfast parlour.

"Good morning, Miss Newby. You are an early riser."

"I always am, sir. When the weather is warmer I walk in the garden before breakfast."

"Ah, a little cold and dark at this time of the year."

"Indeed, sir."

"I understand Elizabeth asked for you to help her with the Christmas houseparty."

"That is not entirely correct, sir. Elizabeth did not ask. Mrs Wilson intimated it was her younger daughter who kept saying Elizabeth could not cope. Mrs Petersford only asked for her sister to be called home."

"Why would she do that? Without her she would not be able to manage."

"That is what I am intending to find out. What is your understanding of the matter? How much time do you spend with your wife, sir?"

"Well I see her at lunch and dinner, of course. She is usually busy with the household in the morning. It does take a good deal of her time now. Things are often going awry, not like before the baby."

"Do you visit her at nights."

He looked askance at being asked such a question. "That is very personal, Miss Newby."

"Do you still love your wife?"

"What personal questions you ask. Why should I tell you such personal information?"

"Because often a wife has trouble when she feels unwanted, unloved."

"I love my wife as much as I always have. It pains me to see her like this. She has locked the door between our rooms so it is not my decision."

"Do you ride out in the morning like many men?"

"Not very often in the winter. I normally spend my time in my study. Sometimes I hear the arguments my wife has with the servants, she seems unable to manage them."

Diana paid attention to her breakfast. "I will make my own decision on who is at fault, sir. If I am not needed to plan the houseparty then I will see if I can save your marriage."

"Save my marriage. What are you talking about? My marriage is a happy one and I intend it to stay so. That is why I am so worried about Elizabeth."

"Then I will make sure the difficulties are eliminated. "

"When you are ready I will show you the picture gallery."

"Thank you, sir. That would be very pleasant."

They climbed the first set of stairs and passed a personal maid almost running. As she opened a bedroom door a voice could be heard chastising her for being tardy.

"Is that your wife's maid, sir?"

"No, it is Miss Eleanor's."

"Do you always accompany her on her visits?"

"She is not part of the local ladies and needs some assistance."

"I wonder what the ladies think of you accompanying her while your wife stays at home?"

He stopped suddenly and looked at her. "What should they think?"

They had reached the next landing. There were walking down the long picture gallery that ran most of the length of the house.

"This is a very pleasant place to walk when the weather is inclement. I have heard of such before but never seen one. Do you use it often."

"Not very often although I used to walk with my wife, especially when she felt the need to ease her back during her confinement."

"That was kind of you, sir. Many men would not be so accommodating."

They paused at various paintings for him to explain who they were. When they came to one painting they stopped. "This was Elizabeth when I first met her. I had it painted when we were first married."

"I thought it was Eleanor, her sister."

"They were alike at that age it is true."

The painting of him showed he had changed little.

Diana thought the likeness might be the problem. She would investigate that.

She found Elizabeth in the parlour giving instructions to the housekeeper. She seemed quite capable to her. She joined her and sat quietly until she had finished.

"Why do they think you cannot cope with the housekeeping? You seem very capable to me?"

"If they would do as I ask there would be no problem. The maids seem to think they can ignore what I say."

"What does the housekeeper say?"

"She says they are only doing as I told them. I keep changing my mind so they get confused."

"Do you change your mind?"

"No. I don't. I spend a great deal of my day checking they are doing what I have asked. Even the cook changes the meals and says it is what I ordered. Sometimes I think I must be losing my mind."

"Have you spoken to your husband about it?"

"It would make him worry even more."

"Does he not mention it at night?"

"At night? You mean when we retire? He no longer comes to my room."

"Do you never go to see him?"

"He has locked the door. He no longer wants me." For the first time Diana saw the tears in her eyes. She had the desire to put her arms around her and assure her it would all come right, but it was too early to be sure."

It was later in the morning when Elizabeth had seen to the flowers for the hallway, a large arrangement for the hall table, that she first understood the problem. The footman carried the large vase into the parlour and placed it on a table.

"Why did you put it there, I thought it was to go in the hall." Diana queried.

"She changed her mind, Miss. She wants them in here now."

"Who told you, was it your mistress herself?"

"No, Miss, she sent a message with Miss Eleanor." That made things much clearer.

The weather was inclement so coffee and tea was ordered in the parlour where they often sat to discuss the arrangements for Christmas. Arthur Petersford was the first to arrive. He accidentally brushed against the over-large flower arrangement and it crashed to the ground. When Elizabeth and Diana entered he was enraged.

"Why was that put in here? That vase was worth a fortune."

Elizabeth was distressed. "I asked for it to be put in the hall not in here."

He rang the bell for a footman to fetch the housekeeper.

"Why was that put in here when my wife instructed it to go in the hallway?"

"Your wife changed her mind. She often does, sir." She looked a little anxiously at the broken vase and the scattered flowers. "I will have this cleared up immediately, sir." She gave Elizabeth a strange look as she left.

Arthur stared at his wife.

"Why did you change your mind?"

"I did not. They should have been on the hall table,"

"Then you appear to be losing your mind, Madam." He turned and stalked out of the room. The tears were streaming down her face and Diana put her arms around her. She now understood everyone and the real problem. She must talk with Elizabeth and make plans to alter the situation.

Chapter 21

Lunch was uncomfortable for everyone except Eleanor who chattered and sparkled.

"I thought we would go to the Bristows this afternoon. I know she has several ladies attending with their husbands. It would lift your spirits to get away from this house, Arthur. You do seem a little down."

He made no reply.

"I think Mrs Petersford and I have work to do this afternoon. Something you are not capable of, Miss Wilson."

"I can assure you I am capable of anything I need to do."

"I am sure you are, but this is nothing that includes you."

Eleanor held her head high. "Tell them, Arthur. You know what I am capable of."

"Indeed, I don't know what you think her incapable of; she has kept this house running while you have been unable to."

Elizabeth's head dropped as she fought back the tears. Eventually she stood and excused herself, leaving the table in an unforgivable way as far as Arthur Petersford was concerned. Eleanor made some uncalled for remark with glee. Arthur looked pointedly at Diana.

"If you will excuse me, I will see to your wife, sir. I see your statement this morning was untrue, you no longer care for her."

Anything Eleanor said was not heard by Arthur as he fought with his emotions.

Diana tapped on the door. "Elizabeth, may I come in?"

"Why did you say that? Now he thinks even worse of me."

"That is not true Elizabeth. He told me this morning how much he loves you and how worried about you he has been. We do need to talk privately about what to do. I want you to answer me some questions."

"What about?"

"May I see in your wardrobe? Show me what gowns you have for Christmas. I understand there is to be a ball, what will you wear?"

"I don't know." Her misery was too deep.

"Do you have any new gowns?"

"No. I have enough already."

"What might you wear to the ball?"

"I expect the cream, if it still fits me."

"This one, have you tried it on recently? You may need it altering since the baby came." Elizabeth put her head in her hands.

"Then I won't go."

"Yes you will, Elizabeth. You will go and be the most elegant lady there. Your husband will be unable to take his eyes off you."

"He never looks at me now."

"He will, I promise you. How long have you had this gown?"

"It was my engagement gown; it has such happy memories for me."

"It is very pale and innocent, like the young lady you were. You are a wife now. Your figure is fuller, you are allowed to wear lower necklines and deeper colours. What colour does your husband favour?"

"I don't know, he has never said, although he bought me a necklace of rubies. He said it suited my colouring."

"Then ruby it is. What you need is a dress to show your charms and which matches your jewellery. Do you have a good dressmaker? Could she work quickly, or is there a modista in the nearest town who could design a gown for you?"

"The dressmaker takes a long time. There is a modista in the town but how would I get there?"

"We ask your husband to provide a carriage for us. If it inconveniences your sister then so be it." Elizabeth hiccupped a laugh.

"Now, about the flowers – the footman who delivered them to the parlour was told you had changed your mind. I believe they are often told that by your sister. You must speak to your housekeeper and tell her only orders from you, or those you give to her may be carried out. Anyone who accepts an order from your sister, even if it purports to come from you, will be dismissed. That should make them listen."

"I doubt the housekeeper will listen. She believes me to be incapable of running the house, now."

"Then include her in the order. If your orders are not carried out exactly, when the houseparty ends she will be dismissed. The cook also."

"They will go to my husband. They have worked for him for years; they were his parents' retainers."

"Then it seems I must intervene. After you make it clear to her I will ask to speak to her. Let us see how she feels then."

"What will you say?"

"Nothing that she will take to your husband I can assure you."

"Come downstairs, I think we both need some tea. You can ask to see the housekeeper while they are out, or do you want Eleanor to believe you have given up without a fight?"

Elizabeth gave her a strange look. "No, of course not."

"Then let us begin to spoil her triumph."

"Tea, Mrs Peterford?"

"Yes, tea. I feel the need for refreshment. Have my sister and husband left?"

"Yes, Madam."

"Then tell the housekeeper I wish to speak to her."

"I believe she is very busy, Madam."

"I beg your pardon. Are you refusing to give the housekeeper a message? Do you not enjoy working here, young man."

He looked bemused. "Yes, Madam."

"Then keep a civil tongue in your head and do as you are instructed or you will find yourself without a position." He bowed and left hurriedly.

The housekeeper was not as bad mannered as the footman. She curtsied and stood awaiting orders, not expecting what came next.

"Mrs Walton, do you enjoy working here?"

"Of course, madam, I have been here for many years."

"And during those years you gave your loyalty to your mistress. But now it seems you are prepared to cause trouble for me."

"No, Madam. I would never do that."

"But my husband thinks me incompetent because of you. I give you clear orders do I not?"

"Yes. Madam."

"Contrary to what my husband thinks I do not change my mind or contradict my orders as you told him. My orders are countermanded by my sister. I have not given her the right to give orders in my house. I understand she is giving orders in my name. They are not my orders, Mrs Walton and anyone who takes orders from her in the future will be dismissed.

"Dismissed? That is a little hard, Madam."

"Is it? This household seems willing to damage my marriage in order to placate a seventeen year old girl with no rights here. She has never had the running of this house whatever you think. Of course I will continue to give you the orders daily and I expect them to be carried out. Any deviation from them will result in dismissal. That includes you and cook, Mrs Walton. I will be mistress in my own house."

"The master will not like this."

"Are you threatening me, Mrs Walton?"

"No, Madam. I will instruct the staff not to take any orders from Miss Eleanor. Or face dismissal."

"Thank you, Mrs Walton."

The housekeeper left the room in a far worse mood than she had arrived. She would go to the master. Mrs Petersford could not dismiss her without his permission and he would never allow it. However, the mistress could make trouble for her. Was it true that the orders from Miss Eleanor were not from her? She would speak to the staff."

"Come in." Mrs Walton sat in her room mulling over the ultimatum.

Diana entered with a smile on her face. The poor woman had no idea what was going to happen.

"I understand Mrs Petersford has spoken to you."

"Yes, she has." her face said everything she needed to know about her attitude.

"It is such a shame. Will you be here after the Christmas houseparty?"

"Oh course I will." She frowned.

"Well at least there will only be one mistress by then. Will you continue to stay here if he chooses to keep Miss Eleanor as his mistress? She has no idea, of course, but both she and Mr Petersford will cease to be part of the community if he takes her as a mistress and his wife is forced to leave. The only guests you will be serving then will be his friends and their mistresses or whores. It will be such a shame for him.

"I have no doubt Eleanor believes she will be able to marry him. She is putting about such lies; I believe she is trying to make Mrs Petersford so unhappy that she takes her life. How guilty will you feel if you are part of that conspiracy?

"Will Mr Petersford be happy with you when he knows what is happening for he will know. I will tell him everything I have seen and heard."

"I never meant to undermine her authority."

"But that is what has happened because you do not seem to be able to manage your staff."

Mrs Walton looked shocked. "But ..."

"But then you never tried, did you. Have you always disliked Mrs Petersford?"

"No. She was always a good mistress. But she has made Mr Petersford so unhappy lately."

"Unhappy because she was weak from bearing his child: his heir. You would have thought he would have been happy about that. I believe her pain hurt him more than you realise.

"He is being taught that she is unable to cope by a girl who knows nothing of life, but who wants her sister's husband for herself. If you go to him with your complaint about his wife I will tell him everything I know of your inability to control your staff and have orders obeyed."

"I had no idea the orders were not from Mrs Petersford."

"Well now you know I suggest you make sure the servants understand. The first one will most certainly be dismissed. It will make the others realise how seriously this is to be taken. Do you understand me, Mrs Walton?"

"Yes, Miss Newby."

"If you are asked again by Mr Petersford, I suggest you tell him that the conflicting orders had come from Miss Eleanor, not his wife."

"I feel dreadful. Diana. What do I do now?"

"You ask your husband for a carriage tomorrow morning to take you to town. You have errands to do for Christmas."

"Do I?"

"Of course you do. You have not forgotten you need a new gown, at least one perhaps more."

"What if he refuses?"

"Then I will ask to see him and tell him exactly what has been happening and what I will tell his guests when they arrive."

"What will you tell them?"

"You would be surprised. Now make yourself look like the mistress of this house and be ready and confident when you go to dinner."

Eleanor was in high spirits at the dinner table. She recounted everything that had been said at the afternoon visit including, or especially, what had been said about Elizabeth.

Elizabeth sat and listened in misery. It was up to Diana to give her some support.

"I find it very strange, Miss Eleanor, that you are prepared to talk to strangers about your sister in this way, especially as they have known her for quite a long time. You have only just met them, I understand."

"They know the problems she has and are very understanding."

"I wonder how understanding they are, given that the problems are all related by you. In their position I would expect a sister to be supportive, not spreading unsubstantiated rumours."

Arthur looked up suddenly and blinked. What she had said had struck home.

While her husband was looking at her Elizabeth took the opportunity to speak.

"I have errands in town, Arthur, will it be possible for me to have the carriage tomorrow morning."

"Well you will have to be back by lunch or it will delay our afternoon visit, will it not Arthur/"

Arthur stared at Eleanor in surprise.

"Of course you may have the carriage. Do you need me to accompany you?"

"I have Diana and both our maids plus footmen, Arthur, so there is no need for you to accompany us."

Arthur looked a little hurt. "If you are sure. You know I would willingly come."

"Thank you, Arthur, that is good to know."

Eleanor was looking from one to the other wondering what to say to break the strange bond that seemed to be between them.

Diana smiled to herself. She was right, Arthur had no idea what was happening and it would be no problem now to make him take notice of his wife again.

Going into such a large town without male companions was quite daunting for Diana. They left the carriage at the coaching inn and walked down the main street, two maids and a footman following behind.

"Oh look at the gowns in the window." Diana was almost overcome by the display. "Do they have them already made, do you think? How could they be made to fit you?"

Elizabeth laughed. "You have never been to a modista before, Diana."

"No I have not. I have always had my gowns made by a dressmaker."

"Then this is a new experience for you. Arthur took me to one in London after we were married. I still have those gowns but they are rather tight now."

"Then you definitely need more making. When Arthur sees you at the ball he will insist you have a whole new wardrobe."

They entered with some misgiving, leaving the footman outside to wait for their return. The maids both stayed by the door.

The modista was very polite at first until Elizabeth mentioned needing a ball gown, at which point she became much more attentive. Bales of ruby coloured cloth were brought out, velvet, satin, silk, lace. It seemed the colour was very in vogue in London. Patterns were shown and debated and in a short time the decision had been made and they took Elizabeth into the fitting room to be measured.

"I think you should have more than just the ball gown, Elizabeth." Diana called. "After all you need to be well dressed the whole time."

When Elizabeth came out she was looking stunned. "Do you really think so?"

"Oh yes. Your husband will appreciate it with his London friends there."

The modista visibly expanded.

"Can you have them made in time for Christmas? The party starts in just over a week."

"Of course, Madam. That will be no problem. It is such a pleasure to dress a local lady in such elegant gowns. I am afraid few of the local ladies are willing to purchase such fine material."

"Then I will choose some other designs and you can make them as soon as possible. The ball gown at least must be ready within the week. As many of the others as possible would be appreciated, but I understand I will not be the only one needing new gowns."

"Thank you, Ma'am, I appreciate that. I will see as many as possible are completed. You will need another fitting to check for alterations and to set the hem."

"Oh, I had not realised that."

"Is that difficult for you?"

Diana was not going to let Elizabeth back out now. "What day would you suggest? We will need to see the carriage is available."

"Shall we say one week from now? The dresses will be delivered a day or two later."

Eliza had come to stand by Diana and was whispering in her ear.

"Why don't you buy a new gown, Miss?"

"I don't need a new gown, Eliza."

"You are going to an old lady during the winter, Miss. It could be cold there and there was that beautiful green material."

Elizabeth heard her. "What a good idea, Diana. You should have a gown made. It need not be a ball gown for you have a very excellent wardrobe, but your maid is right. You are going to a house where your elegant clothing might not be to your advantage."

In the face of such determined supporters Diana gave in. Yes she supposed they were right, she would need warmer, more serviceable clothes when she went to Lady Farthingdale. So Diana was dutifully measured and two winter dresses were picked. She also ordered a new warm stole and petticoats.

It was a very jolly party of ladies who took lunch at the inn. More than one young man asked the innkeeper who they were but he had no intention of giving away their direction.

The next week was busy. The Christmas decorations were found from the attic and put it place. Many looked rather tired.

Elizabeth made a note to buy a few new ones when they went to town again. Perhaps something with a baby to remind Arthur of the son he never seemed to visit.

Vases were found and prepared for the last days when the greenery was cut and the flower arrangements were made. When the weather was not too wet they ventured out in to the garden to look for which greenery should be cut. The gardener was involved and the plans made.

In all this time Eleanor went visiting and never once took any interest in what they were doing.

There was one bad day when Eleanor tried to say something was wrong, that Elizabeth had made a mistake, but when the housekeeper was summoned it was proved not to be so.

"But I gave orders for it to be done." Eleanor appealed to Arthur. "You see, she is unable to allow me to help anymore."

"What exactly is wrong, Eleanor?" Arthur queried.

"I asked the cook to provide partridge for you today. I know how you like it, Arthur."

Elizabeth was forced to intervene. "Cook had already been given the dishes for today. Something like partridge needs to be ordered several days in advance, Eleanor. Did you not know that? There will be partridge but when it is available. Please do not try to change the dishes again. It is difficult for the servants to obey two sets of orders and this is *my* house."

Both Eleanor and Arthur looked up at the tone of her voice. Eleanor was angry and irritated; Arthur was surprised but not upset in any way.

A week later the carriage was ordered again. Arthur was intrigued. "What is so important you need to visit town again?"

"We need more decorations, Arthur. I know they are precious to you but some of them are rather sad. I think for the houseparty some new ones will be needed. I never knew last week or I would have bought them then."

So Arthur was put off from asking any more difficult questions.

The week had passed quite quickly with everyone being so busy. The journey to town was quite an exuberant excursion. There had been no real disasters for the whole week. The servants were terrified of being dismissed, especially just before Christmas and had adhered to the housekeeper's instructions. The dresses were to be fitted, which was exciting in itself.

The modista had prepared all the dresses for fitting. Mostly they needed only the hems setting. Everything would be delivered in two days' time.

"I wonder what Eleanor will say when she knows?"

"I hope she does not see them arrive."

"I suggest we have them sent in my name. Could you do that, Madam? Could they all be sent with my name on them?"

"Indeed, Miss. It is not unusual to hide the arrival of new gowns. I will have them addressed to you, Miss Newby."

They walked around the shops oblivious to the cold wind and found some carved wooden decorations painted in red and green, one of them a carving of the Christ child.

Lunch was again taken at the coaching inn. This time they were not alone in visiting the town. Two of the local ladies were also taking lunch with their husbands.

"Mrs Petersford, what a surprise to see you here. I had not though you well enough." Mrs Turpster was genuinely surprised.

"Mrs Turpster, how nice to see you. Mr Turpster, Mr and Mrs Walting, I do not understand, I have not been ill, merely busy preparing for the Christmas houseparty and tending to my child. You will all be at the ball, I hope."

"Indeed we will. But your sister said you were not well after the birth."

"I was very weak for a short time but I recovered quickly. It is difficult for a girl as young as my sister to understand the problems that can arise in giving birth. I am afraid she has little understanding of the running of the house and the responsibilities a wife has. I think she still believes in marrying a prince and living happily ever after without any such responsibility. Any slight query in the house she sees as a problem of enormous proportion. Are you here for a special reason or just to see what the Christmas shops have?"

"We are here to meet a friend who is coming on the stage. It is so nice to have friends for Christmas and knowing she will not be alone makes it all the better."

"You will bring her to the ball, of course?"

"Are you sure, Mrs Petersford?"

"Of course. If we can make her Christmas even better is that not what Christmas is about."

Two days later the gowns were delivered. Eleanor was astonished and made haste to pour scorn on Diana having gowns made.

"Why should I not? I will no doubt need warmer gowns at Lady Farthingdale's."

"But how can you pay for them?"

"My dowry is invested. It provides me with an income."

"You have a dowry?"

"Of course, Eleanor, what gentlewoman has not?"

Eleanor's response was an open-mouthed silence.

Chapter 22

The guests were arriving. Many came from London or their estates quite a distance away. Mr and Mrs Wilson were overwhelmed by the nature of the guests their daughters were mixing with. There were a few of the local gentry there also, who came with their sons and daughters to add youth to the festivities.

The first time they were all assembled was at dinner when the talk was general, some making new acquaintances, many meeting old friends.

When the men had returned from their port and the tea trolley was finished Diana noticed Eleanor speaking with Arthur and encouraging him into the hall. Elizabeth had risen to give them the suggested entertainments for their stay, but finding Arthur absent, she was forced to give the information alone.

Everyone seemed pleased with what had been suggested. There were enough card games to please the gentlemen; there was even a billiard tournament. The ladies had games to play, some of which could be played sitting down and so included the older guests. If the weather was good they would have a treasure hunt, if not it would be in the house. In the evening there was to be a play reading by a local celebrity, some country dancing if there was someone willing to play for them. There was an evening of music provided by the young ladies and of course the ball. Everyone was looking forward to the ball. Many local families were invited so it would be quite a large affair. If anyone could not remember what was happening then they could ask her or her husband. The butler would also be told each morning if they needed to enquire.

By the end of the first full day many of the guests were beginning to ask questions.

Albert Bursted had known Arthur Petersford for many years as had Phillip Carstairs. They cornered him in his study on the second morning.

"What the hell is going on, Petersford. Your wife is running this party on her own while you mope around, led by the nose by a girl still in the schoolroom. Who is Diana Newby, where does she fit in here?"

"Eleanor is Elizabeth's sister, she came here to help because my wife could not cope after the birth. She is having trouble running the house. Diana Newby was sent by Elizabeth's parents to organise the houseparty."

"So all this is organised by this Miss Newby? I thought she had only recently arrived?"

"Yes, a couple of weeks ago."

"You can hardly organise this kind of gathering in two weeks. I think you are deluding yourself."

"The problem is I think Elizabeth may be losing her mind and I can't take it."

"Petersford, Arthur, a more capable wife I have yet to meet. She is no more losing her mind than I am. I know how you feel, don't forget I lost Madeleine. I suggest you pay her more attention and ignore that pushy young girl. I have suffered from someone like that, remember."

"Who is this Diana Newby, what is her background?"

"I don't know much about her, Carstairs. She has a dowry but no home. She goes as companion where she is needed, apparently she has sorted out problems in a couple of houses and has nowhere to go until after Christmas. She is going to Lady Farthingdale as a companion."

"Good grief! Aunt Wilhelmina. I thought she already had a companion. I must get to know this young lady better."

Carstairs encouraged Arthur back into the party and steered him to his wife. "What do we have for entertainment today, my dear?"

"It is on your list, sir."

"My list?"

"I left in on your desk several days ago. I had thought to discuss it with you but you are so often out with Eleanor."

"I wish you had said."

In all this time, Phillip noticed, she never raised her eyes to her husband and she called him sir."

He made his way to Albert Bursted. "This is more serious than you know, Selgrove. Find out what you can from that Diana girl, she seems to be the key to this."

After lunch Albert Bursted, Earl of Selgrove, used his experience to isolate Diana and steer her into the empty library.

"I hear you are to go to my great aunt as a companion. Lady Farthingdale."

"Oh are you family? Then perhaps you can tell me something about her and how she may need my help."

"Your help?"

"Yes, sir, everyone needs help of some kind. Often they are unaware what it is. I understand she is irascible and somewhat immobile. Perhaps I could help ease her joints in some way." Selgrove was staring at her.

"Who are you, Miss Diana Newby? Where exactly do you come from?"

"Where I come from is my business, sir. I am only here to help others."

Selgrove was an Earl, not used to being refused in this way. He drove her against the door, one hand on her arm the other on the woodwork caging her, hoping to make her more subservient. Diana panicked, blindly opening her mouth to scream. He put a hand over it to silence her but she kicked out with her feet and knees. This was not the normal reaction. He let go and stood right away from her. She made to open the door.

"Please, Miss Newby, I just want to talk to you." He waited until her breathing was normal. "That was not the usual reaction I get from ladies. Something has happened to you in the past."

"Yes, sir."

"Come and sit down before you collapse, and tell me what happened for I mean you no harm, I am merely concerned to know my great aunt's new companion."

Diana sat for a few moments, still trembling. He went to the table and poured a small brandy which he put into her hands.

"A man tried to …"

"Steady, I understand. Where was this."

"At the Cobdens, sir, during the night when I was asleep. I kicked him and hurt him and he tried to suffocate me with a pillow. I am sorry if I reacted a little badly."

"Only to be expected. So you came from the Cobdens. Are they friends of Petersford?"

"The Wilsons live close by and were at the houseparty we had."

"Why did you leave?"

"Miss Beatrice was married and Miss Gertrude hates me. It was her hopeful who attacked me."

"Ah. Were you there long?"

"Too long in that house. It was a dreadful place, Mr Cobden insisted Beatrice marry Lord Langdale and she refused."

"Langdale. Why would any Father give him his daughter. The man is unacceptable in the ton. You would not believe things I know about him."

"Yes I would. I discovered about his wife and mistress. Cobden had made a contract and I knew it could bankrupt him but Beatrice could not marry him. It was left to me to make him withdraw from the contract."

Selgrove sat back, his eyes wide open in surprise. "How did you do that?"

"I found she had a suitor who had been refused by Cobden because he was a second son, so I organised a houseparty with everyone there and encouraged her chosen suitor to give the appearance of compromising her. Langdale would never know if the child was his."

Selgrove laughed out loud. "What a capable girl you are."

"That's what Mr Smeaton used to call me."

"Who was he?"

"I was there before the Cobdens. His daughter had refused ever to marry when on the verge of signing. She was broken-hearted. Her intended had also withdrawn which I found strange until I met Victoria, a recent addition to the area. She had told lies to each of them about each other, bad enough to break them apart. She was in the process of trying to compromise him into marrying her."

"And you prevented it. How did you know it was her?"

"I had met someone like that before." She seemed to withdraw from him, this was very personal.

"Where do you come from, Miss Newby?"

"I tell no-one that, sir. I am a helper with no home."

"Do you have no family?"

"Not any more, sir."

"Where did you learn to be so useful?"

"I was taken in by Mrs Fortesque who trained me to be a hostess. She knew in the future I would need a skill. She left me a dowry which is invested to give me enough income to dress myself adequately. I was with her for four years before she died."

"Taken in. That's a strange way to describe it. What happened?"

"I never talk about it, sir."

"Well tell me. Is that when you met this girl you recognised. What did she do?"

"She told them I had stolen an ornament. She had planted it in my room so when they looked they found it and believed her. They threw me out three weeks before I was due to marry. I understand she married him."

"Did Mrs Fortesque know about this?"

"Oh yes, sir, she was there. She understood everything that had happened. They were part of her family, but she never had any contact with them again."

"Did you not know the girl before?

"No, sir. She came from London. We were never told where; she talked about a big house. She just had this incredibly cutting voice and she always had to be in the centre of everything."

"What was her name?"

"Lucy, sir. Lucy Firbeck."

Selgrove sat up suddenly. "Firbeck, are you sure?"

"Yes. Her father rarely came out with her, and her mother had no control over her."

"Did she have a sister?"

"Her mother said something once but her father looked sternly at her and nothing more was said."

"How old was she?"

"Not much older than me. It was over four years ago."

He was looking pensive. "Yes, that would fit. Lucy Firbeck. But she is married now. What is her married name?"

Diana looked hesitant. "Pennington, sir."

"Thank you, Diana. Now tell me about the Petersfords. What is happening here?"

She looked thoughtful. "He is your close friend."

"Yes, I know, that is why I need to know. So tell me."

"This is how I understand it. When Elizabeth had the child I believe she was very ill, the doctor thought she might die. Mr Petersford was very upset; he has never been able to understand that she is completely well now. Mrs Wilson sent her younger sister Eleanor to be with her and help but she has no idea about running a house like this, she is still an untutored child. She countermanded every order Elizabeth gave which caused problems as you can imagine. Elizabeth wrote to her mother to ask her to fetch Eleanor home but they had letters from Eleanor saying Elizabeth could not cope, how ill she was, how needed she was to run the house.

"They never understood. The grandeur of this house and lifestyle has turned Eleanor's head. She thinks Arthur her dashing prince who will sweep her away in place of her sister, so she continues to upset the house by giving orders in Elizabeth's name and telling all the local ladies how ill she is, reinforcing Mr Petersford's pain.

"Nobody has visited, Eleanor goes out and takes Mr Petersford with her every day. He thinks he is allowing

Elizabeth to rest but Eleanor is unaware how the neighbourhood are beginning to see her as his mistress. She has no knowledge of just how a mistress is treated by society. I don't think Mr Petersford can see what is happening; it could ruin his standing, it is ruining their marriage. They are both so unhappy.

"I came here until Lady Farthingdale was home because I was needed to help with the houseparty, it was a married couple with a new baby and I would not have the problems of broken love affairs. I seem fated to be faced with affairs of the heart."

"Where is Lady Farthingdale now if she is not at home?"

"In Bath, I understand. Her companion wishes to marry and will be staying there when she leaves after Christmas."

"Then I need to see she is protected on the drive home. Perhaps I should send my travelling carriage."

"That is kind of you, sir." Selgrove smiled.

"In comparison to you, my dear, I feel inadequate. Thank you for the information, I will act upon it."

"If you wish to help, perhaps you could pay special attention to Elizabeth at the ball."

"Is there a particular reason?"

"Oh yes." Diana smiled. "I intend Mr Petersford to be extremely jealous of any man who pays attention to her."

Selgrove raised his eyebrows. "You aim to make my friend call me out?"

"I'm sure you are capable of coping with that, My Lord."

Selgrove was gradually making his friend understand that there was no problem with his wife's health. How to introduce the problem of Eleanor however, was difficult. Perhaps he was thinking of her as a mistress, she was very similar to Elizabeth when she was younger. Selgrove had hoped he could avoid these kind of problems now, he had suffered them enough in the past, but Arthur was his friend. If Diana Newby could work to save the marriage of complete strangers then it behove him to at least try.

"Arthur, why do you insist on paying so much attention to your wife's sister? She is still a child."

"She needs me to introduce and support her with the ladies."

"Introduce her to what. She is a bit young for you; surely you don't intend to keep her in this house with your wife. At least put her in a house of her own or your reputation will be lower than it is."

Arthur stared at him. "What are you implying, Selgrove?"

"I am not implying anything but the local ladies appear to have made their decision. Have any of the men said anything yet?"

The horror of the situation swept over him. "It's not true! What do I do, Selgrove? No wonder Elizabeth doesn't want me."

"I think you should try to avoid Eleanor as much as possible. Sit with your wife; speak to her as often as possible. I will try to stop her sister from bothering you."

Diana had a special mission. She waited until everyone was down for breakfast and the maids had left on their daily routine. She opened the door with hesitation and crept into the room. It was no different from any other room except for the private things spread about. Where would she look; there were so many places where you could hide it, she must think like Eleanor. There was a small jewellery box on the dressing table sitting against her brush. Now that was just where she would have expected it to be. She lifted the lid; there was very little jewellery in it, but then the Wilsons were not rich and aristocratic, they probably had very little to spare for such fripperies. And there it was. Eleanor had been so confident in her success she had never thought to find a more secure hiding place.

Carefully she removed her prize and closed the lid. Now all was in place she merely had to wait until the ball.

The evening before the ball Eleanor escaped from Selgrove and came urgently to Arthur Petersford.

"Arthur. You must come and organise the footmen. They refuse to set up the tables for cards and it is getting late."

"Have you spoken to your sister?"

"Of course not. She is incapable of coping with everything, she has made no provision for tonight; no tables, no cards, no extra brandy and glasses. It is intolerable."

Arthur went to the library where the footmen were standing in confusion.

"Is there a problem? Why do you not put up the tables as you did before?"

"The mistress has not given us orders, sir. We may only take orders from her."

"There you are, you see. Tell them."

"If you will excuse me, I will check the reason."

"You mean you won't tell them. You are the master here, Arthur. Do you need your wife's permission to make a decision?"

The door opened and Selgrove entered with Elizabeth.

"Are here you are, Petersford. We wondered what was so important for Eleanor to drag you out so urgently."

"She is instructing the footmen to put up the card tables and they refuse. Apparently only your orders are acceptable."

Selgrove winced. Not the way to win back your wife.

"Of course they refused. We are not having cards tonight; the young ladies are to entertain us. It was on the sheet of entertainments."

"I seem to have lost it, I'm afraid."

"You seem to have lost a great deal more than a paper, Petersford." Selgrove muttered.

"I'm sorry, Elizabeth. I should have asked you for another copy when I realised a few days ago. I was just enjoying everything you have achieved so competently." He looked at Eleanor. "Next time, ask what is needed and don't try to take over. This is not your house, remember."

The retort was to his credit, because everyone there stared at him in shock.

Chapter 23

The day of the ball and everyone was brimming with excitement. Most of the morning was taken with the younger girls being told of previous balls their elders had attended, who was there, what everyone wore. There was much discussion of what each of them was to be wearing.

Elizabeth floated between them all, chatting to each one seemingly carefree to anyone not involved.

Diana was often close to her encouraging, chatting to people. Selgrove caught her attention. "What are you planning?"

"I told you, he will see her in a different way tonight. If not then I fear when her parents leave she will be going with them."

"She is that distressed!"

"Indeed she is."

"He is equally upset, he fears just that. I hope your idea works whatever it is. I will do my part, I have asked Carstairs to assist in keeping Eleanor away from him."

"That was kind of you, sir."

Elizabeth floated close to them and curtailed their conversation.

Lunch was a light affair in a buffet style the main meal of the day being the dinner prior to the ball.

Tea was taken early and the ladies retired to rest and prepare. The dinner would be the start of the formal evening and everyone would be wearing their most beautiful gowns and most expensive jewellery.

Elizabeth was nervous. "Are you sure he will notice me, Diana, I am so worried."

"You will look like a dream to him in your ruby dress with the jewels he gave you showed to their best. Everyone will ask about them and you can say 'My husband bought these for me.' and they will all know how much he loves you."

"But ..."

"No buts, Elizabeth, it will come right, I know it will. Now stop worrying or you will have tired eyes before the night begins. Get some rest. I will see you downstairs at dinner."

The gong sounded to dress. Elizabeth's maid arrived to prepare her. When she was washed and dressed in her chemise and petticoats her maid began to dress her hair. They had practised this before but even so tonight was the important occasion. Her hair was piled high as in the picture she had brought from the modistas of how the ladies wore their hair in the London balls. One piece had been damped and rolled in rags to create a long ringlet. Both of them were nervous. It was getting late when she was ready for the dress. It fitted so beautifully she could barely believe that the woman looking back at her from the mirror was really her.

"Hurry, Madam, or you will be late for the gong. Put on your perfume before the jewels." she complied as the maid went to the case laid ready on her dressing table. She heard her gasp and followed her eyes as she looked into the case, it was empty.

"But they were here earlier, Madam. I checked."

"Did you take them out, could you have dropped them?"

Elizabeth was getting more and more upset.

"Don't worry, Madam, they will turn up. You look wonderful just as you are. You don't need jewels."

"You don't understand, they were the reason for the dress, they were the reason for everything tonight. It's all going wrong, I can't bear this any longer. It was all for nothing. "She collapsed on the bed in floods of tears.

"Please don't cry, Madam. Your face will be all patchy. Here let me put some cold water on it to calm it down. You can't go down looking like this."

The gong rang and the maid worked to calm her mistress and make her face presentable. Downstairs in the drawing room they waited.

Arthur stared down at the key sitting beside his hair brush: the key to the door between their bedrooms. A wave of emotion swept over him. She wanted him, it was not too late. He finished dressing in a daze.

"Are you ill, sir?" His valet saw the sudden change in his master and began to worry; he seemed unable to connect with anything around him.

Arthur floated down the staircase to the drawing room to await the dinner gong but mainly to await his wife – who wanted him.

The room was beginning to fill with guests talking happily, the younger ones excited about the coming ball. Selgrove came to speak to him but he seemed unable to take in anything he said. She still wanted him.

Everyone seemed far away. The dinner gong was sounded, the butler put his head around the door to see if he should announce dinner. A hand came onto his arm and he looked down at the woman beside him. She looked exactly as she had at their betrothal, the cream dress, the same hairstyle. She wore the diamond and ruby necklace he had bought for her.

She urged him to go in, but something was wrong. The room had become silent. He looked around at the shocked faces. Diana Newby came towards him and spoke. What about his wife. He looked down again at the woman on his arm and the shock hit him.

"Eleanor, why are you wearing Elizabeth's necklace? You are wearing her dress. Why are you dressed like my wife?"

"I thought it would please you, Arthur."

"Please me?"

"Well Elizabeth is so unable to cope these days; she has not even arrived for dinner."

He stared in horror. Selgrove stood close and was staring at her also. It was Diana who spoke.

"Eleanor, what are you trying to do?"

"Well someone has to take care of Arthur, Elizabeth is not able to. You see, she has not even come down to dinner."

The door opened slowly to admit a vision. It was exactly as Diana had hoped. Everyone stared at the voluptuous woman in ruby red who seemed to have stepped out of a Paris salon. Her hair was piled high on her head with a curl hanging by one ear. The neckline was low and revealing, the dress fitted around the bust with leg of mutton off the shoulder sleeves. The skirt hung straight at the front accentuating her body with a full train spreading behind her.

She looked around the room. "I am sorry to keep you all waiting." And to Arthur "Are you waiting to go in?"

Arthur walked straight to her and took her hand bringing it to his lips. His eyes said everything his voice could not.

He led her in to dinner. He should perhaps have led in a more senior lady but there was no way he was willing to let go of her now. She still wanted him.

The dinner passed Arthur by. He must have eaten the food but he remembered nothing of it. People talked to him but all he knew was that Elizabeth was there beside him looking magnificent, and she still wanted him.

They left the dining room and went to the ballroom. The visiting neighbours were arriving and being greeted. Arthur kept Elizabeth's hand on his arm. Her sister came to stand with them as if she were part of the reception line. Diana watched for problems.

"Don't they look wonderful. Elizabeth looks so well, I can hardly believe how ill she has been." Mrs Wilson had picked up none of the mutterings of the guests where Eleanor was concerned.

The local ladies stopped in surprise as they saw Elizabeth looking healthy and on Arthur's arm. They greeted Eleanor in some confusion.

The ball began as expected with Arthur and Elizabeth leading the way. Selgrove was true to his word in dancing with Elizabeth to make Arthur jealous, but really it was no hardship, she was outstanding. Carstairs waited for his opportunity, she was in great demand with gentlemen of all ages.

Diana avoided the dancing and stood by the Wilsons.

"You would think more of them would ask Eleanor to dance. They are all so fond of her. Obviously they are being kind to Elizabeth."

"Who are fond of her, Mrs Wilson?"

"Well, everyone. Even Arthur has not danced with her. Frankly I am surprised, it is not well done of him."

"Well I am relieved for Elizabeth's sake. It reflects on a wife when a man takes a mistress. When the mistress is her sister it must hurt even more. I don't think Eleanor realises how she will be treated if he openly acknowledges her. It would be the end for Elizabeth, of course. After all these weeks trying to send her home while she disrupted the house, drawing him away purposely. It would not have surprised me if she had taken her own life. Perhaps that was her sister's hope, to enable her to marry Arthur. Of course they would be cut by the whole district.

"If Elizabeth returned with you tomorrow would you take the child as well. I doubt Eleanor would want to bring him up and if left behind he would have no love and no status. It would be a terrible life for a child to feel unloved."

Mrs Wilson was speechless. Mr Wilson was eyeing her seriously.

"Is that what they are saying? Is it true?"

"It is what many are saying. Whether Arthur has succumbed yet I am not sure. You only have to look at her to see; she was given the loan of one of Elizabeth's gowns, any except the cream betrothal dress. As you see she is wearing the betrothal dress."

"She does look exactly like Elizabeth did at their party."

"Except for the rubies, of course. Elizabeth's dress was designed to wear with the ruby and diamond necklace Arthur bought her. No doubt she was late because she was searching for it and I know how upset she would have been. Eleanor is wearing it. It does not even match the gown. It was done to hurt her sister and make Arthur think she did not care for his gift."

"Eleanor will be taken away tomorrow morning." Mr Wilson was adamant.

"Are you sure, dear? What if Elizabeth needs her to stay."

"It seems to me Elizabeth never needed her to stay in the first place. She has no place here. All we can do is take her home and try to repair her reputation."

Mrs Wilson looked at him without understanding.

"But I thought she had so many friends here?"

"Who told you that?"

"Well Eleanor did."

"Do you want your daughter to turn into a whore, Madam?" Mrs Wilson went white. Mr Wilson took her arm and escorted her out of the ballroom to where the refreshments were being served. When she was enough recovered he escorted her to their room and rang for her maid, returning downstairs to speak with Eleanor. Judging by the exchange between them, he had announced her return home in the morning.

The Earl of Selgrove requested the next dance with Miss Diana Newby.

"Well, my dear Miss Newby, it appears your plan has worked. By the way what did you say to the Wilsons?"

"I just explained what the neighbours thought and asked if they were happy for their daughter to be a mistress and her sister to take her own life for unhappiness. It was Mr Wilson who asked his wife if she wanted her daughter to turn into a whore. Mrs Wilson is the daughter of a vicar of very high morals, I understand."

Selgrove laughed. "You say it all so innocently. Do you really think Elizabeth would have taken her life?"

"Not if I had anything to say in the matter." She laughed. Then suddenly more seriously "There was always the possibility, especially with the housekeeper acting so unhelpfully. I doubt we shall ever know if that was Eleanor's intention but I don't think she had thought that far."

"I think you are right. She is probably too naïve to have thought beyond her fairy prince dream."

The dancing finished and no-one was surprised to see Arthur still firmly attached to Elizabeth who looked like she, too, was floating in a dream.

The problem with a ball in your house with visiting guests is that the host and hostess need to stay to the end to see everyone away into their coaches.

It was a happy pair who made it to their rooms to prepare for bed. Elizabeth was not surprised when the connecting door opened and Arthur arrived.

"May I come in?"

"Of course you may, Arthur. You have always been welcome."

There was no discussion of the reason for the locked door. Arthur was too full of emotion and physical need while Elizabeth was even more responsive than usual. He had never felt her body since the birth but he explored it now, stroking her soft skin, enjoying her enlarged breasts and more prominent nipples.

"Oh Lizzie darling I have missed you so much." He was nuzzling into her neck and kissing his way down her throat and onward to her sensitive breasts. His erection was pressing into her leg, his hand wandering down to her soft warm cleft with its promise of paradise. He needed her to enjoy this so he spent more time than his body wanted, stroking her to full desire. She was panting with need when his hand stroked the hard nut between her soft cheeks. Then she erupted and he nearly embarrassed himself. She shook under his hands and gripped his shoulders.

"My you did enjoy that, but don't fall asleep yet, I want my turn." he kissed her hard and possessively. "You looked magnificent tonight. Wherever you bought that dress you must have many more made. I want you to look that womanly and desirable for me all the time. You are mine, Lizzie, and I can never let you go. I have hated every minute without you."

She reached up and put her arms around his neck to pull his face to hers, his mouth on hers. When they surfaced she was as needy as him.

"Arch for me, my darling." He slid into her in triumph as her legs wrapping around him. His body moulding to hers he began to ride her with an all-consuming need, harder and deeper until she cried out and her body gripped him as he spent himself inside her. In total bliss they lay together as sleep overcame them both and they drifted into oblivion wrapped together in each other's arms.

It was rather late when they arrived for breakfast. They glowed.

"I see you had a successful night, Arthur." Selgrove arched his eyebrows and his eyes laughed at him.

"You have no idea how good it feels, Albert. I am not sure I could have born it much longer."

"Did she refuse you?"

"She locked the connecting door after the birth. It has been torture to know she was so close."

"Has she given you a reason?"

"I dare not ask. I have no intention of upsetting her again."

"I wonder if the oracle will know."

"The oracle?"

"Our Miss Diana Newby. She was determined it would all come right. Perhaps she knows."

Some of the guests were late down after the ball; some were going home, including Mr and Mrs Wilson.

"Mama, Papa, you are going this morning?" Elizabeth was concerned. "I have been so busy I hardly had time to talk with you. Could you not stay?"

"No, child. We are leaving this morning, it is for the best. Eleanor's maid has been packing her gowns. See that she has returned your betrothal gown and necklace before she leaves." Mr Wilson was more serious than Elizabeth had seen him. Mrs Wilson was pale and tired from lack of sleep. By the look of her eyes she had been crying.

Eleanor was trying to resist but was being helped on her way by several of the servants including the housekeeper.

By lunchtime all was peaceful. Those who had chosen to stay another day were sitting relaxed in the parlour. Selgrove inclined his head to Diana to indicate that he wanted to speak to her alone outside. She went willingly into the library, no longer apprehensive of him.

"A success I believe, Ma'am." Diana inclined her head. "Can I ask you one thing? Why did Elizabeth lock the door between their rooms?"

"But she did not. She thought Arthur had, that he no longer wanted her."

"But Arthur though she had."

"Yes, I found that out when I first came. There had to be a reason and it became clear as the days went by. Who wanted to break apart their relationship?"

"Eleanor!"

"Indeed. I searched her room and found the key in her jewellery case. Neither had wanted the door locked, only Eleanor. It was obvious really."

"What did you do to bring them together, apart from the dress, of course? That *was* you?"

Diana laughed. "Yes, that was my idea. When I found the key it had to be replaced at the right time to have the full effect. I put it on his dressing table yesterday before he dressed for dinner."

"Ah, that would account for the happy bemused attitude on his face when he came down. I don't think he heard a word I said to him."

"I am so relieved they are together again. It is not good for a happy couple to be driven apart like that. I don't think anyone will ever manage to come between them again. Perhaps I should tell them before I leave."

"I have to say, Diana, may I call you that." she inclined her head in acceptance. "I have every confidence that Great Aunt Wilhelmina will have a much happier and more comfortable life with you there to take care of her."

Diana was very moved and had to turn her head away to hide the tears that welled in her eyes. "Thank you, sir. It makes my existence worthwhile."

Less than a week later the letter arrived stating when Lady Farthingdale would be home and that Miss Newby was expected forthwith. At least she knew she would be returning in comfort. She was sure that Albert Bursted, Earl of Selgrove would make good his promise for his Great Aunt Wilhelmina.

Chapter 24

After a pleasant evening with the Petersfords Michael was up early the next morning. Perhaps today he would see Diana.

The day started out overcast but dry but during the ride the rain began to fall increasingly heavily. When he reached an inn a few miles from his destination he was forced to stop and take shelter.

It was not far short of lunchtime so he ordered food and took his drink to find a table.

The inn was crowded with others taking refuge from the downpour.

"May I join you?" Michael indicated a vacant seat at a small table with only one occupant.

"Of course. Let us hope the weather improves shortly."

Michael settled himself in the chair with his ale in front of him. "Indeed. It is not pleasant riding in this. It will be bad enough when it stops with the roads nothing but mud."

"I take it you are on horseback, do you go far?"

"Not far, only as far as Hesket village."

"Hesket, are you here for the funeral, if so you are a little late."

"Funeral? No I am here to see an old acquaintance. She is companion to an old lady."

The fellow traveller perked up. "To Lady Farthingdale?"

"Yes, are you acquainted with her?"

"I take it is Miss Newby you are here to see."

It was Michael's turn to be surprised. "You have met her?"

"Several times. I think you should know; it is lady Farthingdale who is being buried."

Michael slumped back in his chair.

"At least I am not too late this time. I have followed her progress through several houses and each time she has moved on. She seems never to be given any rest, everywhere a problem to be put right. I hope at least the last few months gave her some respite.

"Well she was of great help to the old lady I know that."

"At least no broken hearts and broken marriages." The stranger raised his eyes.

"She has been with an old lady before, I understand, she certainly seemed to know how to make her life easier. She was a cantankerous one by all accounts."

"She was with my Great Aunt for several years."

"Oh, so you know her well."

"Not recently, I have been away in France."

"I thought you looked like a soldier. Did your aunt have swollen feet and a painful back?"

Michael laughed. "I have no idea, I never saw her after I went into the army over four years ago. It is possible."

"Miss Newby seems a very capable young lady but even so I am glad she will have someone there when the family hear the will."

"Are you the lawyer, sir?"

"I am, but only Miss Newby knows that, the family have a local man who believes he holds the will. They are in for a surprise." He leaned forward to avoid being heard. "They expect everything to go to the two boys, well, men now. The whole family were less than helpful to their relative, the sons only visited to bully money from her. They were quite aggressive to Miss Newby, I understand, accused her of trying to take the old lady's money."

"Diana has her own money; Aunt Letitia left her a dowry."

"So I understand. Still, I am relieved you will be there."

"Can I ask, is the money going elsewhere?"

"There is a much younger daughter, sister to the boys. They appear to be training her to be a housemaid. She has been given no education even though she is gentleman's daughter. She is to inherit all the money. A school has been arranged and she will be removed from the family who find her a nuisance; they have just used her as another way of making money."

"Can I enquire if this was Diana's doing?"

The lawyer laughed. "It seems you do know her, sir."

Michael's food arrived and he concentrated on eating.

"I do believe the rain is abating. Would you care to ride in my carriage, sir? I believe it will be a little drier and allow us to arrive together."

"It would allow me to arrive a little less covered with mud. I thank you, sir."

He paid the bartender for the food and followed the lawyer out. The carriage was being attached to the horses harness and Michael waited for them to bring his horse and tie it on the back.

He turned to the lawyer. "Arnott, sir. Michael Arnott."

The lawyer took his hand. "Stephen Barnam of Wilford, Barnam and West."

"This was a fortuitous meeting. You obviously know where you are going better than I."

"Indeed."

They climbed up and pulled the apron over them and Michael settled to a comfortable ride.

They arrived in the village as the party were leaving the church. It seemed the heavy rain had caused a problem with the interment. The carriages were plodding slowly to the house filling the roadway and prevented their arrival.

As the mourners alighted each coach moved away for the next to pull up. Nobody intended to walk even a few steps in the mud.

Michael was craning his neck in his eagerness to see Diana. Mr Barnam waited patiently trying to suppress a smile at this young man's obvious anticipation.

They had some difficulty in finding somewhere to secure the horses there being no stableman. A local workman saw their plight and showed them the unused stable where he agreed to take charge of their horses for a small payment.

There was a path from the stable across an orchard area to a side door of the house, where a small vestibule allowed for the removal of cloaks and muddy boots. It was from this unexpected direction that the two men arrived to the surprise of the parties gathered there.

"Who the devil are you!" Mrs Bristow pulled herself to her full height and looked down her nose at them. "You were not in church."

"We have only just arrived, Ma'am. Mr Barnam and Mr Arnott."

"Arnott! I might have known one of you would turn up to see if there was anything. Well you can turn around and leave. There is nothing here for you to get your hands on."

"I did not come for the funeral and I have no knowledge of Lady Farthingdale, Ma'am. I came to visit Miss Newby."

Diana was staring at him. He had changed he knew but he thought himself still recognisable.

"Mr Arnott at you service, Miss Newby."

Diana closed her open mouth. "Michael?"

"Indeed, home safely from France and searching for you."

"But I don't understand."

"I went to Grandfather Arnott and he has helped me search for you. I will explain more later." He gave her a warning look to prevent her saying more. "Miss Newby." He finished firmly.

Mrs Bristow took charge of the small repast none of which had been any of her doing, as Diana and Eliza had received no help from anyone. The family were like locusts; they devoured everything and once they moved about Diana noticed the ornaments were gradually disappearing. Still, they were not her concern.

The kitchen maid cleared the table with the help of Eliza as the family returned to sit solidly around the table waiting.

An elderly gentleman stood to address them. He cleared his throat. "I will now read the last will and testament of Lady Wilhelmina Farthingdale."

Mr Barnam stepped forward from the side of the room where he had been quietly watching.

"When is the will dated, sir?" The old man looked surprised.

"What business is that of yours?" Mrs Bristow interjected.

"Because unless it was in the last six weeks then I hold the current will of Lady Farthingdale."

Everyone stared at him in horror.

"I am Barnam of Wilford, Barnam and West and Lady Farthingdale consulted me about a new will in February."

Everyone looked at Diana.

"You knew about this. This is all your doing."

"I can assure you, Madam, that Miss Newby does not know the contents of the will. It was witnessed by my clerk."

"She was delirious, not in her right mind."

"Lady Farthingdale seemed extremely lucid to me. She knew exactly what she wanted and why she wished it. If you wish to know the contents I suggest you allow me to read it to you."

He walked to the end of the table and took out the will from his pocket. He began to read the first page.

"I, Lady Wilhelmina Farthingdale as the widow of the late Lord George Farthingdale wish to dispose of the inheritance from my husband in the following manner. My capital assets are to be invested and administered by the firm of Wilford, Barnam and West to provide schooling and dowry for Miss Constance Bristow, youngest daughter of my niece Mrs Lilly Bristow. No part of the money or any access to it is to be given to any other members of her family. She is to be placed in the care of the Bath Academy for Young Ladies and any interference will result in the removal of any other bequests from said family."

There were arguments beginning amongst the Bristow children, especially the boys. Mrs Bristow had turned extremely pale.

"She promised me the boys would be looked after."

"I understand she has funded your sons on a regular basis, Mrs Bristow, some of them under extreme duress."

"Do we get nothing!"

"If you will let me finish. The house and contents will go to the Bristow family to dispose of as they wish. However!" he had to stop until their glee had subsided. "However the house will remain furnished and for the free use of Miss Diana Newby until such time as she marries or decides to leave of her own free will at which time the family may take possession of it."

Mrs Bristow turned on her. "I knew this was your doing. You only came here to see what you could get."

Diana went to answer but Barnam interrupted.

"Miss Newby knew nothing of this. Lady Farthingdale was adamant she should not be told. I understand Miss Newby has no family and no home and she wished to reward her for the *free* assistance she has given her."

The two sons, both in the twenties, had started to move aggressively towards Diana. Michael strolled purposefully forward and stood beside her. Barnam assessed the situation and decided to give them a little warning.

"Captain Arnott is an old acquaintance and will no doubt be here as her protector until she decides her future. I suggest you curb your aggression unless you wish me to call the constable."

"He won't do anything."

"In the circumstances I believe he will when I give him the reasons; unless he wishes the magistrate to deal with him also.

"There are no further bequests, Lady Farthingdale rewarded her previous companion when she left her employ, her maid has been paid off." He folded the will and replaced it in his pocket.

"If you will excuse me I have another call to make."

He made for the side door, pausing only to bow and smile at Diana and Michael.

The next hour was chaos as the family stripped the house of any removable object that could be sold.

Diana was jostled and harassed until Michael stood guard in front of her, his coat front pushed to one side to reveal his pistol. Eventually they left.

"I take it I am staying, Miss Newby." Michael laughed, smiling into her eyes.

"If they have left us enough bedding, sir. Perhaps we should investigate."

Eliza emerged from her attic room where she had been avoiding the mayhem downstairs.

"Eliza do we have bed linen or have they taken everything of use?"

"Oh the best linens are kept upstairs, Miss. The staff were too free with it when the Bristows came to visit."

"How sensible. I gather they did not find that closet."

"No Miss."

"Cook will be in the kitchen preparing dinner; I must tell her there will be one more."

"How many servants do you have, Miss Newby?"

Diana looked at him pointedly.

"Michael, I believe you should call me Diana, we both know my name is not Newby any more than yours is Arnott."

Michael smiled. "There you are wrong Diana. I have officially added my grandfather's name to mine. It is my decision if I ever use my father's name again and I choose not to. But I am more than happy to use your given name. Where is the young lady in the will, is she in any danger?"

Diana and Eliza looked horrified.

"Surely not, she is their sister."

"Eliza, she may not be wanted by the family but I am sure she will suddenly be their favourite daughter now. But as to being safe ..."

"Where is she?"

"She has lived with an old lady, a Mrs Dawson for two years. There is a lady comes in to cook for her but Constance does everything from making fires and peeling vegetables to dressing Mrs Dawson's ulcers and emptying her chamber pot."

"Does she have no maid? Is she that poor?"

"Oh no she is not without funds but she has no maid. Constance is paid, although she receives none of it. Reginald and Wilfred collect it regularly. Lady Farthingdale helped to clothe her as she outgrew her worn clothes."

"The more I hear of them the more I dislike those two boys."

"So did Lady Farthingdale. That is why we looked for a plan to leave them out of her will."

"Then you did know about the will."

"Some if it." she smiled. "I helped decide on a school for her where she would be safe. We have assurances that she will be protected from the family and need never leave between terms."

"I thought you must be involved, it was too much a coincidence that a wrong was being redressed."

Diana smiled and blushed. She changed the subject. "In answer to your question, our cook comes in daily so does a maid, or did. The only permanent servant we have is the kitchen maid who sleeps in a room at the side of the kitchen. She is very close with the Bristows so I am never sure how much to trust her."

"Then we must keep her uninformed of what happens in here."

Eliza laughed, putting her hand over her mouth and turning away. At last, someone prepared to defend her mistress.

The noise of an arrival in the side porch had them turning to see Barnam ushering a small girl into the room. Diana held out her arms as she crossed the room.

"Constance."

Eliza busied herself preparing Michael's bed and one for Constance in the room previously occupied by lady Farthingdale's maid, in the attic with her. The two attic rooms were reached through a wooden door to one side of the huge fireplace that divided the house into two.

The house had two distinct sides, each reached from the front hall which was situated in the centre of the property and ran from the front door to the side of the great fireplace with doors opening on either side to Lady Farthingdale's private rooms and the main living area.

In the main room the small door at the side of the fireplace was to the attic rooms, another led into the back hall with access to the kitchen and back into Lady Farthingdale's parlour. Diana had always imagined that in the past small children would have had fun running round and round until they were chastised.

The main living area was not exactly a parlour but a large room used for everything. It was part parlour, part dining room and part hall. There were three doors which led off the rear of it. One to the side entrance vestibule, one to a guest room, now Michael's, and one to Diana's room.

With few people living there it caused no problem but how they would manage with so little privacy now Diana had no idea.

A hushed discussion concluded Constance's presence there should not be known, therefore she should not be seen by the servants. Mr Barnam informed them he intended to bring his wife in a day or two to accompany Constance to their house where she could arrange to have suitable clothing made for her departure to Bath.

Eliza took Constance under her wing to make sure she was not overwhelmed by the changes now happening in her life.

"I must see to my horse. A local man working on the field came to our rescue and showed us the stable. He may have left by now."

"I will walk with you Michael. I expect it was Dick, he lives down the lane with his son Dicky. They have a horse so we could arrange fodder from them. I will fetch my cloak."

She went swiftly to her room to put on her half boots and cloak. Michael leapt to attention as he heard her cry out. She appeared in the doorway, distressed and white faced. "They have taken my horse."

A few minutes later when she was calm enough to explain she told of the bequest in his Aunt's will which left her a very old bronze statue of a horse.

"Aunt Letitia always said it was worth a great deal of money. If ever I was in financial difficulties I could sell it."

"It was an investment of a different kind?"

"Yes."

"Describe it to me."

Diana waved her hands showing the size, described the colouration and most of all the weight.

"I never saw them with anything that heavy."

"Nor did I."

Michael went into her room and looked around, then he went to the window and opened the casement. In the wet ground outside there was a deep indent surrounded by footprints. He returned to Diana.

"They threw it out of the window then came back for it. Is there a Constable nearby?"

"Yes, about five miles away, but the Bristows know him well so I doubt he would do anything."

"Then I will ride to the Bristows. Give me the direction."

"Be careful, Michael."

"Don't worry, Diana. I have managed to survive four years of war, I am sure I can survive the Bristows."

"A Mr Arnott to see you, Mrs Bristow." The butler ducked away leaving Michael to enter the room.

"What do you want?"

"I am here on a friendly mission, Mrs Bristow."

"Friendly. Why? Is she leaving?"

"While the house was being emptied of ornaments someone, one of your sons I believe, entered Miss Newby's room and stole a bronze statue of a horse. It is too heavy for a lady to have carried away. I wish to ask for its return immediately."

"You call that friendly!"

"Indeed I do. I am giving you the chance to redress their mistake. The alternative is to go to the Constable and the Magistrate, have a letter sent by a lawyer and a court case brought against your family for theft."

Mrs Bristow sat quietly. "How do I know this statue even exists?"

"There is a will in which it was bequeathed to Miss Newby, which can be produced in court."

"You can't prove they took it."

"Miss Newby is very distressed. I doubt she will be leaving until the horse is returned. If it is not returned she could decide to spend several years here which would be a constant reminder to all of you. In the circumstances she may decide not to leave at all; she does have the right to stay."

Mrs Bristow was at a loss as to what to say. She walked about the room for a time then faced him. "I do not believe anyone in my family took it but I will inform them of its loss. It may be they could root out the thief for you and have it returned."

"I am grateful for your help, Mrs Bristow."

"You told them that I was staying!"

"It seemed a good way to force them to return it. Whether Mrs Bristow has any authority over her sons I have no idea, but it will make them consider the options I gave."

"I could never bring a court case!"

"But I could on your behalf."

The next couple of days were busy with concealing Constance. Dick and Dicky were enlisted to provide for Michael's horse and it did not surprise him to find how well thought of Diana was.

For some part of the day when it was safe, Diana spent time with Constance teaching her simple reading to help her feel less awkward when she arrived at school.

Mr and Mrs Barnam arrived in a carriage to take Constance to school once she had clothing. Constance was a little tearful at leaving Diana and Eliza but was looking forward to becoming a lady like Miss Newby. It was Diana's turn to bite back the tears.

Chapter 25

Now there was just the three of them. In the eyes of society, of course, it would be seen as scandalous for Michael to stay there with only Diana's maid. He intimated as much but was firmly told he was there as her protector and the gossips could go hang themselves. Once she moved on who would know anyway.

Michael felt a pang at her words.

Eliza was as tactful as she could be. In the evenings she sat in one corner of the room and kept her face to her sewing. Diana and Michael played cards, or some board game they had never played before and spent long hours discussing the rules and laughing over their confusion.

During the day Michael exercised his horse by riding around the area, seeing where all the houses were and talking to the residents. It was on one of these rides that he met the local doctor.

"You are at Lady Farthingdale's, I understand. Well I am pleased Miss Newby has a man around, I do not trust the Bristows even if they are one of the senior families in the area."

Michael told him about the will and how threatening they had been. He also mentioned the stolen horse.

"I doubt you will see that again if it is valuable. I never knew a family with more avarice than them. I have real trouble being reimbursed for my time if I have to call there. How any parent can treat their daughter as they have treated Constance I cannot imagine. Mind you, they treated Lady Farthingdale just as badly and still expected her to leave them her money."

After a week there had been no visits, no threats but no horse either. Michael began to wonder how long he should stay, but was loath to leave. He needed to know if Diana had any plans for her future.

One evening he sat and told her of Newman and his promise to take his pocket watch to his son

"Is it far, Michael? Are they expecting you?"

"Less than a day, I hope. No they are not expecting me. I doubt I will be welcomed."

"Why ever not!"

"Newman's home was as unhappy as mine and very similar. He married a young girl who he adored, but who came to see him as a way of bettering herself. They had a son. When his father died and his elder brother returned home as head of the house, he fell in love with Newman's wife and she with him. His brother said he withdrew his support for his family; he must go into the army to support them or they would starve, so he had to go. I dread to think what I will find when I arrive. Yet it is no surprise them hoping he would die in France, it is what my own father hoped."

"The last few years I hardly saw you. When you were younger my governess and I would often come across you sat under a tree by the river reading. She used to say it would be better if I were more like you." Diana blushed a little and turned away.

"Did you not believe all the lies they told about me. If so you were the only one."

"I was not told all of them but they never seemed to fit your character. I never saw you even argue with anyone. I remember seeing a large bird land in a tree and knock a precariously built nest to the floor. You carefully picked it up, chicks and all, and climbed the tree to replace it. I thought then what a kind and gentle person you were."

Michael looked down at his boots in embarrassment. "I never did anything wrong, Diana, and that is the truth. I was a boring swat if truth be known, but the boys at Eton loved to wind up Frederick to get me into trouble, and Frederick believed them. Like father, he never checked. Just as he never questioned what Lucy said about you."

It was Diana's turn to stare at the floor.

"I'm sorry. Does it still hurt that much."

"Sometimes, yes. My life was planned. I was looking forward to being a wife, having children, then suddenly nothing. No future, no family. Always hiding who I was to prevent anyone learning what had happened. I never took it, but society would find me guilty, even now I could be accused and punished and who would speak for me. Even Aunt Letitia is gone."

Michael put out his hand and covered hers. "I would speak for you. I know more than you think. Smeaton would speak for you, so would Cobden and Petersford. You are not alone any more, Diana."

Michael began to plan. What should he do next? What would Diana do next? If she decided to leave would he lose her? The longer he stayed the less he wanted to leave but he knew he had the pocket watch to deliver. What if she decided to leave and he was not there when she went. He could not bear the thought of that. He must take the watch and then talk to her about the future: Their future.

He announced his intention of leaving for the Newman's the next morning. He would be away for at least one night, he said, possibly two. It depended on how easily he found their house and if they were at home. The evening was heavy with sadness.

The morning brought an early start for everyone. Diana had risen to see him away; Eliza had risen early to make sure he ate breakfast before he left. His saddlebags were packed and laying over the back of a chair in the main room.

Diana was hovering near him. She wanted to sit quietly but was too disturbed to settle. The sooner he went, the sooner he would return, well that was the how it was supposed to be, wasn't it. But she didn't want him to go.

Michael rose from the table.

"Make sure you keep all the doors locked, Diana." He looked over to Eliza too. "Especially the side door. You must keep yourselves safe while I am not here."

Eliza cleared the plates from the table, leaving them to say goodbye without her there.

"Diana. I hate leaving you."

"You will not be gone long, Michael." She stood close to him and he turned to face her. He was looking into her eyes which had a misty look in them.

Could he hope, should he hope?

He lowered his head to touch her lips with his as she looked up at him. He wanted to hold her, to wrap her in his arms and press her to him. To bury his face in hers and meld her mouth with his. To feel totally one with her.

He let his arms slide around her as his lips pressed firmer against hers. Her mouth opened slightly and she felt his tongue touching the inside of her lips. She tasted wonderful. He was having difficulty controlling his desires. This was all new to him. He had never been with a woman, never wanted one before. Diana, only Diana. It had always been only her.

Her neck and back must be at a strange angle so he stepped forward to lean her against the wall to give her support. He leaned into her, the desire roaring through him.

Suddenly he was holding a tiger. She was kicking and fighting, scratching and punching him. He let her go and stepped back in shock.

Diana was in panic, on the verge of screaming.

"Get off me! Get out! I am not one of your whores! I thought you were different!"

"My whores?" Michael stared in disbelief, his voice dead. The cold was spreading through him again. He had thought she cared, that she had understood and believed in him. "I mistook you, Madam. I see you did believe the lies. You are no different to my family, Miss Newby. I will not trouble you further."

He walked across the living room and picked up his saddlebags. Eliza came in from the kitchen.

"Goodbye, Mr Arnott. How long will you be away? When can we expect you?"

"I will not be returning, Eliza. I am no longer welcome."

Michael never knew how he made it to his horse. He just found himself riding away. The need to put space between them was urgent and he kicked his horse into a gallop. The dust swirled behind him, blotting out the past.

Diana stood frozen where he had left her. Michael had gone. What had she said to him, she had no idea. She had just panicked.

"He said he was not coming back, Miss."

Diana wanted to cry. She was trembling now, shaking from head to foot. Michael had gone, she had lost him, driven him away. She would never see him again.

"Are you ill, Miss Diana."

She stared through tears at Eliza's concerned face.

"I have to go after him."

She ran from the house, through the orchard to the stables. It took time to saddle a horse, he would still be there, he had to be.

The stable was empty, the road was empty. In the distance there was just the swirl of dust.

Chapter 26

George Pennington sat in his chair where Michael had left him. At first his mind was a blank with horror that his son had dared to speak to him in that way but then his recollections began to flood in.

George's father had been a hard, domineering man and George had been an only child destined to inherit and brought up from an early age to learn how to rule the surrounding area as the most powerful landowner and the future magistrate. He remembered walking by the river with a man following, always a man following. He had no freedom, could do nothing that was not known or reported back to his father. Every misdemeanour was punished with the cane. He swore when he had a son he would never cane him for such simple wrongs.

He had never caned Frederick, even when he went scrumping in old Finbers's orchard. But Frederick had apologised and promised it would not happen again. He remembered the scene in the study with Finbers and Frederick, his head hung in shame. They were both there, Finbers had said, so Michael was sent for to answer for himself and he had not been contrite in any way. But then he was barely five years old. He imagined the scene, Frederick climbing the tree and tossing the apples down to Michael who stood below. Michael had been far too small to climb an apple tree, too young to know it was wrong.

But still he had felt the need to punish someone and had caned him. He remembered the look on the boy's face, hurt like a wounded animal, but no tears. If he had cried perhaps it would have been different. But Michael never cried he just took whatever punishment he handed out to him. Oh he tried to say things were not true, that he had not done it, but he had never listened. Michael was punished for everything Frederick had done wrong, for every wrong George's father had punished him for. Michael had become a way to punish his now dead father for his own treatment and he had not even noticed what he was doing.

When Frederick wrote to him from Eton he remembered the pain he had felt that first year, thinking his son had turned out so bad. He needed to punish him even if he was away at school, so he told the neighbours. He was the magistrate, he would not treat lightly anyone doing anything wrong and he would prove it with the punishment of his son. To make sure they knew and understood he repeated everything Frederick wrote.

By his second year at school George had ceased to feel the pain. He reduced the allowance to Michael, paid only for the meanest of rooms. He would bring him to heel. Still Frederick wrote and every time they returned home Michael was caned. But still the reports kept coming.

When Frederick went to Oxford he seldom wrote, perhaps with no Michael there was nothing to say. Most of his letters had always been about his brother. When the letter came describing the brothel affair he was incensed. Arnott, his father-in-law was there.

'Attacked women in a brothel, Michael! George you do not know your son, he is not interested in women he is a gentle scholar. Have you never had a conversation with him? You must know how intelligent he is.'

He had not listened. He had not wanted to hear it, he knew his son. Everyone knew what his son was like; the whole neighbourhood could tell him. He was a wastrel, a bad apple, you only needed to know what Frederick had reported from school.

True he had seen little of him during his holidays. There was that incident when a group of boys had rampaged around the area and stolen food and things they could sell for money. Turnbull had come to him with several of the neighbours saying it was Michael who had led them. It was just what he would do. Wilson had been sent for to find Michael. He remembered the stunned silence when Wilson had reported that Michael was not at home, he was in Kent with a school friend and had been for more than two weeks.

How could you not notice that your son was not there? Easily it seemed.

The candle gutted and went out but still he sat there, his mind reaching into the past.

Arnott had gone to Eton over the brothel affair. 'Don't you ever check anything, George. I would hate to be brought up before you if you never check if an allegation is correct. How many have you sent to hang or be lashed for things they never did? Have you ever given anyone the chance to defend themselves?'

He never gave Diana Butterwick a chance to defend herself. He never let anyone speak for her and he never checked if any of it was true. Frederick had come to him and Frederick did not lie. Surely Frederick had checked, but had he? Had he checked at school? Michael had said Frederick was naïve and gullible and everyone at school knew that and fed him lies. It was a joke to them.

What if he had not checked that day? Diana had been a lovely girl, not one you would imagine would steal. What had Michael said, if she had wanted it she only had to wait a few weeks and she could see it every day, it did not make sense, but sense had never been his strong point. Was that true? What had happened to Miss Butterwick? He knew nobody had taken her in. He knew her family was no longer accepted amongst the local gentry and he heard of the items stolen with which Lucy reinforced her guilt almost every day. He had become a little tired of her vindictiveness, you would have thought after four years she would have stopped complaining, but then that was Lucy's nature, nothing was ever good enough she always wanted more.

Like the London trip. He knew he should not have moved Michael's money, that if it was discovered he could face some stiff questions. Michael was a minor, he needed help in dealing with it, that would be his argument but how could he account for giving Frederick his money. How could he answer for the money spent on London gowns at such high prices, the cost of the best hotel?

Had he hoped Michael would be killed in France?

Yes.

The cold shock washed over him. How could anyone want their son to die to save them from having to face up to what they had done? Michael had known; that was even worse. From the day he left England Michael had known. He had fought for is country knowing his father had taken his grandfather's gift and ruined his life.

What of Arnott? Had he known what had happened with the money? Did he believe Michael had not wanted to go to Oxford and had wasted it? Since the day he had returned from Eton and told him exactly what had happened there none of them had seen him, not even Mary his daughter. She never asked about Michael. Did she ever speak to him; he could never remember them talking together. Not since he told her Michael thought he was a bye-blow. Had he grown up with the hatred of a Mother as well as a Father? Michael had never seen the letters from his grandfather Arnott, he had made sure of that. The same as he had prevented Frederick from receiving the letters Michael sent from France.

The news sheets reported the numbers of casualties and the major battles, but Michael talked of men, real people in terrible situations. After the letter about Villefranche he never opened any more. They upset him too much, made his conscience prick which angered him.

Michael had apologised for surviving, with sarcasm. He had known his desire to avoid having to face him, he understood too much. How could he hold up his head amongst the local gentry if Michael told them everything? But they would never believe him so he would be safe from that. The thought brought him up short. Michael would never be believed, he had seen to that just as he had ruined his life. Could he blame him for wanting retribution?

But why was it so important to him to have someone pay for the life of Diana Butterwick? Could it be he wanted his father punished for everything he had done to him, just as he had blamed his father and punished Michael in his stead ....

Where would he go? To his friends in London he expected, so if he needed to find him he could. What name would he take? He was prepared to forego the title of Captain just to avoid using the family name he was so angry and ashamed of.

The money was mostly gone, what would he do, how would he survive? He had not been trained for any profession which had been his intention. Another way to punish him by having no way to support himself whilst he gave him nothing.

Could he blame him for his anger?

No.

Yet he had not walked out and left them to their fate, he had warned him of what was happening. He had obviously been to see his mother, as he had mentioned a white powder she put on her food, a tonic from Lucy. When people take Arsenic their hair falls out, he said. Was her hair falling out, he had never even noticed. How often did he visit his wife now she was so vague and stayed in her room all day?

There were sounds of the maids moving around in the house but still he sat there in the dark. He heard someone come downstairs and go to the side entrance, speaking quietly to one of the servants. They never responded. It was probably Michael, the servants had been trained by Wilson never to speak to him.

Another deliberate act on his part.

Not a Christian. That had hurt. George Pennington was seen as the most prominent upholder of morals in the district. Is enforcing morals not being a Christian? Michael had looked inside his heart and seen the darkness of what he had become. How could he have done that? When had he become this understanding, this wise?

Arnott had asked if he knew how intelligent Michael was. How did you find out how intelligent someone was, by talking to them he supposed. When had he last had a conversation with his younger son, when had he ever had a conversation with him.

Never.

The room was cold, the fire having died hours ago. The murmur of voices increased as the maids took over the house. Someone opened the door carrying a candle.

"Oh sir! I did not know you were here." She exited at speed. He heard the information being passed on. Wilson appeared in his dressing gown.

"Are you ill, sir? Do you need the doctor?"

"Not physically, Wilson. Has Mr Michael left?"

The butler sniffed. "I will find out, sir. Would you like me to bring candles?"

"Yes please, Wilson."

He heard the butler talking down the hallway to the servants.

"It appears he left some time ago, sir. We will all be the better for that."

George winced. He had done a good job in making everyone hate the boy.

The candles now lighted, the study became familiar. He remembered his father in here caning him just as he had caned Michael, but never Frederick. How much did Frederick know and would he now hate him as much as Michael did. Frederick knew something because of how silent he had been since Michael's arrival and the walk they had taken in the garden.

Lucy had become even more vindictive since his arrival. Perhaps she knew more than she was saying. Would she accuse Michael of something dreadful enough to make him stop his allowance. She knew he would never check; he never did. Well this time he would, and he would make sure they all knew.

Wilson arrived fully dressed. "Do you wish me to call your valet, sir?"

"Why not, Wilson. I feel the need for a bath. Would you inform him?"

Wilson bowed his head and retreated.

He felt totally soiled. If only he could wash the inside as well as the outside.

Bathed and dressed George Pennington made a call before breakfast. He went to his wife's room; it was still quite dark so he lit the candles in her private parlour. Her maid was not yet around so he pulled the bell and sat to wait.

"Oh, sir. I thought it was the mistress."

"Has Mr Michael been to see his mother?"

"Yes, sir. Yesterday when she was having dinner. He waited but she would not speak to him."

"What did he say to her?"

"He said he was leaving and she would never see him again."

"Nothing else." The maid looked embarrassed.

"He said a better son never existed but she would never believe that."

"Did he mention some white powder."

"Yes sir." She went to the table and brought the box. "Mrs Lucy brings it for her to help her recover. She said her mother used it. He said I should not give it to her and that I would be without a position soon." She hung her head as if she had said too much.

"Thank you. I will take the box. If Mrs Lucy brings any more do not give your mistress any unless I say so. Do you understand?"

"Yes, sir."

Putting the box in his pocket he went down to the breakfast room but ate hardly anything.

"Wilson, have my carriage brought round will you."

He went up to his room to put on his outdoor clothing. On his way down the stairs he came upon an argument.

"Well if you won't tell him then I will. Do you want to be poor all your life while he gets given everything?"

"He is not given everything, he gets very little."

"Look how he behaves."

"You can't be sure it was him."

"Of course it was him. Everyone said it was him. Just because he is your brother you are willing to forgive him. Well I will not."

George arrived at the bottom of the stairs where the two stood arguing.

"My study!"

Once inside away from the servants he turned to both of them.

"What has happened?" He asked. Frederick said nothing.

Lucy jumped in with her accusation. "Michael went to the local inn last night, you heard him say he was going. Well my maid told me something dreadful happened. Michael was so drunk he attacked a girl in the village. He defiled her! How can you put up with someone like that? Why don't you do something to stop him?"

"What do you propose I should do?" He raised his eyebrows in question.

Lucy had obviously thought this through and continued with the diatribe against Michael. "Well stop his allowance for one thing, that might help. We have much more need of the money than he has. You only have to look at his clothing to know he is getting money from somewhere and I expect it is not honest. We all know what he is like."

Frederick looked at her in shock.

"Lucy, Michael has been fighting in France until recently."

"Fighting! Carousing with the French women I expect."

George walked to the door and called to Wilson.

"Wilson, have Mrs Lucy's maid fetched, will you."

It was Lucy's turn to look shocked.

"We will see who told her about this." Her father-in-law said.

"You do not accept my information. You think a maid's testimony is better than mine!"

"I merely wish to hear from where she acquired the information."

"So you do not believe your own daughter-in-law!"

"Enough, woman! I happen to be the master in this house and I will not have you question my rights." Lucy was stunned.

The maid arrived with fear written on her face.

"I understand you know about a problem at the inn last night."

She stared at him. "Yes, sir."

"Were you there?"

"No, sir."

"Who told you?"

She had trouble answering. She looked at Lucy and her eyes pleaded.

"Who told you!"

"Mrs Lucy, sir." Lucy jumped in.

"Don't be ridiculous, you said the downstairs maids told you."

"Oh, yes. Ma'am. The downstairs maids told me."

"Which ones? What are their names?"

"I don't remember sir." The girl was trembling.

"You may go." She left gratefully, taking a quick glance at Lucy.

"You see …" Lucy began.

"No, I don't see. Madam"

Wilson knocked on the door.

"The carriage is ready, sir."

"Come, Frederick, we have calls to make."

Frederick looked surprised but stood to leave with him.

In the carriage neither of them spoke. Frederick never asked where they were going and his father never volunteered any information. They arrived at the local inn and George encouraged his son to follow. It was well before nine in the morning and early for any but villagers and estate workers to be there.

"Good morning, sir. Good morning Mr Frederick. You're early birds, is it a new family routine." Willy joked.

George looked stern. Then turning to his son said "You ask him, Frederick."

Frederick looked horrified. Swallowed hard and stared at the inn keeper.

"Was my brother Michael here yesterday" He avoided asking about last night.

"Yes, sir. T'were good to see the Captain again and looking so fit and healthy. We had thought he might not survive in France. So many seem to have been killed."

Inside George winced.

"What happened last night?"

"Last night, sir. Well nothing much, just the normal crowd as got a little drunk, it were old Lodi's birthday, if he really knows when he was born. I think he just wanted them to buy him some drinks."

"What about my son. Was he here celebrating?"

"Captain Michael, sir. No, not last night."

"So when was he here, Willy?"

"Yesterday morning, Mr Frederick. He come in about this time asking questions." He stopped a little short.

"Questions, what questions?"

Willy was embarrassed now. "Well, about that girl that disappeared four years ago."

"Diana Butterwick?"

"Yes, sir. About what had happened to her and where she went. But I don't know anything." He hoped he had not said too much. Pennington was known to be quite nasty if you were in any trouble.

"Was there a problem with a girl yesterday?"

"A girl, Mr Frederick. No not that I know of. What sort of problem?"

"Someone has reported that a girl was attacked last night." He omitted to say in what way.

"Not that I heard. I would have by now."

"And my brother was definitely not here last night?"

"No sir, I only saw him this time yesterday, had an ale, asked about what happened and then left. He seemed busy, if you know what I mean. Like he was going somewhere."

Frederick seemed to sag in relief.

"Thank you, Willy."

"Come, Frederick, I have another call to make." and they left the inn with Willy wondering what that had all been about.

Chapter 27

They sat in silence again. Frederick wondered if they were visiting another inn to check, he hoped not.

The doctor was at home, the butler informed him. Was it urgent as he had been out all night and he had another call to make shortly.

He assured him he would only take a moment of his time but that it was important. He was shown into his waiting parlour.

"Pennington. What can I do for you?"

"Good morning, Dr Gordon. Your butler said you had been up all night."

"Three hours sleep, but that goes with the profession. A country doctor is always on call."

George took the small white box out of his pocket and handed it to him,

"Do you have any idea what this is? I take it you did not give it to my wife."

"Not in a box like this. This is an apothecary's box. How would your wife come by this?"

"My daughter-in-law gave it to her as a tonic. She has been putting it on her food." He paused for a moment. "Tell me, doctor, is it normal for someone's hair to fall out in clumps, for that is what is happening to my wife."

Dr Gordon stopped to look in surprise then opened the small box and inspected the white powder inside.

"How long has she been taking it?"

"I have no idea I could ask her maid. I am loath to ask Lucy."

"No. In the circumstances say nothing to alert her. I will get this checked while I am out today. It might be a good idea if I call to see Mrs Pennington on my way home this evening."

"Thank you, doctor, it would put my mind at rest."

Frederick had stayed in the carriage during the visit and now worried over the cause.

"Is mother worse?"

"She is certainly not improving. Dr Gordon is going to call in and see her."

The rest of the journey was silent until they were almost home.

"Frederick, do you intend to tell Lucy where we have been?"

"She will ask."

"Will you tell her?"

"She won't believe me."

"Of course she will. She knows it is not true. Last night Michael called to see his mother then came to see me. He stayed talking to me until late, then retired and left extremely early this morning. I knew he was not there but I wanted you to know for yourself."

Frederick looked at him in surprise.

"Why did you not tell me? I would have believed you."

"Enough to stand up to your wife?"

"I was sure Michael would not do that."

"But you believed them at school."

Frederick sat silently.

"He said I was naïve and gullible. It's true, I believed everything they said. I never knew friends could lie like that, I trusted everyone. Except my own brother." He hung his head to hide the pain on his face, the tears in his eyes. "Now I'll never see him again."

"You could go to his friends if you wish to see him. You must know where they live"

"No. I never took any interest. I only know their names were Lansdale and Ashford."

"Wilson might know. He once knew Michael was in Kent."

"Did you not know where he went?"

"I never bothered to ask."

* * *

Lucy left the men to their port, and shortly after Wilson came and spoke quietly to George. The Doctor had arrived and had asked to see him.

"Would you like to see my wife before we talk?"

"That might be a good idea, then we can speak with her maid."

Mary was only just eating her meal so they waited until her maid was in a position to leave her.

"Why does my wife have her meal so late? I would have expected her to eat much earlier."

"Mrs Lucy likes to see to her meal while you are taking your port, sir."

"Why does Mrs Lucy see to her meal?"

"I don't know, sir."

"This is not the meal we had. Is she given different food for a reason?"

"I don't know, sir. She says Mrs Pennington needs her food to be stronger tasting. She thinks the stronger the flavour the more strength it will give her."

The doctor looked serious.

When his wife had finished most of her meal George approached her.

"Mary, how are you today?"

She smiled up at him but he was not sure she actually recognised him.

"Are you any better today, my dear?"

She blinked as if trying to remember something.

"The doctor is here to see you."

Doctor Gordon stepped into her line of vision.

"How are you today, Mrs Pennington?"

"Quite well, thank you sir. Why have you taken my medicine away, my food tastes strange?"

"You are not to have that medicine any more, Madam. It does not suit you; I will give you something better."

"If you think so." Then she lapsed back into a quiet oblivion.

The doctor turned to her maid.

"Is she always this vague now? How long has she been this bad?"

"For some weeks now, sir. She is a little better today, this is the first day she has not been so sick."

"She is sick every day?"

"Yes, sir, and she gets such bad stomach pains. If you could give her something to help I am sure she would be very grateful."

Having the maid so co-operative George broached the question of the white powder. "How long has she been taking the powder from Mrs Lucy?"

"Several months now, but she seems no better. The stomach pains seem worse."

"What did she say the powder was for?"

"When she was unwell her mother used it and it worked wonders, she said. That's why Mrs Pennington was prepared to take it."

The Doctor cut in here. "So Mrs Pennington was still clear-headed when she started to take the powder."

"Yes, sir."

"If Mrs Lucy brings you any more powder do not give it to your mistress. Do you understand?"

"Yes, sir."

"Perhaps it would be best if you did not tell Mrs Lucy, just take the powder and say nothing."

"Yes sir. What do I do if she comes during her meal? She will put it on herself."

"I will arrange for Mrs Pennington's meals to be served at a different time. If you have any problems call someone to fetch me. Do not let your mistress eat it."

"Yes, Mr Pennington."

They were in the study each with a large glass of brandy in their hands. George definitely needed it.

"So tell me. I dread what you are going to say."

"So you should, Pennington. The powder is arsenic. Of course we cannot be sure your daughter-in-law knows exactly what it can cause but she seems intelligent enough. Could you find out from her mother what she took it for?"

"Her parents left the area shortly after her marriage to Frederick. I have no idea where they went; I don't think Lucy knows either."

"This gets worse. Could she be doing this purposely?"

"It is possible. Michael recognised it as arsenic because of the hair loss. He made various predictions about what would happen, all caused by or involving Lucy. They are already starting to happen."

"If she finds out the meals are changed and the powder gone what will she do?"

"I dread to think. What do I do now? How do I protect Mary?"

"In this house it may not be possible. Is there anywhere you could go close by? I doubt she is well enough for a long journey?"

"Only the neighbours and they all think so highly of Lucy."

"Have you no empty property where you could keep her safe?"

"There is the Turnbull's farmhouse. I have no idea how suitable it is. He left this winter to live with his son Alan in London."

"The Turnbulls. Not a bad house if I remember rightly. I visited Mrs Turnbull several times before she died. It is not like this, of course, but large enough to prevent any untoward visitors."

George raised his eyebrows. "You think she might try to interfere there."

"It is possible. You need a small household loyal to you and your wife. Preferably not keen on Lucy. Cook, maids and footmen with muscle enough to keep her out. Beware visits in the kitchen or you could all suffer if she thinks we suspect something."

"Michael said to beware of stomach upsets. Lucy is demanding more money."

"He was right. Move fast, Pennington."

"I will go there at first light and check how quickly it can be done. Wilson will help me find those who are not attached to Lucy, I'm sure."

"Try not to leave this house unprotected, you have Frederick to consider."

George covered his head with his hand. "Michael said Mary first, then me, then Frederick. It depended on the amount of money the estate has."

"He saw then. You can often see clearer when you come from outside. Where is he now?"

"I have no idea. I doubt I will ever see him again but please don't ask now. I have enough problems to deal with."

The last thing George did that night was to send a note to his steward who looked after the tenant farms and ask him to meet him at the Tuckers at first light. Then he arranged for his carriage to be ready before breakfast.

* * *

The steward hammered on the door. "Mrs Benson, Mr Pennington is here to see you." He continued to hammer until they heard footsteps approaching and the bolts being pulled.

"Gracious me you gave me a fright."

"Mr Pennington is here to inspect the house, Mrs Benson."

"At this time in the morning? Well come in, sir."

"Can you show me exactly the layout of the house and how secure it is, Mrs Benson?"

"Yes of course, sir. Since Mr Tucker left I have had little to do so I spent the time cleaning. You will find it in good order."

"Do you have maids and a cook?"

"No sir, only me now. The maid lived in the village and has another position and cook went to London with Mr Tucker. She was to be cook at Mr Alan's house."

"The house does not feel too cold, considering the time of year."

"I have tried to keep it aired, sir. I lay a small fire in each room every day."

"How sensible."

They toured the downstairs rooms then proceeded to the upstairs.

"These rooms have not been used for some time, of course. What with Mrs Tucker gone and Mr Alan in London."

"You seem to have kept them in good order."

"Of course, sir. I had no idea how soon someone might take the tenancy and want to move in."

"You have done well. Can you now show me the kitchens?"

They descended the main stairs and went through the servants' door to the kitchen.

"The kitchens are not very big, sir, not in comparison to at the Hall, but cook was happy enough. She said nothing was too far away but the kitchen maid never got under her feet while she was cooking. We still have some winter stores Mr Tucker laid in last autumn."

"If you were given staff how long would it take to have the kitchen working, feeding a household?"

"A visit to the village for stores and a decent cook could give you a meal tonight, sir." Mrs Benson thought she was impressing him.

"Do you have good linen?"

"Not up to your standard, sir, but good enough for a tenant."

"If I send someone later I want you to prepare the house as quickly and quietly as possible. Only the staff I send are allowed in and you tell nobody who is coming. Do you understand?"

"Mrs Benson looked stunned. "Yes sir. Who is coming?"

"For reasons I cannot tell you, I have need to isolate my wife and I where she can be safe. I will send servants and strong footmen to keep everyone away. The kitchens especially must be secure. The food must not be interfered with."

Mrs Benson was staring at him in amazement.

"Munford, if there is no tenant do we have enough men to look after the land?"

"We still have Mr Tucker's labourers in the village hoping to be employed by the new tenant. We can always organise it with the main estate work."

"Good, do that. I don't know how long we shall be here, but we need to keep the land in production."

"May I ask, sir, who is to be kept away?"

George stopped and looked directly at him.

"Mrs Lucy Pennington."

* * *

The stables were informed the small carriage would be needed all day and if Mrs Lucy wished to go out they were to use the travelling coach. He spoke to the stable-master as to which grooms did not like Mrs Lucy, which brought up the first problem, nobody dare admit not liking her. Two grooms were picked who had been there before Lucy had arrived and were of strong physique.

He would have to deal with the problem of Wilson and the household servants.

"Wilson, are there any servants who do not like Mrs Lucy?"

"Oh no, sir. Everyone thinks the world of her."

"So if Mrs Pennington recovers enough to run the household they will all listen to Mrs Lucy rather than my wife."

"No, sir. Of course not. They are all very loyal to Mrs Pennington."

"Are there any who are more loyal than others? Has there been any problem with any of the servants where Mrs Lucy is concerned?"

"We have had to dismiss one or two of the maids, sir. Then there is Johnson and Dotty." He stopped.

"Johnson, I thought he was the under butler?"

"Yes he was, and because he was so good I kept him on in a position mostly below stairs. He has been walking out with Dotty for a couple of years now; that is until Mrs Lucy saw them together. She believes the servants should not have any attachments. She wanted them dismissed."

"Were they supposed to be working?"

"Oh no, sir, they were outside at the time. Dotty was the senior maid but she is working in the kitchens now."

"Have them brought to my study immediately, Wilson."

He bowed and complied. Wondering if he would be chastised for not adhering to Mrs Lucy's instructions.

Dotty was apprehensive but Johnson stood straight and fearless. George studied them,

"I understand you have been walking out together."

"We have." Johnson was not prepared to back down. If need be they would go to London to find work together.

"You were under- butler. Can you run a house?"

"Yes sir." He looked perplexed.

"You, Dotty. You were the senior maid. Have you been here long?"

"Nine years, sir."

"So, you worked for my wife. Would you prefer it if Mrs Pennington were running the house again?"

"Yes sir."

"Is there another who is not very happy working under Mrs Lucy? Don't worry, she will not be dismissed."

"Quite a few of them, sir, but Betty is terrified of her. Ever since she cleaned her room and knocked a box from the top of the armoire." George stored this information until later.

"You will be going to another house where you, Johnson, will be the butler. I am leaving you to organise the move. You will need two or three sturdy footmen who are loyal to Mrs Pennington. You, Dotty, together with Betty will help pack some household linen then you will be taken in the small carriage. Tell nobody except Betty. I expect the new household running by this evening."

"If Mrs Lucy finds out, what am I to say, sir?"

"Make sure Mrs Lucy does not find out."

The cook was easier to deal with. Lucy had installed one of the kitchen maids as assistant cook to take charge of Mrs Pennington's food. She interfered with the running of the whole kitchen under the threat of informing Mrs Lucy. Cook would take a kitchen maid the assistant cook hated.

The hardest was the housekeeper. Would she say anything? After all she would not be going.

Mary's maid came in handy here. She had access to all the linens needed for her mistress and had the ability to fetch them without causing any comment. Johnson arranged for his footmen to fetch trunks from the attics for her to pack for the household and for her mistress.

Lucy went out in the travelling carriage which allowed for the small black coach to make several trips to the Tucker's house.

Cook had organised dinner but sent pies which could be cooked when they arrived. She left a stunned assistant cook to deal with the evening meal as she would not be there, she informed her. She was warned Mrs Lucy would hear of this. She hoped she would, indeed she did.

The last to leave was Mary and her maid. She would leave with George in the travelling coach when Lucy returned home.

* * *

For all the comings and goings during the day, Frederick had no knowledge that anything was amiss. George found him reading in the library.

"Frederick, could you assist me. I have a little problem."

Frederick shot to his feet.

"Is it serious?"

"I'm afraid it is. I need you to help me check something."

Frederick was concerned when they went to his wife's rooms.

"I just want you to see if there is anything on top of the armoire."

Frederick reached up but the carved ornamentation on the top caused him a problem. George brought a chair for him to stand on.

"Lucy will be very annoyed, sir."

George ignored him.

There was a small wooden box tight against the carving where it was impossible to see from any angle.

"We should not take it. This is wrong, Father."

"Come into my study and we will discuss this."

"Frederick, what I have to say will upset you a great deal." He opened the small box to show several small white apothecary boxes. Frederick stared down at them. "These boxes contain arsenic. Your mother was persuaded by Lucy to sprinkle it on her food, since when she has been increasingly ill. Your brother warned me what was happening. He also warned me of the danger to me and eventually to you. It all depends on the money your wife is allowed to spend.

"Here I have to make an admission of doing something of which I am not proud. Your grandfather gave Michael money which angered me, and I withheld it. For the last year I used it to increase your allowance, I also used it to pay for your stay in London and all Lucy's gowns. Michael now knows about it and it has been removed. When she finds your allowance is reduced she will no doubt react badly.

"Your mother and I are leaving the house today as it is the only way I can keep her safe and alive. Finding this box will help. Hopefully she will not now have the means to cause you a problem."

Frederick was stunned, horrified, unable to speak.

"I know how upset you must be. When Lucy returns we will take the travelling coach for your mother's comfort but it will be returned. I leave you to deal with your wife."

Mrs Pennington and her maid were brought downstairs to the small parlour near the front door and when Lucy swept in and up the stairs, Wilson assisted them into the travelling coach.

"Will you be out for long, sir?"

"Indeed, Wilson. We will not be returning. Frederick will give you any details."

The carriage drew away and George Pennington patted his wife's hand.

"I am taking you away for a change, it will help you improve, my dear."

"The doctor."

"The doctor knows, my dear. It was his idea."

He hoped it would have the required effect on his wife's health.

Chapter 28

Frederick was frozen within himself. He found it impossible to speak even to Wilson. He dressed for dinner in whatever his valet had put out for him. Michael had never had a valet. Where was he now? His father said Michael had been given money and he had taken it, that Michael knew about it. All those demands from Lucy had been answered with Michael's money.

Lucy had lied on purpose to stop Michael's allowance to give them more to spend. Michael didn't have an allowance, it was his money.

Arsenic, surely arsenic killed people. Why would Lucy give arsenic to his mother? His father had thought she might be a problem to him; why would she want to poison him, she would get no money from him if he died, Michael would become the heir so what good would it do her? Unless she was being vindictive.

What would he say to her? How could he tell her his father had left because he believed she was poisoning his mother?

Ice cold fear ran down his back.

Lucy had made Diana into a pariah. Everyone hated her. For four years Lucy had continued with the onslaught. Vindictive, yes Lucy was vindictive. How could he protect himself?

Revulsion washed over him. He had married a potential murderess. He slept with a murderess. What a good job they had no children. Lucy had some strange ideas; she never allowed him to stay in her bed nor stayed in his. He had wondered about a conversation he had heard with her maid. Something to do with being free, not have entanglements like children. Surely all married women wanted children. He wanted children.

The gong sounded for dinner so he walked mechanically downstairs to where Wilson waited.

"If I could have a word with you later, sir. About your father."

Frederick stared at him blankly.

"I don't know where he is. He never said where he was going."

Wilson looked concerned.

"Mrs Pennington is not well enough to go travelling, Mr Frederick. Why would he go now, at this time of day? It is not long to the cold of the evening."

"I cannot tell you."

Lucy was already in the dining room.

"Good evening Frederick. Your father is late."

"Father will not be coming."

"Oh. Never mind. We can well do without him."

Dinner passed with Frederick saying not a word and Lucy never stopping. She continued the diatribe against both Diana and Michael. Would she never stop? Did she never have a good word for anyone?

"Where did you go so secretively this morning with your father?"

"To do what I should have done four years ago. To ask questions and verify the truth. Michael never went to the inn last night and no girl was attacked, it was all a lie."

"They are obviously friends with him. They were lying for him. What did you father say?"

"He said Michael was in his study with him last night. He knew it was not true but I had to have proof to be able to see you were lying."

Lucy narrowed her eyes, her mouth a tight straight line.

"No wonder he is not here. He dare not face me with such lies." She rose to leave. "If you will excuse me, I will retire to the parlour."

She did not go to the parlour, she went to the kitchens to see the under cook. Her father-in-law was getting too suspicious. She had to finish this soon. She found the girl in tears amid the chaos of a disorganised kitchen. There were burnt dishes of food which a maid was trying to remove from the dish in order to scrub it. The food for Mrs Pennington sat on the side unfinished, some of it only half cooked.

"What is going on here? Why has Mrs Pennington's food not been finished? Where is cook?"

"Cook has gone and left me to do everything. I can't do both meals at once."

"Nonsense. Tell the girls what to do. What of this is ready?" She looked at the unappetising meal waiting on the tray.

"This will do, she will never notice the difference. Bring it."

It was an order. She pointed to a maid.

"You, bring it."

The room was empty. Where was her mother-in-law? This was dreadful. All the planning she had put into this and now she had gone. Perhaps she had died. No, Frederick would have said, although he was very silent during the meal. She had to find out where she was and why she had been taken away.

Wilson hovered in the hallway waiting to speak to Frederick.

"I wondered if you knew where your father had gone, Mr Frederick?"

"I have no idea, Wilson. I only know he has left and taken my mother with him. He seemed to think she was in danger here."

"Danger! I don't understand."

"Nor do I, Wilson, but I think is has something to do with the boxes of arsenic we found in my wife's room."

He walked away leaving Wilson rigid and wide eyed.

Lucy searched. It took her two days to find out where George and Mary had gone. She now had plans to be worked out. First she needed another box from on top of her wardrobe, then she would pay them a visit.

"I thought we would pay a visit to your parents to make sure they are well. I am not sure the house is suitable for your mother's health, Frederick."

"You know where they are?"

"Of course, they told me. Did they not tell you? They are in the Tuckers' house."

"I believe my father wants my mother to be totally quiet, Lucy. I doubt we would be welcome at the moment."

"Then I will go alone. I would hate them to think we did not care."

"I have a call to make this morning so it will have to be after lunch."

"But of course, Frederick, ladies always visit after lunch."

Frederick had his horse saddled with speed and made for the Tucker property. He gave his horse over to a groom and made for the rear door.

"You won't get in that way, sir. Go around to the front and see if they will see you."

"Am I not allowed in, Johnson? I need to see my father with some urgency."

"Stay with him." He ordered the over-large footman who had waited at his elbow.

His father was prepared to see him on one condition. "How did you find out where we were? Is Lucy with you?"

"No, Father, but she found out. She says you told her, which I know you did not. She intends to visit this afternoon. How can I stop her? What do I do now? Do you definitely think she was trying to poison Mother?"

"Yes, I do. The doctor does. He says all the illness your mother has had points to arsenic poisoning."

"I can't go on living with a murderess! What do I do, you are the magistrate."

"You do realise what this will do to the family name. Everyone will be implicated. The whole district will shun us especially after Michael's reputation."

"But that is not true, he was never like that. If only I could put right the wrong I did him."

"What difference would it make? Michael has gone, changed his name and thrown off his family; you have to deal with your wife. Has she discovered the loss of the arsenic yet?"

"She seemed normal enough at breakfast, so I can't answer that."

"See how she is, but know that even if you come with her, she will not be allowed into this house."

"I will try to dissuade her. I need to think what to do."

Frederick needed to think without any interruption from Lucy so he went where any man would, to the inn, to sit with a pot of ale in his hand. As every man knows, even sitting alone in an inn does not mean you are allowed to think.

"Morning, Mr Frederick. Nice to see you again so soon."

"Good morning, Willy, a glass of your best ale if you please.

"Right you are, sir. Funny weather this spring. It's playing havoc with the planting, I'll be bound."

"Yes, indeed it is."

"You off to London again this year?"

"No. Why would you think that?"

"Well your wife did seem eager to go, if you know what I mean."

"Yes, she did, but it's expensive to live in London for the season. We don't have a house or family there and the hotels cost a great deal, well the good ones. There are any amount of inns but the accommodation would not be up to my wife's requirements."

"You could always rent a house, I suppose."

"Rent a house. That would mean servants and cooks."

"I suppose it would. So, no London for Mrs Lucy this year."

Frederick took his pint and went to sit in a quiet corner.

A house in London. How much would it cost to rent a small house with a few servants? It must be cheaper than any hotel, especially if it was only a small house. If he could take Lucy there she would be in heaven. If he could leave her there, so would he.

He would need to speak to his father again to see about financing it. Could he afford it on his allowance? Possibly, if he went without. Without Lucy what would he spend his allowance on, the odd tailor's bill, a few ales. Surely it was worth it to be rid of her. How would he stop her from returning; save from closing up the house and leaving himself he could not imagine, but the alternative was to tell Bow Street they feared she was trying to commit murder, and how would they prove that? Who else knew who could help him?

Doctor Gordon. His father had said the Doctor recognised it was arsenic poisoning and checked the white powder. That must have been why they had visited him.

The Doctor had just arrived from a morning call and was preparing for an early lunch before leaving again.

"I am glad I found you in, doctor."

"You look serious Frederick. What is this about?"

"My mother being poisoned by my wife."

"Your father told you."

"I was with him when we found a wooden box full of white boxes of arsenic."

The Doctor whistled. "How many?"

"Five."

"Five boxes! That would poison half the county."

"What do I do? My father will not allow me to have her publicly accused, but I can't live with her now. For one thing, any argument and I would not feel safe."

"No, I can see that."

"How could I take her to London and make her stay there?"

"London, I suppose that is a good place. Where would she stay?"

"I thought I could take a small house with staff."

"Would you stay there?"

"No, definitely not."

"If she has friends there, perhaps that might encourage her to stay. If you were not there she may take up with some man which would enable you to throw her off."

Frederick looked enlightened.

"I should warn her, perhaps, that if she soiled the name of Pennington she would be publicly denounced and left penniless. Would that be too strong, do you think, or would it make her circumspect?"

"I doubt it. I fear your wife will enjoy the pleasures of London to the full, which will play exactly into your trap. Do not be too firm, be careful she does not realise what you are planning. She is a vindictive woman."

"So everyone is now telling me. Would that they had said that four years ago before I married her. How expensive is it to rent a house?"

"Whatever you are able to pay. There are houses of all sizes and if it were not in the best of locations it could be quite cheap. How do you think the Londoners afford to live? Tucker has a house and a wife to keep and he manages."

Frederick shook his hand warmly. Now he knew what he must do. First a return journey to his father to check on the money.

He slowed as he neared the Tucker house. The travelling carriage was pulling away from the house. So Lucy had not waited, she had tried to visit herself. Luncheon was going to be a trial.

"Father, I need to tell you what Doctor Gordon and I have discussed. Do you think my allowance would afford me to rent a small house in London, with a few servants?"

"You want to go to London again?"

"No, I want to take Lucy there and leave her."

"She will expect money."

"I need to work out if I can afford it. I am prepared to use all my allowance to be rid of her."

"I will give you a note for Wentworth to allow you a sum to achieve that. If you call around later or tomorrow I will let you have it."

"I saw the travelling carriage leaving. Has she called?"

"Yes and was turned away. I hate to think what your day is about to become. Good luck, son."

Lucy was incandescent with rage. She never stopped the whole of the lunch, even when the servants were there.

When she left the dining room the servants almost ran to avoid her. When he had arrived home and gone to his room to change his coat, her maid was cowering against her wroth and the upstairs maids were being screamed at. She had obviously found the box with the arsenic was missing.

"We were supposed to go later, Lucy. Why did you go this morning?"

"Because I knew you would try to avoid going. I know you too well."

"Obviously not well enough. You have not yet asked where I went this morning."

"Of what importance is it to me?"

"Because I was asking advice on taking a house in London for you."

Lucy stopped. "A house in London, Frederick. When did you decide this."

"Quite recently, but I wanted to surprise you. I will go up in a day or too and see what I can find."

"Oh, but I will go with you."

"No, Lucy. I am not going to an expensive hotel and I shall only be there a day or two. Write to your friends, if you like. Tell them you will be there very soon and you will let them know where you are living and when you will arrive. You can start packing your London gowns."

"Oh no, Frederick, I must have new gowns for this season. The fashions change every year."

"Can they not be altered in some way?"

"Good gracious, Frederick, of course they must be new. How could I hold up my head if my gowns were not from the best modista?"

Frederick knew this was going to be a problem but he was in too deep to go back now. She was going to London and she would have to make do with the gowns she owned. The allowance she would have was to run the house and she would never afford what she expected.

The following morning Frederick picked up the letter to Wentworth. During the afternoon his valet packed his saddlebags and fussed about not being allowed to go.

Very early the next morning Frederick left for London, hoping he would be successful. The alternative was unthinkable.

Chapter 29

Frederick arrived in London in a highly nervous state. He took a room at the Star and Garter and sat in the tap room planning the coming day. He needed to see Wentworth but should he do that before or after finding a house? Where did he go to find about renting one, he was not used to London, even though they had been there for a season; most of his time had been spent waiting at the modista's for Lucy to pick her gowns, or at Gunters being seen. He knew Lord Williams, a cousin of Harwood, plus Alan Tucker was there with his father, but he had no idea where either of them lived.

If he had been at home he would have asked Willy at the inn, or one of the local gentry. Would the inn keeper know of how to find a house? Would Wentworth know? That was a thought. Wentworth would know.

He called the barman for another brandy. It was not the same quality as at home, but at least it was drinkable.

"You staying long, sir?" The question jolted him out of his reverie.

"No, probably not. I am here to find a house to rent."

"Been to the agency have you?"

"No, not yet. Where is the agency?"

"There's one up the road here. Caters for all sorts like you, sir. Nice area places, if you know what I mean."

"I will try them in the morning. Thank you that was helpful."

The barman nodded and moved away.

"This is the smallest we have in this area. We have others, but they are rather outside the desirable areas for the ton.

While in good repair it is sparsely furnished. I am sure with a little addition it will be suitable, perhaps some colourful throws to brighten up the seating which is rather worn. Is it for yourself, if so it is an admirable bachelor house."

"It is for a single lady on her own."

"Oh I see your need for a small house in a good area, sir. This is a very acceptable area, I am sure she would be very comfortable here. Being small with insufficient rooms for a family it is a very inexpensive house for such a sought after district." Did all such men ooze like this, people like him made his flesh crawl. Still, this was a price he could afford and in an area Lucy could not object to.

"I will take it."

"The lady will be pleased, I am sure."

Frederick doubted she would.

The agency dealing with staff was much less obsequious.

"A small house with a single lady, you say. So you will need a cook-housekeeper and a butler, plus a maid. Would you be needing an additional footman?"

"Not to begin with. I feel I should warn you, she is a very demanding lady."

"Ah, elderly ladies can become rather crotchety, sir."

"She is not old and she can be very aggressive. I hope you have someone who will not leave at the first insult she sustains."

"That difficult?" She searched through a box containing names and lifted one out. "I have a couple, the Jomens, a cook-housekeeper and her husband. He is a very capable man with a pleasant disposition, but I am afraid the cook is not easily cowed and their last position was not a success. While I can place the husband the wife poses some difficulty and they obviously wish to be together."

"They sound perfect, madam. The cook cannot be dismissed without losing the butler as well which would leave her with no staff. Are they available at once, if so I would like to see them."

"I will send for them for interview, sir. Would three o'clock be suitable?"

"Indeed, there might even be time to see the house."

Was it really that easy to rent a house in London? Well if you were not fussy then it seemed it was.

Feeling very pleased with himself he took himself to Bond Street to walk among the shops. Perhaps he could allow himself a whisky. He rarely drank it but this seemed a good day. Wentworth had been much more friendly than usual. He had seemed genuinely pleased to help him. Almost as if his small request was a relief.

The clientèle in this bar were of a much higher strata.

"Pennington? It is Frederick is it not." He turned to see Lord Williams with a friend, looking his way."

"Indeed it is, my Lord."

"What brings you to London? Is your wife not with you?"

"No, I came alone. "

"Have you met Carstairs."

"No I have not. It is a pleasure, sir."

"Pennington, I have heard the name before but I cannot for the life of me recall. Do you have a large family?"

"Not that I know of, Carstairs. There are only my father and brother. I have never heard of any others."

A group of soldiers were standing close by and reacted to the name.

"Excuse me, did you ask after a Pennington."

"Do you know of anyone of that name?"

"We had a Captain with us in France; perhaps that is where you heard the name. Captain Michael Pennington. A good man, cared for his men, lost hardly any of them."

"Perhaps that is it. Did he have family?"

"None that he cared to talk about. The most intelligent Captain we had. Colonel once said we could all go back to England and leave him with the men, and the war would be finished within a week."

The officers around laughed. Frederick cringed inside.

"Should have been a major now. Colonel said he would have his job within three years. Pity he sold out."

"Whatever for, if his advancement was that secure."

"A shame really. Colonel Finch said he came to see him, told him he was changing his name."

"Obviously that branch of your family are not up to the mark, eh?"

The conversation continued but Frederick let it go over his head. His pain became more acute the more they talked. Lord Williams glanced at him, a frown on his face.

"I never knew you had a brother, Frederick. He was never mentioned when I have been there."

"No, he was away much of the time, in Kent."

"Ah, that would be it then." Still he looked a little thoughtful. Next time he saw Harwood he would ask.

The Jomens were perfect. He warned them of Lucy's temperament and how she would react to living in a small house on a small income. He installed them in the house with an advance on their remuneration and left them to prepare for his wife's arrival. A bank account opened with her first allowance and he was free to go home. Within the week he hoped to be on his way back. That arrival he was not looking forward to.

* * *

Lucy stormed and shouted. She threatened and screamed.

"I will make the name of Pennington hated among the whole ton!"

"Indeed you will, Lucy dear. If is it known my mother is suffering from arsenic poisoning the family name will be ruined. You are being given the opportunity to live a quiet life among your friends. You can always draw attention to yourself and be arrested by the authorities, if that is your wish."

She stood frozen to the spot.

"We found your stock of arsenic. Enough to poison half the county, the doctor said. It is only because of the family name that you are being given this chance. Any blackening of the name and your small allowance will be withdrawn. Any attempt to return to the hall or cause any problems and you will be denounced to the Bow Street authorities. Father suggested we leave a letter with our solicitor in the event any of us die suddenly."

Lucy was still staring with horror as he turned and left her to her future.

"Goodbye, my dear."

Frederick rode as far out of London as he could, that day. He never wanted to see or hear of her again, although he doubted that could be achieved. She was still his wife however much he wished it otherwise.

Five days later Mrs Turnbull arrived to enquire why no-one had seen Lucy at their afternoon gatherings and why Frederick was the only one in residence. The following day an invitation arrived for a dinner at the Turnbulls, no doubt caused by their avid need to acquire more information.

Frederick's first thought was to send his apologies and stay isolated in his own house. If they knew any of what had happened he would be ostracised anyway. On the following morning Webbly just happened to call, to check out what was happening, no doubt. It seemed he would only have any peace if they were given the information they craved. Well why not; perhaps he could use the occasion to redress some of the hurt he had done to Michael. It may not be what they were expecting, but he dare not tell them the whole truth, it was too unbelievable and his father would not allow it. He sent his acceptance.

The dinner was tense as everyone tried to pry information out of him without being too obvious. Lucy was in London, he had taken a house for her; it was what she wanted, to be near her friends for the season. Why he was not there he left rather open.

When the meal finished and as the ladies were about to leave Frederick stood and requested to be allowed to speak. He engendered eager attention.

This would be the most difficult few minutes of his whole life, but perhaps he would feel a little better about himself afterwards. He cleared his throat.

"Everyone here believes they know me. I doubt they do. You all watched me grow up the perfect boy, the perfect son. When I was small I was not perfect but when I was caught I apologised and was forgiven. Often I took Michael with me. He was too small to understand why I was not punished but he was. I never asked my father why. Once Michael could read he spent all his time with a book. When I fell into the river trying to take the boat out I was not punished, but Michael was. He was not even there, but I said nothing.

"At Eton Michael had his own friends, I barely saw him. When I did he was in the library studying, he always had a book with him. When my friends came to me with tales of what Michael had done we laughed about it, but I never checked. I never ever checked. Father expected me to write to him every week and I had nothing to say, so I wrote about Michael and he never checked either, he just caned him when he came home. When I wrote from Oxford about the brothel attack, the only person who checked was Grandfather Arnott. Michael had never been in trouble. I know you will not believe me, but Michael spent his time at school studying. I never visited his room, I never knew what allowance he had, I never knew his friends. I let him down. Every word I wrote from Eton was a lie, Grandfather proved it. You all hate him now, because of me."

Harwood went to interrupt. He put up his hand.

"That is not the worst part. Four years ago Lucy was heard telling her maid she had *dealt* with someone's betrothal. That was just before she told me about Diana Butterwick and the ornament." He looked around at them. "Did any of you hear Diana enthusing over it the night before? No? I doubt it happened. I never asked. Lucy said it was missing, stolen, a maid had told her. Why not broken? I never checked. Lucy said to check Diana's room, why? Because she had put it there and I never asked any questions. I believed every word she said, just as I had believed about Michael at Eton. Two people whose lives have been ruined because of me.

"I have the life of Diana Butterwick on my conscience. What of her family? Which of you have ever spoken kindly to them? Through you I have ruined their lives too. I will not take part in your dinners and parties any more. I have to find a way to live with my conscience."

Harwood stood to attract his attention. "Why has your father moved to the Tucker's house?"

"My mother is ill and needs total quiet. Father thought it necessary."

"But there is only you there."

"They moved before I took Lucy to London. Mama needs total quiet."

It was Mrs Turnbull who asked. "When is Lucy coming home. Mr Frederick?"

"I am not sure she will, Mrs Turnbull. I would be happier if she did not, after what she did. She has spent the last four years making you hate Miss Butterwick when she was innocent, and Lucy knew it. I am not able to accept her as my wife any longer. You will have to do without your weekly dose of venom.

"If you will excuse me I will leave now. I will wish you all goodnight, and possibly goodbye."

Chapter 30

Michael rode all day. He stopped only to rest his horse and drink. He ate nothing. He felt cold and sick - again. He tried to think of Newman, of where he was going, of what he was going to say.

The house was not pretentious. Just a normal gentleman's house with gardens surrounding it. It did not appear to be part of an estate, so they must live on their investments. Perhaps they could not afford to support two families. Given what Captain Newman had said he doubted that, his father had left him money but his brother was controlling it.

He felt the anger wash over him. It was his father all over again, controlling the money and hoping he would be killed in France. Well in this case they had been successful.

The butler opened the door.

"Captain Pennington to see Master Christopher Newman."

The butler looked puzzled. "If you will wait here, sir."

He was shown into a parlour where the sun was shining and a lady sat quietly with her embroidery on her knee. A man sat in a fireside chair holding a book. He rose to meet him.

"Pennington. What brings you here?"

"I have come to see Master Christopher Newman with a message from his father."

They both looked confused.

"My brother is dead."

"Indeed he is. He died in my arms, leaving a message for his son."

"I will tell him. What is it?"

"I will speak only to his son."

"I find you high-handed, Captain."

"I find you exactly as your brother described you, sir. I presume you have married his wife, once you had him killed."

"He died in the war."

"He died because you sent him there with that intention."

"I find your attitude disgusting."

"I find yours to be tantamount to murder, sir. How a brother can act as you have is unconscionable. Have you also banished his son?"

"He is at present my heir. He is well cared for."

"More than your brother was." He turned to the lady sat contemplating the floor. "I presume you were his wife?"

She looked up with a haughty stare. "I am the mother of his son, who I care for very much."

"And now the wife of his brother. I can only hope you do not treat his son as you treated your husband, Ma'am."

"I loved my husband."

"I believe you did when you married him. He loved you to the end, Ma'am. It caused him real anguish that you could turn away from him to his brother. In our circles that is not acceptable, but I believe you were not from our circle originally."

"How dare you insult my wife."

"How dare you hold up your head after what you have done? Do you dare to go to church each week, listen to the commandments and call yourself a Christian? If you refuse me access to his son I will call again next year, and the year after. I will keep coming until I speak with him. I made a promise to your brother and I will fulfil it however long it takes."

Newman pulled the bell and asked the footman to have Master Christopher fetched from his schooling.

"You will not be allowed to see him alone."

"I would not wish to. I believe what I have to say will be surprising to you."

Master Christopher Newman was shown in and marched across the room, stopping in front of the stranger. He was six years old and must only have been two when Newman last saw him. He had his father's fair hair and slight build and carried himself with the bearing of a soldier.

"Christopher, this man has something to say to you."

"I am Captain Pennington, and I was with your father when he died."

"Why are you not wearing a uniform, Captain? I am going to be a soldier when I grow up."

"The war is over now. Many good men like your father died."

"Did he kill lots of Frenchies."

"He killed those who he needed to, Christopher. It is not good for a man's soul to kill other men, even in war. He hated having to do it. He hated war. He was a peaceful man who cared for his men and kept them safe."

"Was he killed by a Frenchie, did you kill the man?"

"Listen carefully, Christopher. Your father was an excellent Captain who, like me, would rather not have had to shoot anyone. He was shot by a coward. We drove out some French soldiers from a village where they killed the men and attacked the women and took all their food. We gave the women and children the food we had. There was one boy, old enough to be a soldier, who was a bully. He shot your father in the back while he was washing in a stream. There are bullies in every country, son. There are good people in every country. The women and old men in that village were good people. Your father was buried in the churchyard with the help of the French villagers who cared about him.

"He would not want you to be a soldier. He talked about you every day; his last thoughts were about you. He wants you to be happy."

He put his hand in his waistcoat pocket and drew out the pocket watch.

"He asked me to give you this. It is for you to remember him. Keep it with you always, never let anyone take it from you, and remember never to give in to bullies. You will meet many in various guises during your life. You must resist them to prove that, like your father, you are better than they are."

Christopher was thoughtful looking at the watch.

"What happened to the boy?"

"He made himself out to be a general, so we gave him a court- martial, put him against a tree and he was executed by a firing squad made up of your father's men. He died in fear. No death is good, however it happens."

The other two occupants of the room were fidgeting uncomfortably.

"When you are older you may wish to visit where he died. It is a called Villefranche. There was no fight there, only one enemy. Study well, Master Newman. Become a man of knowledge and wisdom and make your father proud of you."

"I will. Sir."

Michael took a step back and saluted smartly.

Christopher stood up straight and saluted back. He looked down at the watch in his hand.

"Thank you, sir."

Michael left a silent room. However you considered it, in this case the bullies had won. Newman was dead and they had married. He could only hope the boy would not encounter problems from them because of who his father had been.

* * *

Every mile on his journey south tore at his insides. If he just went down that road, or this road he could be in Hesket village, with Diana. He was no longer welcome there; she had made that very clear.

He rode until he was past the turnings that would take him there. He had turned his back on his hopes, his dreams. He would stay the night in Nottingham and then go home to Grandfather Arnott. He felt guilty, he had not even written to him.

The coaching inn was busy so he went to find a quiet place to drink his ale in peace.

Nottingham was a busy place during the day. It had all the shops to cater for the surrounding area. Diana would shop here if she needed anything not found in the village.

Stop thinking about her.

He passed shops selling meat and cakes, cheese, anything you could eat. He turned a corner. Here was a solicitors' office, Wilford, Barnam and West. He wondered if Barnam was back from Bath yet. Now the shops sold a different kind of merchandise, Paintings, tableware, materials, clocks and ornaments, a bronze horse ... Michael stopped. A bronze horse, the correct size and colouring in a shop full of clocks and ornaments that were not new. It had to be Diana's horse. How had it landed up here? He cast his mind back to the room at Lady Farthingdale's house when he had first arrived. What could he remember? Not much, except the ornate clock on the mantle shelf.

He peered into the dark interior. There on a cabinet was the clock just as he remembered it. This was Diana's horse and the Bristows had taken it and brought here to sell. The shop was closed but he would return in the morning.

He had trouble relaxing with his drink so he returned to the coaching inn and settled himself to write a long and detailed letter to his grandfather Arnott.

"Is Mr Barnam back?"

"Who shall I say is calling, sir?"

"Michael Arnott."

The clerk disappeared into the bowels of the building and returned to take him to a pleasant room overlooking a small garden.

"Mr Arnott. How can I help you? I am Herbert Wilford, I am afraid Barnam is away at present."

"I was hoping he had returned from Bath. I met him at Lady Farthingdale's funeral."

"Then you know his mission."

"Indeed. I met Constance when she stayed with Miss Newby until he fetched her away."

"We are expecting him back tomorrow but that is by no means certain. Is this a courtesy call or is there anything I can help you with?"

"I do not know how much Barnam told you, but Miss Newby had a statue of a bronze horse stolen on the day of the funeral. We were certain it was taken by the Bristow sons; the family cleared the house of everything moveable they could sell, including Diana's horse."

"I do remember Barnam mentioning it. After all the help she had given to the old lady, it was a dreadful thing to happen. Have you spoken with the Bristows?"

"Their mother, yes, but the horse never re-appeared. Now I have located it in a shop just around the next corner. I wondered if you could give me any idea of how to proceed. It is an expensive piece and I prefer not to pay a large sum for someone to profit from a theft."

"At Warley's! I am surprised. Warley is usually very careful he never buys anything stolen. We once had to act for him over an item; he was innocent of any criminal action, he had no idea it did not belong to the seller, but it has made him very wary. Perhaps if I accompanied you we could come to some arrangement."

Warley was indeed concerned, especially with the lawyer there.

"I understood everything came from his aunt's house after she died."

"Lady Farthingdale's house. Yes, there were ornaments there which were probably brought to you. They are legally theirs. The horse, however, is not."

"You are sure? You say the other items are legal."

"I never took notice of the ornaments they took but I do remember that clock." He indicated the ornate timepiece sat prominently displayed."

"How can you be sure who owned the horse."

"Miss Newby was left it in the will of my Great Aunt, Mrs Letitia Fortesque. She found it missing immediately after everyone had left. They had thrown it out of her bedroom window and gone round to retrieve it. There was a deep indent in the soft earth and footprints."

"Did you report it to the constable?"

"No. He is a friend of the Bristows. I went and gave a quiet threat to their mother in the hope they would return it. Nothing happened, obviously, because the horse is here."

"I paid good money for it."

"And I will reimburse you for any loss. Although I am not prepared to pay for a large profit. Mr Barnam will reassure you when he returns that we had discussed the loss and the possibility of a prosecution, when he visited the house more than a week ago."

Maybe it was the mention of a prosecution that sent Mr Warley to retrieve his account book.

"Here it is, Mr Wilford. It is as the young gentleman said. Mr Bristow brought a large number of items from his Aunt's house. He said Mr Barnam had the will and they owned the items. He never mentioned the horse, of course."

"You paid ten pounds for it!"

"It would be worth a great deal more than that in London. Mr Wilford"

Michael took out his note case and drew out two notes.

"I believe it will be easier for everyone if I reimbursed you for what you paid. If you wish to check with Mr Barnam when he returns he will be able to reassure you. My name is Arnott."

Michael sat on the bed in his room. Now he had the horse what was he going to do? He had to take it back to Diana, and that meant seeing her again. Half of him wanted to go, half of him dreaded the dismissal he was expecting. He could deal with the rejection of his family, the attitude of the Newmans. The Bristows had just brought out his determination for retribution, his willingness to fight against all bullies. The rejection by Diana, however, was more that he could handle. Had he the heart to go back and face her. Perhaps he could ask Wilford to have it delivered.

He had a meal while he thought. He was hungry. Why was he so hungry? When had he last eaten? Not since breakfast at Diana's.

The barman was remonstrating with the middle-aged waitress.

"When have I ever hit you, Maudie? Just because he hit you, you think everyone will. Get back in the kitchen and stop making problems."

She had not seemed a timid woman. He indicated he required another drink. The barman brought it himself, quicker than waiting for the woman to return.

"She doesn't seem the complaining kind."

"Problem is, if anyone lifts their hand near her she reacts badly. I only went to lift down a glass. She'll apologise later, she knows she can't help it." Michael finished his meal and was enjoying his drink. The waitress came out of the kitchen and cleared away his plate. "Sorry about that, sir. I don't seem to be able to stop it. I just panic."

"At least they understand."

"Yes, sir. I am grateful for that."

He stood from the table. He was no nearer to making a decision. He climbed the stairs slowly. When he was half way up it hit him. Diana! Diana had been attacked, pinned down in her bed, fought for her life. The waitress had said she could not help it. What if Diana could not help it, if she had just reacted to him leaning her against the wall to kiss her? Why had it not occurred to him before? She was such a capable young woman who would imagine she would react like that. He needed to know, to find out. Decision made. He was going back with the horse.

It was late when he unsaddled his horse. It had taken him longer to ride there with the horse balanced in front of him. The night was dark but the moon had just started to rise, casting an eerie light over the orchard as he carried his saddlebags over his shoulder and the horse under his arm. He walked without thinking to the side door, distracted by something laying on the ground. Bark. Long thin strips of willow bark newly peeled from the tree. He hoped they did not intend to burn them for a good long time, they made nothing but smoke when they were this green.

He tried the side door and it opened. How strange. He had expected to have to wake someone to get in. He had specifically warned them to keep the doors locked.

He struggled in, pulling the bolts on the door before entering the dark, silent room. Everyone had retired.

He went into his room and put the horse on the dressing table, thankful to let it down. His saddlebags he put onto the bed. The moon was just starting to shine into the room, touching the bed. Something was wrong. He lit the candle and looked around; the bed was not made up, they had not expected him. There was a smell that permeated the room. A smell of smoke. He had not smelt it in the main room. Someone had lit a fire in here with that willow bark. It must have been choking, the smell was stale but it still hung about. He went to the window and opened the upper casement for fresh air.

He removed his coat and boots and placed his pistol on the table beside the horse. Tomorrow he would give it to Diana. What would she say? Would she dismiss him before looking at the horse? What if he put the horse in her room and she saw it when she awoke. He liked that idea.

Chapter 31

In his stockinged feet Michael walked quietly to Diana's room carrying the horse. He caught his sleeve on the key in the door. Why was the key on the outside? Silently crossing to her dressing table he lowered the horse, misjudged in the dark, and it made a clunk as it landed. Michael held his breath.

"Eliza. Is that you Eliza?"

No help for it. He was discovered. "No, it's Michael."

The bed covers and hangings moved and Diana, wearing only her night rail, erupted from the bed, flew across the space and threw herself at him, clinging to him with her arms around his chest as if her life depended on it.

"Michael, you came back. I'm sorry, I don't know what I said but I'm sorry!"

Shock made him hesitate, but only for a moment, before he closed his arms around her and leaned his head on the top of hers.

"I realised this morning. You reacted when I pinned you against the wall. I'll know never to do that again, I thought you hated me."

"Hate you. If only you knew, Michael."

"Perhaps I do. If you have suffered even a part of what I have been through in the last three days. I forgot to eat for two of them."

Diana realised the position she was in and tried to pull away, but Michael was not yet ready to release her.

"I can't let you go, Diana, I love you too much. Marry me. Never send me away again. Let me take care of you."

"What if I react that way all the time?"

"I need to find out what it is that causes that, and avoid doing it. I have to tell you, I have no experience with women. You are the only one I have ever wanted, so we might have to experiment. Be patient with me. At least I know not to leave next time."

She eased back a little and tilted her face up to his. "Perhaps if you kiss me we could start now."

Eyes shining he bent his head to touch his lips to hers. "If I feel you reacting I shall stop immediately. By the way, you never answered me."

"Answered you?"

"Will you marry me?"

"Of course, Michael. I thought we had come to that decision before you left."

"Then I will now proceed to attempt to compromise my fiancée. Like I said, this is the blind leading the blind. I know what happens, I've listened to the men talk, I have just never done it. Now I intend to see how far you will allow me to go."

He felt her giggle turn into a satisfied sigh.

Michael turned his mind back to the day in France when the men gave Simons a talk on how to seduce a woman. He had paid special attention.

Stroke her hair, kiss her, try to get her into your arms where you could get your hands on her. Well he had managed that without even trying. He stroked her hair, and she buried her face in his chest, she liked that. He speared his finger to her scalp and massaged, she was enjoying that. He held her head in his hand and gently eased it away to give him access to her face in order to kiss her again.

It started out as a gentle kiss but what happened next surprised both of them. Were kisses supposed to be like this? The tingles began in his chest and surged up his neck and into his jaw as he pressed further into her mouth. She parted her lips which allowed him to run his tongue over hers, stroking it. He only lifted his head when they both ran out of breath.

Stroke her back, nuzzle her neck, women like that. So did he. He buried his face in her neck while she laid her head back in pleasure. He let his face lower to her throat and felt her body tremble.

"Are you all right?"

"My feet are cold."

"Oh. Should you put your slippers on?"

Diana giggled. "How romantic. I thought you were trying to compromise me? My feet would be much warmer in bed."

Desire spiked through him.

"If you are sure." He walked her to the bed and pulled down the bed covers.

"Are you keeping your clothes on?"

"Oh. I suppose not."

"A fine lothario you are." she laughed.

Diana started to unbutton his waistcoat and shirt. If she continued like that he would not need to unbutton his breeches, he would burst the buttons off. By degrees they stripped him of his clothes, leaving them lying where they dropped. The first problem was when he tried to lift her night rail. Diana froze.

"Ah, we have a problem. Perhaps you should remove your nightgown yourself, you seem to react when I try."

She settled, calmed, then tipped her face up to his to be kissed. Then she pulled up the material and raised it to her head, he helped her remove the last of it.

She climbed into the bed and he followed her causing her to roll into the hollow, and into him. "Oh!" He took advantage of it and wrapped his arms around her.

This was like nothing he had ever experienced in his life. No wonder the men talked about it. The feel of a naked woman, one who was to be his wife, was almost more that he could handle. Next move. Stroke her. Stroke her back, her bottom, her legs, her stomach, her breasts. Then kiss everywhere, especially her breasts. Apparently women liked that, they were sensitive. Suckle the nipples. Surely not. He would have to try.

He started stroking; apparently she intended to do the same to him. Her bottom brought a reaction to both of them. She was soft, smooth and he wanted to hold it and pull her closer. Close to his now very erect member.

When he stroked her legs she wrapped them around his, pressing into him while his fingers moved to the inside of her thigh.

She was trembling.

"I'm not upsetting you, am I?"

"Don't stop now!"

Obviously not then.

When his fingers reached the top of her inner thigh she leapt, her fingers gripping his arms. A moan escaped her. She was not the only one, he wanted to moan. He was beginning to throb.

Keep control.

He gently pressed her onto her back and ran his fingers down the front of her, she was squirming. He lowered his face to kiss her neck and upper breasts, stroking one with his fingers and gradually running his mouth over the other. Lower his fingers stroked and lower. He flattened his hand on her stomach and his mouth accidentally touched her nipple. He felt the tremor that went through her. Oh, obviously she did like that.

He was having difficulty remembering what came next. Something to do with the curls between her legs, a little hard nub to stroke and putting a finger inside her. A finger! He wanted more than a finger there.

His hand seemed to know what to do. He stroked as he suckled at her breasts and she grew uncontrolled, grasping at him, thrusting her breast into his mouth. When he pushed a finger inside her he found the little hard nub with his thumb. Oh, that was it. He rubbed and felt her body lift and shake, covering his fingers with juice. Her breathing was uneven, her hands gripping at him. He was still suckling her and stroking between her legs. She was still needy, but he had forgotten what he should be doing. There was only one thing he wanted to do now.

He removed his hand and rolled onto her, lifting himself onto his arms and knees to avoid trapping her with his weight. His body seemed to know where he wanted to be. He used one hand to steer himself where his finger had been, then thrust home.

She cried out.

He should stop, he knew there was a reason he should stop, but he could not. He let his body take over and rock into her. Withdraw, and press in, withdraw and press in, riding her. Suddenly she began to answer him, to grip him with her body, to answer each invasion, moaning and panting. He had no control now, he could not stop. He pressed in one last time and felt his body empty into her. Her body was arched as she gripped him and they collapsed together into the rumpled sheets, entwined together in the hollow in the mattress.

Mine

In total contented exhaustion they slept.

And Michael dreamed.

He was in Villefranche, laying by the camp fire in the dark. In his arms he held the body of Newman. He had to get him away to safety. Where were his men, they should have been there. Someone was there; he could hear them in the periphery of his hearing.

His men had gone, they had put out the camp fire but it still smoked. He knew he had to move, to take Newman with him. He tried to move but he kept rolling back. He heard a click, was that a gun being cocked. His instincts brought him to awareness. Where was he?

The body in his arms coughed and he was wide awake.

The room was full of smoke, it was getting hard to breathe. In his arms he held his future wife; he had to keep her safe.

"Diana, wake up, my sweet."

"Mmmm." cough

"Diana, wake up, the room is full of smoke, we have to get out. You have to get dressed."

Diana blinked her eyes and coughed.

"Get dressed, my darling. We have to get out. There is a fire of some kind."

He hauled her out of the bed and stood her on her feet. She moved towards the chair in a sleepy daze and started to dress.

Michael went to the window to give them some fresh air. He had to be careful, too much air could cause the smoke to turn to raging fire.

The window was stuck. He tried another. By the time he had tried all the casements he knew. The windows had been nailed shut. This was serious.

He drew on his breeches and shirt and went to the door, it was locked. The floor was hot to his feet. He went to the bedside table and lit the candle, inspected the floor and realised. Beneath the door fronds of green willow had been pushed and they were smoking.

They had to get out. He wished he had his gun he could have shot the lock off, but that was in the next room. He would have to break the window.

"Wrap yourself in your cloak and hold this to your nose." He wetted his handkerchief in the water in the pitcher and gave it to Diana. In crossing the floor he kicked his waistcoat and it made a noise. His pocket knife.

He needed to break the glass but the noise would alert whoever was doing this. What if there was anyone outside. He would have to take that risk.

The windows were much painted but the wood beneath was not in good condition. His pocket knife was sharp and easily cut through the glazing bars. Carefully he prized out the small panes of glass and laid them against the wall. Once the first came out fresh air flooded in, but drew the smoke towards them.

He sat Diana on the upright chair within the protection of the curtains, closing them isolated them from most of the smoke. When he had removed enough to allow his shoulders through, he prepared to climb out. One last thought made him fetch the bronze horse and put it on Diana's knee.

"Don't come out unless you have to. It could be dangerous. If anyone tries to grab you, hit them with it." He leaned down and kissed her.

"I love you."

Then he climbed feet first out of the window in the hope there was no-one waiting to attack. He felt a sliver of glass scrape his arm, the blood running. If that were the worst he sustained this night then he would not complain. It was a pity he had locked the side door but at least he had left a window open in his bedroom where his pistols were.

The open casement was quite high up. At first he could not understand why he was struggling to climb in. Why was he so tired. Then he remembered the last few hours. Oh! Well he could not complain about that.

He landed head first on the floor and rolled as quietly as possible. On the table sat his pistol. Then he thought of the small pocket pistol he had in his coat pocket. Best to be prepared.

He sidled around the partly open door, a pistol in each hand.

The sight that confronted him made him breathe in with anger.

There was a good fire burning in the grate and before it a man with a scarf around his mouth and nose was poking fronds of green willow into it. They gradually took light and began to smoulder, giving off quantities of smoke. By Diana's door there was another man, feeding the fronds beneath it, his progress lighted by the kitchen maid holding a candle, a cloth held at her face. Michael stepped forward.

"What the hell do you think you are doing!" He virtually shouted it.

The maid dropped the candle and fled, the man by the door let out a yelp as the hot wax fell on him. The man at the fire turned towards him and Michael saw the light from the fire glint on the metal of a gun. He fired. Anyone who was listening would have only heard one reverberating shot, but Michael felt the sting of pain in his side as the man before the fire fell.

The second man had now sprung into action and drawn his pistol. Michael was nearer to him and fired his small pocket pistol into his right shoulder, making him drop his gun and scream with pain.

A stream of cold air flowed into the room from the kitchen. The maid had obviously made her escape. If she fetched help he could be in trouble. Judging by the pain in his side he already was.

To the side of the fireplace the small door from the attic rooms opened to admit Eliza carrying a candle.

"Eliza. It's Michael. I need help. Light some candles will you."

She went from candelabra to candelabra gradually lighting the dreadful scene.

"This one is still moving. What can we tie him up with? Is there any cord?" The man from near Diana's door was gradually trying to edge his way towards the front door, his scarf still in place.

Eliza brought the curtain ties and they secured his hands and feet. While Michael tied the chord Eliza tried to hold him still and was kicked. Whilst she was not looking Michael kicked him in his bad shoulder. He wailed and passed out.

"Open a front window, Eliza." he started to draw the fronds from under Diana's door, then he threw them out into the front garden where they could smoke all they wanted. He unlocked Diana's bedroom door and called inside.

"You can come out, Diana. All is safe now."

Diana came out brandishing her horse, looking around the room with wide eyes. She put the horse on a table and went into Michael's arms.

"Oh Michael." He swayed. "Michael, you're bleeding!"

"I took a bullet in my side. I feel a little weak, my love. Would you mind if I sit down." He subsided into a chair.

"Eliza, go to Dicky and tell him to fetch the doctor. Mr Arnott has been shot. We need the Constable as well."

Eliza needed no second telling. In her dressing gown and slippers she was running down the road. Mr Michael needed help.

Within minutes both men were on their cart and away for the doctor and constable.

When Eliza arrived back at the house, Michael was laid on a chaise, his shirt removed, Diana pressing a wad of cloth to his side. He looked pale even in the candlelight.

"Is there any brandy Eliza, or did they take it."

"I think they took it, Miss."

"Then can you find a way to make some tea. I doubt the kitchen fire is still in but this one should be good enough to boil a kettle."

"Where is the kitchen maid?"

"Gone. She was holding the candle for him." Michael's voice was weak. He had lost a lot of blood.

Eliza bustled about boiling water, closing the kitchen door and bolting it. They would not be surprised from that direction. She checked the side door and bolted it. Stepping daintily over the man by the fire, Eliza studiously ignored him. The sooner someone arrived the better.

It was nearly an hour before the doctor arrived, having had to be roused from his bed, and have his gig brought out.

Eliza let him in the front door and he walked in to a battle scene. He took in the motionless man by the fire, the semi-conscious man bound hand and foot and Michael Arnott laid on the sofa. Diana was holding a wad of blood-soaked cloth to his side with one hand and spooning tea into his mouth with the other. The house smelt of smoke and blood with an underlying hint of gunpowder.

"Let's have a look at you." He sent Eliza for a bowl of water and more cloths and began to wash the blood away. "Looks like you took a bullet. It seems to have gone right through, that's why it bled so much. Which one shot you?"

"The one by the fire."

"Who are they?"

"No idea. Never looked. They were feeding smoking willow fronds under Diana's door. The window has been nailed shut."

He whistled "How did they get in?"

"The kitchen maid. The side door was unbolted when I arrived late this evening."

"It's last evening now."

"Oh. Lost track of time."

"For all the blood you have lost, it is not a bad injury. I have not had to dig out a bullet which helps. Judging by the pain I would say it bounced off your rib, could have taken some bone off. It saved worse internal damage. Some brandy might help."

"The Bristows took it after the funeral."

"Is there much the Bristows did not take?"

"The best sheets. That's about all. They never found those."

The doctor stood up and stretched, looked down at the two men but left them for the Constable, he should be here soon. "It might be best if I wait." He walked to a chair and dropped into it. His eyes alighted on the horse.

He went to it and ran his hand down it. "Is this the famous disappearing horse. When was it returned?"

"Michael brought it back last night. He brought it to me and we put it back on my dressing table, then they locked us in. They didn't know Michael was here they thought it was only me in there."

The doctor looked at Michael. "That was lucky. If she had been alone."

"Don't remind me."

"Get some rest if you can. The Constable will need you to be alert when he comes. I will see to the wounded one shortly. He seems out of it at the moment."

It was daylight by the time Constable Pinter arrived. He was of the opinion this was a case of an attempted theft, until he came into the house.

"Who are they?"

"We have no idea. We left them as they were for you. One is dead, the other is not conscious. I was loath to revive him."

He looked around the room. "Why are they here, there is nothing to steal?"

"To kill Miss Newby."

"You don't know that."

"Yes I do, Constable. I found Miss Newby's stolen bronze horse in a shop in Nottingham. It was with the ornaments taken from here by the Bristows. The man admitted he bought the ornaments from a Mr Bristow. Most of them were theirs but not the horse; that belongs to Miss Newby and the Bristows knew that. I brought it back late last night."

He went on to describe exactly what had happened after he arrived, leaving out the most personal information, and how he had come to shoot the intruders and in his turn be shot in the side "I shot that one in the shoulder to disable him when he also pulled a gun."

Michael slumped back on the sofa.

"What happened then?"

Eliza answered. "I heard a noise and came downstairs. Mr Michael asked me to help him and light the candles. He had been shot but he put the smoking bark out of the front window. We opened the door for Miss Diana and I went for Dick and Dicky while she helped Mr Michael. We made tea for him to drink."

"Tea. Brandy would have been better, surely."

"We don't have any. The Bristows took everything after the funeral."

The Constable looked a little mortified, they knew he was friendly with them.

"Perhaps you are a little upset at the moment." That was an understatement.

The doctor harrumphed.

"Perhaps we should see if we recognise these two."

The Constable walked over to the man laying by the fire and pulled at his scarf.

They heard his intake of breath.

"I presume he is dead? I never bothered to check. I was too busy dealing with Mr Arnott."

The doctor walked over to the man by the fire. He looked down and blinked. He knew now why the constable had been shocked.

"The other one is still alive. He just has a bullet in his shoulder."

310

Constable Pinter went reluctantly to the other man and removed his scarf. Now they all knew who both men was. This one was Wilfred Bristow. The dead one was Reginald."

Chapter 32

The doctor made sure Constable Pinter wrote everything in his book. Then they found Dick, outside taking care of the doctor's gig, and sent him to fetch Dicky back with the cart to transport Reginald's body to the Bristow house. Wilfred, now somewhat more revived, was examined and pronounced alive enough to have the bullet removed. It took some time and a great deal of blood, the bullet being of small calibre from the pocket pistol it was difficult to find. Wilfred was loaded into the doctor's gig, still bound to prevent escape, and taken with the Constable to be locked up.

Strangely, it was the Constable who made the last remark.

"Lock all your doors. The Bristows will come and you are in no condition to deal with them."

They locked and bolted the doors, they locked Diana's bedroom door until Dick was able to bring some wood and nail it over the window. They prepared Michael's bed, and the attic room for Diana. They checked all the windows were shut and even locked the doors to Lady Farthingdale's rooms in the off chance that someone might break in there.

The cook had to knock on the back door but found it was not the kitchen maid who answered but Diana herself. The door was bolted after her and the silent house waited.

They heard the Bristow coach arrive followed by hammering on the door. They closed the curtains to stop them from looking in. It took only a day for the whole area to know what had happened. Gradually the neighbours came calling, asking after Mr Arnott's health and offering assistance. It seemed they were not the only family the Bristow boys had upset.

Michael was too weak to travel to the Coroner's court but the doctor went. Constable Pinter reported accurately everything he had seen, including the dreadful smell of smoke that permeated the whole house.

The Coroner gave a verdict of self defence against felons caught in the act of a criminal offence. Wilfred was sentenced to hang for the 'intent to murder' of Miss Diana Newby. The district was in shock. The Bristows disappeared. The maid had left the area.

Michael regained his strength quickly but was advised not to ride for at least two weeks. The wound was healing well but the pain from the damaged rib was a problem.

Diana sat and read to him until he refused to stay in bed. He kept hauling her against his right side to kiss her. Eliza tried not to notice.

A week later a large travelling coach arrived with a coat of arms blazoned on the side.

Eliza opened the door with some trepidation as the Earl of Selgrove strode in with all the confidence of his position.

"Diana, Miss Newby. I have just returned from Cornwall where a letter reached me saying my Aunt has died. If I had known in time I would have been here. Is there any way I can help you."

He looked around at the empty surfaces. The furniture still stained with blood, the air of neglect.

"What happened here!"

Michael had risen from his chair and introduced himself.

"Arnott, sir. Miss Newby and I are to be married, but at present I cannot ride." The Earl took his hand.

"Arnott. I have heard the name before. Have you known Miss Newby long?"

"Since we were small. We lived in the same area."

Selgrove looked intrigued but asked no more questions for the time being. He subsided into the cleanest chair and listened with horror to everything that had occurred.

"You intend to leave soon?"

"We would have been gone before but the doctor forbade Michael to ride and we need to send for his grandfather's coach to transport us."

He turned to Michael. "Are you well enough to move, sir?"

"Indeed. I believe the doctor is being over cautious. While I accept I cannot ride yet, I am otherwise quite well."

"Then the least I can do is to offer my carriage."

The Arnott household was thrown into a frenzy with the arrival of the Earl's carriage carrying a wounded Mr Michael, a young lady with a maid both requiring a room, not to mention an Earl and his entourage.

Grandfather Arnott was relieved to have Michael back safely if not completely sound. Miss Newby he had met before but the Earl was a surprise to him.

The Earl stayed the following day although he gave no reason, announcing he would leave the day after. After dinner Grandfather Arnott retired and they relaxed in the parlour that had been little used in recent times. Selgrove seemed thoughtful, occupied.

"Diana, Miss Newby. I have a favour to ask. Since talking with you before Christmas I have been searching for any sign of a Pennington in London. I need to find if the girl I am searching for it is this Miss Firbeck. If you know she is in the country could you tell me where?"

Diana froze, Michael dropped his glass.

"How do you know the name?"

Selgrove looked shocked at Michael's sharp tone of voice."

"Diana told me a little of what happened to her when we were at the Petersford's Christmas house party. I have been looking for a girl named Lucinda Ferndale for over four years.

She sounded just like this Lucy Firbeck who married a Pennington."

Michael turned to Diana. "You told him the name?"

Diana was in tears now. Michael went to comfort her, drawing her up and putting his arms around her, locking her against him, her head in his chest. Selgrove, to give him his due, looked concerned.

"I had no intention of upsetting you, Diana. I just need to find her. I will not mention you."

"How do you intend to do that, Selgrove? You want to find some girl from the past and you are prepared to put Diana in grave danger."

Selgrove looked perplexed. "It is four years, they will have forgotten."

"No. You have no idea. If they knew Diana was even alive they could have her arrested and hanged for a theft she has not committed. Lucy is a powerful woman, vicious and vindictive. I was there less than a month ago. Every week she announces she has found another ornament Diana is supposed to have stolen. The ladies look up to her, the men think her a paragon of virtue. George Pennington is the local magistrate and never checks anything. If they knew where Diana was she could be put in danger, just for you to see this missing girl from your past."

"Is there any way I could see her without meeting her. I would know her immediately. Do you know where her parents are?"

"No. they left the area. I am not sure even Lucy knows."

"That makes it even more likely it is Lucinda. To reassure you, Arnott—it is not me who wants to find her, it is Bow Street. They are still looking for the girl who poisoned my wife four years ago."

Michael and Diana turned to face him, she with wide eyes, Michael with a strange look on his face. He gently seated Diana and walked over the decanter to pour himself a brandy. The room remained quiet.

He turned to face Selgrove."Tell me."

It was Selgrove's turn to look distressed. Michael walked over to him and put his brandy glass in his hand, returning to pour himself another.

"When I met Madeleine my life changed, I had never been so happy. Her family were not wealthy, nor did they have a house in London. I made the mistake of inviting them to come and live in my London house where she could see them daily. It pleased her. After six months the doctor advised me she was carrying my child, I was ecstatic with happiness. Then she began to be ill. At first the doctor thought it just caused by her condition, but gradually she became worse. It was nearly four months later when she died. She could not even recognise me at the end, her sister was having to feed her. When she had become ill I tried to encourage her by buying her favourite pastry from the nearby shop, those our cook made were not the same, she said. Nor were the ones I bought. When her sister brought them they were sprinkled with what looked like sugar. After she died they cleaned out her room and the housekeeper came to me with a small white apothecary's box found behind a chest. The maid had said her sister brought them, and that they had often seen them but now they had all disappeared.

"The doctor checked. She had been feeding her sister Arsenic. She tried to take over my house. I believe she coveted the position of my Countess. The family had taken a house of their own after Madeleine died, but the doctor had questioned them so they knew there was a problem. I went to Bow Street but when they arrived the family had left, very suddenly. I have been looking ever since."

"Do you really think she and Lucy are the same person?"

"It is very possible. I just need to see her, I will do no more."

Michael sat thoughtful, head in his hands.

"You must be careful to mention neither of our names."

"I am aware you are in some way connected, Arnott. You said Diana was companion to your Great Aunt, but Diana had said she had been family to the Penningtons. Logic tells me that Arnott was not originally your name. Can you give me any information?"

"I believe you are right, I have reason to believe Lucy is your wife's sister. What a dreadful situation, all because I left one hour too early."

Both of them looked at him in surprise.

"I heard her say she had dealt with someone's betrothal but I thought it was that of Lord Williams. She had been trying to attract him the week before at Harcourt's dinner, apparently. The men were laughing about it."

"Lord Williams. You know him?"

"No, I was never invited."

"But Harcourt—Williams can't stand the fellow. He used to be reasonable but recently he has become dreadful. He calls him Hang them Harcourt."

"Now perhaps you understand the danger to Diana. Lucy has instilled into them how guilty she is."

"Perhaps I could enrol Williams, get him to take me to Harcourt's to meet this Lucy Pennington."

"She would recognise you."

"True. If it is her she would disappear again. This will take some thinking through."

Diana was still distressed. "I think I will retire if you will excuse me." They acknowledged the bow of her head. Michael took her hand and kissed it. He looked deep into her eyes. She was frightened. Perhaps tonight he might test his recovery, even if it was only to hold her close.

"What do you know, Arnott? You are family to the Pennington's, I believe. Now Diana has retired what can you tell me."

"That Frederick never checks anything. He is, or was, naïve and gullible and Lucy told him Diana had gone into raptures over an ornament and now it was missing. She directed him to have her room searched. They found it, of course. He always believed anything he was told. His father is the same, especially if Frederick, his perfect son, tells him. They threw her out on the spot. If it had not been a house party he might have had her hanged then, but her family were there and all the local gentry. That is probably what saved her."

"Who is Frederick?"

"Diana was betrothed to him. They were due to marry in three weeks' time."

"Why would she take the risk of stealing an ornament when she would be moving in?"

"My point exactly. I told Frederick that a month ago. He knows now. Little use it will do him, married to a viper like Lucy."

"Have you always loved Diana?"

"Yes, I suppose I have, although I have never had the means to take a wife. I'm not sure I have now."

"Will you not inherit from your grandfather?"

"No, Frederick will." Michael stopped, realising what he had said.

Selgrove's voice was quiet. "Frederick is your brother."

"Not any more. Diana was not the only one he never checked on the truth. Hers was only once, mine was my whole life. The only person ever to check was Grandfather Arnott. He knew it was all lies but nobody will ever believe good of me."

"That's why you went into the army." Michael looked surprised. "Eliza said you were an officer in the army. I had wondered why you did not use the rank you held."

"Wrong name."

"I can understand that now. Perhaps if I talk to Williams he could find information for me, or even introduce me to this dreadful Harcourt. At least I could find out more."

"I'll give you more information. She has been giving my mother arsenic until she is barely lucid."

"Good God, Arnott. Are you sure?"

"Pretty sure. I told my … Pennington. It is up to him what he does with the information."

"Does anyone else know?"

"No. Please don't let my grandfather know. It is his daughter. I doubt he would survive the shock.

Later that night Diana felt a warm heavy body slide into the bed beside her and turned into his arms. Michael had known, he had understood. Now she could feel safe if only for that one night.

The Earl of Selgrove left later than he had intended. He waited until Grandfather Arnott was downstairs then spoke with him in his study. When they came out Selgrove was smiling. That was one weight off his mind.

Chapter 33

"I wonder how long before Williams returns, Carstairs." Selgrove was idly fingering the glass cupped in his hand.

"You seem in a hurry to see him. I was not aware you knew him that well."

"I admit you only introduced me to him recently, but I need some knowledge from him. Do you remember me mentioning at Christmas wanting to find someone called Pennington? Apparently he knows them, or knows of them."

"Pennington. He does. We met someone of that name a few weeks ago. There is more than one family, I do know. There were officers there who perked up when they heard his name. They had known a Captain in France they thought highly of. He never spoke about his family, there was no correspondence from any Pennington family members, so there are at least two families with that name. It might be this Captain's family you are looking for."

A Captain Pennington. Well Selgrove knew who that was, and he was definitely of the same family.

"Bembridge is a friend of his; he might know when to expect him." Carstairs stood and waved over to Bembridge drinking with friends on the opposite side of the club room. He heaved his large frame out of the chair and came to join them.

"Carstairs. How are you? Not seen you recently, been a bit busy."

"Have a seat, Bembridge, you know Selgrove."

"I do. How are you. Still off the marriage mart?"

Selgrove grimaced. "Things to clear up before I stick my toe in there again."

"After all this time! Not involved in this Wentworth affair are you?"

"Wentworth, not a name I recognise. I am more interested in when Lord Williams will return. I wish to speak with him urgently."

"Williams, well who knows when he will be back. He is involved over Wentworth. Not him personally but a cousin of his. Seems Wentworth's finances are not all they should be. Bit of a scandal brewing, could leave a few in a bad position. Williams has posted down there to warn him."

Whites was agog over the Wentworth scandal. All his clients seemed to have been losing capital for quite some time.

Williams appeared one lunchtime with a very serious older man. Selgrove waited while several approached him for information and when everyone had left them Selgrove strolled over.

"Williams, good to see you back. I understand you were away on unpleasant business."

"Hello Selgrove. Yes I have been. This is a relation of mine, Harcourt. Been trying to sort everything out for him."

The two men nodded to each other. "Don't suppose you were involved with Wentworth?"

"No. I have never come across him. Have you lost much?"

"About half, we think. We were lucky. If Tucker had not alerted Williams it could have been much worse. He was about to decamp abroad with a large quantity in gold and jewels. He must have been planning this for some time."

"Is he being held?"

"Yes. Bow Street have him locked away while we find exactly how much is missing."

"Who is looking in to it?"

"Lansdale, he trained Tucker after he left Wentworth. Wentworth's clerk came to warn Tucker. He suspected something was amiss."

"A blessing for everyone involved. If you have no objection, may I change the subject under discussion?"

"Please do, Selgrove. I fear the constant discussion is wearing Harcourt down."

"I understand you and Carstairs met a Mr Pennington recently."

Harcourt shook his head in disbelief. "At least Pennington has land to recoup his losses."

"Is he involved with Wentworth?"

"Oh yes. Years ago he encouraged us all to use him. Most of us stayed with him. The whole district could be wiped out, except for Pennington. Mind you, he has his own problems. His wife is very sick and his son Frederick, who you met recently," he nodded to Williams "has thrown off his wife."

Selgrove sat up in surprise. "Where is she?"

"Somewhere in London in a rented house. How he will afford to keep her here if they lost much, I dread to think."

Lord Williams had also perked up at the information. "What, that dreadful Lucy woman?"

"I thought you liked her."

"Why do you think you have seen me so seldom in the last few years?"

"Good God, Williams. Why did you not say?"

"You all seemed so enamoured of her."

"Well, we were misled. It seems she has lied to us for years, my wife is distraught. Young Frederick made a clean breast of it. It took some courage to admit how naïve he had been. It also seems he was the cause of his father's anger against his brother, not intentionally, but still he believes it has ruined his life, and driven him away." Harcourt looked rather uncomfortable.

"How can I find out where she is?"

"Why on earth do you want to meet her?"

"I do not want to meet her, only to see if I recognise her. I am looking for a Lucinda Ferndale who fits the description of Lucy Firbeck, who appeared shortly after Lucinda disappeared."

Lord Williams had not known Selgrove long enough to know about how his wife had died. "Is there a particular reason?" Williams could see the tension in Selgrove's face. "You seem very concerned."

"I have been searching for four years and this is the first time I have learned of someone with a similar name and character."

"I can give you what information I have, Selgrove. What do you need to know?"

"Where are her parents and is she their only child."

"The Firbecks? Well I found it strange at the time. They moved out shortly after Lucy married, telling nobody where they were going. As to a sister, there was none when we knew them, but the ladies did say Mrs Firbeck intimated Lucy had not been her only child."

"Thank you, Harcourt. That is informative. I would prefer it if you did not tell anyone of my interest. Do you know what ails the senior Mrs Pennington?"

"She is very much in decline and the doctor ordered complete rest. They moved into an empty house on the estate. Even Lucy was not allowed to visit."

"How revealing. I must make enquiries of Lucy Pennington in London. What kind of house would her husband take, by that I mean what locations could he afford?"

"Not too grand, although Lucy would not stay in an unfashionable area."

"Thank you, that was all very helpful. May I repay by inviting you both to dine at my expense."

"Very generous of you, Selgrove." Lord Williams held up his hand to call the steward and order another drink for them.

"Carstairs, can you make a few quiet enquiries for me. Use any friends you can trust. I have reason to believe Lucinda Ferndale is in London. She may be using her married name of Pennington, or she may have taken another."

"Madeleine's sister!"

"Madeleine's murderer. Be careful not to alert her. She seems to be keeping the name Lucy. I am going to visit the Pennington family if I can. I have the feeling she was removing her mother-in-law in the same way. It will help our proof if that is the case. I will alert Bow Street I might have information for them. At least they will be ready to act if it proves true.

While his friends searched London, Selgrove rode down to the Pennington estate and took a room in the local inn, not exactly his normal level of accommodation. He made a few enquiries about who lived where, and then began to question Willy, the innkeeper.

"You're new in these parts, then?"

"Yes. I know little of the area, although Lord Williams had mentioned it on occasion."

"You know his Lordship then. Do you know Harcourt too?"

"I only met him once recently in London."

"Ah, in London. Been a bit of trouble all round."

"I heard about Pennington throwing off his wife. How do the locals feel about that?"

Willy leaned forward to speak more quietly. "To tell you the truth, sir, she was nothing but trouble. Nasty with it. They do say as Mr Frederick's parents left to get away from her."

"Is that so? She sounds dreadful."

"She had Miss Butterwick thrown out so she could marry Mr Frederick. Captain Michael was looking for her, threatened to have his father charged with murder but she never died around here. No-one knows what became of her."

"It looks such a nice area to live in too."

"It was, sir: in the past. Now nobody will give you the time of day."

"They say Mrs Pennington is very ill. Do you know what is wrong with her?"

"Couldn't say, sir. Even the servants aren't talking. Doctor Gordon is doing the best he can for her, goes in nearly every day."

"Doctor Gordon. Local is he?"

"Yes, sir. The big house down by the bridge."

"Thank you; Willy, is it? Another tankard of your excellent brew, if you will." He found it barely drinkable but he was not about to say that.

Selgrove wandered down the lane to the bridge. It was a pleasant place and reminded him of his country estate. He really should spend more time there, but there was a problem, it reminded him of how lonely he was without Madeleine. Perhaps he should think about marrying again, after all he needed an heir. Maybe if he could satisfy this need in him to find Lucinda, he could find enough peace to move on.

He thought about Arnott, Captain Michael Pennington as he had once been known. His grandfather talked of him being *driven* to find Diana. He knew how he felt, but there was no happy ending for him. Madeleine was gone.

A gig trotted slowly down the road and turned in at the doctor's house. It stopped.

"Are you waiting to see me?" A voice enquired.

Well he had to start somewhere, why not with the doctor.

"I would appreciate it if you could spare me a few moments."

"Come up to the house, I just need to deal with the gig."

He was a pleasant man. Should he tell him first, or ask him for information. He decided to ask first, see what he said.

"Can you tell me what ails Mrs Pennington?"

The doctor was shocked. "I do not disclose details of my patients, sir."

"No, I did not expect you would. Do you actually know what is wrong with her?"

The doctor looked angry. "I suggest you leave, sir."

Try another tack.

"Captain Michael says she had arsenic poisoning."

"You know Michael Pennington!"

"I was with him a couple of weeks ago. He believes his mother is being poisoned by Lucy Pennington. Is this your understanding too?"

Doctor Gordon was seriously discomposed.

"Who are you, sir, and of what interest is it to you?"

Selgrove walked to the window and looked out toward the bridge.

"I am the Earl of Selgrove and I married a wonderful girl, but a little over four years ago she died. The housekeeper found a small white apothecary's box behind a chest. Apparently her sister brought them regularly. The doctor found it to contain arsenic. My wife had been poisoned slowly and painfully by her sister, who intended to become my countess. We gave the proof to Bow Street but when they called the family had fled. Her name was Lucinda Ferndale. Around that time a Lucy Firbeck who bears a strong resemblance to her, arrived here, broke Frederick's betrothal and had his fiancée branded a thief.

"Can I ask the question again, Doctor Gordon? Was Lucy poisoning Mrs Pennington with arsenic?"

The doctor subsided into a chair. "Are you sure?"

"Oh yes, we have signed statements from all the different apothecaries she visited. The writing is the same even if the name is different. She always had a maid with her who she referred to as 'Effie'."

"She still has a maid called Effie."

"I need to know where this Lucy is. I need exact directions. Do you think the Penningtons would be prepared to testify in court?"

"No. Lucy is banished to save the family name. Wait here one moment." He left the room, taking his keys from his pocket as he went. A few minutes later he returned holding a small ornate wooden box.

Selgrove grasped. "That was Madeleine's box. Where did you get it."

"It was taken from its hiding place on top of Lucy's armoire." He opened the box. "Are those what you saw?" Inside were small white apothecary's boxes just as he had been given all those years ago.

"I will keep this safe, Selgrove. If it is needed, I will give evidence of where the box was found. If you can keep to her name of Lucy Firbeck I would be grateful. The family has a great many problems at the moment. Where are you staying?"

"At the inn."

"Hardly suitable accommodation for you."

"It will do well enough."

"Then I will enquire of Frederick for his wife's exact direction and bring it to you there."

"I am grateful, sir."

The two men shook hands solemnly, with heavy hearts. A few hours later Selgrove had what he needed.

With information from the Earl of Selgrove, Officers from Bow Street arrived at a certain house in London to arrest a Lucinda Ferndale, or Lucy Firbeck, or Lucy Pennington, or whatever she was currently calling herself. They took away a Lucrezia Fullerton. When he heard the name Selgrove thought it very apt.

She was incarcerated in Newgate prison to await trial.

* * *

The banns were being read. In three weeks she would be Michael's wife. For a week Diana worried over the future. Where would they live, what work could Michael do, what if they were in London and someone recognised her? Michael had stopped coming to her bed. Did he still want her? Was he as worried about the future as she was?

By day she helped running the house, watching Grandfather Arnott relax and smile with contentment to see Michael so happy.

Diana had learned to deal with whatever she found, so she decided she needed a serious talk with Michael to discuss the future. With her heart in her mouth she faced him.

"Do you regret this marriage, Michael?"

"Whatever makes you think that? Diana, my love, you are everything I have ever wanted. Do *you* have doubts?" A cloud crossed his face and his brow furrowed.

"You no longer come to my bed, Michael."

"My side still pains me, Diana. The doctor warned me not to exert myself for several weeks. I want to be healed when I take you to wife."

"You could hold me, like you did last week."

Michael smiled. "Diana, my darling one, I want you too much to lie with you and not make love to you. I am not strong enough to resist the temptation you pose. Perhaps in another week I will be sufficiently healed. Is that what is troubling you?"

"Where will we live, Michael? If we go to London I am afraid of being recognised and accused. I am frightened, Michael."

"Maybe we could go north, or even to the continent, it depends on what work I can do. I had not realised it worried you so much. We should discuss this with Grandfather, perhaps he will have some ideas. If I need to study there is time while we are here. I hope he will live for a great deal longer and I have no intention of leaving him. It could be years before we need to leave."

"Could we not manage in a small house in a village?"

"Is that what you prefer, if so I will speak to Lansdale about the income I can expect from our investments."

Michael was waiting for an appropriate moment to speak to his grandfather but he found himself drawn into a conversation as the three of them sat in the small parlour to take tea.

"Now, my dear; what has you so worried that it causes dark rings around your eyes just before your wedding? You should be happy."

"I am, Grandfather, but I fear for the future. How will Michael support us? If we go to London someone might recognise me and accuse me."

"Why would you go to London?" He turned to Michael with a worried look. "Are you considering leaving?"

"No, sir, not while you are here. But I do need to address my future and find a way of supporting us when Frederick has this estate."

Grandfather Arnott's eyes opened wide. "Who told you Frederick was to inherit?"

"It was always talked of at home, that your estate was entailed to Frederick."

"Michael, my boy, an entailment goes through the closest male relative. Frederick was never my heir through entailment. When he was born, I promised your mother her son would inherit from me. And so he will. Not Frederick, he has your father's estate. Once you were born this was always going to be yours."

"So I have no need of employment!"

"There will be enough employment here for you, dealing with the estate." He joked. He leaned forward and patted Diana's hand. "So you can stop worrying. You have no need to go to London. You can stay here your whole life, my dear."

Diana slid forward and hugged him. "Thank you Grandfather."

"Just see you provide me with great grandchildren. I would like to see you a complete family before I go."

A week later, as promised, Diana felt the warm male body slide into her bed.

"Let me relieve you of this nightgown, my love."

She was more than willing to allow it. She would allow him anything, especially when he was doing such wonderful things with his hands. When his mouth joined in she was unable to think. His body was close, but she wanted him closer. She knew exactly what she needed, and it seemed he was more than ready to satisfy both of them. He sank into her willing body and drove them both to total bliss. Collapsing together, they drifted into deep sleep.

Diana's eyes had lost their dark rings by the time the wedding drew near.

* * *

I was in a much happier frame of mind that Selgrove arrived back at the Arnott's estate to attend the wedding of Miss Diana Newby and Mr Michael Arnott.

There were guests there beside the locals. He met his friends, the Petersfords, a very confused man named Cobden with his wife and an extremely happy couple called Smeaton. It seemed Diana had engendered good will wherever she had been.

There was a friend of Michael's there called Edward Ashford who had some problem on his estate in Kent, but most surprising was Michael's second, who went by the name of Lansdale.

He made a point of making closer acquaintance.

"Lansdale, I know the name, but you are much younger than I had imagined."

"It is my father you know of, I expect. I work with him but he is the senior partner."

"No wonder. I thought you a little young to be taking on this Wentworth affair."

Michael heard the name and came to join them. "Wentworth, what brings you to mention his name?"

Lansdale looked up at him. "It seems you removed your money just in time, Michael. Some clients have taken exception to his inept management and tried to withdraw their funds. There was insufficient there."

"Has he been arrested?"

"Oh yes, now he has, but not before he tried to abscond with a large amount"

Michael whistled. He turned to Selgrove. "Are you involved?"

"No, thank goodness. I heard from Lord Williams, his cousin Harcourt has lost a great deal. It was Wentworth's clerk who went to someone called Tucker who works for him."

Michael grinned. "Allen Tucker! Your father trained him well, Robert."

"He did indeed."

"You both know Tucker?"

"Oh yes Selgrove. He grew up on the Pennington estate; his father had a tenant farm. He was trained by Wentworth, very badly. He told me of the money Grandfather had given me." He suddenly remembered. "I must make a new will. The one I made before I went to France left everything to Allan. I will have a wife tomorrow."

Selgrove laughed. "You found out about the estate?"

"The estate?" Lansdale queried.

"Apparently I was always to inherit this estate. I just never knew. I thought it was to go to Frederick. Lucy will be angry when she finds out."

Selgrove sat back in his chair, looking deeply into the brandy balloon that rested in his palm. "Lucy is in prison awaiting trial for poisoning her sister with arsenic. We have always had the proof but not the girl."

"Lucy *was* your wife's sister. You did think it possible."

"Did you know Frederick had thrown her off? Your father would not have the name damaged by bringing a case against her."

"Is my mother still alive?"

"I believe so. They have even more proof. Doctor Gordon is prepared to bring it to the trial. She will not survive now."

"Perhaps you would like to be the one to tell Diana. She is still frightened." Michael suggested

"Then it will be my pleasure to inform her."

Diana had been taken over by the families she had assisted. Grandfather Arnott sat and smiled at the love in which she was held. Michael could not be marrying a better person. She would make him happy, bring him peace. Michael obviously adored her. He believed her life would be happier with him than she would have been in the Penningtons' household.

It took some time before Selgrove managed a quiet word with Diana.

"I have news for you." Diana looked worried. Michael stroked her arm. "Lucy is in Newgate Prison awaiting trial for murder."

She looked from one to the other.

"You are free, my love. She can no longer hurt you."

"There are others who might say something."

"Don't look for problems, Diana. I have not told Michael yet. I met Harwood in London with Lord Williams. Frederick told them Lucy had lied, that you were not guilty of theft." He looked at Michael. "He also told me Frederick had admitted to being naïve and ruining your life. He is certainly suffering for his gullibility. The Wentworth affair will leave them all in a very precarious position financially."

"They all know? Do my parents know?"

"That I cannot say."

"I doubt your family were there, my love. They have never been accepted in society since you left. I expect the information will reach them somehow. Poor Frederick, he must be feeling the weight of responsibility very heavily on him."

The day of the wedding dawned bright and warm for all it was only the end of April.

Michael waited in the church eagerly with Robert by his side. Grandfather Arnott sat smiling in the front pew with a footman to assist and Fletcher beaming beside him.

The church was full, the Arnott workers crowding in to see the nice Mr Michael marry his young lady.

Smeaton walked Diana down the aisle. She was glowing with happiness and looked like a princess. Michael though his chest would burst he was so full of pride in this lovely girl. It seemed difficult to accept that she was truly to be his, for the rest of their lives.

The ceremony over, the happy couple walked together out of the church and into their future.

Epilogue

The trial was a sensation. Few had known the Countess of Selgrove had been poisoned.

Lucy tried to deny it. When her maid, Ellie, was called she shouted threats across the court and had to be removed. While there was more than enough proof, the production of the box sealed her fate.

The workman who made it was called. Yes, he made many boxes, but only one inlaid with blue butterflies, which was especially for the Countess of Selgrove. Frederick was called to testify it was found on top of Lucy's armoire, the doctor telling the contents of the small apothecary's boxes.

No mention was made of Mrs Pennington. There was no need.

Lucinda Ferndale, alias Lucy Firbeck, was hanged, but nobody went to watch.

* * *

Michael was busy seeing in the harvest but there was another surprise. Doctor Fisher who had been called to his wife, who was feeling queasy and overtired, announced that she was with child which would arrive around Christmas time. He was delighted, of course, although Grandfather seemed even more overjoyed.

Once the harvest was in, better than expected with the way the weather had been all year, the little family were free to enjoy their quiet times together. When the child arrived everything would change, the house would be much noisier, there would be much more to do. Strangely it was Grandfather who was looking forward to that most of all.

Most days Michael rode with Fletcher, usually in the morning now the days were starting to draw in. The sheep had been brought down from the high pasture, the grass there was no longer good enough and it was time to introduce the ram for next year's lambs. Michael was not expected back until dinner time.

After lunch, Diana retired to rest in her room and Grandfather snoozed in his study.

Tranter seemed to be trying to wake him.

"I am sorry to disturb you, Mr Arnott, but you have a visitor."

Grandfather blinked his eyes and tried to focus on the butler. "A visitor?"

"Yes, sir. A Mr Pennington."

Grandfather might have been alarmed had he known of his daughter's illness. "You had better show him in, Tranter." he wondered what had caused George to come calling after so many years. He was not a man to back down from an opinion. He was somewhat surprised when Frederick was shown in.

"Frederick, my boy, what brings you here?"

Frederick stood stiffly. "Good afternoon, Grandfather. I … I am not sure how to begin."

"Then sit down and tell me how you are."

Still he stood. "I wish to make some reparation for the damage I have done."

"What damage do you refer to?"

"I never realised what I was doing to Michael in repeating what the boys said."

"I know that, Frederick. You never had an enquiring mind, nor did your father. You believed what you were told. Your father should have checked and informed you. You did not beat Michael or poison the neighbourhood against him."

"But I should have checked, seen he was well and happy. I never even visited his room."

"That was remiss of you, Frederick, but you were only a boy."

"I love my brother, Grandfather. Now I have lost him. He will never come home now; he has even changed his name."

"What do you want of me, Frederick?"

"Father always told me I would inherit your estate. He said it was entailed. I have thought a great deal since Michael left. There is no entailment through a daughter. I would like you to make Michael your heir. He needs it. I don't know how to find him, but I will. I only wish I could find Diana Butterwick alive and well. Her suffering weighs on my conscience. I know now how badly Lucy lied."

"Does she know you are here?" Grandfather knew only too well what had happened to her, but was interested in what Frederick felt.

"Lucy is dead, Grandfather. She was hanged for the murder of her sister four years ago. When I realised how badly she had lied to me I banished her to London. That was where they arrested her. She was an evil woman and I have had no peace in my marriage. It was my own doing. Yet again, I never asked any questions."

"Sit down, Frederick. Your standing gives me a crick in my neck." Frederick sat stiffly. "So you wish me to name your brother as my heir."

"Yes, sir."

"Does your father know you are here?"

"I rarely see him now, sir. He and mother have moved to the Tuckers' house. They went originally to avoid Lucy."

"So he has not mentioned the entailment."

"He did a few months ago, when we found Wentworth had seriously depleted the capital and the estate profits would be down this year. He reminded me I would inherit from you. It is not fair and honest that I should inherit both."

"You are not so much like your father, Frederick. He would never use the words 'fair and honest'." Frederick could not answer. "Let us see if I can relieve you of some of your guilt. Your father was wrong about more than the entailment. Once Michael was born this estate was always meant for him, though none of you knew it." Frederick looked shocked. "Will you call Tranter for me?"

Frederick went to the door to summon the butler.

"Tranter, is it time for tea yet?"

"Almost, Mr Arnott, although Mrs Arnott is not down yet."

"Shall we go into the parlour ready for tea when it arrives?."

Frederick helped his grandfather out of his chair. "You have family staying?"

"Oh yes, Indeed I do."

The door was opened by a footman. The young lady was asking for the tea to be sent for. She stopped when she heard the voices.

"Come in, my dear. We have a visitor."

Diana entered the room slowly. A man stood by the window against the light, making it hard to see his face.

"Come and sit down. I would not like you to fall in your condition."

The man near the window was very still. She came forward and sat, gracefully subsiding into the cushions of the sofa.

The man still never moved.

"I believe our visitor is shocked to see you, Diana. Come, Frederick, take your courage in both hands and believe what you see."

"Diana. Miss Butterwick?"

"Not any more, Frederick. If I were still a Miss it would be shocking, in my condition."

He walked forward and bent to take her hands. He lifted one to his lips. "You can never know how it feels to find you alive and well."

"Indeed, I am very well, Frederick. Are you staying? If so I must arrange for the housekeeper to prepare a room."

"No doubt whether he is staying relies on your husband when he returns."

The tea tray arrived and they turned to the business of pouring and drinking tea. Diana was allowed to choose the first of the fancy cakes and pastries.

"I think I am being spoiled, all these cakes."

"I miss such fancies. The cook cannot manage such as these. Father took the cook with him when he and mother left."

"You have not engaged another cook?"

"I make the best of what the kitchen assistants can do. The finances will not allow two good cooks. When I have repaired the finances perhaps I will."

Strong footsteps rang down the hall and a man's voice spoke to the footman. The door opened and Michael entered.

"It is starting to rain, so I came home. I have no wish to catch a cold in case I give it to you, my love." He bent and kissed her upturned face. Gradually he realised there was someone else there.

The two brothers looked at each other as the realisation sank in.

"Frederick!" Michael launched himself across the room to take his brother's hands. "Frederick, it is so good to see you here. How are you? It must be dreadful for you, the court case and everything that has happened."

There were tears of relief in Frederick's eyes as he looked at his brother, taking in the warmth and friendliness.

Michael was just as moved as his brother.

It was Grandfather who had the last word.

"What more could I ask for than my family be reconciled? I take it you are staying, Frederick?"